REALITY
GOLD

Book One in the SHIFTING REALITY Collection

REALITY GOLD

TIFFANY BROOKS

DUNEMERE
Books

NEW YORK
SAN FRANCISCO

PUBLISHED BY DUNEMERE BOOKS

Copyright ©2018 by Tiffany Brooks
Book and cover design by Jenny Kelly
Cover art ©2018 by Jill De Haan

Publisher's Cataloging-in-Publication Data
provided by Five Rainbows Cataloging Services
Names: Brooks, Tiffany, author. | Title: Reality gold / Tiffany Brooks.
Description: New York : Dunemere Books, 2018. | Summary: Twenty teenagers compete on a reality television show to win a million dollars and find a priceless treasure. | Identifiers: ISBN 978-0-9984997-6-5 (pbk.) | ISBN 978-0-9984997-5-8 (ebook) | Subjects: LCSH: Young adult fiction. | Teenagers—Juvenile fiction. | CYAC: Reality television programs—Fiction. | Competition (Psychology)—Fiction. | Contests—Fiction. | Teenagers—Fiction. | BISAC: YOUNG ADULT FICTION / Performing Arts / Television & Radio. | Classification: LCC PZ7.1.B766 Re 2018 (print) | LCC PZ7.1.B766 (ebook) | DDC [Fic]—dc23.

ISBN: 978-0-9984997-6-5

DEDICATED TO MY FATHER,
who introduced me to Tolkien,
but even more importantly, paid all my
overdue library fines without complaint;
TO MY MOTHER,
who proudly framed my first poem and hung it
inside our front door for all the world to see
as if it was a masterpiece (it was not);
AND TO JAMES,
who has supported and encouraged me,
mostly by repeating over and over, with varying
degrees of love and exasperation, *just finish it.*

The Marker Rubbings

Marker #1

Marker #2:
Found at the shrine

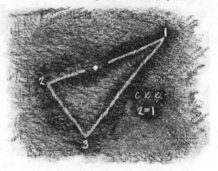

Marker #3

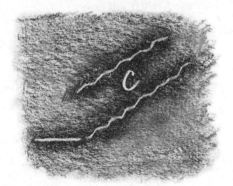

Marker #4:   the final clue

Ilha da Rocha Negra

7

4

7

7 X X

THE WAY SHALL BE EASY

40 VARAS SOUTH

DIG ⊙ △

REALITY GOLD TEAM ROSTERS

SOL TEAM	HUACA TEAM
Alex	AJ
Chloe	Annika
Cody	London
Justin	Lucas
Murch	Maddie
Porter	Maren
Rohan	Oscar
Taylor	Rachel
Willa	Riley
Zander	Sean

REALITY GOLD

1

I'VE GOT MY OWN VERSION OF MURPHY'S LAW, AND IT goes like this: if there's something that will make a bad situation even worse, I'll do it. My ex-friends called it Riley's Law, and it's the best explanation for why I was now crammed shoulder-to-shoulder with nineteen other teens on one of those ominous-looking military-style helicopters that always show up in disaster movies when the worst stuff is about to go down.

Why—*why*—had I thought doing a reality show was the answer to all my problems? Would I ever learn to leave things alone?

My back bounced against the cold metal wall. All the players were wiggling and vibrating against one another like a batch of lottery balls about to be released. I scanned the opposite row of my new rivals' faces, yet not a single other person looked scared, sick, or even mildly nervous.

Keep it together, Riley.

Somehow, a stupid mistake from eight months ago had snowballed into this: me, hurtling toward a deserted island off the coast of Brazil, about to compete in a nationally televised reality show. Back in October—a lifetime ago—my friend Izzy and I did something dumb. I got suspended. Izzy got expelled. My sentence was lighter because my role was trivial, but my progressive San Francisco classmates—always on alert for signs of inequality—decided the school had gotten it wrong and our misdeeds were identical. The only reason I was still around, they argued, was because my parents were big donors to our school and Izzy had been ousted because she was a scholarship kid. There was a petition submitted to the headmaster, demanding my expulsion. The school declined, and the only wreckage would have been my own hurt feelings if I'd left everything alone.

But because of Riley's Law, I didn't. I couldn't.

Instead, I decided I had to defend myself in an op-ed on the school website. The essay was well-written and impeccably argued. No one noticed any of that, though, because within hours the *San Francisco Chronicle* had picked the article up and decimated it. Decimated *me*. There's a whole gentrification thing going on in the city right now, and my words were twisted and held up as proof of the spoiled mentality of the Bay Area's one percent. Their warped interpretation: *Wealthy Private School Student Demands Special Treatment.*

That was definitely not what I'd said, but it didn't stop

people in all corners of the Internet from flooding my Facebook page and raiding my Instagram, suggesting I go kill myself—but before I did, I should get surgery to move my eyes closer together, start a diet to fix my fat face, and grow some boobs.

It was bad enough when it felt like my friends and classmates hated me, but suddenly the whole world was screaming about how worthless I was.

Some creative snake even managed to download some photos of me before I made everything private. He slapped some Marie Antoinette–style comments on them and they went viral. Birthed by the Internet and tended to by trolls, this warped version of myself showed up everywhere. The meme of the girl in the red velvet party dress, holding her white-gloved hands out in disgust, under the caption *You bought that on sale? I can't even!* That was me when I was ten, taken at my middle school's annual holiday dance. It had been a really fun night; the dress was a gift, and when I twirled, the skirt puffed up like a bell. I felt like a princess. That sour expression had probably only flashed across my face for a second or two, and it was nothing more than an exaggerated reaction to the DJ playing "Oops I Did It Again," which I secretly loved.

Now when I hear that song or think of that night, I want to die.

The helicopter suddenly banked right, hitting a rough patch of air. Across from me, two girls wearing tiny shorts

3

with hair longer than their crop tops clutched each other and screamed. The one with the deep red hair looked familiar but I couldn't think of why, which was driving me crazy because I usually remembered things like that.

They were so casually entwined, as if they were best friends already. Once, that might have been me. If I'd been doing this show a year ago, I probably would have been right there next to them, commiserating over the awkwardness of it all, asking the girl with the red hair where she was from and complimenting the blond girl's gold clover necklace.

But now my instinct was to hold back. Becoming the butt of a national joke left me unsure of who I could trust. After the bad publicity prompted the headmaster to start making noise about how it "might be better for everyone" if I enrolled somewhere else, I withdrew and hid in my room while being homeschooled for the remainder of the year. At least, that's what my mother called the rotation of counselors and tutors who cycled through our house. My father didn't call it anything. By then he had basically washed his hands of me.

And now September was coming in three short months, bringing with it a new school for my senior year and a chance for a fresh start. I wanted my future classmates to know something about me besides that garbage online, but countering a rumor is nearly impossible. As my tutor liked to say: *a lie can travel halfway around the world before the truth can get its boots on.* But then I heard about this show. It was the perfect solution. Me, on television every week—the real me, looking friendly and nice and normal and nothing at all like an evil narcissist who bathes in champagne and the tears of poor people.

For that tactic to succeed, though, I had to put myself out there. Be friendly. The girl sitting on my left, who'd introduced herself as Taylor, seemed like an easy person to start with; she'd been chattering away non-stop with nearly everyone else already. But when I leaned toward her to say something, we hit more turbulence and my forehead smacked squarely into hers.

"Hey!" she pulled back, pressing her fingers into the bridge of her nose. The exclamation was hardly fair. I obviously hadn't done it on purpose.

Nevertheless, I apologized. "Sorry," I said sheepishly, internally cursing myself for the false start. Doing this show badly would be worse than not doing it at all.

"Hang in there," Deb, the producer, shouted. She was tiny, but she had a big presence with her loud voice and a wild flash of dark, curly hair. "The wind currents always get unpredictable near the island, but it won't be too much longer in the air. You guys ready?"

There were a lot of nods, some more enthusiastic than others.

"Are you guys dead or what? A little spirit, please. I'll ask again: *You guys ready?*"

This time there were shouts and cheers. A guy in bright red Bermuda shorts near the back door put his fingers in his mouth to whistle, although the wind rush inside the helicopter was so loud I couldn't hear it from that far away. He had short dirty-blond hair, looked very preppy, was named Parker or Porter—one of those first name/last name kind of names. Cute. We'd met at the airport when we'd both arrived at the door at the same time and had a couple of rounds of polite but awkward "You first," "No, you." Too bad I'd watched him later trying to catch the eye of the pair of new best friends huddled across from me.

"Much better," Deb said. "Now listen up, because I've got a surprise."

Oh no. I'd binge-watched enough reality shows in the last few months to know that last-minute bombshells never brought good news. Even more worrisome was how the film crew had suddenly jumped into action, swinging cameras onto their shoulders and scattering among the players to take up their filming positions.

One of them knelt in front of me, so close I could see dark patches of stubble along his cheeks and a few loose threads unraveling from the neck of his black T-shirt. If I could see him in so much detail, his lens must be capturing my every pore.

I swallowed nervously. I had definitely underestimated how unnerving it was to feel this level of scrutiny again.

For a second the aperture in the center of the lens opened up and a reflection of my face flashed in the glass. I didn't see any features, just fear.

Breathe, Riley.

There's a game I play when my anxiety starts to kick in. Since it was a suggestion from my therapist, I resisted at first, but now I use it all the time. It takes up excess mental energy and forces me to be in the moment. It also feels way more productive than plain old deep breathing. Here it is: describe something in opposing ways and then figure out which description is correct.

My participation in this show: ballsy attempt to rehab my reputation or a ginormous mistake that would lead to round two as the Internet's favorite punching bag?

Me: misunderstood girl, or spoiled Internet brat?

I'd find out soon enough.

2

"TRY TO IGNORE THE CAMERAS," DEB ADVISED, WHICH

was virtually impossible. I could practically feel the lens touching me, the sensation of being stared at was that strong.

I didn't know the names of any of the cameramen, and I wasn't about to ask. Part of Deb's welcome at the airport had included the fact that the camera crew was off-limits.

"Don't talk to them, engage them, or worst of all, try to bribe them," Deb had told us. With what? I'd wondered, before deciding I probably didn't want to know much more about what that implied. She'd obviously meant sex or something illicit because we had virtually no possessions to bribe them with. We were hardly allowed to bring anything to the island—just the two bags we'd been supplied: the duffel for clothes and a smaller nylon square bag Sharpie'd with each of our names that we'd been told to stuff with our most important personal items.

Deb clapped her hand against the back of her clipboard, eager to reveal her big surprise. "Guys, come on. Can I have you look over here, please?"

I must not have been the only one transfixed by the camera, which was reassuring. I gave Deb my attention, glad to have something else to focus on.

"As you know, for the next twenty-six days you'll be living on Black Rock Island, competing against one another in challenges and games for a million-dollar prize," she said. "You also know that the island is the long-rumored hiding spot for a priceless treasure, a trove of stolen Inca gold, which is why the contests you'll face in the game are all inspired by the legends of Black Rock."

She paused. As a producer, she worked behind the scenes, but her flair for the dramatic meant she was also at home in front of the camera.

"But here's something you don't know. We've added a twist to the game. Any player who wishes to do so will be allowed—and encouraged—to search for this treasure. All searches and discoveries will be part of the show, and there will be an extra two hundred and fifty thousand dollars for any player who finds the treasure or a substantial clue that leads to its discovery."

Wait, what?

"Yeeeeehawwww," a huge guy in an army-green tank top shouted, tossing his cowboy hat in the air. I didn't usually support the idea of men in tank tops, but I'd make an exception in this case. He had incredibly huge biceps.

I weakly joined in the cheering. Over the past year I'd learned a lot about how to keep a low profile, and the key is to do just enough so that you fit solidly inside the norm of what is expected. Going camo, I called it.

It wasn't that I didn't want to search for the treasure. I did. That was the problem. In fact, the chance to sneak around the island on my own and search for the treasure was another big reason I was here. Finding the gold—now *that* would really be an accomplishment, possibly even more important than transmitting my true self onto television screens across the country. Forget *spoiled*, *entitled*, or *selfish*, if I found the gold, the first ten pages of a *Riley Ozaki* Google search would be nothing but sunshine and rainbows. I'd be celebrated, not shunned. Sought out, not exiled.

I might even—dare I hope—impress my father, who had been involved in the last failed treasure hunt on the island.

But now that part of my plan was in jeopardy. I'd planned to search alone, in secret, without any competition. During casting auditions, Deb had explicitly told me the treasure wasn't going to play any role in the competition, and I'd counted on that. I had some inside info on where the gold was hidden, and I wasn't about to share it with a bunch of yahoos who probably thought all they had to do was run around the island and start digging when they found a giant X marking the spot.

The guy on my right—black skinny jeans, beanie, definitely a hipster—seemed particularly jazzed about the prospect of finding the treasure.

"Maybe I'll just keep the gold," he said. "It's probably worth more than the two-hundred-and-fifty-grand prize, right? Finders keepers."

I was too shocked to respond right away. Just keep the gold? As if finding it would be the simplest thing in the world? The last person who had searched the island for the treasure had been murdered, the specifics of which I happened to know pretty intimately because (a) that treasure hunter was my godfather and one of my parents' oldest friends, and (b) I had been with him on Black Rock Island about three weeks before he'd gotten hacked into a million pieces.

So, yeah, treasure hunting wasn't quite the no-big-deal Deb had made it out to be. People had freaking died doing this. Gold fever was a virus, my father always said, and once people caught it they became reckless—or worse.

"I'm just throwing this out there, but how, exactly, would you keep it for yourself?" I asked my new opponent. It took some work to keep the hysteria out of my voice, because I'd already been thinking of the treasure as mine. It was obscene picturing this guy's hands—or anyone else's—all over it. *I* didn't even plan on touching it. The finding part was more important to me than the keeping part, and in fact, I hadn't thought too much about the particulars of what would happen right after I made the discovery. Instead, my mind always sped past that part to imagine the final outcome: a pile of glinting gold, a crowd of admirers, and exploding flashbulbs.

"I guess I'd take what I could carry," he said. "Stuff whatever could fit into my pockets."

We both evaluated his tight jeans at the same time.

"You might want to wear bigger pants," I advised. "Because, let's say you find it, you'd have to hide it from Deb. You probably wouldn't be able to keep more than a coin or two secret. Not worth it. You might as well take the cash prize."

He nodded thoughtfully. "True. Hey, do you think if some of us work together to find the gold we can split the prize money? I'm Sean, by the way."

I paused for a second. Would hearing my name trigger any sort of recognition?

"Riley," I said, glad we'd only be using our first names on the island. Less identifiable. I waited to see if there would be a reaction, but he just nodded.

"Cool," he said.

I was relieved, although it wasn't totally surprising. Simply hearing my name wasn't usually enough for someone to realize I was the *"Can't Even" Girl*—which was nice, but also only temporary, because the second anyone looked me up online they'd immediately get the goods. There was no way to separate your online self from your real-world self anymore. Both versions converged into one, whether you wanted them to or not. Still, I was going to take it as a good sign that the first person I'd given my name to hadn't reacted upon hearing it.

The trick was going to be getting through today without being recognized. If I did that, I'd be anonymous the entire time I was on the island. I hadn't dared to think too much about it because I didn't want to jinx it, but so far so good. We'd turned over our phones and tablets and computers at the airport in preparation for three weeks in a screen-free, no Wi-Fi zone. Or, rather, everyone else was preparing to be unconnected during our island stay. I had different plans.

My bag held a small Wi-Fi satellite receiver I was attempting to smuggle onto the island to help me decipher clues as I searched for the gold. Designed to look like a makeup compact, it had passed undetected in this morning's search for contraband, which was actually kind of funny. I had spent hours stressing over getting that thing past the security check, and it had turned out to be a nonissue. Instead, it looked like having a bunch of newly deputized treasure hunters to compete against was going to be the real problem.

Just when I nailed one problem, another arrived to replace it. Or, to apply a phrase my mother had grown particularly fond of overusing this year: when one door closes, another one opens. Whenever she said it, I always silently added *and hits you in the face.*

Also tugging at the back of my mind was a growing fear

that Deb had lied to me. I used to be the kind of person who took everything at face value, but not anymore. No way. *Assume everyone is out to get you*, that's my credo these days. So what was up with Deb going out of her way to assure me that the show wouldn't have much to do with the real treasure? Filming on Black Rock was just a gimmick, she'd said. Something to give the show an interesting theme.

Not so much, it turned out. The question was why.

A string of small islands popped into view through the porthole windows above the hand-holding girls. My stomach flipped. There it was, at the heart of the island chain: Black Rock Island. Big black mountains in the dead center, a banana-shaped beach on the right, lots of green everywhere else—a deceptively tranquil view of a place that over the years had soaked up enough blood to earn its cursed reputation.

I nudged Taylor and enthusiastically pointed to the islands, a peace offering of sorts, a gesture she seemed to appreciate based on her squeal of excitement.

Everyone turned to look, even Deb.

"There it is, gang," she called. "The largest island—the one in the middle—is Black Rock, your home for the next twenty-six days. That is, if you're lucky."

Everyone contorted themselves to find a view. I didn't want any of the players to know I'd been to the island before, so I did my camo thing, staring out the window and ooh'ing and aah'ing like everyone else.

When we all slid back against the helicopter walls, I

noticed that Joaquin, the on-camera host of the show, was standing next to Deb. We'd been introduced to him briefly before takeoff.

"Joaquin is going to do another welcome speech in case we don't like the footage we shot back at the airfield," Deb explained. "Double-up filming is probably going to happen a lot, but we need you to play along and listen as if you're hearing it for the first time."

Joaquin was handsome in an outdoorsy way. Dark brown hair with high cheekbones that were naturally ruddy from spending time in the sun. He was wearing what basically looked like a costume, a rugged outfit in the style of Indiana Jones: khaki shorts and a safari shirt with lots of buttons and tabs. He had such a strong presence that his jungle attire didn't even make him look out of place against the stark metal consoles and screens and wires.

A cameraman knelt down on the floor in front of him.

When Joaquin spoke, he gave the exact speech he had made a couple of hours before in the same lilting Latino accent. "You are about to embark on a journey in a land full of rich traditions. My people have lived here since the time of the Incan Empire," he said before launching into a background of the Incas, their bravery, and most importantly, their gold. "Since the early 1600s, treasure hunters have come to this island searching for hidden treasure, and now it is your turn—to find the treasure hidden within yourselves."

It was just as cheesy the second time around, but if

anyone could pull it off, Joaquin could. His earnest, easygoing charm allowed him to say things that would seem fake if anyone else tried.

He kept going, but I was having a hard time paying attention because the helicopter was descending at a rapid rate. We weren't over the island yet, but we were very low and close to the water.

"And so here we are, Black Rock Island, or as my people would say, Ilha da Rocha Negra. For many of you, this will be your home for the next week or two, maybe three, and for a few lucky ones, a little bit longer," Joaquin continued. "And in honor of the bravery and daring of the Incan warriors and the treasure seekers who have come before you, I invite you now to dive into our beautiful waters and swim to your new shore."

There was silence for a second, and then a pop of earsplitting noise as everyone understood what he meant. We wouldn't be landing on the island. We were going to have to jump from the helicopter.

I'd once woken up to ninety-three texts, countless snaps, and even a few missed calls—a true rarity—but that wasn't much worse than the *Oh my God, what have I gotten myself into?* feeling that surged over me when I looked down at the water, a million feet below.

3

REACTIONS EXPLODED AROUND ME, RANGING FROM
fear to excitement.

Taylor turned toward me, as incredulous as I was.

"Did you know we were going to have to do this?" she asked. I had noticed earlier that her rapid-fire way of talking made her sound excitable, but that was nothing compared to how hyped up she was now.

"God, no," I answered.

We exchanged exclamations of disbelief. Taylor used her hands to punctuate everything, and her fingers flew wildly from her temples and down her neck until she finally pushed both palms flat against her chest, as if to keep her heart from pushing through her chest.

"Do you know how long it took me to straighten my hair this morning? I wanted at least one day with good hair. Oh my God. I can't believe this."

Taylor had thick hair even longer than mine, hanging well below her shoulder blades in a crisp, even line. If it wasn't naturally straight it must have taken hours to flat iron.

"Do you have a hair tie?" Her hands flew into prayer position. "Please? I can't deal if it gets ruined so soon."

I had two hair ties on my right wrist, buried beneath a row of leather bracelets. I pulled one off and gave it to her, resisting the urge to point out that there was no way anyone's hair was going to stay dry jumping off this thing. My own hair would naturally dry straight, but I decided to loosely braid it to stay out of my face during the jump. Taylor used the borrowed hair tie to twist hers into a tight bun high on top of her head.

I hoped the cameras caught the exchange. See, world? I knew how to share.

"I'm Riley."

"Taylor, and oh my God, you literally saved my life," Taylor said. "I'm serious. You shouldn't keep those on your wrist, though. I heard some girl got an infection and died from her hair tie being too tight."

Around us everyone was still buzzing. *But I don't have my bathing suit on. How far will we have to swim? Is this danger-ous?* And from Porter and a similarly preppy guy next to him, *Hell, yeah* and some more fist bumping.

Taylor leaned over. "That's Willa Kisses over there, right?"

I started to turn in the direction where Taylor was staring.

She grabbed my arm. I felt her fingernails; this girl was intense.

"Don't look now," she hissed. "The girl across from us, the really gorgeous one."

"Her last name is Kisses?"

"No, dummy. WillaKisses_xo. That's her Instagram!" Taylor released my arm and swatted me gently. "She's got like a billion followers. I can't believe it might be her! I knew some famous people would be doing this thing. I can't believe we won't have Internet this whole time. I can't wait that long to look her up."

Oh, so that was it! I *had* seen that girl somewhere: Instagram. How embarrassing. Back at the airport, I'd almost asked her if she was also from San Francisco because she looked so familiar. I felt a flush of satisfaction at Taylor's no Internet comment. I hadn't brought the satellite to investigate the competition, but looking everyone up would be a nice side benefit. WillaKisses_xo was definitely going to be my first search. Still, I felt a twinge about Taylor getting so excited when she'd recognized Willa. If she was looking out for people worth identifying, she might pin me next.

Deb walked up and down the aisle between us, holding onto ceiling straps along the way as if they were monkey bars.

"Before you arrived, I asked you to dress yourselves as a form of an introduction by wearing clothes that reflect who you are. This is going to be your second chance to show yourself off to the audience, so make a statement," she urged.

I looked around, scoping out the competition. Hard to tell what they'd be like in the context of the game, but as for what we looked like, it was pretty obvious we'd been cast to fill every possible stereotype. Several different ethnicities were covered—Indian, African American, Asian—distributed across a variety of personality types. There were jocks, preps, hipsters, sorority-type girls, and nerds. It wasn't hard to tell who was trying to be what, based on the outfits. I hadn't wanted to stand out, so I'd gone for *average*, wearing simple jean shorts and a light blue V-neck T-shirt. But there were a few who had taken things to the extreme. The guy who'd tossed his cowboy hat exuded country charm, a football fan in a Patriots jersey had the sporty thing down, and the girl with purple-tipped hair was definitely edgy, possibly even a little scary. Maren, I'd heard her say her name was. I made a mental note to stay out of her way.

"Are you ready to show you can be a contender?" Deb called. "Let's see your stuff! Come on, who's first? Porter? How about you?"

Porter nodded, making an *I got this* face. All around him his new friends were raising their fists in solidarity. He started to stand, but Deb held up her hand.

"Great, but hold on," she told him. "Joaquin needs to be the one to get this party started."

Deb retraced her monkey bars walk, ending near the

cockpit, away from the cameras. Suddenly the ramp started to lower.

It only took a few seconds for the ramp to yawn all the way open. Wind and noise and chaos poured inside. It felt a bit like we were inside a giant whale, ready to be spit out.

Wait. My mind flitted to the pile of bags at the back. The compass might survive a swim, but the satellite and my notes definitely wouldn't. I'd have to leave my bag. We all would. But . . . that was fine, right?

Or was it? My trust issues kicked back in. We'd been specifically told to pull out our most valuable things and put them in those small, separate bags. Why? All our stuff was supposed to end up at the same place. What was the point of sorting anything out?

Maybe it was an easy way for the crew to do a more detailed search of the bag where we'd most likely hide any contraband. That was worrisome. The satellite might not pass a close inspection.

I was getting a bad feeling about all this.

Another helicopter hovered a short distance away. The sun glinted off a camera lens in the open door, just in case I had any doubts our plunges would be commemorated from every angle.

"To ease your minds, we're only fifty meters from the beach," Deb said, "and as you can see, there is another helicopter out there. Experienced medics are on board in full scuba gear, ready to jump in. Not that anyone will need it."

Joaquin took over.

"Swim to shore, where you'll be self-sorting yourselves into two teams," he said. "You will find two baskets of bandannas on the beach at the high-tide mark. Since there are twenty of you, each basket holds ten bandannas. The yellow bandannas represent the Sol team, in honor of the sun god worshipped by the Incas. The green bandannas are for the Huaca team. *Huaca* is the ancient word for natural, revered objects like rocks and caves."

He swept his arm toward the door. "Choose well, and let the games begin!"

At the door, Porter did a few exaggerated arm stretches, then turned, gave a wave, and hopped out the door in a straight line.

Naturally he'd gone first. He seemed like someone who'd be right in the middle of everything. I'd been crazy to think I had a chance with him; everyone was clapping and watching his jump in admiration.

Plenty of people were lining up to take their turn, even a couple of nerdy-looking guys who I never would have thought would be at the front of the line. I'd been counting on them to put up a fuss—I really didn't want to be the only one to hesitate. I didn't want to be a troublemaker. I wanted to fit in. Doing what everyone else does is what keeps you safe.

"I'm totally freaking out," Taylor muttered as she stood up. She motioned urgently for me to stand, too. "Come on."

I reluctantly stood, apparently too slowly for Taylor because she went ahead, wiggling through the crowd to slide behind Willa and her friend, who might have been even prettier than Willa. Alex, I was pretty sure her name was. Was she famous, too? She looked vaguely familiar, but maybe it was just that the combo of thick eyebrows and light green eyes was a popular look right now. Even more impressive than the buttery color of her blond hair was how silky it looked, even from a distance.

After Willa positioned herself in the middle of the ramp, she took off her T-shirt and shorts and flicked them daintily at Joaquin. She was wearing a tiny white crocheted bikini. Of course she was—although with a body like hers, I probably wouldn't wear clothes unless I had to, either.

Then she and possibly-Alex held hands and jumped together.

Taylor was next, and there were a few laughs as her wail floated up in her wake.

"The rotor wash is pushing these kids underwater," the pilot's voice said through an intercom. "I've got to go higher."

A heavy guy, the football fan in the Patriots jersey who had called everyone "bro" back at the airport, was next in line. His last name was Murchison but he'd told everyone to call him Murch.

"Say what?" Murch had that slow, deliberate confidence that seemed as if it was issued to sporty guys along with their team uniforms. He wasn't a prize, physically: overweight, with crooked front teeth. Still, his innate swagger meant he probably had a huge group of sports-minded followers back home, wherever that was.

Deb poked her head inside the cockpit and a few seconds later the helicopter rose up.

"Higher. Great. We really have to do this?" Murch asked Joaquin. "Listen, man. I know I look like I'm one big floatation device, but I'm not. I'm gonna sink like a stone, guaranteed. You want my drowning on your head? How about we just land this thing on that flat beach over there so the rest of us can get out, nice and dry."

"Interesting, Murch. I wouldn't have guessed that you, of all the players, would want to look so weak," Joaquin told him.

Ouch. Murch made a skeptical face. "Weak? Hell, no. Fine. Bring this thing higher and let's do it."

I stood, reluctantly. I couldn't risk leaving my bag behind. Arriving without the satellite I'd be just another player in the game. It wouldn't be enough. Not by a long shot. The satellite was my key to success—if I found the gold, or even anything of importance, I'd be able to get online for advice. I'd even set up a cloud storage account so I could upload photos. I had a single chance to get this right, to accomplish something. Once I left the island, that was it.

Deep breath, Riley.

Jumping: no big deal or huge mistake?

Refusing to jump: calling attention to myself for no reason, or a necessary action?

Everyone's eyes were on me. No doubt they were wondering why I was standing there not doing anything. I felt exposed, raw, the way I felt whenever I stumbled unsuspecting onto a nasty comment or a bad picture of me. I couldn't go back to living like that.

"I'm not going to do it," I told Joaquin. "You can call it weak, or whatever you want, and you can bring me back to the mainland, but I'm staying in the helicopter."

For a few seconds no one did anything.

There was only one other guy left on the helicopter besides Murch, and he spoke first. "Me neither," he said. "I've got to protect the foot! I didn't get a soccer scholarship just to lose it when I crack my ankle on some underwater junk down there."

The others joined in, agreeing. No one left wanted to jump. A few girls toward the front of the line quickly sat down.

I relaxed a little bit. Once you weren't the only one not doing something, things got easier.

"It's your choice to jump or not," Joaquin said, quieting everyone down. "However, as I mentioned, the players who already jumped are likely to judge that decision and it may come back to haunt you. Are you still choosing not to jump?"

I nodded. Others joined me.

"Well, if they aren't jumping, then I'm not going to, either," Murch said, obviously relieved despite all his earlier bluster.

Annika, a tall girl in athletic shorts wearing a knee brace, sat next to me. "Thank you so much! I really did not want to do that."

I got a few thumbs-up from the other girls. Okay, good. I had my bag *and* the gratitude of some of the other players. Not a bad start.

Maren was the only one who wasn't looking overly appreciative, and her purple-streaked hair and dark makeup made her look downright gloomy. She had been in the jumping line but at some point she'd sat down. Funny. She looked like someone who would have jumped to look tough, to prove she wasn't scared.

Deb updated the pilot and the ramp began to rise. The wind immediately died down when it was fully closed, although the helicopter still bobbed in the air a bit.

"Perhaps there will be a benefit to your choice after all," Joaquin said. "The eight of you will be allowed to carry your personal packs onto the beach."

Well, well. Validation flooded through me. It *had* been a trick.

"What do you mean? The others don't get to keep their little bags?" Maren asked.

"They will get their clothing bags delivered later, Maren, just like you will. But their personal packs?" Joaquin raised his shoulders. "They left them behind. They must not have considered those packs important."

Maren stood up. She looked excited, or at least as excited

as a girl with black lipstick can. "You're not going to hand them out later?"

Joaquin shook his head. "A good treasure hunter should always keep his tools with him."

"Or her," Maren said. She went to the pile of packs near the cockpit, rifling through them and calling out names.

"Riley?"

I raised my hand, and Maren tossed my bag over.

"Cody?" No answer. "Zander?" More silence.

Maren threw their bags to the side, plus a third. "Porter's. We all know that dude jumped. Maddie?"

A short, friendly looking blond girl wearing a T-shirt with a rainbow-colored cat on it raised her hand.

"You?" Maren asked.

Maddie nodded.

"Okay, but speak up, cat girl. You want your stuff or not?"

After the rest of the bags were claimed by Murch, Lucas, London, Rachel, and Annika, I watched in disbelief as Maren started rifling through the abandoned ones.

"Are you taking their stuff?" I asked incredulously.

Maren looked up. "This is a game, right? I want to win. There might be something in here I can use, and notice no one is stopping me."

It was true. Deb and Joaquin were leaning against the cockpit wall, observing but not showing any indication they planned to stop her. Joaquin even looked amused.

Maren tossed me a bag. "Here. Take this one. That's for saving me a dunking."

I felt a camera swivel toward me. I recoiled; I couldn't do it. I wanted to, but there was no question how bad it would look if I was filmed taking other people's things. That was the root of my infamy, after all. Spoiled, out-for-herself Riley.

I left the bag right where it had landed, praying the camera had caught me refusing to take it.

Maren continued to shove things from the jumpers' bags into her own. I saw a book, a small box, some papers, and then my insides flipped. An orange booklet—I recognized it immediately. The subject was treasure signs and their interpretations, and among the dedicated treasure hunting community (a brotherhood of thieves, really) it was referred to as "the Cipher." It wasn't something a casual reader would come across. I'd only found it myself after months of researching, thanks to a recommendation on an obscure members-only website for treasure seekers. I hadn't brought my Cipher—it was so loud and bright and obvious—but I had copied several of the pages into my notebook. Anyone who used the Cipher knew what they were doing, and even more importantly, the fact that someone had brought it meant they had more than a casual interest in the treasure. Just like me, they must have planned to search for it even before Deb had given the green light. I definitely had to find out who it was.

I glanced out the window. Down below on the beach, the swimmers had made it to shore. Most of them had chosen

Team Sol, judging by all the yellow bandannas being swirled around.

Maren roughly plopped down in Taylor's former spot, her nylon pack stuffed.

"Gotta do me," she said. There was a dark smudge of lipstick on her front tooth. I debated telling her, before deciding against it. She seemed like the kind of girl who would shoot the messenger.

"Whose things do you have?" I asked, trying to sound casual.

She shrugged. "Didn't pay attention to names, just grabbed anything that looked interesting."

At least I knew whose bags they weren't. I scanned the faces of everyone left on the helicopter. We'd probably all be on the same team, but just in case, I took note of who had their bags.

The helicopter landed, sending a cloud of white sand into the air.

"It's go time," Deb said. "Everyone out."

4

I KICKED OFF MY SNEAKERS AND LET MY TOES SINK
into the soft sand, taking it all in. Sparkling blue water, with
a wide band of white beach that sloped up toward the green
jungle. Really, it was a perfect and picturesque backdrop—all
very *Lost*, minus the crashed airplane. Supposedly there was
a storm on its way, but right now the sky was bright and crisp
without any sign of trouble.

This was it: the very spot where my godfather, Miles
Kroger, had been murdered. You would never have known
someone had died a violent death here if this beautiful, serene
view was all you had to go on. It wasn't that I expected to see
signs of a crime scene, or even a memorial, but it was a little
unsettling that something so savage could have occurred in
such a peaceful setting without leaving a mark of some sort.

Or maybe my discomfort came from the fact that in
some ways it was hard to recognize this as the same place.

Two years ago, this beach had been mostly deserted without any man-made structures—just lots of treasure hunting gear piled around a makeshift tent camp. Now it was Disney'd up: Incan-style huts and hammocks, fire pits and torch-lined paths. A giant gold gong glinted from the tree line. The sand seemed whiter, almost glittery. Even the jungle seemed greener, as if it had done nothing but rain since I left.

Actually, in a way it had rained, I realized. Money. The whole reason I'd heard about the show in the first place was because Deb had been drumming up investors and my father had been on her hit list. My father: Oz, the Great Wizard of Silicon Valley. Otherwise known as Albert Ozaki, he was the man who could bring any start-up from poverty to prof-itability—someone whose only disappointing endeavor thus far was, apparently, his daughter.

"There had better be a green bandanna in that basket for me because there's no way I'm partnering with those yellow idiots," Maren said.

Everyone who'd jumped off the helicopter was celebrat-ing about a hundred yards away. They were a mass of activity, almost a single unit, hopping and jumping around either in excitement or in an effort to dry off. Maybe both. It wasn't even nine in the morning yet, so it would be awhile before the sun would get hot enough to do any good.

I held on tightly to my bag. I didn't regret staying on the helicopter one bit.

"Team Sol!" There were lots of celebratory cheers, some

31

with a taunting edge, as if yellow unquestionably represented the better team and those of us on the green team had already failed the first test.

Ha. Little did they know.

With the exception of Murch, who had run full tilt off the helicopter when it touched ground, the rest of us were hanging back, taking everything in, making our way slowly to the baskets.

"What's up, chickens?" Porter heckled us, hooking his thumbs underneath his armpits. His yellow bandanna was tied around his upper arm over his white button-down shirt. "Did you have a nice ride? You like being nice and dry?"

"Jealous much?" Maren asked.

"I know you are, but what am I?" he shot back good-naturedly. I couldn't help smiling. He answered Maren, but from the way he'd been looking at me it seemed like I was the intended audience.

Next to Porter, Murch was tying a yellow bandanna across his forehead, which meant at least one of the jumpers must not have chosen Team Sol. I didn't have to wonder why there'd been an available slot on Sol for very long—hovering near the Huaca basket and sporting new green bandannas were the smallest, least athletic guys in the entire group. Sean was one of them, and so was Lucas, the soccer player who hadn't wanted to risk his foot. If I were them, I'd have skipped out on Team Sol, too. Porter, Murch, and the other four Sol guys high-fiving each other were all the same breed—sporty, big, and loud. My new Huaca brothers seemed to be more of the hipster or nerd variety.

We made our way past Sol to our basket, the six of us girls swapping tentative smiles as we pulled out our green bandannas.

Good: it looked like we had a mix of personalities and strengths to cover whatever challenges Deb might throw at us. Annika and London were sporty, Maren seemed ready to fight, Maddie appeared sweet and fairly malleable, and at least two of the guys who'd jumped looked like they were pretty smart.

We went around the team circle, giving our names. Besides me and Maren, our team included Annika, London, and Maddie, Sean, Rachel, AJ, Lucas, and Oscar.

Variations of *where are you from* small talk bubbled up, and it was obvious we'd been pulled from all areas of the country.

Annika was the first one to start talking about the game. "You guys, help me out. I'm so confused. There are two different prizes now?" she asked.

"One for the winner, or winners, of the game," AJ said, "and then a separate one for whoever finds the treasure. But I guess the same person or people could win both. It didn't sound like there was any problem with that."

Annika scrunched her nose in puzzlement. "So if there are ten of us and our team wins one of the prizes, we'll split it ten ways? Why would we even bother trying to find the treasure? It'll probably be hard to win one prize, let alone two, and if we find the treasure we'd only get twenty-five thousand each. I'd rather focus on the main prize. Wouldn't we all prefer to win the game and get a million dollars? After we split it that's still a hundred thousand for each of us."

Maren snorted. I noticed the lipstick smear was gone and I wondered if she'd figured it out herself or if some brave soul had stepped up to tell her.

Annika, understandably, reacted defensively to the snort. "What?"

I hadn't realized that I'd ended up next to Maren, and people were looking at her and then at me, possibly lumping us together because of the whole helicopter/bag episode. I edged toward Maddie, who was hovering on my other side. I'd definitely prefer to be associated with Maddie. It wasn't like I could go camo with Maren. Getting linked to her would pretty much be the opposite.

"First of all, ten of us won't make it to the end. Obviously," Maren said. "So you don't have to worry your brain with all that pointless math."

"Why 'obviously'?" London interjected sharply, her long cornrows swinging over her shoulder. "Deb hasn't explained every single rule yet. Ten could make it."

London and Annika had been sitting together, and now here she was speaking up for Annika, so it was a perfect illustration of how the same thing could happen with me and Maren. I shuffled even closer to Maddie.

Maren rolled her eyes. "Did you bother to watch a single episode of *Survivor*? Because this show is definitely going to copy at least half of it," she said. "We're going to do a bunch of contests and after each one we vote someone off until one person is left. Duh. If you were on that show, I bet you'd be the one who shows up not knowing how to make fire even though that's literally always how they break ties."

Maddie gasped. "We have to know how to make fire?"

Maren shook her head in exasperation. "For God's sake. This had better not be a contest of intelligence or we're doomed."

AJ jumped in. "Calm down, everyone. I got the four-one-one—"

"Talk like a normal human, please," Maren interjected.

AJ was untroubled by the correction. "I got the deets—"

"Nope," Maren said firmly.

AJ adjusted his account again. "Here's the story. We'll be doing a series of challenges that have a treasure theme to them, but they won't have anything to do with the actual treasure. Then if we want, on the side, we can search—"

He continued talking, going on about team dynamics and strategy and the ratio of optimal group numbers most likely to yield the highest rate of return. Well, at least one of us was smart. He was animated and obviously very passionate, which saved him from being completely boring, but still. No one wanted to think about getting voted off so soon after arriving.

I tuned out. Next to me, Maddie seemed to be ignoring AJ, too. She was staring up at Black Rock.

"Are you nervous?" I asked her, thinking of her anxious reaction to Maren's fire-building comment.

She nodded hesitantly.

"At least you got to keep your bag," I said. "That means you're better off than most of the players on the Sol team."

Maddie smiled gratefully. "Yeah, I know! I brought a photo album with pictures of all my pets. I'd be so sad if I lost that. It's going to be hard to be away from home so long."

Maddie seemed really, really young. She was short, and her oversized cat T-shirt and long-ish shorts made her look even younger than she probably was. We had to be at least seventeen to participate in the show, but if I'd run into her on the street, I would have guessed she was fifteen, tops.

"Plus it's scarier on the island than I thought it would be," she said. "It's pretty, but we're so far away from everything."

I nodded. True. The isolation was going to take some getting used to. When I'd stayed on the island last time, there had been a boat to take us over to the mainland for quick breaks when we got tired of camping. This time, we'd be confined to the island until voted off.

"At the hotel last night the receptionist told me there was a curse on this island. That freaked me out. Have you heard that, too?" Maddie asked.

"Supposedly seven must die before the treasure can be found," I said.

"Wait, it's true? That's so creepy! Have people actually died?"

"Yeah. Six so far." I shivered involuntarily, thinking of Miles. To deflect, I attempted a joke. "Only one to go—"

I stopped talking, distracted by the Sol team. They were huddled together, a few of them stealing furtive glances our way.

Maddie turned to see what I was looking at. She frowned. "Hey, what are they—"

She hadn't even finished her sentence before the Sol boys started running toward us. Maddie yelped and immediately ran, her fight-or-flight instinct obviously more well-tuned than mine, because I froze.

Porter was headed my way. He stopped short right in front of me and grinned. "Riley, right?"

I nodded. What was happening? I felt a flutter of hope. Had I been right that we'd shared a connection? I'd cut myself off from friends and romance for so long that I might have been reading the signals wrong, but it had to mean something that he'd picked me. At least, I hoped it did.

"Don't make this hard, okay?"

I was flustered. "Don't make what hard?"

I didn't know what else to say, but it turned out he wasn't interested in talking, because before I realized it, he had bent down, leaned into me, and flipped me over his shoulder.

He grunted in discomfort, and my immediate reaction was to feel embarrassed. I nearly apologized for my

115 pounds being too much of an inconvenience before I snapped out of it. Still, it was a surreal feeling. Half an hour ago I'd thought he was cute, and now here I was bent over his shoulder, face-planted against his back. It was as thrilling as it was objectionable, because any hope for a normal initial interaction had just been hijacked. I couldn't tell: Should I be glad, or mad, that he had targeted me?

I was still holding on to my bag with one hand, but I pulled on his shirt with the other. I kicked my legs hoping all the movement would make him give up, but he kept walking straight toward the ocean. The cowboy with the muscular gym-rat body—Cody, I'd heard someone call him—had managed to catch Maddie, but the other boys were having a hard time with the three other girls. Maren was not having it, and Annika and London were holding off any would-be captors by going back-to-back and crouching down in an attack position. Well, good for them. As for me, it looked like I was going to be getting wet. When we reached the tidemark, I reluctantly tossed my bag onto the dry sand where it would stay safe.

Porter advanced steadily into the water until it reached his knees, taking rough, giant strides so I was wet from being splashed before he even tossed me in. I hated myself for squealing when my back hit the waves.

The water was warm, even warmer than the air, thank God. I sunk underwater to take a second to collect myself. I had to admit, I felt flattered, but I was pretty sure that wasn't how I was supposed to feel. It was probably a big violation of girl power to smile and flirt with someone who'd just unceremoniously dunked you.

But girl power be damned, because when I sat up and started to undo my braid, Porter was smiling at me, and what can I say? He was cute. I smiled back, but then he turned around and raised his arms in a sign of victory to the girls on his team waiting up on the beach. There were only four girls on that team: Willa, Alex and Taylor, and another blond girl named Chloe. In any other group, Chloe would have been eye-catching, but next to Willa and Alex she was merely pretty. Poor Taylor, though. As predicted, her hair had not survived the jump. Skinnier, shorter, and smaller than the other girls, she looked like a sad, wet cat who'd been caught outside in the rain.

Willa started clapping for Porter and the other three girls joined in.

Oh.

It burned, but had I really thought we'd shared a special moment? Even discounting how he was obviously playing up to those girls, he and I were on opposite teams. We weren't supposed to share moments or anything else.

I realized suddenly that there was a camera guy only a few feet away, standing calf-deep in the waves, capturing every second. Frustration overwhelmed me. Great. Five minutes on camera and I was already looking stupid.

Usually my emotions don't affect my expression—a fact

that everyone is quick to list as a personality flaw—but when Porter turned back around he did a double take.

"Hey, don't be mad. Everyone on our team got wet, now you're wet, no big deal. Now we're even."

He held out his hand. Normally I'd have taken it immediately. I'd have been grateful for it. I would have felt special. A good-looking guy had picked me—*me!*—out of a group of girls. That was something, wasn't it? Something valuable?

Yet looking at him standing there with his wide, confident stance and his arm only halfheartedly extended, his attention clearly elsewhere, I got mad. And when I get mad, that's when I stop thinking straight and do all the crazy things that end up getting me in trouble. I'd pushed that instinct down all year—a relatively easy thing to do since my social life consisted of close to zero interactions—but now I couldn't take the slight.

So instead of allowing him to pull me up, I grasped his hand with both of mine, put my feet on top of his for leverage and then yanked him down into the waves next to me. Through the rush of the water, I thought I heard him yelp.

I waited for him to sit up. "Okay," I told him. "*Now* we're even."

"What the heck? What is wrong with you?" He stumbled up and headed for the shore, but not before staggering and turning back to scowl at me.

"Man, was that a mistake. I should have gone for her instead of you."

He meant Maddie, who had suffered the same wet fate as me, but unlike me, had already pulled herself together and made it back to the beach.

For some reason, the camera stayed on me instead of Porter, and that's when I felt something familiar rise up and wash over me: that feeling of *Oh God, I made a huge mistake*, the residual hallmark of Riley's Law.

I leaned all the way back to dip my head into the water, then lifted my feet to float on my back. I stayed for a minute, maybe more, silently waiting for the cameraman to get bored and leave me alone.

On the far end of the beach, the helicopter lifted itself into the sky, hovered right above me for a few seconds and then zoomed toward the mainland.

Well, there went my ride. No turning back now.

5

I CAME OUT OF THE WATER WET AND IRRITABLE, BUT I

had at least one thing to be grateful for: Deb had been telling the truth when she'd promised the show wasn't meant to be a survival or deprivation experience. The three open-air tiki huts at the tree line turned out to be part of a fully stocked base camp. Hammocks, board games, cornhole, and even a fire pit would help us pass the time. Strings of tiny Christmas tree lights were wrapped around the posts of each of the huts and some of the palm trees. Because it was daytime they weren't lit, but their presence indicated that we'd have electricity. Nice.

I grabbed my zip bag on the way up, relieved to find that everything was still inside.

Everyone was standing around the edge of the largest hut, which was obviously our dining area. There was a full kitchen, too, hidden from the beach side and nestled between the back of the hut and the woods. I stood off to the side of the group, hoping no one noticed my dripping wet, self-conscious arrival.

Joaquin was holding court in the middle of the hut, surrounded by bamboo tables and chairs that were arranged in groups underneath brightly colored strings of lanterns. The decor could have been lifted straight from an actual movie set, it was that elaborate. Lots of wood carvings and gold accents and beachy decorations like you'd see in a casual seafood restaurant or a beachside fish taco stand.

Porter whistled. "Now this is what I call a Snack Bar."

Katya, Deb's assistant, tossed me a beach towel. Green, for Huaca. Maddie had a green one, too. The Sol team members were all wrapped in yellow.

"Nice of you to join us, Riley," Joaquin said with a friendly wink.

The entire group turned to stare. I tried to smile but it was definitely more of a wince.

"I'm about to show everyone something that we're all really excited about," Joaquin said.

I felt like I was supposed to say something. "Can't wait," I tossed out, trying to nail the right level of excitement. Not too much or I'd sound like Taylor, and not too little or I'd seem like Maren. My reaction verged a little closer to Taylor then I'd planned, mostly because I knew what Joaquin was about to show us and I was actually excited.

Joaquin motioned us to follow him toward the back corner.

A row of twenty brightly colored electronic tablets were lined up on a small table, against a wall lined with a fishing net and some buoys. The contrast between the glossy metal phones and the casual driftwood fish taco signs reminded me of home, because that same mix of hightech and natural was everywhere in San Francisco. You'd walk into an artisanal, fair-trade, eco-friendly coffee shop, the kind that referred to customers as "guests," where everything was very stripped-down and earthy, yet you could whip out your high-tech phone to pay with an app.

"Allow me to introduce you to Silicon Valley's newest product, the Demon Tablet and Phone," Joaquin said. "One of the show's sponsors"—aka my dad—"has generously provided them so that all the players of this show can act as beta testers before the product rolls out nationwide."

"I'm down, but what are they?" Murch called out.

"Picture your phone, taken to the next level. Your phone, with all the features you use, but explicitly tailored for your generation. You'll never run out of space again. The Demon will hold all your apps, photos, videos—you name it. Whatever you want, you can add to this phone. Come on over and take a look."

I didn't need to. I knew exactly what they were, and I had an ice blue one of my own back home. The Demons were my father's latest project. I knew they'd be here, which was why I'd gone through all that effort to bring the satellite.

Joaquin went through the rules: the Demons had to be

checked out every morning and returned every night so they could be recharged. Failure to comply by anyone would mean the loss of their use for everyone.

"You won't be able to make calls or use any of the apps yet," Joaquin said, "because while you're on the island you won't have access to Wi-Fi."

Yeah, that's what he thought.

"What's the point, then?" someone called out.

"The point, my friend, is the camera feature," Joaquin said.

Willa squealed.

Joaquin nodded knowingly at her. "I knew some of you would appreciate that. The photos and videos you take on the island will be used in actual footage when the show airs, but not only that, when the show is over, these photos can be uploaded to Facebook—"

"Facebook's dead," Murch called out.

"Fastchat, then."

"Snapchat!" Willa corrected him, laughing. "You're only messing with us, though. You know what they are. And don't forget Instagram, that's the best one."

"Maybe. Or is it? Everything changes so fast, it might be some new hot thing by the time we're done filming."

"Can I put my fantasy football app on this?" Murch asked.

"Yes, once the show is over and they are connected with Wi-Fi, any apps can be installed. Those of you who make it through the game without losing your Demon—or your

Demon privileges—will be allowed to keep the one assigned to you. Furthermore, the company would like to use footage from this show in their commercials, and if you're featured, you'll be compensated accordingly. Certain players may even be invited to serve as brand ambassadors, so treat these phones well, and use them appropriately."

Phil, the assistant producer, passed out the Demons with Katya. I took one, pretended to learn how to use it, and then when everyone else was busy playing with their new toys I went to find Deb.

She was back where the helicopter had landed, sorting a pile of camera equipment.

"Hey," she said, leaning in conspiratorially. "Got your Demon, I see. I owe your dad big-time for suggesting them. The footage is going to give the final edit of the show something really different. So how about that treasure news, huh? You're excited, right?"

Not what I had expected at all. I thought for sure Deb would pretend she'd never said treasure hunting wasn't going to be part of the experience.

"I don't know about excited," I said. "Mostly I was . . . surprised. You told me you were filming on Black Rock just to give the show a theme, that the gold itself would never come into it."

I watched her for signs of deception or unease, but there were none.

"That's what we thought," Deb said, "but then I sprung

for the legal team to do some digging, and it turns out that based on our contract we had a bit more freedom than I was originally told. Treasure hunts aren't allowed on Black Rock right now per se, but if something was to happen while part of the show, well, it turns out that's a different story."

"You have permission, then? Or you don't? I'm confused."

Deb laughed. "Does it matter? Find it, and let me take care of the details."

This was kind of shady. True, I'd technically been planning to look without permission, but that was me, an eighteen-year-old girl on my own. Not a corporate-funded operation. The distinction felt important.

She looked at me in concern. "I thought you'd be all jacked up. No?"

Just because looking for the gold was part of the show now didn't mean I wanted her to know I'd planned to do it anyway. I hedged. "I'll probably give it a shot, but I mean, what are the odds of me finding it? The treasure has been hidden for hundreds of years. Plenty of qualified people have tried and failed to find it."

Deb picked up a small camera and flipped a few buttons, inspecting something before handing it to one of the black-clad men packing up the gear.

"This one's good to go," she told him. To me, she said, "Probably give it a shot? Come on. All those very specific, very treasure-based questions you plagued me with? *Deb, will we be near the first marker? How close will we be to the black cliffs?* You were going to go for it and try to follow the clues on your own, admit it."

I was saved from answering immediately when one of the cameramen carrying a box of gear accidentally backed into Deb.

"Hey, Lou, watch it. Hasn't enough equipment been trashed so far?"

I could have laughed and said *okay, you got me.* Maybe the old me would've done that, but now I kept whatever I could to myself, especially when there was a bit of sketch to it. She really hadn't known about that loophole? Seemed like a big enough deal to have investigated right away. I wasn't buying it.

"Plus, you brought the map with you," Deb pointed out.

I'd forgotten she'd seen my copy of the treasure map in my bag during the contraband search.

"Old times' sake," I said quickly. "I wanted to see the places I'd been to last time, but I knew I'd never remember where we'd been without the map."

She threw up her hands. "Okay, okay. But give it a shot. Maybe you picked up some clues when you were here before."

I had. That was the thing. I had the biggest clue of all: I knew where the treasure was likely hidden. The X, so to speak. In fact, I'd even been at the site of the X—although I hadn't known it at the time.

The trip to Black Rock two years ago had come about at the last minute after an SOS call from Miles. He'd been searching on Black Rock for nearly a year and he'd almost run out of money. He urgently needed more, he told my father, because he'd found something important: a collapsed cave system, hidden from view, in exactly the right area. Funding treasure hunts was my father's side passion, and after hearing the words *important* and *hidden* he canceled our family trip to Paris and hauled me and my mother to Black Rock Island.

It wasn't quite the resort-style vacation I was used to—this was pure camping. Partially constructed tents, threadbare sleeping bags, and no bathrooms. I understood the lack of basic amenities once we spent a few days with Miles. My fun, prank-loving godfather who used to blow into town for a day or two and enthrall us with tales of his adventures before disappearing on a new quest had been replaced with someone serious and grim. He'd become skeletally, creepily thin, and he didn't want to think or talk of anything other than the gold. Even changing out of his wrinkled cargo shorts and stained Grateful Dead T-shirt was apparently too much of a time suck, because he wore that same outfit the entire time I was there.

Get more funding. Expand the search. Renew the permit. Find the gold. Those things were whispered and discussed so much that I expected to hear them churning from the crash of the waves and whispered in the rustle of the palm trees.

The professional search team had quit before we arrived, which meant saw only Miles and a handful of people who were paid by the hour. Miles had a girlfriend, too, but I barely saw her—she was the one tasked with renewing the permit. She spent nearly all her time on the mainland haggling with government officials.

I went to the site on a number of occasions, but it wasn't interesting enough to hold my attention for more than an hour at a time. Dirty, dusty caves can only compete with a perfect white sand beach for so long, but I was there, at what would turn out to be the X, on our last day.

"You need to abandon this project," I'd heard my father tell Miles. I was nearby, using string to mark off the areas that Miles had searched and found lacking. It was hot, boring work and I was glad for the distraction. "This was always meant to be a vanity project to raise your profile," my father continued, "but you've taken it way too far. Even if you find the gold, at this point the payoff you'd get from any public attention is far less than everything you've sunk into it."

Miles was despondent. "A little more time to let Lady Luck find us," he'd begged, but my father was adamant. The dig—and Miles himself—had deteriorated beyond redemption.

"Gold fever has him in its grip," my father explained as we flew home. "At this point, he'd sell his soul to find this treasure. The greatest favor I can do for him right now is to stop enabling him."

I wasn't sure about that, but I did agree that Miles was certainly suffering from something. Miles had somehow come to believe that he was engaged in a struggle with the island itself, and releasing the gold from the depths of its hiding place was his sworn duty. I'd begun to suspect that his girlfriend was off the island so much because she preferred dealing with governmental red tape than listening to him bang on about the gold all the time.

Even so, it bothered me the way my father had cut off his friend so easily.

He'd waved off my concerns. "In the end it's all economics," he'd said. I guess that's why he made the big bucks—every investment, no matter what or who was involved, was made according to a strict cost-benefit analysis. Miles had become a liability. He'd made the mistake of slipping too far into the loss column of my father's affection.

It was something I'd come to experience for myself, and it made me regret that back then I hadn't fought harder for Miles. Taking over his search now would be a way to make things right, for Miles and for me.

"By the way," I said to Deb, trying to keep it light. "Let's say I do remember some of Miles's tips and I find the treasure. You said there's a money prize. That means I don't keep the gold, right?"

"Nope. Any discovery becomes the property of the show. All of that is laid out in the forms you signed." There had been reams of forms to sign. Interesting that this one had been slipped in without any notice or explanation. "Now go join the group," Deb told me. "Phil's starting the grand tour.

I've got to finish a few things and then I'll meet up with all of you in a minute."

FLANKING THE MAIN dining hut were two smaller thatched huts, one for Sol and one for Huaca. They were essentially team clubhouses, and they were decked out similarly to the dining hut in full beach-loving regalia. Once we stepped behind them, though, the frills disappeared to reveal a clearing scattered with some basic buildings that hadn't been tiki-fied at all.

"No filming will occur back here," Phil announced. There was a shed for equipment storage, boys' and girls' bathrooms (showers and toilets, thank God!), and a small medical cabin so austere that Porter took one look and immediately dubbed it the Quack Shack.

"Best not to get sick," he advised the rest of us, and I silently agreed.

The bunkhouses were divided by gender, not team.

"I'll bet it's because some of us are underage. Can't have the unsupervised teenagers hooking up," Willa guessed.

We split up by gender to inspect our respective cabins. Deb joined us for the girls-only tour while Phil took the boys. Our cabin was as stark as you could get, and if the huts on the beach were meant to represent a tourist's dream, this was definitely closer to an orphanage. One tiny window and no decorations at all, only our show-provided duffel bags piled against the wall on one side and a row of bunk beds on the other. There were also ten small safes, stationed two per bunk at the base of each set. These weren't from my dad, but they had a techy vibe to them that suggested they were most likely from one of the start-up companies he worked with.

"I call a top bunk!" Maddie called out, running to the far set of beds and climbing on the top.

"She's so cute," Willa said, in a sweetish tone that was hard to pin down as condescending but was probably meant to be. "And so is this! I never went to summer camp, so now it's my chance. Just us girls, playing with each other's hair and having pillow fights every night."

"Yeah, I'm a no on the hair thing," Maren said. I wasn't surprised to see she was the first one at the duffel bags. She was already going through her own.

"Hey," she said to Deb. "You guys took my *Dropkick Murphys* T-shirt. If my Gov Ball shirt is gone I'm going to be pissed."

"We told you no brand names," Deb reminded her.

"I thought you'd just blur them out."

"That's what we'll be doing with your slogan T-shirts, yes, but brand names are off-limits. It was a simple instruction."

"Slogan T-shirts? You mean like this?" Maren held up a gray T-shirt that read *Cool story, bro. Now make me a sandwich.*

"Nice," Willa said. This time her sarcasm was evident. Taylor, Alex, and Chloe were standing right behind her, barely even attempting to hide the fact that they were waiting for Willa to choose her bed before they picked their own.

Whatever. I wasn't going to be picky. The one underneath Maddie looked fine to me. No one raced me for it.

Deb went into the rules. No boys, lights out at eleven, and there would be a rotation of chaperones staying nearby in the Quack Shack to make sure we complied. "And Maren, for continuity's sake we're going to need you in the same clothes you were wearing on the helicopter."

I hadn't even noticed, but Maren was in the process of taking off her shirt. She was wearing a bathing suit. I wondered again why she hadn't jumped; she had obviously been prepared.

"You can wear your awesome sandwich shirt tomorrow," Deb said. "And by the way, that goes for all of you girls—no changing. Even those of you in bathing suits. Looking at you, Willa."

"If you say so," Willa said. Before this second I had never been sure that *smirking* was a real thing, but sure enough, it was. I wished I could remember if I'd ever seen her Instagram account. Probably filled with lots of artsy staged pictures of her doing trendy things. Faux hiking, drinking lattes, looking angstily toward the horizon, that sort of thing.

"We can keep some of our things in a safe?" Maddie asked Deb. "That's so nice."

She slipped her nylon bag off her shoulder and started transferring things into a safe, including that photo album she'd been talking about.

"Those locks are the newest in fingerprint technology, so

once you set it, you'll be the only person who can unlock it," Deb said.

I quickly unpacked my own bag, putting everything into the safe and locking it right away. I breathed a sigh of relief. Map, compass, satellite, notebook—they'd all made it here safe and sound.

I saw Alex looking around, probably noticing for the first time that her small nylon bag wasn't in the pile of duffels. Chloe caught on, too.

"Excuse me, Deb, I don't see our little bags," Chloe said. She was really polite, the sort of girl who could be cool while also appealing to adults. *That nice girl Chloe* was probably how her friends' parents described her.

"Yeah, about that. Joaquin is going to tell you—"

Deb's walkie crackled.

"Deb, we need you by the staging area. We've got an issue with the C-cam."

"Again?"

The voice came through even angrier. "Worse. I'm telling you, we're freaking cursed—"

Deb cut him off. "Okay. I got it. Flying in."

She clipped the walkie back on her belt, looking exasperated.

"Listen up, gang," she told us. "Time to go back to base camp where you can hang out with the boys and spend too much time on your new phones, so basically it'll be exactly like you never left home."

"Wait," Taylor said. "Our bags—"

"Base camp. Joaquin. Move it."

The other girls didn't need any prodding. If Joaquin knew where the bags were, then that's where everyone wanted to go. We found him at the fire pit, but he told us we'd have to wait for the boys to arrive to talk about the bags. There were a few complaints, mostly from Taylor who had an A+ whine, but nearly everyone took his word and settled in on the logs to wait for the boys. I have a theory that really good-looking people get away with things that less attractive people can't, and I was sure if doughy, overweight Phil in his uncool orange Hawaiian shirt had been the one holding the secret of the lost bags he would have gotten a lot more pushback. But Joaquin was hot, so no one wanted to offend him.

That didn't mean he wanted to walk into trouble, so he stayed near those of us girls who had kept our bags and weren't loudly fuming about injustice.

"I like your Zodiac pendant," Joaquin said to me. "Virgo?"

I nodded and touched my necklace. It had been a birthday gift from Miles several years ago and I'd intentionally chosen to wear it to the island. I hoped it would bring luck.

"So where are you from?"

"San Francisco."

"Ah, a California girl. I live in Southern California, myself."

"Did you move there right from Brazil?" I asked him.

Joaquin looked confused. Then he laughed. "Are you serious?"

"You said your people . . ." My skin doesn't usually flush, but I felt my cheeks go so hot that there was no chance he missed my embarrassment.

"My people are from LA," he said, and I realized he was speaking without even the slightest hint of an accent. A slow grin spread across his face. "You thought I was actually from Brazil? That's great! It's called acting, kid. Thanks for the compliment—you just made my day."

Noise in the distance indicated that the boys were on their way, so Joaquin stood and got ready to greet them.

I didn't know why I was surprised to hear he was an actor. By now I should be used to things turning out differently then they first appear, because after all, that's the story of my life. I could hardly accuse others of being sheep and accepting whatever story they were presented with if I was guilty of doing it myself.

"Welcome back, guys." When they'd all arrived, Joaquin took a minute to show us where to sit at the fire pit. "Let's talk for a minute about how you all shook out," he continued. "Team Sol, it looks like most of you are the danger lovers, the adrenaline junkies. Ninety percent of your team jumped off the helicopter. Do you think that love of danger is going to give you an edge in the game?"

"Damn straight!" Porter called out.

"Are you sure about that?" Joaquin said. He paused, letting that hang for a minute. "It's true that Team Sol might have the brawn, but it's also true that Team Huaca might have the brains. You'll notice that those of you who jumped into the water left your personal items bag behind on the helicopter, but those who walked off carried theirs."

It was hard not to feel a little bit superior as most of the Sol team began to realize that maybe they weren't the team with the edge after all.

"Wait a minute. What? Are you keeping our bags?" Taylor wailed.

A list of lost items floated into the air, with varying degrees of exasperation.

My headlamp, my best bathing suit, my journal.

"Why would you do that to us?" Taylor demanded, arms flying, voice rising. But Joaquin was unmoved.

"Treasure hunting tools left behind." He shook his head sadly. "The best advice I can give you is that going forward in this game you'll need to think like a treasure hunter. Every tool matters. Every clue matters. Don't take anything for granted."

Joaquin's accent was noticeable now. I was starting to get it: when he spoke with an accent it was for the show. A lack of accent meant the cameras weren't rolling and he was off-duty.

AJ was even more agitated than Taylor, which was saying something. "Okay, sure, but seriously, I need my bag." AJ's glasses kept sliding down his nose and he'd push them up with the heel of his hand. "I really, really need it. I actually have important things in it."

"Important?" Maren asked, perking up. "What kind of important things?"

"My map, my Cipher, *things*."

AJ? The stealth treasure hunter was AJ? I gave him the once-over. I guess it made sense that it would turn out to be one of the smart guys.

"You told us to put our most important things in those bags," AJ complained to Joaquin. "You set this whole thing up! You tricked us."

"You set yourself up, AJ. For every action, there is a reaction."

More wails of protest, which, honestly, Joaquin deserved for that lame comment. I was feeling pretty good, though. Who knew that all my previous difficulties would turn out to be good practice for this show? A year ago I took everything at face value, which meant I'd have fully trusted Deb, left my bag behind, and completely lost out.

Murch, representing the ten percent of the Sol team who hadn't jumped, looked at Maren. He leaned over to say something to Justin, one of the other athletes on Sol, then he pointed at me and Maren. "Those two took some stuff out of the bags. See if they've got anything," Murch said loudly to his teammates.

What? No! I hadn't taken anything, but even more importantly, I'd saved his butt from jumping. And seriously, *those two*? If I looked like Willa or Alex or Chloe he would definitely have known my name. I was about to take myself out of the equation, but I got a look at Maren's face. For a tough girl dressed in black from head to toe, she looked worried.

I felt the cameras on us. On me. So much for trying to blend in. How was it that I'd been on this island less than an hour and I'd somehow stepped right into the same problem that got me here? I could see how it would play out on TV: I step away, say I had nothing to do with it, and then the show cuts to a clip of Maren throwing me a bag—eliminating the part where I don't take it, of course. And voilà: there it is, my online reputation in full color. A girl who would do anything to save herself, including hurting friends, if that's what it took.

But if I let myself get grouped with Maren, my "be friendly" strategy was basically toast. She had to be the prickliest person on the island, and I'd be tied to her, which basically meant I was facing two bad options. If I sided against Maren, it would be better for me now—but no doubt I would pay for it later when the show aired, and a big reason I was here was to provide visual proof that I wasn't the troll the world thought I was. My other choice wasn't much better, though, because if I sided with her now, well, I'd become a target. No doubt about that. It could be worth it, though, to get to look at AJ's things. His notes might be helpful.

I'd wanted to avoid attention, but now that I was getting it, let no one say I hadn't learned from my mistakes. I wasn't going to make the selfish decision. I wouldn't throw Maren under the bus.

"Fine. Yes, we might have some things," I told everyone. "When we realized the bags had to stay on the plane, we—"

"Ah, capitalism at its finest," Deb interjected. "Now the rest of you can bargain with Riley and Maren if they've got something you want returned."

I stood there, openmouthed in shock. That isn't what I'd meant, but now it was too late to explain and the crowd was audibly and visibly turning on us.

Why do you get to do that? Who are you to go through our things?

Cody folded his arms across his impressive chest. He spoke in a slow, Texan drawl.

"Y'all, I believe we are witnessing the start of this game. You'd best straighten your backbone, because it's gonna be the law of the wild out here. Kill or be killed."

"On that note," Deb interjected brightly, "how about we play some nice icebreaker games?"

6

AFTER A FEW AWKWARD AND UNPRODUCTIVE ROUNDS
of two truths and a lie, it was time for lunch. Those cute little
groupings of tables with two, three, or four chairs I'd noticed
before in the dining hut? Not so cute when you had a plate of
food and had to awkwardly walk through them looking for
an inconspicuous spot to slide into.

I bypassed the core Sol group, obviously. They'd pulled
two tables together so that Willa and the three other girls
from Sol—Alex, Chloe, and Taylor—were sitting with
Porter, Justin, and Murch. At this point I was glad they were
ignoring me instead of giving me dirty looks, but even so it
was almost as annoying to hear them talking like old friends
already, cementing the fact they were a unified team. And
there really was no getting away from noticing it, because
Taylor's voice was loud and persistent and her idea of conversation was to exclaim *Oh my God* at everything. Justin and

Porter were commiserating about the college sports commitment process—*Dude, you've got to get your coach on those letters!*—while Willa was establishing her social media cred. *Once I moved to LA and started posting a lot of beach and party pics I went over a million followers. Not as many on Snapchat yet but I'm trying.* I could tell that Alex and Chloe's discovery that they were both from nearby towns in Ohio had taken a backseat to Willa's tales of her more glamorous hometown.

Honestly, it was amazing how certain people always ended up together. Like little balls of mercury, pretty people inevitably flow together to merge and form one bright, shiny pool. It happens everywhere. Even, apparently, on deserted islands.

Maddie was sitting alone. I'd have to sit with her—it would look odd if I didn't, but I really wanted to sit with AJ so I could find out what he knew about the gold. He hadn't taken a seat yet. It had to seem natural, so I looped back around to a buffet set up by the kitchen entrance and picked up another spoonful of rice and beans.

This time when I passed the Sol table, Murch leaned his chair right into me, knocking my plate to the ground.

"Oops," he said.

My face got hot. This was the worst-case scenario. Not only wasn't I invisible, I was being actively targeted. I felt a wave of shame crash over me, and I bent down to retrieve the plate, hoping Taylor's latest *Oh my God* was in response to finding out Willa's average number of likes per post.

It wasn't. When I stood up, the Sol table had stopped talking. Taylor was looking at me in wide-eyed embarrassment and amusement, and a bit of something else, too: relief. I had seen it at school all the time after the scandal—the realization on old friends' faces that they'd dodged a bullet by not hanging out with me. Right about now, Taylor had to be feeling pretty glad she'd left me behind on the helicopter.

"Careful there," Murch said warningly to me. "You wouldn't want to get in the way and get hurt."

It was a split-second decision. I faked a stumble and tipped my plate of sandy food right onto Murch's lap.

"Are you freaking kidding me?" Murch jumped up, sending his chair backward. His reaction was so fast, so extreme, that I didn't even have time to pretend to look sorry. My regret was legit, though—he towered above me, huge and quivering with anger, and if Porter hadn't jumped up and put himself between us, it was possible Murch would have hit me.

God, Riley—think!

My knees trembled. I was starting to feel warm and fuzzy again toward Porter for saving me, but before I fully turned into a pile of mush, he said to Murch, "Hey, man, sit down and cool off, would you? It's not worth getting kicked out over an annoying girl like her."

Annoying girl. Oh. He'd done it for Murch, not me.

"Yes, don't mind me," I said, taking a few steps back and retreating for the buffet. "Annoying, clumsy old me."

Willa tossed Murch her yellow towel and the friction dissipated.

Porter catcalled Murch. "Strip, strip, strip!" while Willa laughed and covered her eyes. "Please, no! Keep your clothes on," she pleaded teasingly.

I felt strangely let down. The confrontation had actually been a little exhilarating. But now it was over, and I was back on the outside, watching Chloe dip her towel in a glass of water to rub the stain on Murch's shirt while the other kids laughed at Murch's extreme reaction.

By the time I finished with the buffet for the third time, the Sol team seemed to have forgotten all about me, which was a good thing—but I couldn't help feeling a pinch of bitterness that they'd moved on so quickly. Luckily, I had other things to focus on. Enough people had settled into the tables that the only one with any seats left was Maren's. AJ was right behind me.

"My bag," he said, plopping his plate on the table and not bothering with any niceties. "You guys have it?"

"Nope," Maren said.

I opened, and then closed, my mouth. She was the one holding his things; if she wanted to pretend otherwise, I'd have to let her. I fiddled with the salt and pepper shakers.

"I thought you said you had our bags?"

"I didn't say anything." Maren looked at me pointedly.

"Fine," AJ said, obviously exasperated. "Not you. Riley. Riley said you had our bags."

"Nope," Maren repeated.

"No? Really?"

I felt sorry for AJ. He looked crushed, understandably. I'd have felt the same way.

"What did you say you lost?" I asked innocently. "A journal?"

"Yeah, my journal, and some other stuff. The treasure map, for one thing. And then I had a little book, too. Orange, with lots of notes in it. That thing is key because it's the definitive guide to interpreting the signs."

"Ohhhhh," Maren said, tipping back in her chair. "Those things. Why didn't you say so? I didn't take anyone's *bag*, but I did take some things out of the bags. Orange booklet, you say? That does sound vaguely familiar."

AJ looked so grateful that he didn't even seem to mind she'd been playing with him. "Thank God."

"Here's the thing, though. I don't quite understand why you'd bring any of that in the first place. We literally only found out today that searching for the treasure was an option."

"Deb told us to study the island history," AJ said.

"Yeah, study the history," Maren said. "Not bring a dissertation on the methodology of treasure map reading, complete with aerial photos."

"Oh, so you do have my notes!" AJ brightened up. He lowered his voice. "I got a heads-up this was going to be a thing. Deb found me and convinced me to do this show because she read an independent study I recently published on drone usage to survey and chart the terrain of this island. I used those pictures, plus some open-source NASA images, to graph a series of undiscovered subterranean cave systems"—my heart nearly stopped. He knew about the caves, too?—"and Deb was into it. Finding the treasure will be great PR for the show, while adding a solid footnote to my article. Probably get me into Harvard, actually."

"But if you find the treasure, you'll get a chunk of change," Maren said. "You won't need to go to Harvard."

"Are you crazy? Harvard is the dream. The rest is gravy."

I barely heard the discussion that followed—something about weighing an Ivy League acceptance against the archaeological importance of discovering a priceless treasure. My head was spinning. I couldn't believe the odds of someone else, someone *here*, coincidentally discovering the existence of the caves. I might be way out of my league. While I was going to have to rely on the satellite for assistance with the clues, AJ needed nothing more than his own brain.

I definitely needed to see his notes before Maren gave them back.

MOST OF THE crew had left us alone after lunch, other than a few cameramen who weaved and circled around us, nonstop filming. When Deb had said it would take a while to get used to their presence, I'd thought she'd meant days. But here we were, not even halfway through the first day, and I was already starting not to notice them.

Phil lumbered around the tables, passing out copies of the map. "If you're planning to search for the treasure, you'll definitely need one of these."

I didn't need a map; I had my own copy in my safe in the cabin, but I took one from Phil anyway. I pretended to study it while paying attention to the talk swirling around me. Nearly everyone, thankfully, seemed clueless about how to find the gold. Conventional public wisdom was that the treasure would most likely be found in a grove on the far side of the island, because that's where a silver buckle from the 1500s had been discovered about twenty years ago. Almost all the players had heard of the buckle's discovery and seemed to be trying to pinpoint on the map exactly where that grove might be. Thank God—that was far away from where I planned to go. Any treasure hunter worth their salt knew the buckle had nothing to do with the gold.

"This seems like forced labor to me," Murch said to Phil as he took a map. "You're letting us loose on the island and hoping we find the treasure. We do, and it's a big win for you, but we just get a few bucks. You're basically sending us to do your dirty work."

"Two hundred and fifty grand is more than just a few bucks—"

"Shhhh!" At the Sol table, Justin stood up and motioned for silence.

Angry voices shot out of from the trees.

Deb emerged from the path, followed by Katya. "We're going to have to improvise," Deb was saying sharply. "We don't have a choice."

They stopped short when they realized they had an attentive audience.

"An island to explore, a beautiful beach, and all of you guys are sitting here waiting for someone to tell you what to do?" Deb asked. "Come on. No audience wants to watch a show of you lounging around. We need movement and action. Phil, did you explain the daily jobs? Might as well put them to work if this is what they're going to give us on their own."

"Jobs?" Murch nodded knowingly. "What'd I just say? Forced labor."

"Yeah, this place is basically a prison camp," Deb shot back, waving her clipboard toward the beach. "The daily jobs," she explained, "are minor tasks to get you moving and interacting with each other. I doubt you'll find them too taxing. Every day there will be a sign-up sheet at breakfast, and you can either choose something to do or one of us will assign you a job. We'll have shifts in the kitchen doing light prep—"

"I'll take that." A tall guy with a buzz cut tipped his chair back and he balanced, effortlessly, on the back legs. Everything about him was assured and no-nonsense, from his spiky hair to his sharp cheekbones and the way he observed the rest of us with his intense, dark eyes. He got some surprised looks. "What? My dad has a restaurant in Fort Lauderdale. Might as well stick with what I know."

"Love the enthusiasm, Rohan," Deb said, "but we weren't thinking there would be any need for shifts today so there isn't anything needed in the kitchen right now. There's been a slight change of filming plans, though, so we have an hour or two before our first challenge. Phil, what can we offer today? Firewood collection? Seaweed cleanup?"

"How about both?"

"Great. Both." Deb directed Katya to get a branch from the fire pit. "Katya, hold it up so everyone can see. All right, everyone, see this piece of kindling? We need to keep a pile of similar-sized pieces of wood by the fire pit, because that's where you'll be spending most of your evenings and firelight gives a nice, scenic backdrop. How about each of you finds twenty pieces of wood, or Phil, whatever you want to assign. Okay? Joaquin, get some confessionals going, too."

The two women left in a rush, leaving Phil to explain the chore system in more detail. He showed us how the little bits of seaweed and driftwood that washed up with the high tide had to be cleared so that the beach was pristine for filming. "And no," he added for Murch's benefit, "it isn't 'forced labor.' Crew members are going to be coming by every low tide to do a full cleanup, which includes raking the sand. Your contribution to this effort is very minor, and as Deb said, it's to get some interactions going. We'll use bits from those scenes as filler."

Beach-ready Willa chose seaweed cleanup, striding confidently toward the water. I had never seen anyone so comfortable wearing so little. She hadn't so much as fidgeted with a bathing suit strap or adjust her bottoms, which was a skill, really. And like metal filings pulled by a magnet, a number of players—mostly male—followed her.

"Hold up," Joaquin said, pointing at each of us who were left, his finger finally settling on a quiet girl whose name I hadn't heard yet.

"You're up, Rachel," he told her. "Confessional time."

"One-on-one interviews," Phil explained to the rest of us after they left, taking a path toward the camp interior. Better her than me. The longer I could delay my confessional, the better. I had no intention of confessing a thing.

Instead, I chose firewood duty.

"Twenty sticks?" I asked Phil.

"Sure. Yeah. Twenty sounds good," he said indifferently.

"Don't bother counting to twenty," Rohan said as we walked into the woods. "This is all just a runaround. Just get an armload and be done with it."

"It seems a little strange that they started us off with such a bang, basically throwing us out of the helicopter, but now we're killing time doing chores."

"Oh, it wasn't planned," Rohan said. We'd only gone a few feet into the woods, but we ran right into a dead tree with branches scattered all around. Rohan picked up some of the longer ones and began snapping them over his knee. The sound summoned AJ and Maren. I frowned. Had they been talking without me?

"We were supposed to start the first challenge right after lunch but someone smashed up a bunch of equipment," Rohan told us.

Alex and Taylor emerged from beyond the fallen tree and came around to our side. Alex was using a couple of branches like walking sticks. Rohan held his hand out for them, snapped each of them over his knee, and tossed them to the ground. I threw a branch of my own on top, and Taylor threw one, too.

"Who would do that? What kind of equipment?" Alex asked Rohan. "Like cameras?"

He picked up another branch and threw it onto the pile. "I don't know, but the local guys on the crew are scared. Stuff like that has been happening for a while. They all think that old curse is real."

AJ dropped a branch he'd dragged over to the pile. "I've said this before and I'll say it again. The curse is not real. It was made up to keep people away."

"It's working, dude."

Alex was pensive. "How do you know all of this?"

"I talked to them," Rohan said.

Maren followed up. "How?"

"How do you think? I opened my mouth and the words came out."

"I meant, literally how did Deb and Phil not object to

72

that? Not to mention it doesn't seem like too many of them speak English," Maren pointed out.

"I speak Portuguese, so that's not really an issue."

Interesting: a competitor who spoke the language of our host country. That couldn't be a coincidence. It wasn't as if Portugese was commonly taught in school.

I kept an eye on AJ. There was no way he was going to waste time gathering firewood when he could be checking out the first clue on the map: a stone marker not too far inland. If I'd never seen it in person, that'd be the first place I'd go.

Sure enough, I was right. When the pile of sticks got large enough to start bringing to the beach, he slipped away. I was about to follow him when I realized there was a camera pointed in my direction. I hesitated. I didn't want to be filmed sneaking off. That footage might turn into what Phil had just called a filler scene—and with just a few well-chosen snippets of me looking shady, Deb could shape the audience perception and shift reality, turning me into a villain.

But I could use these filler scenes to my advantage, too.

"Do you guys know where AJ went?" I asked innocently. Everyone looked around, even Maren. Good. That meant they hadn't talked about the clue without me. "I'll bet he started the treasure hunt."

"Little sneak," Rohan said. "But if that guy knows where the gold is, let's follow him."

Perfect. Now following AJ to the clue seemed like Rohan's idea, not mine. I pointed north. "I think the first clue isn't too far that way."

Alex took some of the firewood to the beach on her way to grab some of her Sol teammates. "Some of them are really into the treasure hunt," she explained, which was fine by me. I wanted to see exactly who came along. That's who my competition for the gold would be.

The underbrush wasn't too thick, and we easily found a path. I remembered the trail had been here two years ago, it just wasn't as worn-in as it was now. The crew must have been taking some sightseeing trips between camp and the marker before our arrival.

We had just reached a wide, bright clearing when Alex caught up to us. She had collected quite a group: a cameraman; Cody, Chloe, and Taylor from her team; and Sean, Lucas, and Maddie from mine. Across the open meadow, all of us could see AJ staring up at a giant stone totem pole that angled up from the tall grass like an unseemly scarecrow in a wheat field. I stared at it suspiciously. That monstrosity had definitely not been here two years ago.

"That's the first clue? Doesn't seem hard to find at all. This thing is going to be a piece of cake," Rohan said. I wasn't going to guess out loud, but I was pretty sure Deb had put the stone totem there. The real marker was just a small, flat stone—probably not impressive enough for TV. Furthermore, I took note that Rohan didn't seem to know that the first clue—the marker—had been discovered nearly two hundred years ago. The trail went cold from that point, though.

A small black drone flew overhead, probably with a camera attached, capturing the bird's-eye view of us as we approached the statue. It had been a long time since I'd been part of a group; I hadn't quite gotten the feel of where I fit into this one yet. From above, we may have looked like a cohesive unit, but when you were down on the ground, it was obvious there was no real sense of camaraderie. If there were, we would have bunched up into several mini-groups, not a slim single-file line. That was fine with me; I'd become wary of new people, for obvious reasons. It was better to make connections slowly. Act too quickly and I might misjudge— allowing a new set of people to befriend and then abandon me, just like my old classmates at The Shaw School.

"Got you," Cody shouted to AJ when we were nearly across the field.

AJ didn't seem bothered by our arrival. "If you'd done even the slightest bit of research, you wouldn't have needed to follow me," he called back. "This marker has been public knowledge for years. I'm actually disappointed you had to rely on me to get here. Am I not going to have any real competition in this thing?"

"Don't you worry about that," Rohan muttered under his breath, although he was frowning. Probably realizing that it was not, in fact, going to be a piece of cake.

When we reached AJ, one of the camera guys made sure to zoom in close enough to capture all the disappointed expressions. The unimposing stone square pressed into the dirt at the base of the totem pole had three dots carved into the surface in the shape of a pyramid.

"That's it?" Alex asked. She sounded as discouraged as the rest of the group looked.

She bent down and traced the dots with her finger. I'd done the same, many times. Just as I'd done then, I thought about how strange it was to be so close to something that had been around for nearly four hundred years, and meant so much to so many. People who had touched this marker had died, probably not too long afterward. Maybe even Miles. I imagined him here, asking Lady Luck for guidance.

I shivered. The drone swooped lower, breaking the mood for a second and reminding me there was nothing to worry about. We were under constant surveillance.

On the other hand, the drone hovering above us was a bit menacing.

"What do those dots mean? How are we supposed to know where to go from here?" Taylor asked AJ.

AJ shrugged exaggeratedly. "Got me," he said, not very convincingly. "This marker was the first, but also the last, clue found. No one has been able to figure out where to go next."

"Come on, dude. You must know something." Rohan jumped in and worked on AJ a good while, but AJ held his ground. Good. I was glad the only other person here with any real knowledge of the treasure wasn't going to blab about it.

Even better, it seemed as if everyone was beginning to realize that treasure hunting was going to be a lot harder than they'd thought.

"How is anyone supposed to see three dots on a stone square and know where to go next?" Chloe asked. "It's impossible."

"Seriously? You guys are killing me," AJ said. "I'll let you in on something, but only because this info was freely available if any of you had bothered to look. That stone isn't a clue. It's a marker. Nothing more than that. Think of it as a dropped pin in Maps. It's simply saying hey, start the next round of instructions here."

"What instructions?" Taylor asked.

"The instructions are on the map," AJ told her. "They're hidden, but they're there."

I was impressed. He did know what he was talking about.

"How'd you learn all this for the show?" Maddie asked. "I read about the buckle, but that's about it."

"I didn't know much about any of it until this year, when I did an independent study on the island," AJ said. "That's why I wanted to come. See the place in person."

"Wow. I did this show so I'd have something to put on my college applications," Chloe offered. "I had no idea people had, like, real reasons to come."

"Forget the essays. Isn't the money the real reason why we're all here?" Rohan asked.

"Heck, yeah," Cody answered. "I'm definitely here for the cash. College bills for sure, and besides, who doesn't have a little side hustle that needs some funding?"

"Same," Lucas added. "I thought getting into George-town was hard, but it turns out finding ways to pay for it is way harder."

"So all of you have college plans?" Rohan asked. "Damn. I thought there might be some others like me."

"You're not going to college?" Chloe asked in a shocked voice, as if she had never met anyone who would have considered such a thing.

"Nope."

There was an uncomfortable silence, and I was suddenly aware of the cameras again. The drone was hovering right above our circle, so virtually every angle was covered.

Maddie piped up. "I'm not going to college right away. I'm starting my senior year, but I already know I'm going to take a gap year after graduation. After I leave here I'm volunteering in Costa Rica with Teen Trailblazers to rescue sea turtles, and if I like it, I'll do that before starting college."

Rohan shook his head. "Yeah, Chipmunk? But that's not the same thing, is it?"

No one spoke.

"Look at you," Rohan said. "So shocked. Did you really think we were all the same? Honor roll bots looking to pad their applications and pay for a useless degree? You guys must really live in a bubble. What kind of show would that be?"

"What do you mean, *what kind of show?*" Chloe asked.

"It means filming a bunch of brainiacs without any secrets would be pretty boring to watch. Drama, that's what this show is about."

"Oh my God, that's so not true," Taylor said, hands fluttering. "Deb said grades *are* important. I had to turn in my transcript. She told me my GPA was a big reason why I was picked."

"Then she lied to you." Rohan seemed to be enjoying everyone else's discomfort. "You think ratings will come from watching a bunch of library lovers figure out a puzzle or run around a maze? Nope. Ratings will come from the off-hours stuff. The scheming and backstabbing. Deb basically just admitted it. They have us doing chores so we can 'interact' with each other. Let me help you out. That's code for girls pulling each other's hair and wrestling on the sand in bikinis while the guys get in fights over girls who are out of their league."

Chloe shook her head dismissively. "No way. No one is going to scheme or wrestle or do any of that, because we all want to get into college and if the admissions committee sees us doing any of that stuff on TV we won't get in anywhere."

"Ah, but you won't be able to help it. That's the beauty. Half of you are here because you've got something to prove, and I guarantee the other half has a ton of secrets. They want us to dig each other out, get to those secrets and fears and conflicts. And for those of you smug idiots who think that won't happen, let me advise you that after you sell yourself out once, it'll be easy to do again. And again."

That was ominous—and interesting. It sounded like he was accusing everyone of having a secret. What could the others be hiding?

"I don't have any secrets," Chloe said. And then, defensively, when everyone just stared, "I *don't*. I live in a small boring town with normal parents, and I've never gotten a grade below an A-minus or been grounded or anything."

"Fine. You're practically putting me to sleep, but then you must be here for some other reason. Maybe it's to provoke someone. You're a rah-rah cheerleader, go-team girl. Maybe you're here to get Goth Girl all hot and bothered."

"Goth? I assume you are talking about me," Maren interjected. "I am not Goth. If you start calling me that I will literally smash your head in with a coconut."

"Noted. But do you see how this works? You're playing right into their hands. But getting back to secrets, I know for a fact that at least one person is here incognito."

My heart sank. Me, he was talking about me. He had to be.

I swallowed, getting ready for it. I'd been stupid to think I could be anonymous here.

7

I BRACED MYSELF, BUT ROHAN POINTED TO SEAN. "ANY-thing you want to confess?" Rohan asked.

Sean looked as startled as I felt.

"Yeah. I've seen your videos," Rohan told him. "You're the guy who sets himself on fire on YouTube. You just got *owned*."

Sean's surprise turned to embarrassment, and rightfully so, since Rohan had been able to call him out in all of three seconds. "Used to be Vine, but yeah, now mostly YouTube. And I only set myself on fire once. That was a mistake."

"I knew it!" Maddie blurted out, as if she'd been waiting a long time to let it out. "You're Sean, right? *Boom_Sean_alaka* Sean?"

Sean nodded proudly.

"Your videos are so great," Maddie said earnestly. Was she really a senior? Maybe she skipped a grade. "Well, not the one where you get set on fire, of course."

My relief at not being identified slipped away when I noticed Rohan was watching me.

"It's the quiet ones who need watching. They've always got something to prove," he said.

I swallowed hard. If I'd been nervous before, that feeling had just quadrupled. One of the cameras moved in on me to catch my reaction. No wonder the cameramen all wore black from head to toe. They were basically vultures.

"Not me," I said. "Just like Chloe, I'm a normal, boring girl."

"Says the girl who not too long ago manipulated things so that we'd be in her debt," Rohan pointed out.

Everyone stepped away as if I were toxic, suddenly remembering how Maren and I had "stolen" their bags. Great. Thus far, this show was going to be everything my parents predicted. I was here reinforcing all the old stereotypes, not changing them. My bad reputation was only going to intensify at this rate.

Time to play the question game.

My life: regular teenage tragedy or the eighth circle of Hell?

The hostile looks I was getting were a good indication of the answer. Hell. Definitely Hell.

We went back to camp even more fractured than we'd been on the walk there.

ON THE BEACH, Willa and Justin were putting up a volleyball net. For a second I was torn—everyone was headed there, and the beach activities looked like fun. I shook it off. I had business to attend to; I needed to try out the satellite to make sure it was going to work.

I had some excuses ready—*I was getting my bathing suit, I had to use the bathroom*—but I didn't run into anyone on my way to the cabin. Lots of volleyball fans, apparently. Luckily it didn't appear that there were individual cameras assigned to each of us, because I'd made my exit without any of them trying to follow me. They must just go wherever the action was.

It made me perversely happy that my high-tech satellite hadn't come from my father. He had no idea it existed, but then why would he? He'd barely paid attention to me lately, having allocated far too much of his valuable time to me already. Like Miles, I wasn't producing gold for him, so he had cut me loose and moved on.

Instead, I'd gotten the satellite from Katie, my English tutor. She had a part-time job writing product reviews for a technology magazine and she was always carrying around a few of the gadgets she'd been hired to cover. I didn't quite understand how the satellite worked—all I knew was that it had been commissioned by the government for spying, and its invisible sorcery somehow captured signals even in the most remote places. Since it just so happened I was heading to one, I'd begged Katie to let me borrow the satellite, something she only agreed to if I got a B- on my next paper.

If there was a perfect illustration as to how far I'd fallen this year, that was it. A B- had become aspirational. In any case, our trade had been a success—I had my super-stealth satellite, and Katie was pleased with my B.

I couldn't wait to test it now that I was here, although I was half-scared, half-excited. What if it didn't work? I was so nervous that I flubbed my first two attempts to open the safe.

"Making sure no one stole any of your jewelry?"

The voice startled me. Maren was in the cabin doorway.

"I didn't bring any jewelry here," I told her, leaning back on my heels.

Maren sauntered in, taking her time. "Really? A rich girl like you?"

"What? I'm not—"

"Rich? Sure you are. Look at your clothes. Everything new, everything brand name. Even your shoes probably haven't been worn before. Your mommy run out and buy it all for you from safari trips dot com when she signed you up for this thing? I'll bet she did."

I frowned. That actually wasn't a completely inaccurate description, not that I was going to admit to it.

"Well, thanks for sharing that opinion," I told her. "But feel free to leave now."

"Whoa, calm down." Instead of departing, Maren sat down on the nearest bottom bunk. I couldn't remember if it was hers or not, but she was acting like it was. "We don't have to talk about the La Perla underwear I saw in your bag if you don't want to. I came in here to say I don't know why you didn't tell everyone I was the one who'd taken their stuff, but . . ."

I waited. It didn't seem like she was going to add anything else.

"Is *thanks* the word you're looking for? I can't tell, because you just walked in here insulting me, which is kind of a strange way to say thank you."

"I'm a strange girl, what can I say."

I sighed. "Yeah, I'm getting that idea."

She leaned back onto the mattress. She still wasn't showing any signs of leaving.

I needed to see AJ's notes, and to do that, I needed Maren. I wasn't happy about it, but at this point, it was basically a fact that I was going to be stuck with this nutty girl. I might as well make the best of it.

"We should be partners," I said finally. "Make a pact not to vote each other off."

It was risky, and Maren was definitely not my first choice. Or my fifth, or tenth, or even nineteenth. But, in a way, I'd already partnered with her when I hadn't denied the bag accusations.

"All right," she said, a bit indifferently, which was offensive. She'd come in here looking for me, after all.

"I'd like to see the stuff you took from everyone else. Especially AJ. What else was in his bag besides the map and the Cipher? He said something about notes or a journal, didn't he?"

"That's on a need-to-know basis, and you definitely don't need to know."

"No? I was thinking that one of the benefits of a partnership would be that the partners are nice to each other," I said.

"Please." Maren rolled her eyes. "It's not like we're friends. We're not. This is an arrangement. Totally different."

I winced, but it must not have been noticeable or Maren would have commented. It bothered me that she'd taken friendship off the table. Why? Was it so unreasonable to think I might be someone she could like? More importantly, why was I hurt by her rejection? Maren was exactly the type of person I needed to avoid at all costs—sharp, a lightning rod for negative attention, and no doubt quick to look out for herself.

"Well then, partner, as part of our arrangement I'm going to need to see those things," I said.

Maren left without saying goodbye, which now that I was getting to know her I interpreted as a yes. She'd have argued if the answer was no.

"Good talk," I said to the empty doorway, but actually, this hadn't been a terrible talk. I had a partner now. An angry, Goth, selfish partner, someone completely the opposite of what I had hoped for. But really, did it matter? I was going to need the help. And she was the one who had AJ's notes.

In the distance, the base camp gong sounded. I looked at my locked safe with regret. The satellite would have to wait.

8

BACK ON THE BEACH, PHIL WAS SHOUTING THAT IT WAS
time to load into the two motorboats approaching the shore.

"One team per boat. Let's go, people!"

Phil and the captain, another local man—now I was noticing them everywhere—held on to the stern of our boat while we loaded up.

"Get what you needed?" Joaquin asked me. I had to stop myself from frowning. Nothing was private, obviously. Did he have eyes on the back of his head? I didn't like being watched all the time. I nodded, keeping my expression neutral. He didn't follow up.

There was a lot of excited chatter as the boats zipped around the backside of Black Rock. We slid onto the sandbar of one of the small neighboring islands that had been visible from the helicopter. Everyone in our boat seemed to be using the Demons for scenery pics while Willa and her friends were mostly taking pictures of themselves.

Deb was waiting for us on the beach, clipboard in hand. I wondered if she ever put it down; the thing was omnipresent, and packed tightly with a solid inch of papers, all neatly color coded and annotated with crisp red handwriting.

"Everyone out!" Phil commanded.

There was definitely a team culture evolving already. The Huaca players were slow to disembark, moving forward in neat lines and jumping cleanly off two by two from the point of the bow. The Sol players were not so patient—nearly all of them vaulted off their boat simultaneously into the calf-deep water and splashed to shore in a crowd. Rohan was the exception, hanging back to say something to the boat captain in Portuguese. How was that allowed? I wondered. Deb had told us not to talk to the cameramen, which I had assumed extended to all the crew, but Rohan didn't seem to be hiding it. He finished his conversation and leisurely hopped off the boat, nodding unhurriedly at me.

"Welcome to the staging area," Deb told us. "If we were filming this show on a set, this would be what we call *behind the scenes.*"

Whatever problems she'd been summoned to deal with earlier weren't noticeable. Everything looked perfectly in order. No broken cameras or smashed equipment, at least not that I could see.

We followed her up the beach toward the trees like

a gaggle of ducklings. So far, today had felt like one long museum tour. So much stopping and starting; so many explanations.

There was nothing picturesque about the huts we passed on this beach, and everything had obviously been built for substance over style. Flat, square huts stuffed with giant lights and cameras barely hid a row of blue plastic portable toilets.

Lots of people were here, too. Some of them wore black shirts with the *Reality Gold* TV show logo, but most were dressed casually in regular shorts and T-shirts. A few waved and shouted greetings. Down at the far end, semi-hidden from sight, there was a group of people constructing something, and it occurred to me that I'd never even thought about how many people were actually needed to film these shows. On TV it always seemed so intimate, as if it were just the players there. In real life it was so different.

"Hey, everyone, meet our crew," Deb said. "We call them the B-team. They're the ones who build our sets, run through the test challenges, and drink beer all night in the crew village."

"Sweet gig," Murch said. "How do I get in on that?"

"Become an out-of-work actor, have a relative on the crew, be nice to me. Take your pick."

"Done!" Murch saluted her, pleased, although I couldn't imagine why. He was none of those things.

Deb led us up a path through some trees, past some rocky caves, to a large, open field constructed to look like an arena.

"Wow," Porter said, adding a low whistle for good measure. "*Hunger Games* anyone?"

Silently I agreed. The arena was far more elaborate than our remote surroundings would have suggested. In the middle of the massive field there were two large rectangles of sand, each about the size of a basketball court. One had a yellow banner, the other one had green. Without being told, we split into teams and gathered under our respective banners.

Joaquin faced the two teams and gave an explanation of the challenge. It was hard to follow—something about using metal detectors to find four keys buried in the sand that would be used to unlock a series of nesting treasure chests. Inside the final chest was a *khipu*—an ancient Inca string code—that had to be deciphered.

Pay attention, Riley. Do NOT screw this up.

In addition to the keys, a special medallion was hidden in the sand. Gold, of course, and whoever found it would become the High Priest or Priestess for their team and was safe from being voted out.

"The medallion will be a part of every contest," Joaquin said, "as a reminder of the important role luck plays in every treasure hunt."

That got my attention. Miles was a big believer in Lady Luck. Most treasure hunters were, because a strike of the shovel an inch in the right or wrong direction could make all the difference. It seemed appropriate, then, that the winning team of our very first challenge wouldn't have to be overly brave or strong or smart. Just lucky.

Katya and Phil gave each team a metal detector and a quick tutorial, and then we were directed to line up along the edge of the sand pit for what was essentially a relay race with a metal detector as the baton. I rubbed my necklace pendant and sent a silent prayer to Lady Luck. I needed a win, or enough help so that I didn't make a fool of myself.

Others had more elaborate success rituals. Take Lucas—he was running through a series of complicated stretches that required both flexibility and a desire for attention.

"Wouldn't want to tear a muscle on the first day," Maren said with mock concern.

"For sure. I'm playing at Georgetown this fall." Lucas mimed kicking a ball. "Soccer."

"You guys, did you know Lucas was going to George-town?" Maren asked loudly. Lucas nodded proudly, obviously unaware she was making fun of him for mentioning it at least three times already.

Lucas had long hair for a soccer player. I wondered if he put it up in a man bun when he played. He had to—there was no way he could flip his hair to the side on the field as often as he was doing now and have a shot at playing in college. I lost a little bit of the kinship I'd felt for him after he hadn't jumped from the helicopter. Man buns were the worst.

"You all set over there?" Joaquin called. After a thumbs-up from Lucas, Joaquin lifted his starting pistol. "Ready, set, go!"

The shot echoed around the arena.

Oscar was first on the Huaca team. We'd decided to take an orderly approach, assigning each player a specific square of the sandlot, so Oscar ran immediately for his assigned corner. The Sol team had settled on the opposite strategy. Their first player, Alex, was running around wildly in every direction, swinging her detector wide and fast.

"That'll never work," AJ said, at the exact second her metal detector beeped. He groaned. "Beginner's luck."

Their next player must have had some of that same beginner's luck, and then the player after that, because within the first few minutes Sol managed to find three of their keys before we'd even found one. And if that wasn't enough pressure already, just as I grabbed the detector to take my turn, a fresh bout of cheers indicated another discovery on the Sol side.

"The medallion," Willa screamed in excitement. "I found it! I'm the High Priestess!"

We were getting crushed. This wasn't even going to be a contest.

But then a miracle: I got a beep of my own. I dropped to my knees and began to frantically dig. Buried about three inches down was an ornate, old-fashioned key. It wasn't a medallion to keep me safe from a vote, but at least I'd contributed something to the team.

I held it up in triumph. "Got one!"

I ran back, passing the detector to Annika and the key

to Maren. She unlocked the chest, flipped the lid back and pulled out a smaller one nestled inside.

"Three to go, team! Let's do this," AJ called.

But Annika wasn't doing so well out on the field. She'd run out at full tilt keeping the head of the metal detector too close to the ground. When it hit a pile of sand and stopped short, her stomach ran right into the handle and she collapsed to the ground.

Next to me, Maren winced. "Are you kidding me? What kind of fool move was that?"

A fresh round of cheers from the Sol team told us they'd found their fourth and final key. Great. Now they were moving onto the second part of the challenge: the *khipu*. They were too far away for me to see what exactly deciphering it entailed, but it had to be hard because we were able to send a full rotation of our players into the arena without the Sol team solving its code.

AJ found the next key and Lucas our third. A minute later Maddie found the fourth, and just like that, we'd caught up to the Sol team.

The *khipu* was made up of rows of knotted, multicolored strings hanging from a rod. Joaquin had explained earlier that for the Inca, the *khipu* was a form of communication.

"Each color means something," he'd told us. "Each knot means something else. Your job will be to find a pattern—a series of six numbers."

AJ yanked the *khipu* out. "Stand back, unless one of you

spent the last month the way I did, learning how to make one of these babies."

"Wait, you seriously wasted—" Maren started to say something but pressed her lips together and decided against it, probably realizing it wasn't a smart move to make fun of someone who might turn out to be the team savior. "Never mind."

Under the *khipu* was a fifth chest, but where the keyhole should have been there was an electronic keypad instead, something resembling what an action hero might have to disassemble to stop a bomb from going off.

"How many numbers do we have to enter?" AJ demanded.

Maddie leaned over to count. "Six."

"Talk to me, talk to me," AJ muttered. I was glad he seemed to know what he was doing, because I had no idea. There were strings of every color and knots of every type. I understood why the Sol team hadn't solved it yet.

Suddenly the concern vanished from AJ's face and his shoulders relaxed. "Got it," he said. "Look at the pink strings. The first three have groupings of knots on the top, and then a few inches of space, and then another grouping of knots underneath. The fourth pink string is totally different. See this knot? It's a reverse knot. I think we're supposed to count the top three numbers, then reverse and use the bottom knots."

I still had no idea what he was talking about, but neither did anyone else.

"What are you waiting for, a medal?" Maren asked. "Just count!"

"Okay, okay. Here we go," he said. "Try five five two."

Sean punched them in.

"Now six four one."

The keypad made a long, loud beep. For a second nothing happened, but then the top of the chest creaked open as if an internal latch had been released.

AJ reached in and pulled out a gold cup, carved with symbols.

Joaquin announced our victory. "Congratulations to Team Huaca for winning the first challenge."

Annika started screaming. Rachel and Maddie grabbed each other's shoulders and jumped up and down. Oscar and AJ bumped chests, a move that sent both of them sprawling to the ground. The rest of us stood around, exhausted but grinning.

I'd done it: I'd survived the first challenge! I might be able to do this thing after all.

9

"PLAY IT UP, GUYS," DEB ADVISED US. "WHATEVER YOU'RE
feeling, come on, let it out!"

She was walking around, needling the losers and jacking
up the winners. AJ, in particular, didn't seem to need help in
that department.

"Suck it, Sol!" He hadn't stopped jeering since we'd won.

But me, let it out? No way. Instead, I went camo, high-
fiving my teammates. Deb waited for the reactions to peter
out before announcing it was time to finish the confessionals.

"I'll take Huaca to one of the booths. Riley, come with
me. Phil, how about you take Sol?"

"Oh, yeah! Let the humiliation dissection begin," AJ yelled.

"Don't get too cocky. You'll be doing it soon enough,"
Rohan called back. The Sol players were definitely sulking.

"I don't think so, homey." AJ began to parade back and
forth on the sand in some kind of idiotic duckwalk.

I followed Deb down the beach. Phil and another camera crew took Alex in the opposite direction.

We ended up down on the beach in a small, fully designed set, totally manufactured to look like a natural beach scene. Deb directed me to a sideways-lying palm tree, lined up parallel to the waterline so that the ocean was directly behind me. Deb sat on a stump straight across. Once again I was surprised by how many people it took to create the effortless scenes that showed up on-screen. You'd never know it was me, a producer, a camera guy, and a bunch of ginormous lights.

Deb waved at the lights. "You'd be surprised how many shadows there are when we don't light everything. Seems strange when we're on a sunny beach, I know, but that's television for you. In a couple more hours when those clouds pull in we'll have to light it up even more."

She was holding two bottles of water that she'd pulled from somewhere. One was for me.

"Cheers," she said, tapping the heel of her own bottle to mine. I drank half and poured the rest on my neck.

"It got hot out there, didn't it? You can take a minute if you want. We're just going to sit here for a little while, chatting about things. It's casual. We'll talk about how you are feeling, your impression of the other players so far, that sort of thing."

"So both of us will be filmed? Are you going to be in the show, too?"

"No. Harry's going to film both of us talking—that's Harry, behind the camera—but when I do the final edits back in LA I'll only be using pieces of your answers. It'll end up looking totally natural, as if you're sharing your thoughts with the audience. You've seen it done tons of times on other reality shows without even realizing this is how it's filmed. So how are you doing? Nice win today. You guys really came from behind."

"I know, I really thought we were going to lose."

"Anyone a weak link out there?"

I shook my head. Annika, maybe, but I wasn't going to sell her or anyone else out. Not on camera, anyway.

"What's it like to be back here, on the island?"

"Pretty strange, actually. The base camp looks totally different." I paused. "No one is going to hear our conversation, right? I don't want any of the other players to know I've been here before, especially not now. Some of them will be all over me if they think I have any idea where to find the gold."

"It could be a nice change for you, though, having a ton of instant friends."

"They'd be fake friends. Those are worse than no friends, trust me."

"Ah, yes. I forgot you know a thing or two about the dangers of false friendships."

Deb knew my backstory, which probably meant the entire crew did, too. I wasn't worried about them having that information, but I was concerned they'd share it with my competitors. This was the first time I'd entered a new situation untagged by the scandal, and I wanted the chance to let these new relationships unfold on my own terms, slowly, without any of that baggage tainting the process.

"Well, I'll put your mind at ease, then. No one here will know what we talk about in these confessionals until the show airs, and by then—"

"Everyone will know who I am," I finished.

Deb lifted her shoulders in agreement. "Yup. Nothing I can do about that. Do you think anyone has recognized you?"

"No, I don't think so." If someone had tied me to my online fame, so far they were keeping it to themselves.

"Great," Deb said. "This'll be a good practice round for when you start your new school in September. Get your feet wet socializing with kids your own age again. Homeschooling couldn't have been that much fun."

"The problem with being homeschooled wasn't the school part, it was the home part," I said wryly.

Deb nodded knowingly. "Things still rough with your parents?"

I paused, flustered. "I'm sorry, can we turn that camera off for a minute? I don't understand why we need to talk about all of this personal stuff. My parents and school issues don't have anything to do with the show. Is it really necessary to get into all of that?"

It didn't seem as if Deb even considered asking Harry to put his camera down, which was annoying but not completely unexpected. Deb was a little like Joaquin in that way—charismatic, but also a little pushy.

"What we're doing here is collecting information to give the audience a little color," Deb explained. "Who you are, what brought you here, where you hope to go from here, that sort of thing. We'll end up using only a fraction of what we film, so we try to cover a range of topics so we'll have plenty of material to work with during the edits."

I must have looked skeptical, because she motioned for Harry to lower his camera.

"Listen," Deb said. "You're here because you want the audience to connect with you, and these interviews are how that'll happen. When an audience watches someone on TV, they only root for the people they feel like they know. Really, really know—their struggles and their joys, everything. And I know you don't think so, but your problems are actually very similar to what everyone struggles with. It's just that your issues are writ large and have unfolded in a very public way. We're all looking for the same thing, though. Every single one of us. Love, acceptance, connection. We want to feel like we *matter*. So that's why I need all this background, to give the audience enough of you so they can relate. Understand? It's to your advantage, trust me."

Trust. There was that word again. I didn't fully trust her, but I saw her point.

Deb signaled Harry again and he picked his camera back up. I'd been so transfixed that I'd missed my chance to see his face in full; usually it was nearly covered by that giant lens.

I took a sip of water. "That was quite a speech. Do you give that to everyone?"

"Only the ones who don't like sharing."

"Okay, okay." I put my water bottle down and got ready to talk. "Message received, and to answer your question, yes, things are still rough with my parents. My father, especially."

"You went behind his back to join the cast, isn't that correct?" Deb encouraged.

I nodded. "After you came to him for funding for the show, I decided I wanted to try out. My parents thought it was a bad idea, but I went for it anyway, and since I was eighteen . . ." I shrugged. "I'm a legal adult. In the end it was my decision to make."

"What was their reasoning? Why didn't they want you to do the show?"

This was hard to talk about. Their opposition had taken me by surprise. I thought they'd be pleased I was taking initiative with something for once.

"Television? A reality show?" My mother had actually cried when I'd told her I was going to do it.

"You've been hiding in your room for months because you said the whole world knows who you are. Now you want to reopen the wound by putting yourself out in front of an audience again. Why would you want to do that?" she asked, over and over, desperate to change my mind. To be fair, she was probably tired of driving me around the city to all my various therapy appoint-

ments and didn't want to deal with my mental health deteriorating even further if the show sent me off the rails again.

My mother always came back to the same point. *"You're inviting people to judge you,"* she'd insisted. *"All this notoriety ruined your life, and now you're inviting it right back in."*

Yes, I was. Inviting people to judge me was actually the entire point of doing this show. Doing this show was me saying, *You want to take a piece of me, world? Here you go. But this time, you can only have what I give you.*

My father's objection was more straightforward. *"This isn't going to be a solution to your problem, Riley,"* he'd said. *"This is simply more of the same behavior that got you into trouble. You're not willing to do the hard, everyday work to get back on your feet. Instead, you're doing what you always do—embracing a grand gesture and looking for a clean sweep to fix everything at once. You're essentially doubling down, and if history is any guide, you're about to make things much worse for yourself."*

After that he stopped interfering. That was his word: interfere. But I saw it for what it was because I'd seen him do the same thing to Miles. He'd stopped caring.

I shared most of those details with Deb—and with the world, via the camera—but it wasn't something I was happy about. Thinking too much about the strain on my relationship with my father was a little like staring straight into the sun—painful, and too intense to handle head-on for long.

Deb had been nodding encouragingly while I spoke.

"That's great," she said. "Really good stuff. Exactly what I need."

I liked the sound of that, but I hoped what she needed aligned with what *I* needed. Deb looked up sharply. Oh, no. Had I said that out loud?

"Riley, this is a television show," Deb said. A fair amount of her earlier friendliness had disappeared; she turned a little frosty. "It requires a certain amount of tension. That there will be hurdles to overcome should be implied. How each of you handles those hurdles—or tricks, as you call them—is part of what provides that tension."

"What does that mean? You're manipulating us?"

Deb cocked her head. "Manipulate sounds so . . . nefarious. *Maneuver* is slightly more accurate, but even describing it that way puts a negative spin on it. Look at it like this: you're here to tell your story and I'm here to help you do that. You had to know that your particular history made you an attractive cast member. You've got something to prove. That's not a bad thing—it's exactly what drew me to you, but don't paint yourself out to be so innocent here. You're here to show the world your good side. That means you're getting something out of this experience, too. Remember that."

Was that a threat? I didn't get to ask, and I wasn't sure I wanted to.

"Harry, that's a wrap." Deb picked up her clipboard and made a note on the top sheet with her red pen, effectively ending the confessional.

10

WHEN ALL THE CONFESSIONALS WERE FINISHED, WE
went right to what Joaquin called the Apu Council.

There were lots of torches and an altar, some logs arranged as seats around a fire pit. There were a few large stone statues at the entrance, which AJ instantly bemoaned as more Aztec than Incan.

"There are literally thousands of books written about the Inca. Would it have killed them to consult one or two? I can't tell whether they willfully ignored the distinction, or just preferred the flash of the Aztecs."

In general, that seemed to be a consistent theme. The show had gotten some things right, but then was oddly indifferent toward others. Like personal safety. I didn't want to be babysat, but thus far the crew had launched half of us out a helicopter and hadn't so much as lowered a camera when the Sol boys launched their water attack. And for all the talk of hunting for treasure, I hadn't heard a single word yet about the six people who had died doing exactly that. Accidents, some of them—a wrong turn in a cave here, a fall down a cliff there—but that was the point. The terrain here wasn't exactly a turf playground.

Deb wanted us to file into the Council very seriously, and when some of us—Cody and Murch—didn't display the appropriate level of gravity she had us go out and do it again. And again.

We were waiting to do our fourth entrance when Phil's walkie suddenly exploded with static, sending out a high-pitched whine beneath all the noise. I jumped. It sounded like a scream, and with the jungle so dark it was eerie.

"Damn these walkies," he swore. "They keep malfunctioning, and the weather hasn't even gotten bad yet."

I knew for a fact that Deb had raised a ton of money for this show, so why were so many things breaking and not working?

He left, presumably to get his instructions in person. I noticed Porter and Willa were nearby, looking at me and nudging each other playfully. God. Porter was a jerk, but that didn't mean I loved how into Willa he was.

Suddenly she pushed Porter toward me. "Go on, tell her you're sorry."

"Okay, okay! Jeez." Porter came over and stood in front of me, much like he'd done this morning. I took a step back.

"You aren't going to carry me into the Council are you? Because I can walk, thank you very much."

He shook his head. He almost looked sheepish, but that was probably because he knew Willa was watching. Actually, so were the other girls on his team.

"The girls told me I should apologize. That I probably caused an unforgivable injury to your hair, or something like that, and it wasn't cool. Anyway, I'm sorry I threw you in. I thought it would be funny."

"The hair wasn't a big deal," I told him. I remembered Taylor on the helicopter, begging for a hair tie. Did every girl on Sol obsess about her hair? "The throwing in, though, that's another story. But it's nice of you to apologize to the enemy."

And it *was* nice, but it would have been better if he'd apologized on his own. Was he a puppet, or what? If anything, it made me think worse of him and slightly better of Willa for pulling his string, even if it did smack of a power play at my expense. I knew it was wishful thinking, but I wanted to believe he allowed himself to be pushed in my direction because he felt something for me.

Phil came back and held up his walkie. "All good now. Get in two lines, and remember: be serious. No joking. No smiles."

We must have done it right because Deb didn't call for a redo. We sat on the logs divided by team. Everyone on the Sol side, even Willa and Porter, was silent. I scanned them, wondering who would get voted out. I hadn't heard anyone complaining that a specific person had messed up, the way Annika had on our team. A mess-up like that would have to make that person an obvious target, unless it was Willa.

There was no way the guys on that team were going to vote Willa out. I didn't think any of the girls would, either. Of course, speculating was beside the point. She'd found the Sol medallion, so she was safe no matter what.

Joaquin greeted us. He had a wide smile that connected all the parts of his face—it showed his perfect white teeth, crinkled up the corners of his eyes, lifted his forehead, and deepened the dimples in his cheeks. "Our first Apu Council. Big night, isn't it?"

Lots of murmured assents.

Joaquin flashed that smile again. "You may have noticed that we have a fire pit here similar to the one at camp. Fire was sacred to the Incan people, because of its ability to hold the light, like the sun, like gold. You may have also seen some pyramid symbols. They were carved on the gold cup you won today, Huaca. That's because the Inca power system was in the shape of a pyramid. A leader on top, a king, and underneath him, a high priest."

He paused. Behind him, a burst of heat lightning lit up the stage. Joaquin kept cool, which must be why they paid him the big bucks, but all the players jumped.

"Since no Huaca player found the medallion, we'd like to invite the Huaca players as a team to choose a High Priest for the night. Someone who led you through the challenge today."

"Right now?" Maren asked.

"Please."

We leaned in for a huddle.

"We're just supposed to vote for someone?" Maren asked.

"How about this? AJ solved the *khipu*, so if not for him, we would have lost," I said. "Let's make him the High Priest."

"Agreed," Oscar said quickly. Maddie nodded, and Maren shrugged.

London made it official. "AJ is our High Priest," she announced.

Joaquin called AJ forward and placed a necklace with a huge gold pendant around his neck.

"AJ, you are the High Priest tonight."

AJ folded his arms across his chest and gave a self-assured nod. "Cool."

"You have tremendous power here at the Apu Council. I know you are familiar with the Incan traditions, so you know about their belief that human sacrifices were both necessary and honorable."

"Yes," AJ said. "But that doesn't mean I'm going to throw myself off the top of Black Rock or anything."

"We wouldn't ask you to do that," Joaquin said, giving a half smile. "But we are going to ask you to make a choice. You see, you can decide which team has to vote a member off. And not simply one member. Tonight, you may decide to vote up to three players off."

Everyone gasped. Taylor screamed. "Three? That's insane. Why three people?"

"I didn't say it *had* to be three people," Joaquin said. "I said the High Priest has the option of choosing three."

"And I can choose which team votes people out?" AJ asked. "My team or Sol?"

"You may."

"This is effed up," Maren called. "Why would anyone choose their own team to vote out?"

Joaquin ignored her and continued. "The decision is the High Priest's to make. Tonight, AJ, the honor is yours."

Both sides were buzzing.

AJ finally spoke. "This will be an easy decision."

"So you've made your choice?"

"Yes, but do I choose the players, too?"

"No, once you choose the team and the number of players to be sacrificed, there will be a team vote that will determine which players are voted out."

"Got it. I choose Huaca."

If Joaquin seemed surprised, he didn't show it. He paused to let the news sink in.

"Huaca?" Annika jumped up. "Wait, no!"

"Dude, what? Don't you mean Sol?" That was from Sean.

"Just to be clear," Joaquin said to AJ, "you are choosing your own team to send up to three players home."

"Yes, my own team. And I choose three players."

"This is your fault," Annika screamed at me. "I would have said you, because you'd saved us from jumping, but you told us to pick AJ!"

I felt as if I'd been slapped. What had I done? She was right; it was my fault AJ was High Priest. I easily could have let myself be nominated, but I'd been so worried about looking selfish, I'd cut that idea off before anyone could even suggest it.

Team Sol was erupting into cheers, and their side of the logs turned into a blur of arms and legs and long hair as they all hugged each other. Alex looked stunned. Chloe and Taylor were crying with relief.

"All right, all right. Everyone calm down please. Team Sol, AJ has just given you a gift. But at what price? AJ, I imagine your team would like to hear the reasoning behind your decision."

It was obvious why Joaquin had gotten the job. He was so calm, so good at making you feel like he was a friend.

"Look, guys, we've only got five challenges," AJ said. "We don't need ten people to win them. There are two big prizes at stake here—a million dollars for winning the game, and two hundred and fifty thousand for finding the treasure. I know that's a lot of money, but not when it's split between ten of us. Cutting the team back is the logical decision."

"Are you kidding me right now?" London asked. Half the team was standing, the other half was sitting in shock. AJ faced us pretty stoically considering the hostility directed his way.

"Listen," Lucas said, motioning the team in. "We gotta vote this clown out. That will show him what a dumb decision it was. Are you guys with me? Come on. AJ is the obvious choice to vote out."

Lucas ran a hand through his sweaty hair. He looked worried.

"But he's so smart," Maddie objected. "He was the only one who knew what to do. It would have taken us forever to figure the *khipu* out."

I felt sick. "Don't you remember? Joaquin said that the High Priest has immunity. Or protection, whatever he called it," I reminded them. "So even if we wanted to, we can't vote AJ off."

"Well, making him boss was the mistake of the century," London said. "Thanks, Riley. God! Honestly, I'd like to push both of you off the top of Black Rock."

I tried to catch Maren's eye. Was our partnership even firm? Panic rose inside my chest. Not yet, not now. I wasn't ready. Leaving now would be a huge embarrassment.

"At this point, I'd like to ask Team Sol to return back to camp. The rest of Apu Council will be for Team Huaca only," Joaquin announced.

The Sol players didn't need to be told twice. Nearly all of them immediately ran out of the Council, yelling and laughing the whole way. Deb would get lots of good reaction shots, that was for sure.

"Piggyback? Hop on," Cody offered Alex. "Night, y'all," he said to us.

Alex saluted as they left. "May the best seven win!"

I was filled with dread as they all left. There was no way I'd make it. Even if Maren and I honored our agreement, the two of us would probably be the two with the highest votes. Ugh. I saw Porter's red shorts in the crowd and felt a flicker of annoyance that I even cared. He obviously wasn't interested in me anyway, so what was I thinking?

But then I saw him fall to the back of the group. He turned toward me, and for a second, our eyes met. I felt something stirring that had been buried for a long time—hope. It was enough to remind me that I had a lot riding on this show. I had to stay. My future depended on it.

I made a decision and turned back to my teammates. "If you don't vote me out, I'll tell you where the buckle was found," I blurted out.

"You know where?" Sean asked. "How do we know you aren't just saying that?"

"I brought some pictures with me. There's one with the buckle, and I have notes from an article about where it was found. I'll show you. Why would I lie? If I am, you'll just vote me out next, so . . ."

AJ had returned to his seat and I didn't like the way he was staring at me. Showing my hand could backfire. Even if the other players voted to keep me around, AJ might decide he didn't want any competition looking for the gold.

"Well, well. Look at that," he said. "It appears someone here knows a bit more about the treasure than previously let on."

"I did a little homework," I told him defensively. I wanted to look knowledgeable enough to get some votes from everyone else, but not expert enough for AJ to see me as a threat. "Like you said, we were told the challenges would be related to the island's history so I wanted to be prepared."

Joaquin called for our attention. "Team Huaca, it's time to vote," he said. "Unfortunately, that means that for three of you, these are your last few minutes on the island."

He passed around a bag of gold marbles and instructed us to each take three. The altar held nine gold vases in a row each marked with our names, and one-by-one we were to approach and drop our marbles into the jars of who we wanted to vote off.

"You'll notice there is no jar for AJ, your High Priest," Joaquin reminded us.

My whole body was shaking when it was my turn at the altar. What if I didn't make it past tonight? I didn't know how I could face anyone back home. My marbles went into the jars for Annika, Oscar, and Rachel. I hoped enough of my teammates agreed with me.

None of us made eye contact while we waited for the results. Speaking was forbidden, but I doubt any of us would have tried even without that directive. Even Joaquin, normally so jovial, was stern and serious when he returned after counting the votes.

He dramatically tipped over the first jar. Nothing fell out.

"Maddie, zero votes," he said. "Congratulations, Maddie. You received the fewest votes, and you are safe tonight."

As nervous as I was for myself, I was glad for her.

Joaquin moved to the next jar. One marble rolled out. "Sean, one vote."

London was next—she got three votes. Lucas got two.

I was getting more and more nervous. None of them had gotten very many votes.

"Maren." She got three marbles, which shocked me. I had thought she'd get more. That didn't bode well for my own chances.

"Riley," Joaquin said, lifting my jar. Two marbles rolled out and I nearly cried out of relief. I had mentally prepared myself to see a pile of marbles, so two wasn't bad at all. My last-minute stunt offering information on the buckle must have paid off.

And when Joaquin moved to the next three jars, it became obvious pretty quickly that I'd be safe. In the end, Rachel got five votes, Annika got six, and Oscar got seven.

"Rachel, Annika, and Oscar," Joaquin said, "I'm sorry, but your time with us is over."

The three exiles approached the altar for a short goodbye ritual and then were escorted somewhere out of view to do their exit interviews.

"Tomorrow you and I are going to have a little chat," AJ said to me as we filed out of the Council. "I'm verrrrrryy curious how much you know about the treasure."

I'd bought myself some time by offering to trade information on the buckle for votes, but at what price? I wondered. Now that I'd exposed my knowledge of the gold, I might have made myself a target.

Question time: careless mistake or necessary chess move? I hoped it was the latter.

11

WAKING UP IN A ROOM WITH SEVEN OTHER GIRLS
reminded me that it had been years since I'd had any type of
group sleepover. When you're with people day and night you
learn things about them, and it turns out London talks in her
sleep, Willa likes to use the bathroom during the night, and
Maren is not a morning person.

"No talking before coffee," she'd told Taylor, who'd fool-
ishly tried to start the day with an overly cheery rise-and-
shine camp song. "Not one word. Not even a whisper."

After breakfast, Phil sent the teams off to their respective huts. Now that I knew how important player interaction
was, I understood why our clubhouse had so many bells and
whistles. Designed to make us feel comfortable, there were
bright colors and beachy accents everywhere: shells, painted
driftwood signs, and tiki torches. It wasn't a traditional
building—it only had three walls, but that was enough to

give a certain amount of privacy, and since the open-air side was facing the water, we had an amazing view. The floor was made of a thick netting, which kept our toes in the sand but provided enough of a stable base for the couches, beanbag poufs, and game table.

I'd brought my notebook from the safe, and I sat on the floor with all the pictures and articles I'd brought that had to do with the discovery of the old Spanish buckle. "Anyone who wants to see where the buckle was found, this is your chance."

Everyone came over to look except AJ. He was keeping his distance. No one really wanted to talk to him anyway, so it worked out fine.

"We're right here." On the map, I pointed to the banana-shaped beach. "And the buckle was discovered on the other side of the island, not too far, down on the left-hand tip. Right here, above the eagle's head."

As promised, I had a magazine article that corroborated the location, and Sean, Lucas, Maddie, and London packed some water and snacks and took off to try their luck. Perfect. That was far enough out of the way that they wouldn't see where I was headed—straight north, to the base of Black Rock.

AJ found his voice when the four other players had cleared out. "Are you going to tell me where you learned all that?" he asked. "Or just make me guess?"

"Share your notes and I'll tell you," I said.

"And join our partnership," Maren added quickly.

"It's funny that you guys think you have to convince me," AJ said. "I just watched Riley send our competition to the wrong place but even better, they *thanked* her. Heck yeah, I want a partnership."

Maren and I looked at each other and nodded. When she handed AJ the pile of papers she'd taken from his bag, his reaction was not unlike a toddler reunited with a lost blankie.

He hugged the Cipher to his chest. "Buddy, I missed you!"

Maren looked on skeptically. Her T-shirt this morning read *Shhh! Nobody Cares.*

"If you know about the Cipher, you must know about Smokey Joe, right?" I asked AJ. He nodded.

A few months ago, I'd found a website with the unlikely and unwieldy name of Smokey Joe's: Seek and Ye Shall Find. Gun to my head, I'd never be able to remember how I'd found it. I'd gone down one treasure hunter's rabbit hole after another, until Smokey and his followers revealed themselves. Most treasure hunt communities online were filled with weirdos endlessly debating signs and symbols, and Smokey's had its fair share of those, but it was a little different. It was password protected for one thing, and to get access I'd had to provide my email address and answer a number of identity verification questions. While some of Smokey's theories bordered on insanity—he covered Area 51 and Atlantis, too—there was plenty of solid information exchanged in the map-reading forum, things that I'd later corroborated with my father, back when we were still talking.

"I haven't been to that site in a long time, though. All anyone ever wanted to talk about was that buckle. I don't know why people think it means anything more than some Spaniard in the 1600s went to take a leak in the bushes and forgot his belt."

"There was better info in the general map-reading forum," I told him. "The discussions weren't specific to Black Rock, but most of the clues used on the Spanish maps are universal."

"Makes sense. Oh, wait, now I get it. You were the one posting about coming here."

I shook my head in confusion. "What?"

"Someone said they were going to the island and wanted to know what to do with the treasure if they found it. Where to sell it on the sly, since it would be illegal to be here without a permit. Asking if there are brokers who would fence the gold for them."

"Are you serious?"

"That wasn't you?" AJ looked surprised. He didn't know me, so of course he wouldn't know it, but selling the treasure on the dark web was nearly the exact opposite of what I planned to do. If I found the gold, I'd be screaming the news from the top of Black Rock and handing it over to the government immediately. It was their treasure. Credit was what I wanted, not money.

"I thought you said you hadn't been to the website in a long time," I pointed out.

"I haven't. This was probably a year ago. Maybe more." Understanding crossed his face. "Oh, I see. That is weird. No one was supposed to have been here before this show started. The government closed off this island after that guy got killed."

Ouch. *That guy.* "I knew him," I said, and then I found myself saying the words I had planned to keep to myself the entire time. "Miles Kroger. And I was here two years ago, right before he died. He showed me where he thought the treasure was located."

I tried not to think about how Miles would have disapproved of how quickly I'd shared that information. Rohan was right. It was easy to sell yourself out, once you felt you had no other choice.

AJ slapped his forehead. Literally slapped it. "Miles Kroger? You knew him? Where was he looking?"

"North. Straight up from the marker—same cave system I think you found."

"I knew it!" AJ said. "I freaking knew it."

He did a crazy move—a jump in the air with a midair scissor kick—that I hoped never to have to witness again.

"Anyway." I kept on with the explanation. "Miles was sure the caves had collapsed so long ago that no one even realized they'd been there in the first place."

AJ brought the energy down a level, but even when he was calm, he was always in motion. He paced back and forth, walking two steps and then reversing, like a malfunctioning wind-up toy. "Wow, this is big. Really big. We've got to go up there. Now. Right now. He might have been killed because he found something. I need to know exactly where he was."

"I can show you where he was when I was here, but he searched for another couple of weeks after that."

AJ waved it off. "It's a start. I can cut off a big area knowing which areas he'd already gone through."

Maren was staring at me. "What a coincidence. You were here on this random island in the middle of nowhere, and then you just happened to jump in on a reality show being filmed in the same spot?"

"Not a coincidence at all. That's how I heard about this show. Deb knew—"

"Yeah, yeah," AJ broke in. "We can cover all that later. Right now we need to pick up our five pieces of wood so we can get that out of the way and spend the rest of the day searching at Black Rock."

As it turned out, the Sol team had already taken care of wood duty, so we took the beach cleanup shift. It was a little awkward, because most of their players were on the beach, too. The girls were spreading out towels in front of their hut for tanning, while Murch yelled insults at us he and Justin threw a football around. Their team was a lot less treasure focused. Maybe after seeing the marker yesterday they'd all realized how difficult a search would be.

Phil came down to the waterline to inspect our effort. "Wassup, guys?" he asked. Phil and Murch had the same body shape, big and mushy, but Murch had a bully mentality that brought out a hardness not there in Phil. Essentially, Phil was Murch in twenty years, after life had sanded him down a bit and taken away the sharp edges.

"Anyone holding on to hard feelings toward AJ after last night?" Phil asked. Just like yesterday, he was wearing shorts that went past his knees and well-worn Birkenstocks. I tried to picture Murch trading in his football jersey for a blue Hawaiian shirt, a visual so out there that I actually shook my head to clear it.

"Wouldn't you like to know," Maren said. She was holding a fistful of ocean gunk, and Phil stepped back, as if afraid she might toss it at him.

I wondered what it would be like not to care at all about what anyone else thought. Every time I had a conversation with someone I played it over and over in my head and wondered if it would have been better to say something a different way, or not to have said anything at all. What was it like to do things without ever thinking twice? Maren stuck out, but she didn't care. She didn't overthink everything. I wondered: if I didn't keep things in, and instead simply said them, would I still have this incredibly destructive need to correct things? Maybe not. Maybe getting the words out, no matter how inelegantly, was the important part.

Phil smiled. "A team code of silence. I like it. Well, good news. It's a relationship-building day today. Team bonding, and all that. We'll fit in some more confessionals, but other than that, the day is yours to do what you want."

"Search for treasure, obviously." AJ threw his last chunk of seaweed into the ocean and wiped his hands on his shorts. "You can find me north of the first marker, at the base of Black Rock."

That was annoying. I knew we were going to be filmed, so the crew would know soon enough where we were going, but did AJ have to announce it so casually? And what was with saying *me* instead of *us*? Hadn't we just formed a partnership?

"Go for it," Phil told him. "And don't forget, there are two protection coins hidden somewhere on the island. Maybe you'll find one to turn in at a future Council for immunity."

"Sure. Or maybe I'll find a hundred million dollars' worth of Incan gold."

"And who wouldn't want an extra hundred mil?" Maren said. She was definitely circling something, I could feel it.

"Right, Riley?"

And there it was.

"You won't be able to keep the treasure," Phil interrupted. "You know that, right? You all signed a form signing over the rights of your discovery to the show. You'll receive money instead as a prize—"

"Yeah, yeah, we know," Maren said, curtly cutting him off. And then to me, "I'm still wondering *why* you were here two years ago. You're a treasure hunter or something?"

"Not me. My dad. I came for the ride."

"Ladies, come on," AJ said. "Whatever this is, drop it.

There's gold out there, waiting to be found. Phil, I'm going to need some stuff. Weren't you telling us about some supplies stored somewhere? I want some backpacks for the team."

Phil walked off with AJ, but the camera guy stayed.

"I'm still trying to figure out why you were here." Maren was obviously not going to let this drop. "Your parents said hey, let's go on a vacation to an island where people are searching for treasure? And then you just happened to conveniently drop in two weeks before that guy died?"

"I told you, my father likes to get involved in treasure hunts. He's done some deep-sea ship salvage, too. That's how he met Miles. My father financed the one that found the *Emily Bligh*. Did you hear about that one maybe thirty years ago, off the coast of Miami? After they brought that ship up, Miles invited him to partner on his next dig and it grew from there."

"Your dad 'gets involved.' He's 'done' some ship salvage." Maren used air quotes as she repeated my words. "Is that a fancy way of saying he pays for those things?"

"What does it matter?" I asked defensively.

"I'm curious why you're here, that's all. If you win, so what? You don't need the money. For some of us, probably most of us, this is really important. It matters a lot. It might mean the difference between getting into college or even being able to pay for it."

"So what am I supposed to do? Sit at home and never do anything?"

"Works for me. At least you wouldn't be here instead of someone else who needs to be."

I scowled at her. "Maybe I need to be here, too. There are other reasons besides money."

"Not good ones."

I hadn't noticed Sean behind me until he cleared his throat. I'd thought he'd gone off with the other three players on our team.

"So, not to interrupt, but . . . you guys have obviously formed a group here," Sean said. "Do I have to search for treasure to be in it? Or can I just vote with you? It turns out I'm not so into this whole treasure hunt thing, and since it's optional, I was going to film some tricks on the beach instead. Deb told me I could use some of the pro camera shots for my site, but if you guys want me to come . . ."

"Yeah we do, because who's to say you won't turn on us and form a partnership with someone else while we're gone?" Maren asked.

"Oh, hey, no. I want to stick around as long as possible and you guys seem like the only ones with any real clue what's going on here. London seems cool, but Lucas is a little too full of himself. Maddie seems like a sweet kid but she's definitely the kind of girl who posts too many times a day, you know what I'm saying?"

"Fine," Maren said. "Scram. Just get ready to vote the way we tell you."

She didn't get a chance to start in on me again because

Porter had joined us. Our little square of newly cleared sand was turning into a real hub of activity this morning.

"Nice," he said, evaluating our disagreement with a lazy, knowing smile. "Is that how you're running your team over here?"

"Who says I'm running anything?" Maren snapped.

"Whatever. Do you have any of my stuff from the helicopter?" he asked.

"Maybe."

"Maybe . . . ?" he looked at her expectantly.

"You'll know when you have something to offer me in exchange."

"We're on different teams, so I don't see how—"

"You'll think of something."

Porter frowned. "Like a sex trade or something?"

"Don't flatter yourself."

Porter's expression turned to something more arrogant. His shorts were yellow today, and he had the same type of button-down shirt as before, but this one was white. He could have walked straight out of that *My dad's a lawyer* meme.

"Oh, are girls more your thing?" he asked Maren.

"Literally anyone is more my thing, but more importantly, you're proving stupider by the second. How about I give you the afternoon to think about a game strategy that could benefit me enough to consider your proposal, 'kay? Now run along and go do your lax bro thing with your lax bro friends. Bye."

Porter didn't move for a few seconds. He wasn't used to being turned down flat like that, I could tell. I almost felt sorry for him. A hurt look flashed across his face, quickly, barely noticeable and for a second he looked like a little boy. But then he ruined it.

"Yup. Definitely a lesbian."

Ugh. I'd been waffling on him, but I'd been right the first time: jerk. That realization made it easier not to notice the way his hair swept perfectly across his forehead, a little bit tousled, not overly styled.

"That's not even an insult," I said. "Is that the best you can come up with?"

Porter looked surprised, as if he'd forgotten I was there, and if I was feeling congratulatory, he looked even more pained than he had before. He liked to be liked. I recognized that quality in him after isolating it in myself.

"Ohhhhh, I forgot. You said you're from Frisco, right? Lots of L-G-B-T people there." He drew out the letters. Interesting that he was using that term. Maybe he wasn't so ignorant after all. His use of "Frisco" was another matter.

"You forgot the Q. LGBTQ. And it's not Frisco."

"Sure it is."

"Um, no, it's really not."

Now he was back to his usual smiling self. "But everyone I know calls it Frisco."

"Hmmm. How many of those everyones are actually from San Francisco?"

"What do you call it, then? San Fran?"

I shuddered. "God, no. That's only slightly better. SF, mostly. Or, you know, its actual name."

"Eh, that's too long. Frisco sounds much better."

Maren grunted in disgust, as if offended by the conversation. She hadn't circled back to start in on me about my father again, so hopefully that meant she was dropping it, at least for a little while. Or maybe it was because AJ came back with Phil before she got a chance.

"All right, kids," AJ said, dumping a pile of backpacks and hats and random gear on the sand. "Let's do this. Sign out your phones and let's go."

"Hold on," Phil said, lifting his walkie. "We're sending a different camera with you. One of the big ones." He assigned someone named Harry to cover us, who replied with "flying in." I was starting to understand the filming language. I wondered if the other guy here, the one who'd been filming us all along, was offended at getting replaced or if they were assigned to do different types of filming. Maybe this guy wasn't allowed off camp grounds.

"Smart idea," AJ agreed. "Because we're the only action worth watching."

"I can't believe you actually think you have a shot at finding the gold," Porter said. "No offense, but if the pros haven't been able to find it for four hundred years, what makes you so sure you'll be able to do it?"

"What makes you so sure I'm not a pro?" AJ shot back.

"Because you're twelve?"

"I'm seventeen and three-quarters, you jerk."

"Take it easy," Phil said. "Why don't you guys get going, but make sure to come back for lunch."

"We're good," AJ said. He held up his backpack. "We've got snacks and tons of water. We'll come back later."

"Let me rephrase. Union rules say we need to rotate the camera guys on and off duty, so you need to come back to pick up a different camera. And maybe while you're here, you'll get invited to throw a football around, do some team bonding. Got it?"

AJ hiked the backpack over both shoulders and snapped its belt around his waist. "Do I look like a guy who's going to get invited to toss a football around?"

Phil sighed. "Fair point."

Harry arrived, and Phil waved us off. "Go on then. Get lucky."

12

THE THREE OF US WALKED FROM CAMP INTO THE WOODS
to the first marker, keeping an eye out for any of the other
players to make sure we weren't followed.

There were actually four of us, I realized. Not three.
Harry, the camera guy, counted, too. It was easy to discount
him because he never spoke, and it was amazing how quickly
you could get used to something you originally considered
obtrusive.

At one point, we heard the drone buzzing overhead,
obviously tasked with finding all of us scattered around the
island and filming our different locations. When we reached
a clearing, Harry gave a wave and it zoomed off to pinpoint
another group.

When we got to the marker, AJ dropped the backpack
and pulled out his copy of the map. Like me, he had scrawled
notes all over it. I peered over AJ's shoulder to see if he'd been

able to interpret all of the secret codes. Right away I noticed that he'd circled the cross at the top of the map. Smart boy. Drawn the way it was, with three dots at the top of the cross with the bottom leg pointing at the N in the word *Negra*, it was a signal indicating that all explicitly written directions should be reversed. Like where it said *40 varas south*. The correct way to read that instruction was to go north, not south. AJ had caught a few other things, too, like how the bisected triangle in the fourth line of text meant there would be a triangle marking the final treasure spot.

"Why is some of it written in English?" Maren asked, reading the clues aloud. "'*The way shall be easy, forty varas south, dig.*' Shouldn't all that be in Portuguese, or Incan, or some other language besides English?"

I knew the answer to that. I'd learned a lot by lurking around on Smokey's site. There were a few regulars—Dead-Sea, MrJackSparrow, and Viper5—who'd explained the way subtle clues can affect the way a map is read.

"The fact that it's written in English is a clue in itself," I explained. "It means the Church is involved, so we need to read the clues with an eye toward biblical hints. See the numbers 7, 4, 7? That's a reference to John, Chapter 7, Verse 47: *have you also been led astray?*"

Maren looked skeptical. "So?"

"It means watch out, this map is heavily coded and will be hella hard to decipher," AJ said.

Maren shook her head. "I'm going to do you a favor and

pretend I didn't hear that. *Hella hard.* You've got to be kidding me."

AJ wasn't offended. He pointed toward the Black Rock mountains that rose up ahead of us, smack in the center of the island. "From this marker, we're going to go straight. Forty varas—"

"Varas is basically another word for paces," I explained to Maren. "You can use those two words interchangeably. And forty is another biblical reference. In this case, the number forty doesn't literally mean forty. You know how in the story of Noah's Ark it rained for forty days and forty nights? That's just a way of saying it rained as long as it needed to rain to clean everything up. Same principle here. We walk as far as we need to, which will probably put us right at the base of Black Rock."

"If you say so," Maren said. "This is all clear as mud to me."

AJ was bobbing his head to a silent, happy beat. "Yup, the base of Black Rock. That's where I saw those caves on the NASA images."

"And that's exactly where Miles was searching," I added.

AJ held out his fist for a bump. I complied, and we began walking toward our destination, AJ in the lead.

"What if we run into some pirates?" Maren asked. She was joking; we'd had a whole discussion about pirates last night on the boat back to the island. Someone had seen lights in the distance where there was only supposed to be darkness, and it had set off a chain of freakouts. Taylor's meltdown was still bouncing between my eardrums.

"Please," AJ told her. "Do yourself a favor and take these pirates a little more seriously. Modern pirates are bad news. Thieves who terrorize by boat, sailing around and robbing tourists. They try to instill enough terror so that if you do see them, you'll hand over anything valuable without a fight. They're not a joke. But we won't run into them here. The only thing you girls have gotten right about pirates is that they stick to the water."

"That would be good news, except we'll probably be spending most of our time near the water," Maren pointed out. "So . . ."

"Just walk," AJ told her. "I can only deal with one thing at a time."

There wasn't exactly a clear path, but the route Miles's crew had walked two years ago was implied. There were fewer low branches, and the dirt was flatter, signaling this was the way to go. After about twenty minutes, I looked up. Black Rock loomed large. We were getting closer.

Clouds had drifted in and were collecting around the peak of Black Rock. It reminded me of the fog in San Francisco, the way it would slide in and silently wrap itself around the Golden Gate Bridge. The fog back home was such a presence and had such a personality that there was even a name for it: Karl. I felt a ping of homesickness, which was a little unsettling since I'd spent the last several months wishing I could be anywhere but SF.

"It's probably another ten minutes more," I said. "Not far."

The trees began to thicken, but we were still able to make out a slight trail. We had to slow down, though, ducking under the dense vegetation and stepping over fallen trees.

"What if we lose the next challenge?" I asked. "Who should we vote out?"

"Maddie," Maren said immediately. "She bugs me. All that cutesy-pie stuff."

"I think she's sweet," I countered.

"London or Lucas, then," Maren said. "Don't care which. Both seem like idiots to me."

"Is anyone here not an idiot?" I asked. "Just wondering, because you seem pretty anti-everyone."

"I'm partnering with you and the nerd here, aren't I?"

There was that insistence again that we were partners, nothing more. Fine. I wouldn't take it personally. It wasn't like I was dying to be her friend, either.

"What do we think about the other team?" I asked.

As we pushed through the trees, we discussed the other players. We all agreed that Willa was definitely doing the show for social media followers; Murch, Porter, and Justin were a bunch of dumb jocks; Rohan was a pot stirrer; and Taylor was plain annoying.

"What about Alex?" I asked. "I can't get a read on her."

"I can," AJ said. "I think she'd be one of the last ones alive in a zombie apocalypse. She'd be covered in blood and zombie guts but the guys would still be checking her out and the girls would be jealous how great she looked, even in ripped-up rags."

"She looks tough enough to really get into it with some zombies, too," Maren said. "Like if you came too close, she'd cut you."

"Alex?" I asked with surprise. I hadn't seen that, but it seemed like a strange observation coming from the girl with the perma-sour expression and the purple hair.

"Oh, for sure."

The sky became visible again through the tops of the trees.

"We're almost there," I said. Soon enough, we were. The trees thinned out and we entered a clearing where the ground was uneven and lumpy. I stopped to look at the sky. Up close, Black Rock wasn't so much one large rock as a series of them, piled on top of one another like one of those drip sand castles I used to make at the beach. The fog still circled, ribbonlike, around the tip.

"Hey, look at this!"

AJ, who had gone ahead, was swinging something in the air. A coin on a cord. Weird, I just noticed that Harry had followed AJ ahead without even pausing, as if he knew something was there.

"It's one of those immunity coins Phil was talking about!"

"No offense to your searching skills," Maren said, "but that took all of four seconds. Seems suspicious. Where, exactly?"

AJ hung it on the branch of the tree right next to him. "Here. Like that."

"Very coincidental that it would be waiting right here in the first place you decided to search," I said. Something occurred to me. I remembered how freely he had announced where we were headed. "Did Deb know this was where you planned to look?"

AJ shrugged and had the decency to look embarrassed. "I may have said something."

"Are you kidding me?" I was furious. Deb and her crew had been on the island for weeks ahead of our arrival. They'd come here at least once to plant that coin, probably a lot more than that if they had an inkling of curiosity. For all we knew, they could have already found the treasure. This location was high-value information, and AJ had given it away.

"So what?" AJ said. "She wanted to know specifics. If I said no, she wasn't going to let me on the show."

"What else did you tell her?"

"Why are you so mad? Harry's here right now, filming us, so our secret will be out this afternoon anyway—Deb could ask him where we went or simply watch the footage, so what does it matter if she found out before now?"

It mattered. I shouldn't have to explain why.

"I guess I forgot you're only doing this to get into college," I told him angrily. "I'm used to working with people who have integrity and don't blab about things when they don't have to."

"Ooh-la-la, so fancy, with all those colleagues full of integrity. Hope you aren't talking about your Smokey Joe's pals, though, because I'm pretty sure none of them knows how to spell *integrity*, let alone has it."

"I think she's talking about her father," Maren offered. "The rich guy. He probably has tons of integrity."

"Excuse me for wanting to keep this spot to ourselves!" I said.

"Chill out, Riley. I get it, but I told you, I'm good for this show. They *want* me to succeed. The longer I stay on this show, the better my odds are that I'll find something, which is good for them. This immunity coin is a gift from Deb."

AJ leaned in toward Harry's camera, moving in close as if to kiss the lens. "Thanks, Deb! Immunity, I'll take it!"

"Don't touch the lens," Harry warned, the first words I heard him say all morning.

"*We*," Maren said. "Get that word in your head because the three of us have a partnership, which extends to that immunity thingy. One of us might need that before you."

"Sure, yeah. Of course. It's just a good sign. It means our partnership has been blessed by the Gods of Television."

The coin went into his backpack, accompanied by the more practical statement, "I'll keep it in my safe with the map and we'll bring it out for whoever needs it."

I didn't show it, but inside I was still boiling. He'd pointed the crew here without a second thought. He was right, I had been talking about my Smokey Joe's correspondents, but at least they were purists and would have viewed it as a betrayal to leak that information to outsiders. None of them would have done anything that careless.

But I put all that aside and we spent the next few hours crisscrossing the base of Black Rock. We were searching for anything man-made, as well as possible cave openings. It was hard work and I was glad for our water bottles and AJ's supply of snacks, although AJ never stopped. It was funny: he had the same obsessiveness as Miles when it came to the search, but they both had such different motivations. Miles was driven because he felt a connection to the gold, almost an obligation, but AJ only wanted to find the gold for what it would bring him afterward. For Miles it was the be-all and end all; for AJ it was only a means to an end.

I hadn't realized the treasure could be so many things to so many different people, and what AJ had said this morning about someone looking for ways to sell the gold illegally was starting to really bother me. What if pirates or thieves were the ones to find the treasure instead of someone who cared about what happened to it?

Not only that, but now that I'd seen AJ's obsession up close, I was starting to think my partnership with him wasn't the safety net I thought it would be. I was probably safe as long as I was valuable to him, but if he ever had to choose between me or his chance to find the gold, he'd obviously drop me in an instant. Maren didn't seem to have any particular love for me, so she'd probably side with him. I was going to have to spend some time with Maddie and Sean—London would probably always blame me for Annika getting voted off—so I had ties to teammates other than AJ and Maren. I'd look up Sean's YouTube channel later so we'd have something to talk about.

I saw signs of Miles's presence everywhere: a slightly worn path here, a cleared-out spot there. A bit of frayed string tied around a tree brought a flashback. I touched it, remembering the day I'd helped mark the searched areas. I could have been the one who put this here two years ago. How strange to think of all the things that had happened since then.

We worked quietly, and the only real sound was the birds singing to each other, maybe making fun of our lack of progress. Generations of birds had watched hundreds of searchers come and go. Maybe they passed down the song of the treasure in lullabies to their chicks.

A few times we got our hopes up when we found caves that we were able to squeeze into, but none led anywhere. I wished we had more of that string so we could isolate the new areas we searched. Without it, we had to resort to piling branches in lines to show all the zones we'd covered.

At one point Harry's walkie sputtered, although he was too far out of range for any real communication. The drone came back, circling low and aggressively.

"I think that's a sign it's time to go back," he told us.

I looked at my phone and realized it was almost one o'clock. Great. We hadn't found anything, and our teammates may have spent the whole day bonding and conspiring against us. What a waste.

Maybe I could salvage the day by getting online. I really wanted to go to Smokey's site to see if I could find that old conversation AJ had mentioned, the one about selling the gold illegally. If it really was a year ago, whoever it was may have even found the gold already. We could be wasting our time.

The sun flickered off the rocks, as if saying goodbye. The birdsong was practically gleeful as we packed up and left.

13

"WHOA, WHAT'S THAT?" MAREN SAID. SHE WAS THE leader this time, and we'd taken a different path back, one that went along the water. During Harry's intermittent walkie use, he'd been able to figure out that some of the players were swimming on the north end of the beach near camp. This was the fastest route. Fine with me—I wanted to get back to camp as soon as possible so I could start working on my relationships with Sean and Maddie and get online.

"What?" AJ asked. "Where?"

"Over there. I think it's a boat," Maren said. "Yeah, look! It is."

I saw it, too. "Harry, should we go look?"

Harry put his camera down. "A boat? What kind?"

If he was speaking to us voluntarily, he must be concerned. Even more worrisome, he'd lowered his camera—he hadn't done that the whole morning.

We made our way down to the waterline. It was a canoe, half in the water, half haphazardly covered with branches and palm fronds, almost as if someone had tried to hide it in a hurry.

We all stared at it, not saying anything, then the three of us turned in unison to gauge Harry's reaction. He looked worried.

"Does it belong to the show?" Maren asked.

He pulled off some of the palm fronds. "It could be. We rented a few canoes from a place on the mainland, and look, here's their logo." He shook his head. "But there was a whole warehouse full of canoes just like this available for rent. Anyone could have gotten one," he said. I wondered if it felt good for him to finally speak. Did he have to hold back, or was being naturally silent a requirement for the job?

"AJ, maybe it's those pirates of yours finally making an appearance," Maren said.

"By canoe?" I said skeptically. "They'd have to paddle pretty hard to catch anyone. *Hey, wait up, we're coming to rob you.*"

"It's not pirates. It's got to be other treasure hunters," AJ said anxiously. "Outlaws. And we just led them right to our search area!"

Now AJ cared about other people finding our site? Harry wasn't too interested in calming us down. Instead, he was moving around, trying to get a better signal. He kept shaking his walkie, but it just sputtered.

"Damn these things. They were working fine until we started filming and now they're nothing but junk."

"Shhh! Did you hear that? Up the hill," AJ hissed. We all froze. "There!"

It looked like there was movement further up the path, and then I heard it, too: branches being pushed aside, and not quietly. Someone was coming, and they were making enough noise that they either didn't know we were there or were unconcerned about our presence. I would have assumed it was just another player, but not now, not with Harry staring at the woods with a panicked look on his face. He motioned us to the edge of the path. Maren and I ducked on one side while he and AJ went to the right.

Someone was definitely coming. *What do we do?* I mouthed to Harry.

He held up his palm. "*Stay,*" he mouthed back. "*Low and quiet.*"

Suddenly Maren stood up. I grabbed her shirt but she pushed my hand away.

"Rohan, you idiot!" she said. "You almost scared us to death."

Thankfully, she was right. Rohan was coming toward us. He looked surprised but not nervous. Not like someone who had stashed a contraband boat nearby. I wasn't sure how he could have managed to arrange something like that only one day into the game, but then again, if it wasn't his boat, then it was someone else's. Frankly, I would have preferred it to be his, even if it meant he had a super-pro game strategy going on.

"What are you doing out here?" Maren asked.

"Same as you, obviously. Looking for some gold, or maybe an immunity coin."

AJ and I exchanged looks.

"Yeah, we didn't have any luck with that," Maren said.

"I'm sure you'd tell me if you found anything, right?"

"Definitely."

Were they flirting? I guess it wasn't the worst match in the world. They both had in-your-face personalities.

"Your usual strategy of interrogating locals not working out?" Maren asked him, which was when it hit me. Maybe the boat *was* his. Maybe he'd asked someone on the crew to get it for him. But for what purpose?

Rohan joined us. The path went up a hill and then bent left toward the water, and when the trees thinned out, we could see the beach down below. The rest of the players were gathered in the shallow water. Even Joaquin was there, with Maddie on his shoulders, and they were all staring upward at an outcropping to our left that jutted out from the forest. Some of them were holding their phones up, obviously filming something. We'd basically just passed the point they were looking at, but somehow we'd missed whatever they were waiting to see.

"Is someone jumping?" I asked.

The words were barely out of my mouth when I saw a

figure emerge from the trees. It might have been Sean, but before I got a good look, he wobbled on the edge and plunged downward, his arms waving wildly.

He really was a daredevil, although if I had to admit it out loud, I didn't think his jump was particularly impressive.

But then someone started screaming. It took me a second to realize Sean hadn't jumped. He'd fallen.

And now he was floating motionless in the water.

14

IT TAKES A DISASTER TO REVEAL EVERYONE'S TRUE

colors. At least, that's how it went last year after Izzy and I made that stupid mistake that had led to our expulsions. To celebrate passing our Marine Bio midterm, we'd decided to make weed brownies. Neither of us had ever vaped or smoked or tried edibles before, and we figured it was as good a time as any to try it for the first time. To this day, I have no idea why Izzy would have thought bringing the brownies to school was a smart thing to do, or why she would have eaten three of them on her own *before* the midterm, instead of after school the way we'd planned. But that's what she did, and the resulting bad reaction meant that instead of taking an exam she took an ambulance ride to the hospital.

Drugs on school property meant immediate expulsion, so Izzy was never going to be allowed to stay at Shaw. I didn't eat any brownies—either on campus or off—but since I'd participated in making an illegal substance that had ended up on campus, I was suspended.

Back then it had taken weeks for everyone to stop crying and wailing about how scary and horrible the whole thing was. No question Taylor would have been one of the dramatic girls in my class petitioning the headmaster for my dismissal, and her behavior didn't disappoint now. Harry and another cameraman hadn't even dragged Sean from the water before Taylor was screaming hysterically. Willa and Chloe weren't too much more restrained, but surprisingly, Alex ran right over and offered CPR help. My brain is strange sometimes: while everyone else was freaking out about Sean, I couldn't help but watch Alex and think, wow, AJ was right, that girl probably *would* survive a zombie apocalypse. Maybe I was just surprised that someone so pretty was so . . . I don't know . . . capable.

"But what if he dies?" Taylor was wailing.

I tried not to roll my eyes. A few hours ago, Taylor probably hadn't even known Sean's name, or if she did, would have had no problem voting him out. But now she was acting as if his accident was a personal tragedy.

It wasn't until we were on our way back to camp that I realized this meant our team was down another member. If Sean didn't come back, it was now the six of us to ten on the other team. We were definitely going to be at a huge disadvantage in the next challenge.

WE WERE, OF course, forbidden to leave camp for the rest of the afternoon. I thought it would be hard to sneak off, but everyone seemed preoccupied enough that I found a chance to grab my satellite and slip into the woods unnoticed.

I found a perfect little clearing behind the cabin. It was close to camp, which meant it wouldn't take too much time getting set up, and there was a thick wall of vegetation that would keep me hidden from view. If anyone came close, I'd hear them way before they found me.

When I plugged the satellite into my phone, I counted slowly while I waited for it to connect. Before I'd left home, I'd practiced using the satellite a million times so the process would go smoothly here.

It beeped when I got to six. I frantically pushed the volume button. It was jarring how out of place that sound was. Because I was in the middle of a rainforest, or because I'd been away from tech? It could have been either reason.

Three bars lit up. This thing was amazing. Four stars, Katie. I'd have to make sure she gave it a good review in her write-up.

Of course, I looked Willa up before I did anything else. I'd expected her entire account to be solo pictures of her posed to look sexy in beautiful and improbable settings, but there were only one or two of those. The rest were all of her, having a great time—pressed against a friend as they pointed at the camera, dancing at a party in a tiny black dress with a group of other girls, decked out in blue and yellow at a UCLA football game. She was always in a crowd, and only rarely the center of attention. She looked fun.

I gave her my test. Willa: genuinely fun girl, or shallow princess? Hard to tell. From what I'd seen of her here so far, she wavered equally between both.

Sean was next. Three bars weren't strong enough to hold any of his videos for long, but the little I saw was what I expected: no fancy camerawork, just Sean, goofing around.

I wished I knew some last names. I hesitated, and then googled *Porter New York senior brown hair preppy funny*, which was all I knew about him and was, unsurprisingly, not enough to find anything.

I hesitated for a second before going to Smokey's site. For the first time, it occurred to me that using this satellite might be considered cheating. If caught, I could get kicked off the island, and wow, that would be a bad look. Spoiled rich girl caught cheating with her rich girl device to find gold so she'd be even richer. When I'd come up with this plan, searching for the treasure wasn't part of the game. Sure, bringing technology was forbidden, but it wasn't like having the satellite was going to give me an advantage in the challenges for the show. But now things had changed.

I shook it off. I'd gone through a lot of trouble to get to this point. I couldn't stop now.

I logged into Smokey's site, username AnonGirl, and searched through the Black Rock discussion forum. AJ was right—there was a ton of debate about whether or not the old buckle was related to the treasure hunt, so it took me a while, but I finally found something of interest. The conversation was from last May, just over a year ago. I took a sharp breath when I saw the name of the user making the initial query: MrJackSparrow. I recognized his name. He was a frequent participant in the discussions in the map-reading forum.

MrJackSparrow: Let's say I find the treasure. It's no good to me unless I can sell it. Where would I find a buyer?
ThinkTwice: Depends what it is. I could help with gold coins
Viper5: Jewelry is a European market. There's a guy in Spain who'd know how to clean that
MrJackSparrow: I don't want to clean it, I want to sell it
ThinkTwice: That's what cleaning means, idiot. You're talking about something illegal, which means you have to clean it by passing through certain sales channels. You're out of your league
MrJackSparrow: No need for insults. I'm here for information. You don't want to give it, be quiet
Viper5: I'm out. I don't deal with amateurs

ThinkTwice: I'm still here. What do you have, Sparrow?

MrJackSparrow: Nothing yet. But I have a lead. A good one. I'll be on Black Rock soon and I want to set up sales channels ahead of time

DeadSea: Everyone get offline. You're violating terms of service. Treasure hunting is currently illegal on Black Rock, as is smuggling items of value out of that country. Don't bring this garbage here

And that was it. I frantically searched for more conversations. What had happened? This was a year ago and MrJackSparrow had said he would be on Black Rock soon. Had he found anything? My search for the gold could be over before it even started.

The gong sounded for dinner. Not now! I needed to keep looking.

Slow down, Riley. Think.

I'd had conversations with MrJackSparrow in the past year. If he'd found the treasure already, there wouldn't be any reason for him to be on the site anymore. He'd be over in Europe "washing" the gold with his new partners.

That made me calm down a bit, but still, I couldn't be sure. I reluctantly logged off. I checked the battery—ouch. It had drained a noticeable amount. I was going to have to be more careful about the amount of time I spent online. I had no way of charging the satellite; I couldn't bring the charger because it would have been confiscated, or at least raised questions about what it was needed for.

Of course, there was always the possibility that I wouldn't even need to use the satellite again. The gold could be long gone. It was possible MrJackSparrow had already beaten us to it.

"I'VE GOT SOME good news and some bad news," Joaquin announced after we'd finished eating dinner. "Sean is going to be fine, that's the good news. The great news, actually. He banged himself up pretty well doing that jump, but he's going to be fine after some time in the hospital. Unfortunately, he won't be rejoining us."

"What if you're lying?" Taylor called out. "What if he's not fine, but you aren't telling us because you don't want us to lose it?"

"I assure you, I'm telling the truth, and there's no need to 'lose it.'"

I had to admire Joaquin's restraint for not noting that Taylor was already, in fact, losing it. It was also nice the way he went over to sit with her.

"Tell that to the crew," Rohan said under his breath. I wasn't sitting with him, but my chair backed up to his. I twisted around to ask what he meant. On Rohan's other side, Justin leaned in, too.

"They say nothing's been going right," Rohan told us. "I was helping out in the kitchen tonight with dinner prep, and they told me things have been stolen and broken. Sometimes when it doesn't seem like any people are even around. This island is haunted, they're all sure of it. Deb's already run through an entire staff because the locals keep quitting. Didn't you notice everyone making breakfast today was new?"

I hadn't. I felt mildly guilty, but there were so many new people and things to keep track of.

"Look at Phil and Deb, arguing all the time. This show is a mess, and they know it. That can't be good for us, because if things start going down, they're going to ramp up the drama on our end."

I didn't know how much more drama I could take, and from the look of it, Phil was pretty close to his limit, too. He was standing at the edge of the Snack Bar, taking his baseball cap on and off, off and on.

"Are you feeling all right?" I asked him. "Need anything from the Quack Shack? You're looking a bit nauseous."

"No. Wait, yes." He sighed. "I think I do need something for this headache."

I walked with him to the Quack Shack. Phil used his key, but once inside I wondered why they even bothered to lock it. There was hardly anything here—just bandages and aspirin and medicine you'd find in every bathroom. Nothing hardcore. It seemed like there should be a lot more supplies on site, seeing as this was an isolated island, but then again, it wasn't like anyone from the show seemed overly concerned about safety or health.

Phil found the aspirin and shook four tablets out. "You guys are killing me. This show is so much different from the one Deb and I worked on before, with the Alaskan fishermen."

"You did a show together before?"

"Three, actually. Our whole crew as well. We're the go-to team for the Alaska beat." He waved his arm toward the beach. "Can you tell we wanted to do something different? We put this thing together while we dreamed of escaping frostbite. Went from that set to this one."

"That's quite a change! The weather has got to be an improvement."

"That might be the only thing that's better. The last show followed four crabbing boats. The routines and relationships were already established, we were simply capturing it on film. Here, we're creating everything from scratch, so when something goes wrong, it's our fault. It's not like when a guy from one boat decides he's had enough of another rig creeping in on his territory and then the two of them get into it. That's on them, not us. This, though—Sean jumping. One of us should have tested the depth of the water so we'd know if it was safe, but since we booked this island sight unseen, we're playing catch-up as we figure out the terrain. We've got this whole team of people who run through the challenges ahead of time, but we should have had them live at camp for a few days, too."

"Oh, right. Deb pointed them out."

"Exactly. The B-team. I don't know why we didn't think to have them completely replicate your whole experience, not only the challenges. Epic fail, as you teenagers might say."

It wasn't quite as bad hearing Phil say *epic fail* as when my mother tried. At least he said it right, and not: *that was an epic failure.*

I remembered the hidden canoe. "Would the B-team use a boat for anything? We found a canoe up the path along the beach."

Based on Phil's startled expression and the way he quickly rushed us out the door, mumbling something about finding Harry to see his footage, I was guessing that was a no.

It seemed as if everyone was having a bad day.

AFTER I LEFT Phil, I found everyone down at the fire pit. I felt a pang when I saw Porter hugging Willa. Was he just making her feel better, *hey friend*, or was there more to it? My brain said *I don't care*, but my heart said *I might*.

I sat next to AJ and Maren on one of the logs. It was weird to see the entire group so muted, silently staring at the flames.

"Phil didn't seem happy to hear about the canoe," I told AJ and Maren quietly.

"We've got bigger things to worry about. Maddie just finished telling everyone about the curse, and now people are trying to stop us from going back to look for the treasure," Maren said. "They think the island was trying to get its seventh death and that's what caused Sean's accident or something."

"The island isn't a gatekeeper, you guys, keeping the treasure hidden until a certain amount of blood is spilled," AJ said loudly, addressing the whole group. "You're being crazy. I'm not going to stop looking."

"You will if we make you," Murch said. I put a hand on AJ. That guy scared me.

AJ shook me off and stood up. "How about you do your thing and I do mine, tough guy? Or is that a problem for you because you don't have a thing? Go on, give up. But you're not dropping out of the treasure hunt because of the curse; you're dropping out because you can't handle the fact that it's hard."

I saw the lights of some phones, filming. I wondered if these devices were a smart idea after all—wouldn't they get in the way of the real camera footage, or at least diminish the results? How great was it going to be if the real camera was only filming a bunch of kids holding phones?

"Whatever. I'm not taking crap from a loser like you," Murch said. "Huaca, you've gotta vote this guy out. Get rid of him. You wouldn't want to lose another teammate to an 'accident,' would you?"

AJ jumped up and raised his fists. "You want to fight now? Let's go!"

Murch stood up, a lot more confidently. And for good reason. He wasn't ripped like Cody, but he was large.

"Yeah, boy," Rohan yelled.

"Stop it! Don't encourage him," Taylor screamed.

This set off a round of cries, some in support of a fight and some not, but it ended quickly after Murch cuffed AJ on the head. AJ immediately backed off.

I looked around. Seriously, where were the adults? Murch was huge and AJ was scrawny. This was dangerous. Did Deb know this was going on and not care, or did she not even notice?

"Forget it," AJ said. "I've got better things to do than waste my time on you."

He stormed off toward his cabin in better condition than Taylor, who was nearly hyperventilating.

Willa pulled her up. "Let's go on a quick cabin break, sweetie," she said.

Someone on Sol started a game of cornhole, but I stayed put. I didn't agree that the curse should be a reason to stop the search, but on the other hand, the idea of the island not surrendering the treasure until it was ready was interesting. People thought of the sea that way, too, sometimes. Supposedly "she" guarded her sunken boats and often searchers would return to a dive where they'd seen signs of a wreck to find the ocean floor mysteriously washed clean.

I stared into the fire, probably looking like a moron thinking all these random deep thoughts, when Porter slid onto the log and bumped up next to me.

"Hey, Frisco," he said.

I made a sour face, but inside I felt the thrill of hearing him use that nickname. It was like a code that only the two of us knew.

"I had an idea."

"Oh, is that a new thing for you?"

"Hey, don't be salty. I figured out how we can give your team an advantage without insulting Maren with another sex trade proposal. How about the next time Sol wins, we choose ourselves to vote someone off instead of forcing Huaca?"

"Is this to get your stuff back?"

I'd seen his things; Maren had relented last night. Some terrible notes, mostly. I'd been happy there weren't signs of a girlfriend—no pictures or love notes. Rohan had brought a book, and Willa had brought pictures of friends. Nothing special. The real value in their things lay in the fact that they wanted them. I'd even caught a glimpse of what Maren herself had brought: a sketch pad and colored pencils, although she'd shoved them back in her safe pretty quickly before I could see any of her artwork.

"Can you bring the trade to Maren?" Porter asked. "Think she'll do it?"

I nodded. "I think so. Why not?"

Because I'd been thinking so much about Miles, my godfather, the movie of that name was in the forefront of my mind. It felt natural to reference it to Porter.

I laughed. "I feel so *Godfather*-ish right now. Does this make me Maren's consigliere?"

"You know that movie?"

"Obviously. Who doesn't? My dad and I used to watch it all the time, usually at midnight when neither of us could sleep."

I missed those days, but before I got sad about it, Porter put his hands on both sides of my face. "I know it was you, Fredo."

I flinched in surprise. Inside I was basically screaming, *He's touching me!*

He took his hands away. "That's the best scene, isn't it?"

"You weren't trying to give me the Kiss of Death, were you? Haven't you done enough to me already?"

He leaned into me, giving me a shoulder bump. "Oh, so you wanted me to kiss you?"

I felt my face burning. Was I being played? He had just been hugging Willa.

"Definitely not. I would never kiss anyone who didn't know that scene was from *Godfather II*, not the original."

"*Godfather* is a single canon, no need to divide up the movies."

"You know what my favorite line is? *Leave the gun, take the cannoli.*"

Willa emerged on the other side of the fire, Taylor-less. "You guys, this is crazy. We're on a tropical island. What are we doing moping around? You heard Joaquin, Sean's going to be fine. Later he's going to watch this on TV and feel so sorry for all of us losers who don't know how to have a good time. Let's do something *Boom_Sean_alaka* would do! Make him proud."

Justin stood to join her. "I'm in. No cliff jumping, though."

Willa pulled off her shirt. The girl must have packed ten different bikinis. This one was white with gold trim, all the better to show up in the dark night. It was almost like she'd planned it, which, based on her Instagram success, she probably had.

"No jumping," Willa promised. "Just a little bit of night swimming."

A yellow glow from the moon stretched all the way to the water's surface, and it made the idea of slipping into its dark, invisible depths almost attractive. It was peaceful, actually. Small waves rolled ashore with a rhythmic, quiet swish.

Taylor and Chloe and Alex started taking off their clothes, too.

Porter stood up and held out his hand to me. "You coming, Frisco?"

Was I? I wasn't sure. They were the opposing team. Plus, this could be a ploy. Porter had played me before.

But what if it wasn't? I was suddenly glad for Deb's advice to always wear a bathing suit underneath any clothes. It wasn't skimpy or reflective, but my black bikini worked fine.

"Okay," I said. I'd been waiting for Porter to notice me, so why not?

I let him pull me up.

Willa danced between us. For a second I thought she might be there to separate me from Porter, but she put her arms around both our backs and it felt friendly, warm. It was easy to imagine the three of us pictured in one of her posts. One of her long red curls spilled over my shoulder, and it was so light, glinting gold in the firelight. No wonder she was so confident. Hair like that could make anyone feel special. My own hair felt weighty and boring compared to that single, bouncy curl.

"Yes, come, Riley!" she said. "Join the fun group!"

"Only if I get to push him in this time," I said, reaching across Willa to elbow Porter.

He broke free and splashed ahead. "Gotta catch me first."

We went far enough in so that the water was over our waists, the boys predictably taking turns brushing against the girls underwater enough times so that eventually we were all giddily grabbing each other and squealing *What was that?* until Phil rushed to the edge of the water in a panic and made us come ashore.

"One of you drowning or a shark attack is just what I need right now. Time for lights out! I need to call a wrap on this day."

"What's the matter, Phil? Your B-team never went night swimming?" I called out.

He went from frantic to weary. "Just come in, please, and don't forget to log your Demons in. I put the job sign-up sheet out for tomorrow, too, if you want to pick your shifts."

No one did, but it was smart of him to invoke the word *shark*. There had been enough unclaimed flicks to our feet and legs that none of us really objected to coming ashore, not even Willa.

We splashed onto the beach. I thought of the first day, when we'd all walked to the marker together and I'd realized it was the first time I'd been part of a group in a long time. I'd been so nervous, not knowing how or where or with whom to walk, but tonight I didn't feel any of that.

Later, when we were all getting ready for bed, I slid onto Maren's bunk and told her about Porter's proposal.

"Had fun skinny-dipping with all of them, did you?" she asked, ignoring the trade details.

"Yes, actually. But he came to me with that plan. What was I supposed to do, ignore him?"

"It's just so predictable, that's all." She turned her back to me after adding, "I'll think about returning their stuff. Maybe I'll do it. Maybe not."

I sat there for a second, confused. She'd been so clear. We were not friends, she'd said. Many times. But now she was mad because I'd possibly started making friends elsewhere? And the other weird thing was that I was pretty bothered by the idea that she might be mad at me.

Everything was upside down. I didn't know who meant what to me anymore.

15

IT WAS A CHALLENGE DAY, WHICH MEANT THE GONG
woke us up bright and early. We grabbed our phones from
the charging station and had a quick breakfast. It was hard to
believe this was only our third day here.

Because the sun was hardly more than a dark pink ball
above the horizon, there wasn't much talking. Thank God
for coffee. I managed to suck down two cups before Joaquin
herded us onto the boats and over to what we'd all started to
call Challenge Island.

I wasn't sure what today would bring. Maren was obviously mad, and I was nervous how that would play out. Her
T-shirt today—*Good morning. I see the assassins have failed*—
was not a good sign.

The arena had been transformed by the hardworking
B-team, who had replaced the sand squares with two giant
piles of rocks. It would be a wall-building challenge, Joaquin

told us. He had to be filmed four times doing the instructions. Definitely off his game.

Deb finally stepped in to make sure we were clear on what to do.

"So does everyone understand what we are doing here? The Incas were masters of stonework. Their villages were supported and protected by their well-made walls. They also had a sophisticated network of messengers to get information from town to town. Those two things are the inspiration behind this challenge. First, each team is going to construct a wall made from stones without any mortar. Your wall only needs to be three feet by three feet, but it has to be sturdy enough to hold Joaquin's body weight, because he's going to come over and sit on it to test it out. When that's done, you are going to run a relay race, and the first team to plant their flag at the finish line wins.

It was pretty clear that Huaca was at a disadvantage. We had only had six team members left, and with four needed as messengers that left only two to build the wall. I looked over at Maren, trying to see if there was any clue she'd decided to make a deal with Porter. If not, we were definitely toast.

"We don't need all ten players," London mimicked AJ. She was obviously still upset at the loss of Annika, and based on the size of our pile of rocks, rightly so. I was pretty peeved myself. This was going to be a tough one.

I was the one who'd be constructing our wall. "I want all the big rocks first," I directed the team. "And all of them should be as flat as possible, no matter what size. I also want a pile of the really small rocks, because I can use those as filler in the cracks."

I like doing puzzles, and that's really what this was—a 3D puzzle. I got absorbed in the work and time passed quickly.

"You a stonemason back home?" Lucas asked me at one point. "You might have a career waiting when you get off this island."

But it turned out Justin, the Sol builder, was the one with a future in stonemasonry. Not only was his wall finished way before mine, but when he let out a victory yell, I knew he'd found an immunity coin.

Ugh! Oh, well. I kept building, but in the distance I could see Deb arguing with Phil and Katya, stabbing the air in the direction of the walls, and then the trail. I didn't need to know how to lip-read to understand the challenge had been a bust. Sol would probably finish their relay race before our wall was even finished, which turned out to be exactly what happened.

I called Joaquin over to test my wall right as Willa was running the last leg of the relay. She planted the Sol flag in theirs and gave me a sheepish look.

"Sorry," she said apologetically.

"Do we even have to run?" Lucas asked Joaquin. "They won. It's over. I'd rather not exert myself unnecessarily, if you know what I mean."

Phil came over, red-faced and bothered. "Yes, of course you have to run. We'll have to use film magic to make it look more competitive than it actually was."

Joaquin was still sitting on my wall. "Very nice," he complimented me. "It can probably hold you, too. Come see. Sit."

He patted the wall, and the stones barely even shifted when I sat next to him. I felt weirdly proud of this silly accomplishment, but despite Joaquin's urging to take a break, I couldn't sit still. Alex was looking at me with concern, which made me realize: Justin wasn't part of the group who'd made the deal with Maren for their things. Porter had promised that if they won, they'd vote someone off their own team instead of ours. But as High Priest, Justin could overrule that decision. He could easily decide to send our team to Council, and really, why wouldn't he? He had nothing to gain by honoring the deal with Maren.

"Let's go watch the runners, if you can call them that," Justin said, leading the group toward the course.

I waited for Joaquin to get up before using my phone to take a picture of my wall.

"What good is a picture if you're not in it?" Willa asked. "If you aren't going to take a selfie, at least let me get one of you sitting on top."

I sat on the wall and she directed me. "Oh, that's cute. Cross your ankles, and hold up your arms in a shrug, as if you're saying *I made this,* but in a really modest way."

She laughed when I attempted the pose. "Great. Look." She held out her screen so I could see the result. "See? I'm good for something around here: photo advice."

She took a quick selfie of herself as if to illustrate the point, holding the camera high and tipping her head to the right with a wide, openmouth smile. It was a pose that looked awkward when it was happening in real life right in front of me, but when she held out her phone, the image she'd caught made it look as if she was mid-laugh, listening to the funniest joke ever. She looked so carefree and happy, palm trees and blue sky in the background. I wondered if I'd ever have the guts to casually fake a pose like that in front of other people. I'm sure I could do it alone in my bedroom, but if there was any sadder visual than a lonely girl making faces at her phone, pretending to laugh and have fun with imaginary friends, I couldn't think of one.

"Now one of us," Willa said, leaning in close. She smelled sweet, like the freshly cut fields in Golden Gate Park. It hadn't even occurred to me to pack perfume. I smiled. Me and Willa. Maybe someday people would be scrolling through their feed and they'd see this picture and envy me, the way I'd done last night.

"Don't worry," she said, after she inspected the picture. "We can still honor the deal. I'm going to convince Justin to pick our own team for the vote. The only thing is . . ."

I frowned.

"I'm worried for Porter. He and Justin haven't really hit it off. Justin thinks Porter likes me, so it's a little awkward."

Oh. My face flushed. Wait, were she and Justin together? Not her and Porter?

"Well, does . . . Porter . . . like you?" I managed to stammer out.

Willa laughed. "No! I think he's got a thing for you. Didn't you realize? It would be so sad if he left before you guys got together."

I couldn't help but smile. So much for my nonexpressive face.

"Aw, you're so precious. I'll work on Justin, don't worry. Come on, let's go watch them come in from the race. Plus I want to get close enough to hear Deb reaming Phil and Katya out for making this challenge so lame."

She grabbed my hand and pulled me into a run. Harry, the lone cameraman who'd stayed behind from the race, moved to follow us.

I definitely didn't want to go home, not now. For a split second I didn't even care if I never found the treasure because I was holding hands with Willa, a social media star, and she'd called me precious and said a guy liked me. I felt an exhilaration I'd thought I'd never experience again—yet it felt scary at the same time, as if I was teetering on the edge of something. Was I ready to start trusting people again?

Maybe. For the first time in a long while I wanted to.

There were tons of flights to LA every day. I imagined flying to visit Willa for weekends. We'd go shopping, run into some paparazzi, post pictures on Instagram together.

Willa laughed and pulled me to go even faster, and we left Harry in the dust.

Take that, SF friends. Or to use AJ's eloquent words to Team Sol: Suck it.

16

TRUE TO WILLA'S WORD, EVEN THOUGH SOL HAD WON,
Justin announced at Council that he was going to allow their
team to cannibalize itself. He was honoring the deal Porter
and Maren had made—Willa must have convinced him. I
was relieved that my team wouldn't be voting anyone off, but
I was worried Porter might end up a target. If Justin saw
Porter as competition for Willa, the odds were pretty good
Porter would be voted off. Bad news for me. Of course, if
Justin saw Porter as competition for Willa then that probably also meant Porter wasn't into me anyway and I should
just bury myself under my perfectly made stone wall and be
grateful his disinterest hadn't play out on camera.

Either way, it was hard to sit around the fire pit waiting
for Sol to return while worrying about what was happening
at their Council. The lightning was back, sporadic and scrag-

gly in the distance. I couldn't tell if rain would follow. So far the weather didn't really follow any pattern I was used to. Heat lightning, or storm lightning? It was unclear which one we were witnessing, but if a storm was coming, I hoped the boat returned before the rain arrived.

"I see the boat!" Maddie exclaimed, pointing toward the water. It was late, or maybe it just seemed as if the night had dragged on. I didn't know what time it actually was because I'd left my phone at the charging station.

I looked across the beach where she had indicated, but I didn't bother getting up the way I had the first two times someone had thought they'd seen a boat's lights blinking in the distance. We'd already wasted a ton of time thinking it was the Sol motorboat, which led, inevitably, to worrying whether all the blinks were a pirate code. I was ready for Sol to come back already.

"For real this time, you guys," Maddie said. "Look!"

The lights floated closer and closer until we could make out the boat. Maddie let out a sigh of relief when it was clear it was the Sol team, not a pirate ship. I scanned the group, trying to see who was there, but more importantly, who wasn't. Willa was there in the bow, but that wasn't a surprise. I spotted long blond hair; that was Alex. She was sitting next to Cody. He was so tall, he was hard to miss. The boat slid ashore and everyone got out, a lot more subdued than usual.

Porter was there. I let out the breath I hadn't realized I

was holding. Even better news was that Murch was gone. A quiet guy named Zander was missing, too.

"One of the girls is gone," Maddie said, surprised.

"Must be Taylor," I guessed, but I was wrong. Taylor was there, but not Chloe. That was crazy—how had Taylor survived but not Chloe? Pretty, normal, nice Chloe. I hadn't seen that coming at all.

It must have been a tough Council. They walked toward camp single file, not really interacting, except for Willa and Justin. He had his arm around her, and her head was on his shoulder. She looked upset.

Porter looked happy to see me. "Glad you made it," I told him.

"Worried about me, Frisco?"

"Maybe."

He reached for my hand. I felt his fingers intertwine with mine and we moved closer together.

One of the cameras targeted us, something I felt rather than saw because the light that accompanied the camera crew suddenly hit me like a blast of sunlight.

We split apart, and I didn't expect to feel so frustrated at the separation.

The beleaguered Phil ushered us all off to our own cabins. He must have been tired if he didn't care about filming something potentially juicy like that.

"Save all strategizing and fraternizing for tomorrow," he said. "Plenty of time then. Tonight, it's lights out."

I WONDERED IF Maren had seen the hand-holding incident because she was extra snippy in the morning. I'd noticed her black mood in the cabin—she was wearing a *You Discussed Me* T-shirt and it seemed like she pointedly turned in my direction when she put it on—but the fact she was targeting me didn't really come out until after we signed out the phones and headed off into the woods.

A few minutes later, we ran into Porter, Cody, Willa, and Alex, a meet-up that they tried to play off as random but was obviously staged.

"Mind if we join you?" Porter asked innocently. "Or should we just follow behind at a discreet distance?"

"Heck yeah, join us. The more eyes the better," AJ said, at the same time Maren gave a loud "No."

She looked at him in disbelief. "You threw three of our own teammates off the island for no reason because you didn't want to share. But now you want to let these guys in from the other team?"

AJ shrugged. "I've seen the error of my ways. More eyes are a good thing. Maybe even necessary."

"Oh, isn't that nice. Would've been helpful if you'd figured that out before. Anyway, the three of us have an alliance, remember?"

"When it comes to the game, sure," AJ said. "But for the rest of it, I'm Team Treasure. Team Trillion Pounds of Incan Gold, Team Get into Harvard."

"Team AJ, you mean?" Maren meant it as an insult, but AJ didn't take it that way. He held up a finger and then opened his backpack.

"That reminds me. I've got a waiver here that everyone needs to sign, basically agreeing that by going on this search you are admitting that it is part of an effort directed by me, I'm the one in charge, it's my proprietary information that will lead to any findings, that sort of thing."

AJ held his pen out expectantly. Willa waved it off and slipped away toward the beach after announcing her lawyer never let her sign anything without reviewing it first.

"A lawyer, huh? Must be nice to be so fancy," Cody observed as she walked back to the beach.

"This, you saved?" I asked Maren, because it must have been one of the things she'd rescued from his bag. "I can see salvaging his notes, but a legal waiver?"

I meant it to be an inside joke, but she glowered at me.

AJ answered instead. "Nah, Maren never saw this. I had this in my duffel. Anyone who signs can come with me. Oh, and I'm going to film myself reading this as you sign it, so there's no confusion later."

"Dude," Cody said, shaking his head in wonder as he took the pen. "You are one of a kind. You know this doesn't even matter, don't you? The show owns all of us, including you."

"Then it won't matter if you sign it."

Alex signed next while AJ used his phone to film us. Not that he needed it, because Lou was holding his camera, capturing the whole thing. Rohan had told me that Deb intentionally rotated the cameramen so we didn't form relationships with them.

Porter winked at me and signed, too.

"Even me?" I asked AJ.

"Yeah," Maren interjected. "Even special Riley has to sign? But her daddy is the reason you even know your theory is half-right. You're going to hold her to the same standard as the rest of us mortals?"

I stared at her. Why couldn't she drop this obsession with my father? It was as if she'd been at my school and signed the "Fair Is Fair" petition to get me expelled. Had Deb told her to get under my skin?

"This again? Are you going to go after me every morning?" I grabbed the pen. "Whatever. I'll sign it, I don't care."

Everyone took in the Riley and Maren Show. It was really poor form to be arguing in front of the competition.

Maren watched me sign. "You know what? I'm going to take a break from the treasure thing today. Think I'll get my work shift over with early. You guys go without me."

AJ followed her out of the Snack Bar with the waiver. I could hear him telling her that it was retroactive, that she needed to sign because of the previous search.

"Awk-ward," Alex said, in a singsong.

"Yeah," I agreed. It was hard to keep my expression neutral because Maren's comments echoed the views expressed by most of my online harassers. There was such malice lurking behind those tiny screens. I really hadn't expected it to bleed into the real world in this setting halfway around the world. So far, my image repair efforts were doing more to reinforce my reputation than correct it.

AJ came back, holding up his waiver in victory. "What are we waiting for? Let's go. Time to par-tay."

17

THE MORNING SEARCH WAS UNPRODUCTIVE, AND because we were being filmed, we didn't even really talk about anything interesting. Worse still, it seemed like Porter was keeping his distance, staying near his Sol teammates whenever we split into groups to cover different areas. It was a bust all around.

Everyone felt it. AJ kept giving the finger to the drone whenever it appeared overhead.

We returned to camp for lunch, sweaty and tired, and immediately split apart to pull ourselves together. For that, I had antagonized Maren? Definitely not worth it. The others went swimming or to nap in the hammocks, and when it was all clear, I slipped away to see if I could find out more about MrJackSparrow.

His name popped up a number of times when I searched the archives. He was a regular contributor to various discussions, but not a regular one—there were plenty of gaps between posts, which meant there were blocks of time where he could have come to the island.

And then I found something from April, just two months ago.

Think Twice: Hey @MrJackSparrow. What's the word? Find anything?
MrJackSparrow: I will
ThinkTwice: Is that a no?
MrJackSparrow: I didn't find it yet, but I found some caves that no one else knows about. Something's there, I'm sure of it. When I can get back to Black Rock, it will be quick. I know right where to go
ThinkTwice: How did you get on the island? I've heard of hunters getting arrested and sent out of the country and never allowed back again. I wouldn't want to risk it
MrJackSparrow: and that's the difference between us, and why I'll be rich while you spend all day online on the couch in your mother's basement

MrJackSparrow wasn't afraid to burn bridges, apparently. After that, his name came up in a few conversations, but nothing too interesting. I'd have to look more later—it was hard to concentrate on anything but the realization that he hadn't found the gold. It was still there, and not only that, we were on the right track. He had to have been talking about the same caves we were looking for.

I hurried back to camp, running smack into AJ—who was refreshed, ready, and appeared to be on his way toward Black Rock.

"Are you going without me?" I asked, not really expecting him to say yes.

At least he looked sheepish. "Early bird catches the worm and all that," he said.

I'd been right—he was only out for himself. I knew he'd leave me behind when it suited him.

"Nice try, but I'm coming with you," I told him sharply. "So you might as well wait for me to get my sneakers and backpack."

"Fine. I'll wait ten minutes, but that's it."

I left him sitting under a tree. He didn't seem the least bit embarrassed, and I realized immediately why I was annoyed. I'd been accused all year of going behind my friends' backs for my own benefit, but it hadn't even been true. And now here AJ was, actually doing it, and he didn't even feel bad about it.

I had just collected water bottles and sunscreen and grabbed some extra sandwiches from the Snack Bar when behind me Lou's walkie crackled.

"Lou, that's a no-go for you. I need two on the beach this afternoon," Deb's voice came through.

"Flying in," Phil's disembodied voice broadcast. He arrived in a minute, huffing up from the beach. Deb followed. They pulled Lou out of the Snack Bar into what escalated quickly into a heated argument about camera assignment.

Deb was throwing around a lot of sass: *I don't care. Not important.*

Whatever they were arguing about, Phil must have lost, because he was the only one of the three who came back. He looked mad.

"Bring your Demons," he told me. It was cute how the adults all kept referring to them by their proper name instead of just saying *phones.* "I need someone filming at all times. Got it? We'll download your videos later and hopefully find something to use. And don't avoid the drone."

So Lou wasn't coming with us—we'd be on our own. That meant two things: we could search without Lou reporting back every detail and every discovery, but it also meant that Porter and I might have a better chance of getting together if Lou wasn't right there in our face.

No way was I going to leave without Porter. AJ wouldn't like it, but too bad. He wasn't thinking of me, so why should I think of him?

I hurried on the back path to the Sol hut, weaving this way and that to avoid Maren on the beach and AJ in the woods.

I burst out of the trees, nearly running right into the hammock strung outside their hut. Most of the Sol team happened to be right there to witness my ungainly arrival.

"Oh. Um, hey, Porter," I said, as casually as I could. "Can I talk to you for a sec?"

Justin hooted, but Porter didn't seem to mind. He came over and plopped down in the hammock, keeping his feet on the sand so he could swing gently.

"What's up, Frisco?"

"Lou's not coming this afternoon," I said. "That means no camera. I think you guys should come back."

"You think we should come back because there won't be any cameras? That sounds like you're suggesting something off-limits," Porter said, teasingly. He pushed off with his feet a little harder and the hammock rocked a little higher. "I don't know. I might need some convincing. It was pretty hot up there."

"What if I asked nicely?"

"Hmmm. How nicely?"

Oh. This was getting into uncharted territory. I'd had boyfriends before, but casual ones, boys I'd see mostly at parties or in the park after school if a group was getting together. Conversations like this weren't exactly the norm for me. Just as I was cursing my rusty flirting skills, Cody bailed me out.

"Let's continue this on the road, shall we?" he said, walking by and giving the hammock a push as he passed. "Alex and I agreed, we're all going. Get your water bottle, son."

"You heard him. Hurry up, or we're leaving without you," I told Porter, back to business. Then I pointed at the beach where Joaquin and Maddie were setting up a volleyball game.

"Or maybe you'd rather stay and play volleyball with everyone who's not tough enough to search for the gold?"

"I'm coming! Jeez." When Porter hopped off the hammock, we were so close our faces nearly touched. It should have been awkward, but it felt . . . nice. Normal. It lasted just the right amount of time, and then Porter waved his arm toward the trees in an exaggerated gesture. "Lead the way. Ladies before gentlemen."

HALFWAY THERE, WE took a break at a familiar clearing. Black Rock loomed above the jungle, so dark it seemed almost pasted onto the flat blue sky.

"Picture time," Alex said. "Come on, don't even try to complain. Phil specifically said we had to document our every move. Everyone smush together."

Alex seemed lighter today. Friendlier. Was it escaping camp or the lack of cameras that had brought about the good mood? Hard to know, but since she was being nice, I didn't really care what the reason was. She held her phone down low and we crowded around, trying to get all of our faces and Black Rock into the screen.

"Willa would not approve of this angle," I said. Only parts of each of our faces made it in, and not really any of our best features. Alex's forehead, my right eye. We all laughed and made fun of AJ's glasses dominating the center. We looked like friends in that pic, even if the reality was something different.

It was definitely starting to be a much better day now that we'd shed the film crew. Even AJ had managed to shake off his annoyance at seeing the Sol team with me.

He studied the map while the rest of us scrolled through the photos we'd just taken. "We're going to go that way, off to the right," he said, even though no one was really listening. He halfheartedly gave the finger to the drone again; he'd started to do that whenever the buzz announced its presence.

"Ugh, delete that," I told Alex as a picture appeared with only my nostrils in it.

"Come on," AJ said, trying to grab Alex's phone. "I need everyone to focus."

"Fine." Alex put her phone in the back pocket of her shorts and we dutifully followed AJ off to the right, picking our way through rocks and fallen trees.

Cody held up his phone. "Why do they call those things Demons, anyway?" he asked. "Seems like something adults decide on because they think we're going to run with it and make it a thing."

"I actually know the answer to this one," I said. "The original name was spelled *Daemon*, with an *A*, inspired by a computer program spelled the same way. But no one could pronounce it right, so they dropped the *A*."

AJ looked back. "I know that program. But why?"

"Because the Daemon program is always running in the background and that's what our phones are doing now.

They're always there, doing everything. Waking us up in the morning, taking pictures, connecting us to friends, logging us into our school portals. Email. Everything."

Porter was ahead of me. We'd reached a narrow rocky part, and he held out his hand to help me up and over. "And you know this how, Frisco?"

I made a show of dropping his hand when he said Frisco. "Because *San Francisco* is so close to Silicon Valley, that's how. And because—"

"If you're about to say your father invented them, then it's a good thing Maren isn't here," Alex called from the back of the line.

Everyone laughed, even me. It had been nice not having judgy Maren around.

"Not invented, but yes, good point. He helped develop them after he got in during the first round of financing."

We passed over another outcropping. Porter held out his hand again, holding mine for longer than necessary. Yes, it was definitely better not having the film crew here.

"That's a lot of input from a VC," Cody said.

"People like having him involved," I said defensively. I was sure they'd recognize his name, so I didn't offer it in case it summoned a memory of my own scandal.

"He's the one who donated the phones, obviously," Alex noted. "But doesn't that give you an unfair advantage?"

"How?" I shot back.

She shrugged. "I'm not saying it does, but Deb might

want to return the favor and help you out somehow. Quid pro quo."

"Hey, easy," Porter said, coming to my defense. "It's not like these things are necessary to play the game or anything. They're just gizmos to mess around with, not a big deal. And I'm sure Riley would never cheat. Right, Riley?"

I nodded, but my stomach was in knots. This was why I had to keep the satellite a secret. It *did* give me an advantage, and if I revealed it, everyone would be upset for the same reasons everyone was last year at Shaw—only this time, it would be justified. I didn't want to fend off that same anger again, but more importantly, I'd get kicked off the island for violating the rules, and what a sad twist that would be! I went through all this effort to disprove my reputation, but instead I would have confirmed it.

"Interesting," Cody said from ahead. He took his cowboy hat off and slicked his hair back. "But y'all know what's even more interesting? I think that's the most I've heard Riley say since we got here."

I exhaled in frustration. Cody heard me. "What? You should talk more, that's all I'm saying."

Talk more, smile more. Look friendlier. Yeah, I'd definitely heard all of that before. If I could make a list of things that people said to me all the time, at the top would be *You're so quiet. When I first met you, I thought you were a snob/a bitch/ stuck up.* These days everyone is all about putting yourself out there all the time, in every way. Being quiet, or wanting privacy, is something contemptible. Likes and comments are the only currency that matters, so if you like to stay invisible, you're worthless.

Also, there was nothing more annoying than feeling like you had to do something because someone told you to. "All right, I'll talk more," I said to Cody. "And to start, I'm dying to know if you have a ton of different tank tops, or whether you keep wearing the same one."

"He's got two," AJ offered.

Cody confirmed it. "All my other shirts had logos, so they were confiscated. I alternate and wash the dirty one in the sink at night."

"That's gross," I told him.

"They're quick dry. For out in the woods. Came in pretty handy, I have to say. Thought I'd be on the beach most of the time, but this is like home."

"There are trees in Texas?" AJ asked. "I thought it was just oil fields."

"You never heard of the Piney Woods?" Cody was incredulous. "Get your nose out of the books, son, and try seeing the world instead."

"I'm in South America right now, aren't I?" AJ pointed out. "And if you're so in touch with nature, how about you pick where we search next. I'm stumped. There isn't really anywhere left to go."

It did seem as if we were at a dead end. The rock face was ahead of us; and at our sides, nothing but trees and rocks, old ones that had never been touched. We surveyed the surroundings and suddenly it hit me how far into the woods we were. It was the middle of nowhere. And then I noticed something else—there was literally no noise or movement at all, as if the forest was holding its breath. When I had been here with Miles and his crew, there was so much activity—people coming and going, lots of talking, birds getting flushed out of the branches and into the sky. There had been so much movement that it didn't seem so isolated. And back then, I didn't associate this place with death, so any pockets of quiet had seemed soothing, not sinister.

We all moved closer together, instinctively feeling the same vulnerability. My hand brushed Porter's by accident, but he held on and our fingers hooked together, an act that must have sent an urgent message to my brain because suddenly I felt all gooey and warm inside. I squeezed his hand and he squeezed back, bumping his hip against mine before letting go.

It took the sting out of not finding anything so far. I thought of Miles, and I tried to picture him here. Where would he look? He'd try to summon Lady Luck, I supposed, but how? Treasure hunters were creatures of superstition, but I'd never paid attention to any of his rituals when I was here before. I rubbed the pendant on my necklace, the last gift from Miles, and wished for a sign.

Just then, a line of sun shot through the trees to our left and snaked down the face of Black Rock. Okay, then. That out-of-place glimmer of light was as good a sign as anything else that Lady Luck was showing us a direction.

"How about over there?" I suggested.

"Fine," AJ said. "But I hear the drone coming back. Let's walk the other way and let it see us and then circle back when it's gone."

We executed the misdirection, and then Cody took the lead when we turned back toward the rock face. A few yards in, he stopped. "Y'all, I think someone's been here recently."

Cody knelt and pointed to a patch of grass that had been flattened, as if something heavy had been placed on it. He led us farther, pointing out more signs of recent traffic. A footprint here, a snapped twig in the vegetation there. It became obvious this area had seen some action lately.

"We should be careful," Alex said nervously. "Whoever it is could still be here, and if they're here looking for the treasure, they've got to be bad guys."

"But we're looking for it, too," Porter pointed out. "And we're not bad guys."

"We're here legally! No one else is supposed to be here."

"Semi-legally," AJ corrected. "I'm not convinced Deb actually has the right permits. I think she subscribes to the *better to beg forgiveness than ask permission* way of doing things. But I'm going to find the treasure spot if it's literally the last thing I do. Anyway, Cody can take anyone down, right, Cody?" He added sternly, "No matter what, we're not stopping."

But two seconds later, we did just that: stop.

"Holy . . ." Cody said. The line of sunlight had winked and disappeared, but right where it had been there was a crack in the rock face. A crack big enough to walk inside, but even more interesting, the ground in front had obviously been disturbed. Footprints were distinctly visible.

I sucked in my breath. Porter was standing in front of me and I moved closer. He put his arm back, as if to shield me, and I held on to his shoulder, peeking over to watch Cody step inside.

My heart was thudding. I didn't want to hope.

Cody stuck his head out a minute later. He was smiling broadly and holding his hat to his chest. "Y'all have got to see this."

18

WE HAD TO SHIMMY THROUGH A NARROW SPLIT IN THE rock. Luckily it didn't go too deep, and after a tight squeeze, we found ourselves in a cavern. It was big enough to fit all of us, but without the lantern AJ had stuffed in his backpack, it would have been pitch black.

"Sweet Jesus," Porter said.

I thought he meant it as an exclamation of surprise, but inside the cavern there was an actual stone Jesus statue, next to an ornate altar carved into the rock wall. We'd entered a shrine. The air inside was so still, it felt like we'd stepped into a bubble. And in a way we had: the priest who'd originally hidden the treasure must have created this space four hundred years ago. This was a holy site, created to protect a priceless treasure.

AJ was looking wildly around, not saying anything, just taking it all in. I made sure to take some pictures of him before he noticed and turned back to his swaggering self. It was nice to see him awed for a change. He knelt at the base of the statue, which would have made a good picture if it wasn't so dark: AJ, kneeling for mercy. But then I realized he wasn't praying. He was inspecting a pile of dirt.

I knelt down next to him. "Someone's been here."

"Looks like it," AJ grimly agreed.

Cody bent down and ran his fingers through it. "Dirt is dry and fairly loose, but there are still a few chunks of damp soil. I'd say this was dug up a few weeks ago. More than several days have passed, that's for sure."

We pushed the dirt aside—no digging required, the ground had only been loosely replaced—and found a square stone marker. It was nearly identical in shape and size to the original marker, but this one featured completely different carvings. It featured a triangle with the numbers 1, 2, and 3 at each of the points. Instead of a solid line, the longest length of the triangle was broken up with a dot in the center so that it looked like a bit of morse code: dash, dot, dash. Below that was some sort of equation: $2 = 3$, the letter C, and two X's.

"I think these are further instructions," I said, dumbfounded. In all my research, I'd never heard of a treasure map leading to more clues instead of an actual treasure. I got my notebook and pencil out of my backpack to make a rubbing of the stone marker.

AJ stood up. "This is incredible." Some of his swagger

was coming back. He raised his arms in an awkward victory sign. "Andrew Jacobson Jr. has entered the history books, my friends. To all those who doubted my mission, they can all—"

"Suck it," Cody and Porter said in unison.

"Hate to burst your little bubble there, Mr. Andrew Jacobson Jr.," Alex said, "but we all got here the same time as you. Not that it matters, because someone else obviously got here before all of us, which means they probably have the edge when it comes to history books."

"MrJackSparrow," I said under my breath. It was him, it had to be. Sparrow knew about the caves. He'd been in this same area, and he'd planned to come back. It had to be him.

"Are you kidding me with the Jack Sparrow reference?" AJ asked, letting his arms fall and dropping the triumphant pose. "Captain Jack Sparrow is neither real, nor from a decent movie. And in general, can everyone please forget the word *pirate*, because it seems to be causing a lot of confusion. The pirates we need to worry about aren't running around the island with a cryptic map in search of a treasure chest filled with hard to sell gold coins. Think *thieves*. Bad guys with weapons who rob other people for whatever they've got on them at the moment. Money, jewelry, cameras. Just regular old thieves, only they're on boats."

"Speaking of thieves, I heard a drone was stolen. Rohan told me Deb was losing her mind about it. Those things cost a fortune," Cody said, standing up and dusting off his hands.

"There's a ton of stuff going wrong in general," I said. I

looked around the shadowy cavern, the lantern light flickering eerily on the walls. "And now we know there's someone sneaking around looking for the gold. Do you think it's the same person? Someone from the film crew?"

"The film crew?" AJ scoffed. "Those rubes don't even know the difference between tikis and totems. Their set decor has Polynesian masks next to Native American tomahawks dipped in gold paint."

The show did play fast and loose with certain details, and it made sense that no one involved knew too much about the island's Inca history. Then I remembered Phil saying that nearly their whole crew had come with them from their Alaska show, never having seen the island. MrJackSparrow had definitely spent time on the island before this trip.

"But only people from the show are supposed to be on this island," Alex said. "If someone's looking for the gold, wouldn't that mean they had to be someone from the show?"

"*Supposed to* is the key term," AJ said. "You think someone looking for treasure is worried about what they're *supposed* to be doing? The chaos of this crazy show is the perfect way for someone to slide in and get busy."

I thought of the canoe, hidden next to Sean's cliff. Someone could have easily rented it on their own and arrived on the island. If anyone noticed activity on the island, it would simply be attributed to the show. AJ was right; the show was a great cover.

"Another possibility is that it's a crew member who accidentally stumbled onto it," I said. "Like I was worried about before. Remember? They got here before we arrived to set up. They could have been walking around and randomly seen the cave opening. And we know they were up here to plant your immunity—"

Oops. I'd forgotten for a minute that we were on opposing teams. It was bad strategy to let Sol know we had it.

Cody and Alex exchanged looks.

"Immunity say what?" Porter asked innocently.

"You're lucky Maren isn't here. She'd kill you," AJ warned. "But sure, someone theoretically could have accidentally discovered the shrine. We'll know when we see the next clue. If we're first to find it, then this discovery was a one-off. Only someone who knows how to read a map and has studied the rules of treasure hunting will be able to find the next clue."

True. I wasn't even sure we'd be able to find it. I held up the rubbing to make sure I'd gotten all the details. "What do you think of these clues?" I asked AJ. "The C and the X's are probably meant to be Roman numerals. C is fifty and X is ten, so that equals seventy."

"Sounds right," AJ said cautiously. "But seventy what? seventy varas? And where do we start? The triangle must mean that we need to find a triangular area somewhere on the island and start there, but where and how would we find it?" He frowned in frustration. "Offhand, I don't know how to read the rest of it. How about you?"

I shook my head no, and he started to rummage through

his backpack before looking up, dejected. "I didn't bring my Cipher. How could I be so stupid? It's back at camp."

"Dude, didn't you learn anything from the first day here?" Cody had been inspecting the altar, but he had stopped to mimic Joaquin in a mock-serious accented voice. *"Never leave your treasure hunting tools behind."*

Porter nodded. "He's got a point. No doubt Maren's got it now. Hope you have something to trade and I definitely don't mean in the sexual favor department. She shot me down pretty quick, which means you have, like, no chance at all."

I barely paid attention; I was thinking of all the things I needed to look up online.

Porter nudged me. I realized everyone else was ready to leave. "All good?" he asked. "We should probably get back to camp."

I nodded, hanging back so I could take one last look around.

Outside, it was much lighter than it had been in the cavern, even though it was early evening.

"We gotta do one last thing before we leave," AJ said. "Take a video of all of us here so that everything is documented."

AJ held his phone out and rotated around to capture the full area, narrating the scene and describing our discovery. At the end, he faced the rest of us and we instinctively moved together to face the camera.

"Hashtag team treasure," Alex called out.

"Hashtag fearless five," I added, and the two of us burst out laughing at the shared joke.

"Hashtag I need my Cipher," AJ said, which made Alex and I laugh even harder.

"Great idea," Cody said. "Now we'll have a video for Deb. This definitely has to count as a substantial clue, so we'll win the—"

"Wait, what? You think this is *a substantial clue?*" AJ repeated, incredulous. "They're not going to give us a pile of money for finding a shrine that someone practically led us to. Anyway, no thank you. I want to find the treasure, the actual treasure. We're not telling Deb or anyone else anything. Zero. Zip."

"He's right," I added quickly.

"You two are suffering from a strange obsession with this treasure," Cody said, "so I'll excuse y'all for not thinking straight right now. But yes, we will be telling Deb. I'm here for the money, and two hundred and fifty thousand is a lot of it."

"Not split five ways," Alex helpfully pointed out. "Fifty thousand for each of us is still a lot, but there'll be taxes."

"Whatever we get, it will be more than zero," Cody said, "which is what it'll be if we keep this a secret."

"Hold on," I said to Cody. "You just said you're here for the money, and the real money will come from winning the show. We bring this video to Deb and Phil, and everything ends. The show becomes collateral damage. No show, no mil-

195

lion-dollar prize, no college essays. The government will shut us down in five minutes and bring a bunch of treasure hunting experts in."

Cody frowned. "But if we wait, whoever found the shrine first might publicize it. Then we'll lose the treasure prize, *and* the show. It's lose-lose."

I thought quickly. "Whoever is on the trail of the gold isn't looking for publicity. They're sneaking around, and if they find it, they'll probably sell it on the black market. The public will never know. Why don't we keep the news to ourselves and try to find the next clue? The more we have to show Deb, the more likely it is we'll get the treasure prize, plus we'll keep the show running."

"Seems fair to me," Porter said.

Cody nodded. "A day or two, how about that? Show me that you can figure out the next clue. If you can't, I'm going to Deb with this. I don't want to risk losing that prize money."

AJ and I quickly agreed. "No problem," AJ told him. "I'm sure we can figure out the next clue."

Porter shook his head. "If you say so. I have no idea how a bunch of shapes and numbers tell you what to do next, but go for it."

"But what about the phones?" Alex asked. "The crew picks them up every so often to download our pictures. I saw Harry grab them the other morning. We all took pictures, so Deb will see the shrine."

The light was dimming, and it felt as if we'd overstayed

our welcome, but we couldn't leave until we'd hashed everything out.

"Good point," AJ said. "We can't let Deb see those pics. I guess we keep the phones."

"Keep 'em? That's a terrible idea, son. Deb will instantly know something is up," Cody pointed out.

I felt my stomach clench. We were looking at a choice of two terrible options. Turn the phones in, and Deb would see the shrine and that would be it for the show. Keep them, and we'd call attention to ourselves. Deb was smart—she'd send a crew up here to see what we'd been up to, and if she found the shrine, well, at that point it would be her discovery. Not ours.

"We have to delete all the shrine pictures off every phone," Alex said. "It's our only choice."

AJ didn't take that suggestion well. "No way. Delete all evidence of the ground-breaking, history-making centuries-old shrine we found? Sacrilege." He defiantly shoved his phone down the front of his shorts. "Sorry, I'm keeping mine."

Alex looked at him skeptically. "You think that move will stop any of us? I don't want to reach around down there, but if I have to . . ."

"Hold on," I said. I wanted to keep the pictures, too—at least until I could download them. "Let's just think. Ideally, we want to keep the pictures. We might need proof we were here. But we can't risk holding on to all the phones. How about we keep one of them?" I tipped my head toward AJ. "His, I guess. AJ has the most pictures of the shrine, anyway."

"But Deb said if any of the phones didn't make it back, she'd yank all of them," Porter pointed out. "I personally don't care too much about the phones, but I don't want to be punished some other way."

It was hard to argue with that. "How about this. We tell Deb that AJ lost it. That's not completely unreasonable, right? People lose things all the time."

It was our best option. Once everyone agreed, AJ took his phone out of his shorts.

"But any problems with Deb," Cody warned him, "that phone gets returned. Understand? I'm not risking the game for a couple of pictures. I'd rather just tell Deb about the shrine and collect that finder's fee, anyway. Don't push your luck."

I WASN'T HAPPY about the extra pressure. As if finding the gold wasn't hard enough, now we had to do it on Cody's timeline? But at least we'd found a temporary solution. On the walk back, everyone dutifully deleted their pictures. Or, rather, the others did. I only pretended to. I'd delete them later, after I'd safely uploaded them. I thought about the conversation we'd had earlier, about cheating.

Uploading the pictures wasn't cheating, I told myself. *Not exactly. After all, I wasn't doing this for money, and if I benefited, we all would, so what was the harm?*

We were almost at camp when I felt Porter's hand on my waist.

"Shhh. Stay back for a sec," he said quietly. We waited for the others to go ahead. "Come on, let's take the path back to the north end of the beach. Just us. I want to tell you something."

I nodded, not trusting myself to say something that wasn't completely dumb.

In the distance, the gong rang out.

Deb's voice came through, amplified by a bullhorn. "Everyone return to base camp. New schedule today: there will be a nighttime challenge after dinner."

Porter let out a groan. "Seriously?"

I couldn't believe it. Tonight? What miserable, wretched timing.

"We probably have a few minutes before Deb starts screaming ultimatums," Porter said. "Come on, let's make her find us. She can't start the challenge without us. We'll pretend we didn't hear."

I wanted to go. I really, really did. Things changed so fast on this island, I might never get this moment back. But I had to download these photos before I returned my phone, and now that we were being summoned to a challenge, I had limited time.

"I don't know. I think we should go back," I said. "But we'll meet later. After the challenge, okay?"

He looked disappointed. "Am I not as irresistible as my mother always told me I was?"

"Stop," I said, laughing. "Later."

I hesitated, though. I had signed up for this show so that I could present myself to the world looking good, but right now I was *feeling* good. I hadn't really understood, until this exact minute, that there was a difference between those two things. An eternity had passed since the last time I'd felt any sort of acceptance. For so long I'd been on the outside looking in, feeling unwelcome, but here on the island things were starting to feel different. I was starting to feel like I might actually matter.

Even so, I couldn't simply drop everything that had brought me here, and that's what I'd be doing if I didn't get online.

"I'm sorry," I told Porter. "I really am. But there's something I need to do, and if I don't do it now, I might lose my chance."

Annoyance flashed across his face. I wondered if I'd blown it, but then it disappeared. "Mysterious," he said. "I like it."

I prayed he meant it. If I had just ruined things between us, I'd regret it.

19

WHEN WE GOT TO CAMP, I GAVE PORTER A HURRIED—
and reluctant—goodbye, then ran to the cabin to grab the
satellite. As I headed for my spot in the woods, I noticed
Maren in one of the hammocks on the beach. She was staring out at the water. I nearly didn't recognize her. She didn't
have her black lipstick or heavy makeup on, and her hair was
pulled into a loose knot on top of her head. When I got close,
I could see brown roots at her temple, which was interesting.
Forget the purple tips—not even the black part of her hair
was real. Her sketch pad was facedown on the sand with her
box of pencils.

I had wrapped a sweatshirt around the satellite so no
one would wonder why I was bringing my "makeup" into
the woods. I looked at it for a second, weighing my options.
I was going to need to talk to Maren sometime to make
things right between us. Despite my rush, now would be

a good time to do that, seeing as how we might be voting later tonight.

I had this whole speech prepared in my head, but I didn't say any of it when I saw her. She took her earbuds out when I approached.

"Hey," I said.

"Hay is for horses," she said absently. I waited for something more biting to follow, but nothing came.

"You look . . . relaxed," I said.

"Yeah," she agreed. She was still staring at the water. "I used to go to the beach a lot when I was little. I forgot what it was like to spend all day in the sand, just hanging out."

I waited for her inevitable reminder that I was spoiled, that I took beaches and trips for granted, but I was wrong.

"I guess I wanted to take a day off, and just . . . I don't know . . . be." She looked at me and I nearly died, because she was actually smiling. "I know. So cheesy."

"Well, maybe a little," I agreed, somewhat cautiously.

Maren seemed to suddenly realize we were being nice to each other. She frowned at me. "What are you looking at? Take a picture, it'll last longer. Are you here to give me a report on the day or what?"

I told her about the cave, the shrine, and the carvings.

There were a few seconds where we bonded again over the excitement of our find.

"We really might find the gold and win that money," she said, morphing back into the nicer version that had slipped out a few minutes ago. Predictably, though, she flipped back quickly to her old self when she realized that some Sol members had been there for such an important discovery.

"I told you it was a bad idea to let them come," she snapped. "No one ever listens to me. Now we're stuck with them, the same way I let myself get stuck with you."

She put her earbuds in and leaned back in the hammock. Fine with me. I had things to do.

I WAS PROBABLY going to end up missing dinner, but so be it. Preserving these photos was more important.

My hands were shaking as I logged in. So much was at stake. I felt a wash of relief once I transferred all the pictures to the server—a process that seemed to take forever—but saving these photos represented something tangible. They'd be mine, and I'd have them when I left the island no matter what happened after this point.

In the distance, the sounds from camp indicated dinner would be starting soon. Quickly, I logged into Smokey's site, checking the battery first. The icon had drained even more. I frowned. How could that be? It had just been sitting in the safe. I still had plenty of life left, but it was frustrating that I needed to monitor it.

DeadSea was online, as usual. I didn't need to ask him the basics. I knew the number seventy would be involved, but there were two things I needed help with. I wasn't sure what the broken lines on the triangle meant, and I'd never seen an equation like this, not even in the Cipher.

I described them both.

DeadSea: First things first. That dot in the center of the broken lines will be your starting point. Is there a number on this marker? That will tell you how far to go

AnonGirl: 70. But what direction?

DeadSea: General rule: when given a triangle, walk in the direction of the topmost point, the point with the number 1 written next to it. But in your case, the presence of an equal sign means replace. Therefore, the phrase 2 = 1 means that Point 2 of the triangle replaces Point 1 in importance.

AnonGirl: ??? I don't understand

There was no reply for at least thirty seconds, maybe longer. DeadSea was probably banging his head on the keyboard the way I did whenever I had to watch my mother try to copy-paste something on the computer.

DeadSea: It means stand at the center dot and walk 70 paces in the direction of Point 2

AnonGirl: Got it. But I don't know where the triangular area is. How do I find it? Will it be

near the spot where I found the marker?
DeadSea: Not necessarily
AnonGirl: ???

There were several seconds of silence. DeadSea had to be doing the keyboard head-bang thing again.

DeadSea: Context. Treasure hunting always comes down to the context of your search. Whoever hid the treasure left clues for you to find. Use the environment. Use whatever got you to the marker. Examine those things and you will find your triangle

Context—that made sense, and it meant that something in the shrine or on the map would show us where to look for a triangular-shaped area on the island. I started typing again.

AnonGirl: Last question. How about shrines? What would it mean to find one during a treasure hunt
DeadSea: Hugely important. Signifies direct involvement of the church, which means the treasure is of great value. Did you find a shrine? Tell me which treasure you are searching for. Are you in Spain? The Falklands? Where?
AnonGirl: I'd rather not say

DeadSea: There was a shrine in the Abacos, the Friar Josef hunt. Is that where you are right now?

AnonGirl: No

DeadSea: I need to know where you are

I quickly logged off. DeadSea asking for my location so boldly made me incredibly nervous. It also made me certain we'd found something very, very important.

I headed for the cabin to return the satellite to my safe. I stayed out of view from everyone in the Snack Bar, but even from far away I could tell dinner was ending.

"You have exactly half an hour to get yourselves camera-ready for the challenge," Phil announced. "We'll be meeting at the fire pit. We're filming here tonight—not going to Challenge Island."

Oh, God. The challenge! I'd been so intent on getting to the satellite that I'd forgotten for a moment that we had to earn our stay on the island. Losing a challenge now would be devastating. Right after we'd found the shrine, to have to go home? We were so close to something huge.

This must have been what Miles felt. I pictured him, gaunt and intense, arguing with my father, desperate to continue searching. Anger flared inside me—I should have convinced my father to help him. I knew now what it was like to feel the need to keep going. *Just let me finish*, Miles had begged my father. *I really need to finish this.*

Cody had called me obsessed earlier, and the realization startled me. No doubt about it, I was starting to catch the gold fever.

WE ALL MET at the fire pit. Sol sat on one side, Huaca on the other. Joaquin held court in the middle, the ocean at his back. It was a little weird that he always stood on the slant, thus putting himself lower than us, but the ocean backdrop probably looked better on film than the forest.

"Tonight we are going to do things a little bit differently," Joaquin said.

"It's only the third challenge," Rohan shouted. "Everything's different."

"Zip it, Rohan," Deb called from the sidelines. "Joaquin, take two."

It took two more takes, but Joaquin finally made it to the explanation.

"We are going to have an evening challenge for the first time. It's time to play Truth," Joaquin told us. "This is where you show us how much you've been paying attention, and how well you know your competitors. Everyone will be given a piece of paper and a pen. I will then ask a bunch of questions. The winner will give his or her team an edge in tomorrow's main challenge."

I let out a breath. This wasn't terrible. I wouldn't be leaving tonight.

Joaquin passed out some gold paper and pens.

"And now for the first question. List at least three states where players are from."

Oh, okay. That was easy. I'd heard plenty of talk about hometowns. I wrote *Ohio, Florida, and California.*

"Which player's family trains search-and-rescue dogs?"

I held my pen up but didn't write anything yet. Cody would be a good choice, but he had talked about his ranch and hadn't mentioned anything about search-and-rescue dogs being part of it. Who else? Wasn't Maddie going on to Costa Rica after this to rescue sea turtles? She'd brought pictures of her pets here, which made her an animal lover. That would fit with having a lot of dogs around. *Maddie*, I wrote.

The nightly heat lightning was back, fizzing in the distance behind Joaquin. No one reacted. We were all getting used to the strangeness of the island weather. Tonight it felt like storm lightning—the air was cooler than it had been, and even before the sun had gone down the sky had started to darken.

Joaquin wasn't bothered, either, but that was usual. He soldiered on, trying to make his questions sound as mysterious as possible.

"Who owns several patents and invented something successfully sold in stores?"

Hmmm. That one was hard. AJ was too obvious, and he definitely would have said something about that. What about that nerdy friend of AJ's who'd gotten voted off the first night—Oscar? He seemed smart and math-oriented.

But then I remembered how Cody had said something the other day about everybody having their own "side hustle" that needed funding. It was an oddly specific phrase to use, unless you were familiar with the funding process. And earlier today he'd called my father a VC, a venture capitalist. Maybe he'd needed funding for something he had a patent on. I wrote his name down. It was as good a guess as any.

"Third question. Which three players have more than ten thousand social media followers?"

Everyone would get the first two. Willa and Sean. But who else? I went through everyone one by one, and then I remembered how on the first day Murch had been talking about a fantasy football app. Maybe when he'd said *my app* he'd meant it was literally his. Had to be him, unless Maren was running some weird Goth Tumblr.

"Who was in a skiing accident, nearly died, and broke his or her back?"

Oh. That one was terrible. Who might have broken their back? Everyone here looked healthy. Athletic, even. Wait . . . athletic. Porter had told Justin he hadn't committed anywhere for lacrosse yet. And he'd staggered and made that yelp when he'd thrown me in the water. Too flimsy? I looked at Porter quickly—he looked fine. Murch loved football, but he was a bit overweight. Maybe he'd been fit once, before the accident. No. He hadn't really said anything about ever playing sports for his school. I didn't want to, but I wrote Porter's name down.

There were a few other questions that might have been

hard if they'd been asked earlier in the game, but by now all of us knew Rohan spoke Portugese and Lucas would be playing soccer in college.

"Who was expelled from school last year?"

I tried not to react. I was sure this question referred to me, although technically it wasn't quite true. I'd been given the option to withdraw so the expulsion wouldn't show up on my transcript. I wrote my name down anyway.

"We're going to tally up the answers, and when we come back we're going to set up bowls with each of your names in front," Deb told us. "Every time you get an answer right, Joaquin will put a gold marble in your bowl. The most marbles wins. If there's a tie, we've got extra questions."

When Joaquin and Deb left, crew members filed around the campfire, all of them dressed in gold robes and wearing gold face paint. They didn't say anything, just stood in the firelight. It was haunting, and the fact that Deb hadn't announced or explained their presence made it even eerier.

We all stayed very, very quiet.

Some of us, like Maddie, kept our gaze down, but I couldn't take my eyes off the costumed crew. Oddly, even with the gold face paint one of the women looked familiar. Then I remembered Deb had told us that actors made up part of the B-team, and I gave a silent prayer that I had realized that I'd probably recognized her from an episode of *SVU* or *Grey's Anatomy* before trying to smile or signal her, the way I'd almost done with Willa.

When Joaquin appeared to announce the results, the crew silently disappeared into the woods.

"Nope. Not creepy at all," Cody said, which lightened the mood a little bit.

Joaquin said some host-speak about community and knowledge, and then dispensed with the easy questions first. Nearly everyone was rewarded with marbles.

"Now for some of the trickier questions. Which player raises search-and-rescue dogs?" Joaquin paused. "Maddie. Only two of you got that right. Maddie, of course," he said, dropping a marble in Maddie's bowl, "and Riley."

"The patent owner? Again, only two right. Riley guessed correctly again, as did the mysterious patent owner himself: Cody."

Lots of surprised whispers.

"Most of the rest of you guessed AJ," Joaquin told us. "Cody, feel like sharing your invention?"

It turned out to be an obscure tool that hunters used to line up the crosshairs on a scope. Impressive, but not really applicable to any of the rest of us, so Joaquin moved on quickly.

"Congratulations, Cody, for what sounds like a clever invention, and to Riley for guessing correctly," Joaquin said. "How about the three players with the social media followers? Most of you knew about Willa and Sean, but only a few of you knew about Murch's football app."

"Oh, football," Willa said dismissively as Joaquin distributed a few gold marbles. "I never would have paid attention to that."

"You sure about that, Willa? How about for three point eight million followers?"

Her mouth dropped. "Three million?"

I had a feeling that if Murch was still around Willa would be circling him.

"As for which one of you suffered a catastrophic injury—"

"Me," Porter interrupted. Oh, wow. It *was* him. I tried to make eye contact but he didn't look my way until Joaquin announced I'd guessed correctly, and that's when he shot me a quick glance, frowning and confused. And then—did I read this right?—maybe a little bit mad. But why would he be angry?

"Are you all wondering who the troublemaker was who faced expulsion?" Joaquin asked.

"It's me." I gave a quick outline of the story. Everyone was impressed, which just proved how easy it was to manipulate reality. Just a few key words—*edibles, busted, expelled*—and suddenly I seemed a lot edgier than I did five minutes ago.

"You? Damn, girl," Rohan said. "Got that one way, way wrong."

"Apologies to Murch, in absentia, because most people guessed him."

There was a lot of laughter. Not from Porter, though. Or me.

"Congratulations, Riley. You, of all the players, guessed every answer right. For your attention to detail, your team will be rewarded with an advantage in tomorrow's challenge, which will be announced then."

I got a hug from Maddie, a fist bump from AJ, and nothing from Maren. Predictable responses, all three.

In the distance, thunder rumbled.

"Uh-oh, that's not good. Haven't heard thunder here before," Deb said. "Quickly, let's do some confessionals. Riley, AJ, and Taylor—you guys are up. Taylor and AJ, how about you wait with Katya in the Snack Bar while I start with Riley. The rest of you, please return to your team huts or your cabins."

"Hey, Riley." Porter had gotten up from his side of the fire pit and was coming over to talk to me, but I went cold hearing him say my actual name. What happened to *Frisco*?

"How did you guess that about me?" he asked. And not in a friendly way, either. Even worse, before I could even answer, he shot out, fairly accusingly, "Have you known the whole time?"

"What? No!"

"Seems like something that would be hard to guess. That's why it was one of the hard questions. But you knew it."

What the heck? Or, more appropriately, WTF? Since when did being a good guesser become a crime?

"I didn't *know* it. I guessed. I don't understand—are you mad about something?" My mind skittered around, trying to think what I could have done. "Because I didn't come to dinner?"

"I'm just trying to figure out if you were being real with me before, or if that was some kind of, I don't know, story line. I heard some things tonight that got me confused."

"Things? About me?"

It looked as if he was going to say something but decided not to.

What? I wanted to scream, but I kept myself in check. Or mostly in check. My voice was a little shaky.

"What is going on? First you get all formal and *Riley* me, and then hint at a strange rumor, which is probably a lie, so . . ."

"Riley," Deb called out. "You're up."

Great. Deb and her perfect timing.

"Just a minute," I snapped, but Porter had already taken a few steps backward.

"Better go," he said, in that condescending frat boy voice he'd used the first couple of days. "Duty calls, and you can't disappoint Deb. Or yourself. Right?"

And then he turned around and walked toward the Sol hut, leaving me standing there unsure what had just happened.

Wait! Tell me what's wrong, I wanted to call after him. *Tell me what I did, and let me explain. Don't shut me out. Don't try to bring me to the beach alone this afternoon and then refuse to talk to me a few hours later.* But no self-respecting girl says things like that in real life, let alone in front of an eager line of cameramen. That would be social suicide. Screenshot heaven.

So I stayed silent, turned around, and pretended everything was fine.

I'd had a lot of practice doing that.

20

"TROUBLE IN PARADISE?" DEB ASKED. SHE MOTIONED
me to sit on the log across from her. I took my time, going
around the long way instead of stepping over it. Sitting for a
one-on-one interview was really not ideal right now, not if I
wanted to keep pretending everything was fine.

"This whole paradise is trouble," I said after I'd sat down.
"So yes, you could say that."

"Whoa. For someone who just won a challenge, you're in
a pretty bad mood."

"But that's the way you want it, right?" I asked. "All of us
feeling a little bit like we're on the edge?"

"Is that what you think I want?"

"Don't you?"

The air had gotten noticeably cooler, and a breeze was
starting up. I wished I had a sweater.

I brought my knees up to my chest. "There's been some

speculation that the best outcome for you is one where we're all rolling on the sand punching each other out and calling each other sluts," I said.

"I'm not going to lie. That would be pretty great television," Deb shot back. "*Reality gold*, as they say. It would certainly live up to our show's title. Is a scenario like that in the works? Let me know when and I'll make sure our best crew is there to capture it."

"Yeah, I'll get right on that." The camera light was shining on me, lighting up my face and every bit of my sour expression. I didn't care. It actually felt good to be openly cranky.

"Whoa. Joking! Did your sense of humor fly back to San Francisco?"

I flinched. What a cruel trail of words: San Francisco led to Frisco which led to Porter, which led to, what? Dumped? Ignored? Ditched? Nothing good at the moment, that was for sure.

"Porter asked me if I was running some story line with him. Where would he get that idea? It sounds like something you or someone on the crew would say. And he seemed to know about me. You said you wouldn't tell."

Deb was silent for a minute. From the team huts I could hear Porter's voice and Willa laughing. Not the most pleasant soundtrack.

"Let me ask you something, Riley. Put yourself if my shoes for a second, and look at what we're doing here from my point of view."

"What do you mean?"

"What do you think I want from you and the other players? If you were me, the producer of a television show, the very first one that you are getting executive producing credit for after many, many years working way down low on the ladder, what would you want?"

"I'd want the show to be good."

"Obviously. And not just good: great. But specifically, what would you hope for so that the show turned out great?"

I thought for a second.

"Everyone to do what I say? I don't know."

"Nope," Deb said. "Bad producers micromanage the story lines. The good ones let interactions unfold. Yes, you go into filming planning things out, mapping the bones, structuring some of the action, but the bottom line is that for a great show to come together, great things have to happen along the way. Sure, sometimes we prod people along, but this isn't a scripted show, which means the way it'll jell is *not* because everyone starts doing things I order them to. It'll come together when the cast finds its own chemistry. And yes, that chemistry could come from everyone calling each other names, but the point is that I don't know, and it's not up to me. It's up to you. And Maren, and AJ and Porter. And Willa. And Cody. Cast members with charisma who become central to the daily action."

My mother pulled this move all the time, where she'd talk to me like an adult after I'd thrown a fit about something, as if to shame me into immediately seeing her point.

And then she'd throw in a compliment for good measure. Me, charisma? Nice, but Deb was going to have to do better than that. She wasn't my mom. It was going to take more than this for me to feel like we were on the same side.

"You weren't one of those cast members at the beginning, I'm going to be honest with you. But now, I'm interested. I don't often say that, because I really don't like surprises, but look: you just won a challenge. You, the girl we barely filmed two days ago because we thought you'd be the first one gone. No one else even came close to touching you tonight."

"Oh." I felt myself softening while simultaneously hating myself for it. Two compliments? That's all it took for me to turn to mush?

"The best advice I can give you right now is that everyone has strengths. Everyone. And not all of them are obvious, which you saw tonight with yourself. You're an observer, a collector of information. Put that to good use, because whatever you are good at is what's going to keep you around, and that's what's going to make interesting television. That's what I want, bottom line. I want great TV. The players—you—finding your strengths, well, that's the recipe for great TV. Not slutty catfights."

"But what if slutty catfights are another one of my hidden strengths?"

Harry snorted behind the camera.

"Well then," Deb said, "by all means, don't hold back. But now it's time for some housekeeping. Anything you want to tell me about today?"

218

"No."

"No? You sure? How about the Demon? We're one short at the charging station. Whose is missing?"

I tried to be casual. "Oh, that was AJ's. He thinks he dropped it when we stopped for a water break. We're going to go back and look for it tomorrow."

"Tomorrow? The deal was that if any Demon wasn't returned, I'd take all of them away."

Porter had been right—Deb wasn't afraid to threaten punishment to keep us in line.

"I'm sorry," I told her. "I really am. But it's unfair for all of us to lose our phones just because AJ is always hopping around like an idiot. It probably fell out of his pocket on the trail. Just give us a couple of hours to look for it tomorrow. Please?"

Deb frowned, but then relented. "Only because it was the first time this happened. Next time, that's it. No second chances."

My mind was racing. I'd assumed she wouldn't really care about one lost phone. Now what? AJ couldn't keep the phone, that much was clear, and what was equally as clear was that AJ intended to hold on to that phone. Cody would be our first problem. He had said he didn't want any problems when it came to Deb and the phones, so he'd want it returned. If AJ refused, Cody would probably go straight to Deb and tell her about the shrine, and then it would be game over.

Even if Cody didn't tell Deb anything, we still had a Deb problem, because if AJ kept his, she'd take all the phones,

219

which would mean that I wouldn't be able to get online any-more. The satellite wasn't much use without a phone. Good-bye, DeadSea chats. Farewell, insightful tips on map reading.

Of course, I could tell AJ about the satellite and down-load his photos. I could also attempt to borrow his phone and use it with my satellite as needed. But then I'd have a whole new problem: AJ would have leverage over me. What was to stop him from turning me in? Sure, we were on the same side now, but it was early in the game. Things could change. He'd already shown signs of having an allegiance only to himself.

But what worried me most of all was that if Deb found out about my satellite—ouch. She'd bounce me in three seconds. It would be another classic case of Riley's Law in action: do the show to prove myself a trustworthy person, and instead, ruin everything by cheating.

I'd have to convince AJ, somehow, to delete his photos and return his phone. I got up to go when Deb tossed another grenade at me.

"One more thing. I saw you guys hiding from the drone camera. Don't do that again. And if you find something juicy, don't get any crazy ideas. You're contracted with the show—whatever you find belongs to me. I'll be watching you."

Deb: evil genius manipulator, or someone who just wanted to succeed?

No matter which answer was correct, I already knew one thing: she was someone I didn't want to cross.

The rain started just as I left.

21

THE RAIN KEPT UP THROUGH THE NIGHT AND RIGHT ON through breakfast. AJ and I both had rain jackets, but Maren hadn't brought one. She decided to skip the shrine trip.

"Wouldn't want to get this beauty soaked," she said, pointing to her T-shirt which read *Sorry I'm Late, I Didn't Want to Come.*

I hadn't made any headway so far this morning in my effort to convince AJ to return his phone. As of now, he was flat-out refusing to even discuss it, so I decided to table it for the time being. I'd work on him while we were at the shrine searching for clues to the triangle's location.

But AJ and I hadn't made it more than a few steps from our hut when Deb appeared.

"Nope," she said, spinning her finger around and then pointing toward the Huaca hut. "We're waiting for the rain to clear and the second it does, we're filming, which means no escaping into the woods today."

"But we've got to find AJ's phone," I complained. "You said you'd take all the phones away if we didn't get it back. It's not fair if you take them away without giving us a chance to find it."

Deb did a doubletake. "Are you in preschool? Life's not fair, honey." She paused. "But you know what? I'll succumb to your persuasive argument and hold off on confiscating the phones."

"Really?"

"Yes, to holding off. No, to you having a persuasive argument. Lucky for you, though, I'm in a good mood, and I came over here to propose that exact proposition. See how nice I am? Since you can't leave camp today, I'll suspend my deadline and make it tomorrow by noon. You have a small reprieve, but that is a final, absolute deadline. If all the phones aren't charging at twelve on the dot, I'm taking every single one of them back."

That was a relief. It made up for not being allowed to go to the shrine.

Maren and Maddie went to sign up for double chore duty to give AJ and I time to study the map. We cleared off the table in the Huaca hut and spread out all our papers and notes. I found the section on triangular symbol interpretation in the Cipher and explained what I learned from DeadSea about the starting point and direction. I had to push the guilt down while I did it—AJ was throwing all kinds of admiration my way because he thought I'd figured all of it out on my own.

When I was done, he spun his pencil in the air absent-mindedly. He dropped it after the second toss and didn't bother picking it up.

"What's wrong? You don't think I'm right?"

"That's not it," he said. "All of that is perfectly logical and makes sense. But so what? Start in the triangle's mid-point, walk a certain angle. All good. But where's the actual triangle? We have literally no idea—it could be anywhere on the island, and until we figure that out, we're pretty much screwed."

He was right. We had no leads, and limited time to search.

"I need a break." He went a few yards away onto the beach. He didn't do much, just stood there, facing the ocean. AJ, mellow? That was the surest sign yet that we were in trouble.

But that didn't mean I was ready to give in. I picked up AJ's map and thought back to DeadSea's last piece of advice: context. All right. The only things that could give us context were the shrine and the map, and I only had access to one of them right now. The map. I'd start with that.

Maybe it was because I was looking at AJ's map with his own notes on it, rather than my own familiar notes, but something struck me.

"AJ!" The excitement in my voice pulled him back inside without needing to ask why. "Look at your map. Notice anything? You circled areas that looked interesting. I thought it was a bad idea because it made an unnecessary mess. Or so I thought."

I picked up a pencil. "See these three hills at the top of the island?" I drew three quick lines connecting the three hills on the upper left side of the map. "Look at that—now it forms a triangular-shaped area."

He exhaled. "Freaking brilliant," he said, a giant smile spreading across his face. "That's it, that's got to be it!"

I was pleased, too. We had a lead! Even better, this development solved something that had been bothering me, which was that if someone—anyone—simply stumbled across any of the markers, they could immediately jump in on the trail and start searching for the treasure. What was the point of the map, then? Whoever had hidden the treasure had gone to a lot of trouble to hide it. Needing the map to interpret the markers made sense, because it tied them together. You needed the map to solve the markers, and vice versa.

After lunch, the rain cleared. We got word it was challenge time.

"I can't believe we've been here five days already," AJ said. "That means we only have a max of twenty-one days left, and possibly even less than that. We really have to get up to that triangle."

"We'll have time," I reassured him, although I was worried, too. One of us could get voted out, or Deb could put a stop to our island exploration time. We needed to get up there as soon as possible.

Deb and the B-team had set up Huaca and Sol docks off the beach, and then as a team we were supposed to paddle a canoe back and forth to the beach, filling up a hollow golden idol with sand each time. Back at the float, we had to pour the sand into a second empty idol perched on a pedestal, and when it was filled with enough sand to reach a certain weight a door in the pedestal swung open, revealing a key that was then used to open a locked treasure chest on the beach. My so-called advantage was that we got one scoop of sand ahead of time in the pedestal idol, which hardly mattered because strong, giant outdoorsy Cody made the Sol canoe fly between the float and the shore. They lapped our canoe more than once.

In any case, I barely noticed that the canoes were the same as the one we'd found hidden by the beach, barely paid attention when Huaca lost, and barely cared when we voted off Lucas and London later at Council.

Here's what I did care about: Porter hadn't looked at me during the challenge, not even once. Even worse was how much fun he'd been having with Willa and Alex. At one point during the canoe races he'd stood at the bow of the Sol canoe, balancing his feet on each side. Teasing and laughing, Willa had pushed him off and he did an exaggerated wobble before diving in.

Way to take care of your back, I almost called out.

Even Alex had completely ignored me, which was cold considering everything we'd gone through yesterday. Cody did say something to me, but it was a warning to "get cracking on the next clue." It was pretty disheartening to be in a position where I was back on the outside looking in. The day was one big steaming pile of déjà vu, basically.

Not to mention, we'd lost two out of three challenges so far, and with Sean out of commission from his accident, it meant we were down to four players: me, AJ, Maren, and Maddie. Sol still had seven players left.

"Tough day," Joaquin said as we boarded the boat after Council.

I definitely agreed. It had been a very tough day, and without a challenge designed to suit our strengths, tomorrow was likely to be even tougher.

FOR THE FIRST time, we didn't congregate by the fire pit after dinner. I don't know what the Sol team was doing, but whatever it was, it sounded fun, and a lot rowdier than anything happening on our side of the beach. AJ was nowhere to be found, presumably off somewhere avoiding me. Our earlier excitement over cracking the triangle clue had been replaced with a disagreement over returning his phone, and after the challenge he'd shot down any attempt I'd made to convince him. And Maren . . . well, Maren was just being

Maren: making herself scarce because she was grumpy that we had lost the challenge and overly annoyed that "cutesy-pie" Maddie had been the one to survive the vote. If I had to guess, she'd probably retreated to the hammock I'd seen her in yesterday.

That left me and Maddie in the Huaca hut alone, so Joaquin offered to entertain us with stories from the production side. He got a pack of cards out of the game corner, and I cleared all the treasure notes off the table.

"This is all a costume, you know. My outfit. The costume designer picks out my clothes every day. Usually the things she wants me to wear are fine, but I drew the line at the shark's tooth necklace," Joaquin said, touching the plain tooth-free leather cord he wore. "That was a little much, you know? No one wears those anymore."

That was about as deep as his "gossip" went. We played a few rounds of cards, and he didn't offer anything more salacious than a few passing observations on the cameramen, none of whom we knew well enough to find interesting. I hadn't thought of it before, but Joaquin was something of a floater. Not really part of the crew, but not part of the cast, either.

Terrible card player, too. Maddie was killing him at crazy eights.

"I think I'm going to take a walk," I told them, and it wasn't a lie. I did take a walk—right to my cabin to get the satellite. If I wanted to keep getting help from DeadSea, I'd have to answer his questions about the shrine eventually.

The Wi-Fi was quicker than before, which meant I wasn't wasting a ton of battery while the satellite searched for a signal. I'd noticed the battery was draining faster than I expected it to. I had no way of charging it, so when it ran out, that was it.

I hesitated. I really shouldn't waste time online, but on the other hand, the Internet speed was so fast that I could do a quick sweep of social media to see what was going on back home.

I'd gotten rid of my Snapchat account—it had been too painful to see all my former friends goofing around together in their stories, and no one was sending me any direct Snaps. But I could still log into Facebook and Instagram. I didn't bother going to Facebook, but Instagram didn't disappoint. Some funny memes, a couple of birthday posts. I stopped scrolling. Wait a minute. My pulse quickened. Someone had tagged me in something. That hadn't happened in a long time.

I clicked. I saw the picture first—me, of course, in my famous red dress, and I let out the breath I'd been holding. What a letdown. I'd been tagged by Hanna Bilter, a girl from Shaw. People tagging me on my own picture had happened a lot at the beginning of the scandal, and back then they could semi-plausibly claim they were doing it to alert me of its existence. But at this point, eight months later, tagging me like that was obnoxious. It was just a way of reminding me that I'd messed up.

But then it got worse. She had tagged three other people, too. Two of them were private, but AnnieBellaForTheWin's profile was visible.

Oh, God. One of her posts was taken at my new school—I recognized one of the buildings in the background. The other two girls must be students there, too, and one of them had commented *Is this her?* followed by the laughing-crying emoji.

I felt sick. I knew my new classmates would hear of me somehow, but I didn't expect to actually witness someone identifying me. It was so mean-spirited. If I showed my mother she wouldn't understand the intent behind it, because adults didn't get it. *You already knew that picture was out there, honey, she'd say. What does it matter if girls from your new school see it? They'll probably see it soon enough anyway.*

All of that was true, but it was the *why* of the interaction that was so upsetting. Hanna must have been telling people about me, and by AnnieBella's comment, it was obvious that my former friend wasn't saying anything nice. And furthermore, Hanna didn't just tag those girls and let it go at that— she'd tagged me, too, so that I knew. She might as well have added *Good luck at your new school, loser* followed by that same emoji.

Great. Life in SF was still terrible, and now I'd messed things up with Porter here. I logged off. I wasn't in the mood anymore to face DeadSea's questions about the shrine. I'd get back to him tomorrow when I found something new to report.

I wrapped the satellite back up in the sweatshirt I'd

brought to hide it and went to the beach. I wasn't ready to call it a night yet.

The sky was clear after the rain, as if it had been scrubbed clean. It seemed as if the stars were shining brighter than any night so far.

I buried my toes in the sand and listened to the waves sloshing quietly onto the shore. It was strange, but for the first time, I was missing my old friends. I'd missed them before, of course, but there had always been a layer of anger at them for abandoning me. Now that anger was aimed at Porter, so only the feeling of loss remained, undiluted.

"That guy is so not worth it," a voice said from behind me. Maren wasn't exactly who I had hoped would join me, but it seemed like she was in a good enough mood.

"Who?"

"Nice try. Mr. Preppy the Third."

"Oh. Him."

If Izzy had been here, she would have sat me down, pulled out her mini blender, whipped up some chocolate milkshakes, and called out all of Porter's flaws.

"He's a goofball, and I don't mean that in a good way. And that's just for starters. Ever notice how Mr. Preppy is always making sure people are paying attention to him?"

It startled me. Had I said that thing about calling out flaws out loud?

"It's like he's putting on a little bit of a show, you know what I mean?"

I snorted. "True."

I went silent for a minute, remembering all the things I'd shared with Izzy. I missed that. I missed *her*. I said to Maren, "My friend would always do that. Find the tiniest things wrong with a guy after he'd been a jerk."

"Well, sure. It's a solid strategy."

Maren flailed her arms and wobbled around, mimicking Porter on the canoe. "'Whoa, whoa, whoa . . . SPLASH!' I mean, come on."

"I definitely hope they filmed that," I agreed. "And from a bad angle."

"You know, I actually started to like that guy a little better when I thought he was into you. I thought he might be different, cooler, since he preferred you to those perfect girls on Sol."

"Wow, thanks," I said sarcastically. "Huge compliment."

"Oh, come on, you know what I mean." Maren flopped down next to me.

"Actually, that's the nicest thing you've said to me." I picked up a shell and tossed it into the water. "Come to think of it, it might be the nicest thing anyone has said to me since we got to Black Rock."

Except for Willa. She'd said a few nice things. Not that I was going to mention her to Maren. Anyway, proportionally speaking, Maren's "compliment" was probably nicer, since it was harder for her to say.

"Take it when you can get it. I might not be feeling so friendly later."

Were we getting along? It was a miracle. We sat for a few minutes, tossing shells, listening to the waves.

Doing things that friends might do together.

"Is your hair really that color?" I asked. "Not purple, obviously. Is it really black?"

Maren's disdain was palpable. "What's it to you?" she asked. And then, just like that, she got up and left.

Ouch. She really was like Izzy, actually: willing to ditch me so quickly for a tiny mistake.

I kept tossing shells, but not so mindlessly anymore. Faster. Harder. Now I could hear them hit the surface.

Unbidden, a memory of an early morning I'd spent on the island came back to me. I remembered waking up one morning during that trip two summers ago when it was still dark. It was so quiet. No talking, no city noise, just the quiet slosh of the waves sliding onto the shore. I'd unzipped my tent as silently as possible so I didn't wake anyone and tip-toed down to the high-water mark. I'd sat there for a while, all alone. It was so peaceful. The sun wasn't out yet but then suddenly it was, a bright orange ball bubbling up through the horizon. A bird began to sing, loud and steady, almost as if it was talking only to me.

I had felt happy then. No, wait: I didn't *feel* happy. I *was* happy. There was a big difference. I hadn't been truly happy like that since I'd left the island. What a strange thing to realize, and how sad. Then it hit me: maybe that was partly why I'd wanted to come back here. Two summers ago, on this beach, I'd felt like myself—and that was the last time I had felt like me for a very long time. I hadn't appreciated it at the time, but our time on Black Rock was a last gasp of normalcy before everything changed. If my life events were laid out on a chart, the trip to Black Rock would be the high point, followed by a series of points marking a severe downward trend: Miles's death, my father's shame and grief after failing his friend, my expulsion, and so on.

Now that I thought about it, it was clear that's what had pulled me back here—the desire to recapture that better time and to feel like *me* again. To remember what it was like to feel comfortable and free from worry, to remember that there had once been a me who didn't do dumb things, who didn't wake up feeling the aching blankness of loneliness.

You know what? Growing up sucked.

Behind me, I heard the sounds of camp. Phil hit the gong aggressively three times, his signal for everyone to make his day by getting to bed.

Fine with me. I was happy to call time on this crazy day, too. I was the last one; no one was in the huts or by the fire pit, not even Maddie or Joaquin.

"Get a move on, Riley," Phil said. "Tomorrow's a new day. You can spend all day figuring out the marker's clues, but for now it's lights out."

I was startled. Why would Phil have said *the marker's clues* like that? Had AJ said something in his confessional last night?

Phil must have noticed something was wrong. "What? Isn't that your plan?"

I was probably being paranoid. AJ wouldn't have said anything.

Still, something about the way Phil was watching me made me think he really did know we'd found something.

Maybe it wasn't AJ who had told him. There had been such a clear division between the Sol and Huaca teams today, it was conceivable that Cody, Alex, or Porter could have said something to the crew.

God, how stupid. Maren had been right. We never should have let anyone from Sol come.

22

I GOT MY CHANCE TO CONFRONT ONE OF THE SOL TRAI-
tors sooner than I thought.

I'd just squeezed the toothpaste onto my brush at the bathroom sink when Alex slid through the door. Sneakily, I noticed.
I was still mad about today. The way she'd ignored me had
seemed pointed. Was a simple *hi* really that hard to manage?

"Did you tell Deb or Phil or anyone else about the
shrine?" I asked, watching her in the mirror as I started to
brush my teeth.

She frowned. "What? No. Why?"

I kept her waiting while I finished and spit into the sink.

"Phil said something odd. It seemed like he might know
we'd found something."

"If he does, I wasn't the one who told him. What did he say?"

She seemed genuine, but even if she wasn't, it was obvious she wasn't going to admit to it.

235

"Never mind, it was probably nothing."

I rinsed my mouth and let the water run. I was still watching Alex through the mirror and I noticed she didn't have any bathroom stuff. She didn't wear—and didn't need—makeup, so it was hard to tell the difference between when she was going to bed and when she was ready for the day. Unlike me, where it was obvious. I looked like a shiny naked Martian after I'd washed my face and gotten ready for bed. She did have one telltale sign, though: her blond hair was always in a ponytail during the night. It was like that now, so she must have already done her bedtime routine.

So what was she doing here? I didn't say anything else. I wondered if she even noticed I was giving her the cold shoulder.

"I saw Joaquin with you and Maddie tonight. After the council," Alex said. "What was he doing with you guys?"

"I wasn't telling him any game secrets, if that's what you're accusing me of," I said, still watching her through the mirror. "He was just playing cards with me and Maddie."

"Cards?" she repeated incredulously.

I was sick of this. I thought we'd become friends the other day. Well, maybe not friends, but we'd gotten along to the point where I thought things had overarched the team divisions. But now she was in here going on about Joaquin. Was this another way for everyone to accuse me of getting unearned advantages from the crew?

"Yeah, cards. Crazy eights, go fish. Ever heard of them?"

It suddenly occurred to me. "Wait, are you the one who said something to Porter about me?"

"What is with you tonight? Why are you suddenly so paranoid people are talking behind your back? I don't even know what you're talking about."

"The other night Porter was acting strange. He said something that hinted at how everyone is obsessed with determining how much help I've been getting from Deb, and now here you are, all concerned about Joaquin talking to me, so . . ."

"Oh. Wait, no," Alex said. She leaned against the sink, looking relieved. "You're talking about game stuff. That's not why I'm here. Listen, forget about the game for a second. This is serious."

And unexpected.

"Joaquin is . . ." She cleared her throat. "I mean, you can tell he's kind of a perv, right?"

I frowned. It was true, at the beginning I felt a little uncomfortable around him. There was that time where he'd made fun of me for not realizing he wasn't actually Portuguese, but he'd never made me feel dumb for it after that, and it had even seemed to connect us in a weird way. Like how he'd come into the hut to play cards. He'd been funny, but even more, he'd been acting like a friend, which was more than I could say for some people.

"I don't like the way he behaves with the girls, especially Maddie." She held up her hands in a defensive gesture. "I don't mean that in a team advantage way."

"What do you mean *behaves*? He hangs out with us, that's all. Isn't that literally his job?" I asked.

"Not exactly," Alex said cautiously.

Now she was the one making me feel dumb. Dumber than Joaquin ever had. Whatever she was trying to do was backfiring. Or maybe not—maybe she was intentionally trying to mess with me, make me doubt one of the only people who'd felt like a solid ally.

"He's old. And kind of famous. Why would he do anything weird?"

She sighed. "Maybe this was a mistake. I wanted to help. Let's pretend that you and I are here on vacation, and I came in here to give you a heads-up about some guy at the all-inclusive bar who might be a creep."

"Thanks, I guess?"

"Better safe than sorry, right? Grab me if anything ever feels off. Forget about any of this team BS and just say I'm supposed to be somewhere else. Like the girls are all taking a picture together and you need me there, too, or something. Okay? Same goes for Maddie."

"Sure," I said, pretending I didn't know this had to be a game ploy to mess with my head. For good measure, I added, "I'll tell Maddie."

Alex nodded and left. It wasn't until the door swung shut that I realized I probably should have told her that I'd do the same for her, in case she'd meant it for real. Oh, well. It didn't matter; nothing like that would ever happen to pretty, self-sufficient, zombie-apocalypse-survivor Alex.

Anyway, I had bigger things to worry about. It was pretty clear that I was going to have to tell AJ about my satellite if I wanted to preserve access to it. I felt sick about it. I was definitely worried how AJ would react to the news: Would he get mad? Would he tell everyone? If he did either of those things, it was all over for me. At the very least, he might find a way to use the satellite for his own advantage at my expense.

Still, even with all that looming over my head, I held on to hope that tomorrow couldn't possibly be worse than today.

23

FOOD POISONING. THAT'S WHAT CAME WITH THE NEW
day. So yes, if that was any indication, then today was definitely going to be worse than yesterday.

AJ, Maren, and I were going through the breakfast buffet
when Phil suddenly ran past us with his hand over his mouth.
He left a trail of knocked-over chairs in his wake.

Justin was next, and he didn't make it to the trees. He
threw up into the sand outside the Snack Bar. Maddie ran
off toward the Huaca Hut, wailing about how if she even
saw vomit it would make her throw up, too, and the next
thing I knew almost everyone who had been sitting at the
tables was now leaning over, clutching their stomachs. Porter,
too, I took some satisfaction in noticing. He ran out before
he did anything too embarrassing, though. Rohan and Cody
followed, although not as urgently. They were both big guys;
maybe the sickness wasn't affecting them as fast. I didn't see

Alex, Taylor, or Willa. They were either fine, or they'd gone down before Phil.

The Snack Bar looked like a crime scene. Muffins and sliced fruit were splashed across the tables, mimicking the trails of vomit on the ground.

"Riley, step away from the muffin," Maren instructed. I hadn't realized I was still standing exactly how I'd been when Phil ran out, holding a blueberry muffin in midair. I didn't even put it back, I just dropped it. There was worse in the sand at this point.

The three of us stood on the side, like late arrivals to a car wreck, unsure what to do or how to help.

"Let's go," AJ said, low and urgently.

"Now?" I asked. "We can't leave everyone like this."

"Oh, are you suddenly a doctor?" Maren said. "Yes, we can, and besides, I definitely don't want to eat whatever it is that's zombifying everybody."

"Okay, okay," I said. It had to be from the food. I felt fine. It looked like Maren and AJ did, too. If it was an airborne illness the odds were at least one of us would be feeling it.

The camera crew was busy capturing the scene in all its glory. They hadn't been afflicted, which supported the idea this was a food-based incident because they never ate with us. It actually seemed like they might be enjoying the chaos. This was probably a highlight for them—it was their job to get good footage, and the buffet scenes this morning were anything but boring.

Deb and Katya, on the other hand, were not having a good time. They were deep into what looked like a heated argument. Deb was waving her clipboard around without regard to some of the pages that were fluttering loose and floating to the floor.

Deb. Oh no. What if she confined us to camp again?

"Quick, you guys," I hissed. "Let's go before Deb sees us."

It was tempting to run, but we kept calm and the three of us quietly made our exit. We slipped away unnoticed, or at least, that's what we thought. We had just passed the first marker and we were on the straight shot up to Black Rock when we heard Willa's voice.

"Wait up," she called.

"Are you freaking kidding me?" Maren said, not even quietly.

"I know, I know," Willa said, when she got closer. "You probably wanted to be alone, but I think you'll be happy to see me. I've got something good."

Somehow Willa always had the perfect outfit for every occasion. I pictured her at home packing for the trip, creating and laying out entire outfits and photographing them the way magazines do. Today's attire must have been conceived as the "hiking look." She was wearing a white button-down safari top, a variation of the ones Joaquin wore, but hers was flimsy and sheer and revealed a cargo-green bikini top underneath. Her jean shorts were like mine, if you didn't count the four inches' more coverage I had past my crotch. Oh, and aviators and a messy bun pulled everything together. It was hard not to be jealous, because even if all those things were lifted off her and attached to me in a paper-doll move, I still wouldn't look the same. Hair too straight and thick to be messy-casual like that, face too heart-shaped for aviators, boobs too flat for that bathing suit top to even stay up, and so on.

She held out something electronic: a black square with a charging cord attached.

"While you guys were at Council last night, Cody got Rohan to persuade someone from the crew to bring him a charger and cord that would work for your phone."

"Man, Rohan's got connections," Maren said. Admiringly, I noticed.

"Yeah, he's always talking to the crew when no one is looking. Paid off this time, too. Since you can't bring your phone to the charging station, you can use this."

AJ plugged his phone in. "Yessssss! It works."

I hadn't even thought about AJ's phone battery dying—I'd been so worried about the satellite. Good for Cody for thinking about it.

"I wasn't going to come," Willa said. "Plowing through the jungle isn't really my thing, but since everyone else on my team is sick, they sent me. I'm supposed to deliver a message, too. Cody says *find the gold, or we'll have to gamble that the shrine counts as a substantial clue.*"

I shook my head. "He's not thinking straight. He wants to win the most money he possibly can, but pointing Deb

243

toward the shrine isn't the way to do it." Willa hadn't been there when we'd found the shrine, but I assumed since she was here now, her team had pulled her into their side of the partnership and she knew about our discovery. "The second anyone official hears about this, a bunch of archaeologists will swarm the island and we'll be kicked off. No more show, which means no million-dollar prize. Sure, Deb *could* award us the treasure prize—which is a big if, since we weren't technically there first—but even if she does, it's small and it'll be split up a bunch of ways. Not worth it."

"Yeah, I get it, and that's why I brought you the charger," Willa said. "Solve the puzzle, find the gold, and we're all a lot better off."

"Great," AJ said. "I can't let you come, though, unless you sign my NDA."

"Got a pen?"

So much for all Willa's prior legal concerns. When AJ produced the form, she signed it without a second thought.

"Let's get a group selfie before we start," Willa said, which we posed for, some of us more reluctantly (Maren) than others. That wasn't the last selfie. Or the last video. All along the trail, Willa tried new angles and new backdrops. She pulled me in for some, which made me self-conscious, even though a few days ago I'd been fantasizing about this exact scenario. It was Maren, sighing loudly every time, who was ruining it.

Eventually we made it to the upper left-hand side of the

island, and we easily found the wide-open area marked on the map. The rolling hills covered in long grass reminded me of the headlands across the Golden Gate Bridge back home. Willa had her camera ready, of course, but I didn't hold it against her this time—the colors in this view were meant to be captured. Blue water sprinkled with glints of yellow sun, wind-whipped whitecaps, and a bright green edge of land. And best of all, no tourists contaminating the scene.

AJ was less patient. "Selfie time is over. Let's fan out," he said. "What we're looking for first are the three triangular peaks pictured on the map. They could be hills or rocks, so basically please pay attention to anything that sticks out of the ground, okay? Once we find them, we'll be able to find our starting place, go seventy paces, and hopefully that's where we'll find another stone marker."

"Hills? Rocks? A stone marker?" Willa said, as if hearing those words for the first time. "I thought we were looking for gold."

A look of remorse flashed across AJ's face; he was obviously regretting his decision to allow Willa to tag along.

"Uh, I'm going to look over there." He pointed to the right. "Maren, you take the spot below me, and why don't you two head toward the coastline? Be careful, though, it's likely to be a cliff, or at least a steep drop to the shore."

I loved how he was bundling me with Willa because he and Maren didn't want to deal with her. It's funny how sometimes circumstances, not personality, determine if someone is popular or simply someone to put up with. Up here, Willa was exactly the same, but she wasn't the star. She was actually pretty annoying. I think she was feeling it, too, mostly by her willingness to attach herself to me, the likeliest to be awed by her.

Focus, Riley. I looked for bumps or anomalies in the land.

We *had* to find something today. This might be our last chance to do a search. We'd snuck off; Deb might be mad, and if so, she'd retaliate by either taking the phones away or confining us to camp. Of course, Cody's deadline was hanging over my head, too.

My heart sank when I noticed a drone flying in the distance.

"Get down!" I said to Willa, pointing at the drone. How had it found us? I signaled to Maren and AJ. Hopefully it was too far away to have spotted us.

Willa and I hid under a tree, flattening ourselves onto our stomachs so we could peer through the branches and watch the drone. It was moving slowly, going back and forth in a grid pattern. We settled in for what was probably going to be a long wait.

"What sort of gold do you think it is? I was hoping we'd find some crowns or rings and things," Willa said. "Wouldn't it be awesome if we got pictures of ourselves dripping in all this fabulous jewelry?"

Everything was so visual to her. It was actually pretty fascinating the way she framed every situation in photographic terms.

"I don't really know what the treasure is made up of," I said. "Maybe jewelry. Maybe chalices or little statues? Things that could get melted down easily."

"Why's that?"

"The gold is ransom that a village had to pull together to free their king from a Spanish conqueror," I said. "It's actually a sad story, because they were ready to pay it, but before they could get it to his captors, the king was killed. The local priest confiscated the treasure for the crown and then hid it here so the villagers couldn't reclaim it."

"Harsh," Willa said. "But ransom—that's interesting. Whatever's hidden must be really valuable. I'll bet it is jewelry."

I thought about the origin story again. It *was* harsh. But even harsher was that random people like me could swoop in, find it, and keep things that were, essentially, blood offerings. No wonder so many wanted to believe that anyone who plundered the treasure would end up cursed. I'd gotten so caught up in the logistics of the hunt itself that I'd forgotten the sacrifice and loss that had been at the heart of the backstory.

Was this right? What I was doing . . . was it fair? I had never questioned the ethics of my search before, but now that I was actually in the mix, literally getting my hands dirty, small doubts were bubbling up. What gave me, of all people, the right to claw it from the ground where it had been kept safe for hundreds of years?

Miles had looked at it differently, of course. He believed it was his duty to find the gold. He felt tied to it, and he'd tried to convince my father that he'd been *chosen* to find it— which had only made my father more certain that Miles had lost his mind.

The drone must not know where we were because it had stopped its methodical searching and had begun flying in a random pattern.

"Ugh, this is going to take forever." Willa wiggled into a sunny patch. I joined her, and the two of us lay side by side on our backs, knees pointing to the sky.

"I wish this place wasn't so far away," Willa sighed. "It's so pretty here. I'd love to bring Justin up here for a photo sesh."

I ignored the sesh part and focused on the non-Porter part. "Justin?"

"Look, we got the cutest pictures on the beach the other day." Willa held up her phone so I could see the screen and started swiping through her photos. Willa and Justin on the beach. Willa and Justin swimming. At the Snack Bar, horsing around. In the hammock, and on top of Sean's cliff. That one surprised me. I thought we'd all been avoiding that spot out of respect for Sean, but apparently not.

"You should go there with Porter sometime," she told me.

"Oh, I . . ."

"What?"

"I don't know if there's anything there with Porter." It felt odd saying it out loud. I was glad we were facing the sky and not each other, because seeing those images of Willa and Justin made me realize how far away I was from experiencing something like that. Even when we'd been "together," if it could be called that, Porter and I hadn't been sharing time so openly the way they had.

I paused. "Anyway, I had this weird thought that you guys might be together?"

In light of the pictures she'd just showed me, it felt like a stupid observation, made even stupider by her reaction.

"Us?" Willa laughed. "Me and Porter? Oh my God. No. Porter's like a brother," she added dismissively. "But why'd you say there was nothing there? Is this about the other night? When we took that quiz?"

My heart beat a little faster. What did she know about that?

"He was so mad at me after that," I admitted. "I don't get it. I guessed it was him, that's all, and even if I had known, what does it matter?"

"Oh, you know guys. They like to be all manly. I think he was worried you'd felt sorry for him and that was the only reason you were paying any attention to him. Or that Deb had told you to do it. I told him he was being stupid, don't worry. You should talk to him when we get back."

"Maybe."

It looked like the drone was moving further away. Not too much longer until we could start searching. Willa laughed and put her hand over her eyes to get a good look at me. "I can't believe you thought I might be with Porter."

I frowned. "Why? Is that so crazy? Is there something bad about him I need to know?"

"Oh, no. Porter's totally cute. But you're so sharp about nearly everything else. I'm surprised you got that so wrong."

That startled me. "What?"

"It's true. You're so quiet and sometimes it's hard to even know if you're paying attention, but then bam! You come out with something that shows you're way ahead of everyone else. Like the bags, that first day. You'd solved the problem before anyone even knew there was an issue."

I hated compliments because I never knew how to react, but I was saved from saying anything dumb when Willa noticed the drone was actually leaving.

"There it goes," she said, standing up and brushing herself off. "Back to work."

Willa and I didn't end up spending too much time in our assigned area; it was pretty flat, so it wasn't hard to search. We checked in with AJ, who assigned us a new place a little further toward the water.

Willa wasn't up for it. "Let me have the map for a minute," she asked AJ. "I'm going to take some scenery shots with the map and this gorgeous background, okay?"

Maren had been taking a water break with one of the few bottles we'd remembered to pack before our hasty exit. She threw a disparaging look at Willa, who was now arranging the map on top of some scattered wildflowers.

"What's the matter?" Maren asked. "Your milkshake can't

bring all the boys to the yard unless your Snapchat story is perfect?"

"What would you know about milkshakes?" Willa shot back. She waited until Maren was out of earshot, and then said to me, "Actually, she's sort of growing on me now that she's starting to look edgy in a cool way instead of like an outcast dreaming about the day she becomes a school shooter."

Oh, God. I winced, but there was a smidge of truth to the description. All that dark makeup and Maren's affinity for black—her clothes, her hair, her lipstick—had been a distraction. But now, with her toned-down hair pulled up in a high ponytail and any heavy makeup hidden by a pair of round, mirrored sunglasses, she looked actually interesting. Not strange. Even her T-shirt was a little mellower today. It just said *Nope* in big block letters.

From a nearby hill, AJ was waving us over. Willa opted to ignore him, but Maren and I went to see what he'd found, walking and then breaking into a run when we saw how excited he was.

AJ stood next to a pile of moss-covered rocks. Not rough, natural rocks—perfectly rectangular blocks of stone that had once been stacked on top of each other to form a tower. The years had taken their toll, and the pillar had crumbled and allowed the island to overtake it.

"This is it, one of the points of the triangle," he told us excitedly, and now that we knew what to look for, it didn't take too much longer for the three of us to find the other two points. They marked out an area about as big as a baseball field, and we quickly identified the midpoint spot and which direction to go.

"Ready?" I asked AJ. "In seventy varas, we'll know if we're on to something."

"Let's do it," he replied.

My heart thumped as we counted off the paces.

24

WHAT HAPPENED NEXT WAS THRILLING, ALTHOUGH IT

brought equal parts excitement and frustration. First, the excitement: we found the third marker just over the crest of a nearby hill. It was exactly where DeadSea had said it would be—seventy paces from the center point of the triangle. Our frustration came from the fact that the marker had been dug up already, and it was out in the open, fully visible. A shovel, a discarded water bottle, and a few giant piles of earth immediately told us that someone had gotten there before us— and from the look of it, possibly not too long ago.

AJ let out a string of curse words, grabbing the shovel and banging the flat end on the ground over and over.

It was official. The shrine and the marker had been discovered by someone who knew how to read treasure signs. MrJackSparrow—it had to be. How far ahead of us was he?

If he'd been here weeks ago, the black market might already be lit up with the gold. I watched AJ slamming the ground with the shovel and I felt the same rage when I realized that if it was true—if the gold was really gone—Miles would have died for nothing. I felt wronged, suddenly, the same way I'd felt after that article had come out.

Not fair, not fair, not fair.

AJ spent some time in panic mode, throwing the shovel around and generally freaking out. I knelt down to inspect our new clue. The marker itself was just like the first two— just a small, flat, square stone. There were fewer carvings on this one: two squiggly lines that were obviously the sign for a river. There was a *C* inside the river, and at the bottom was a straight line. That was it.

Cody had guessed how long it had been since MrJack-Sparrow had found the marker in the shrine by feeling the dirt, so I tried it. These piles were more like soil. Darker, and not at all dry and dusty. A light coating stuck to my fingers.

I had to yell AJ's name a few times to get his attention. "Can you stop?" I asked, when I finally had his attention. "This is important. Look at these piles—they're still a little damp. I think the marker wasn't dug up too long ago."

AJ calmed down and took a handful. "You're right. It feels pretty fresh, even being exposed to the sun and air. Only the top layer is dry."

"Someone could have been here recently," I said. "Like maybe even today."

"This is great." AJ said the word *great* at the exact time I interjected with the opposite opinion: *terrible.*

We look at each other in disbelief.

"This guy is *close,*" I said. "Maybe even watching us right now. Someone—most likely this guy—killed Miles over the cave discovery. And now we're in his way? I definitely wouldn't be using the word *great.*"

"Are you kidding me? It's awesome that we're so close. Now we have a shot. You'd rather be safe if it meant losing the archaeological discovery of a lifetime?"

I looked at him in disbelief. "Um, yes?"

"Nah. You're looking at this all wrong. Think of it this way: Cody thought the shrine marker had been found weeks ago, right? That means it took this guy weeks to figure out something that took us a day. A day! This guy is a hack, not some dangerous mastermind. What did you call him back at the shrine? Jack Sparrow? I know I made fun of you for it, but I'm glad you brought him up, because Jack Sparrow is a joke of a pirate and this guy is a joke of a treasure hunter. And if the name fits . . . am I right? Let's see if Sparrow figured out where to go next."

Maren and Willa had been keeping their distance while AJ spun out, but now they came over to look at the marker. I made a rubbing after they inspected it, and then AJ and I both took some pictures.

"You can't really figure out what this thing means, can you?" Willa asked. She nudged the marker with her sneaker, as if afraid to touch it. "It doesn't make any sense."

AJ was suddenly all business. "Sure it does. And not only do I know what it means, I don't even need to look at my Cipher to check. It's simple. We go straight that way until we hit a river."

"Not just *to* a river," I pointed out. "The letter *C* is inside the river, not next to it. That means we're supposed to cross it and go—"

"Fifty varas," Maren cut in. "And I'm going to need some credit for remembering that the letter *C* means fifty."

"Lots of credit," I said, but I was distracted. AJ had begun to walk east in the direction he'd just indicated. He wasn't even bothering to make sure the rest of us were coming.

"We're not even going to discuss whether we should keep going?" I called incredulously.

He didn't stop, just yelled over his shoulder, "What's to discuss? Come on, let's go."

It seemed to me there was plenty to discuss. The presence of the potential murderer, for one thing. We were hungry, tired, and thirsty—not at our best, and we didn't even have Cody or Rohan with us to offer decent protection. Easy prey.

Maren threw up her hands. "Well, what else do we have to do?" she asked me.

"For starters, we could try to avoid getting murdered!"

"Oh, come on. Don't be such a drama queen. This guy doesn't exactly seem to be hiding his discoveries. Kind of seems like someone who's sure he's the only one looking."

I shook my head. "Even if that's true, he's not going to be happy to see anyone on his trail. Look at AJ. He practically turned feral right in front of us. You've never known the history of this treasure, so you don't understand how huge this is, and how far people will go to cover it up. I think we should think about hitting pause. Be safe about it."

"Because you're the expert?" Maren shot back. "Aren't you forgetting it's your father who knows it all? Not you? Just go back if you want to give up."

Willa tugged at my arm. "She's right. Let's go back, Riley. Come on."

Like AJ, she didn't wait for me to answer; she just started walking south. That left Maren and me smack in the middle of two people walking in opposite directions.

"Go on," Maren said. "You're basically her bitch now anyway. *Take one of me in front of this tree, now over here, no not that angle*," she mimicked.

"What do you care? Stop judging me for hanging out with other people. You've made it perfectly clear you don't want to be friends."

"*Be friends?* Oh my God. We aren't five, hanging out in the Lego corner." Maren rolled her eyes. "*Wanna be my friend? Okay cool, now we're best friends forever!* Because that was the last time I remember deciding on my friendships like that."

"That's not what I meant! My point is that you obviously don't care about me, so I don't understand why you aren't just leaving me alone. Let me hang out with who I want to hang out with and stop the commentary."

She gave me a dismissive look. "Whatever. I can do that, no problem. But you need to do something, too. Stop pretending you even care whether I like you or not."

I did care, though. That was the surprising thing. She'd been pushing and pushing at me, but her antagonism was more engagement than I'd had with anyone in months.

"I like you enough not to see you killed by a psycho treasure hunter!" I said. "Isn't that enough?"

There was a mini standoff where we glared at each other before splitting up. She went east, I went south. What were we going to do, argue all day over which of us cared the least about the other? I didn't even understand how we'd gone from disagreeing over AJ to fighting about that.

Willa was waiting farther downhill. I caught up to her.

"Listen, I don't think we should leave them," I said. "I meant what I said before. This treasure is worth millions, and someone is out looking for it. We don't know how far they're willing to go to get it. AJ and Maren could be in danger."

"Yeah, and we might be, too. Which is why"—she tipped her head south—"we want to get going. Back to semi-civilization. So *come on*."

"I don't know . . ." I was torn. If AJ was right and MrJack-Sparrow wasn't smart enough to immediately decipher the clue, we had time to go back to camp and re-group. Which was great, but that didn't solve our Deb problem. She must have sent the drone out after us, which meant she'd likely be angry at us for running off. There was nothing to stop her from confining us to camp for the rest of the game, and this might be the last time we were allowed to search freely. The trail was hot—maybe I was crazy to think about returning to camp now and jeopardizing such a good lead.

"Think about it. What if someone *is* out there?" Willa asked. "What are we going to do, throw a sneaker at them? No thanks. I'm out."

She started to leave. I watched her for a second, and my first thought was that it made a good picture: her back to me, with the jungle as a backdrop and the wide, blue sky above. My second thought was more reasonable, which was that as bitchy as Maren was and as annoying and single-minded as AJ was, there was a good chance they were walking right into a dangerous situation. I couldn't just ditch them.

And I had more than a shoe. I had a shovel. I went over and picked it up. The blade was pretty sharp, too.

Willa kept walking. I was definitely worried about not following her. She was my connection to Porter, but I couldn't abandon AJ and Maren and what might be my last chance to find the gold.

WILLA WAS THE one who reconsidered. She caught up to me just as I was entering the forest.

"You win," she said simply. "But if I die without ever

making it online to find out how many followers this show brought me, I'm blaming you."

"Deal."

It took us about fifteen minutes to reach the river, and we could see AJ and Maren ahead of us. Along the way I kept an eye out for signs of anyone else, or any movement, which proved to be difficult because the wind was starting to blow and everything was moving. I tried not to think what the tree branches might be trying to tell me. *Don't be stupid*, I imagined them saying. *Turn back now while you have a chance.*

AJ and Maren hadn't crossed to the other side yet. On the map the river had been drawn as if it was a narrow stream, but this was a raging, rushing flow of water. From the pounding whoosh that came from downstream, it sounded as if it churned into an impressive waterfall.

Willa and I made our way down the riverbank to join the other two, who didn't seem all that surprised to see us. Nor did either of them bother to say hello. Instead, AJ took off his sneakers and tied the laces together, draping them over his shoulders like a scarf. He stuffed his phone in one of the shoes.

"You're swimming across?" I asked.

"No," he said. "*We're* swimming."

The alternative was to backtrack, or head north until the river either dried up or became more crossable. Either of them would have been a safer option, but AJ was not interested. He had no concern for the rushing water and the waterfall in the distance, no care for anything at all except finding the gold. He'd turned into a treasure bot. *Must find treasure. Must keep going. Must finish this, no matter what.*

Gold fever had consumed Miles, twisting him into a shell of the man he'd once been. It had cost him his funding, his friend, and then his life. I'd been blaming my father for treating Miles unfairly, but now I understood where he'd been coming from. AJ was not even remotely open to reason—it must have been the same with Miles.

There really wasn't much point trying to argue with AJ, but I did silently curse him when I was up to my chest in icy water. Maren cursed him, too, but not silently. Not that he cared—as soon as he made it across the river, he squeezed out his shorts and shirt and wiped his glasses on a patch of grass and was immediately ready to continue.

"See?" he said. "Easy. Now we go east fifty paces. No big deal."

The three of us girls needed a little more time to pull ourselves together. My foot was bleeding from a scrape on an underwater rock, and now we were wet and cold. Furthermore, the heavy overgrowth of trees meant it was a lot darker on this side. No bright, friendly colors or happy cow scenery. Very ominous, and it wasn't only because my mood had crashed. Every swish of the branches, every snap of a twig, every flap of a bird's wings was making me more and more nervous.

Fifty paces brought us to a rocky ridge, and sure enough, right where AJ had guessed we'd find it was the marker. Even from far away we could see the spot, because trees had been cleared and bushes messed with.

Sparrow had beaten us to it. Again.

This marker was bigger and more rectangular than the others. A little like a gravestone, actually. It had been mostly dug out as if waiting for us to finish the job. Or as if we'd interrupted a work in progress. The signs hadn't been fully revealed yet, although I could make out what looked like the top of a very large letter—*E* or *F*.

It was a little strange how two separate groups could be so close to solving the riddle after all these years. Was the island finally loosening its grip on the treasure? I didn't have time to think about it too much before AJ dropped to his knees and broke the peace with a long, loud howl.

"Way to play it cool," Maren told him. "Do you mind not summoning the very smart and dedicated person with unfinished business who probably doesn't want us here?"

AJ stayed on his knees, forehead pressed to the ground. Willa took some pictures before I pushed her arm down. It felt intrusive, as if we were watching him grieve.

"AJ," I said gently. It was late afternoon, getting darker, but even worse, we might be in immediate danger.

But AJ didn't move.

"Loser, it's time to get up," Maren said, not so gently.

Out of the corner of my eye, I saw something move.

"Did you see that?" Willa asked, grabbing my arm. "Is someone over there?"

We stared in that direction. The breeze was swirling leaves and other things around, so it probably had been nothing more than that.

"Really wishing it wasn't so creepy here," Maren whispered.

For a few seconds the wind died and there was utter silence again—that same eerie silence I'd felt the other day, without any branches swishing or birds singing, as if the forest was holding its breath.

Then the wind started up again, stronger.

Willa gasped. Something blew over the nearest rocky ridge, a tumbling spinning whirl of black. For a second I thought it was an injured bird, but it was too fluid. A garbage bag?

But it was neither of those things, and when it finally caught on a tree I realized it was a bandanna, like the ones we were all wearing—except I'd never seen it in a color other than yellow or green. And this one was larger, too, more like a swim sarong. In black, with the show's logo printed in bright white, it looked just like a pirate flag.

We all exchanged looks. It felt like a warning.

"That's it," Willa said. "I'm out."

She started running. Maren and I followed, and I was pretty sure AJ did, too, but I didn't wait to find out.

25

FOR ONCE I WAS GLAD TAYLOR WAS SO OVERLY DRAMATIC.
When we finally made it back to camp, her screams of *Oh my God I thought you were dead* made a decent homecoming.

Maddie, Joaquin, and Taylor were the only people in camp—everyone else was a patient in the mainland hospital. We warmed up at the fire pit while Joaquin filled us in.

"Bad food poisoning," he told us, and because it had hit everyone so hard and so fast, it was considered suspicious. Possibly criminal. "The police are involved now. Deb's over there now begging them not to start a formal investigation, because the network is threatening to pull the plug on the whole 'teen show experiment.' Accidents, illnesses—the bosses at the network don't like hearing that stuff. Deb's got to kiss up to them, and I don't know if you can tell, but she's really not a fan of having to kiss up to anyone, especially not a bunch of risk-averse guys in suits."

Of all of us, Willa looked the most upset by the news. "They wouldn't really stop filming, would they?"

Joaquin shrugged. "Maybe. Maybe not. I get paid either way, so I didn't ask. But you should know Deb is pissed you guys took off," he added. "She thought you'd crawled into the jungle and died, so she wasn't too happy when we finally figured out you'd left to have a nice day exploring the island. If I were you, I'd stay as far out of her way as possible, because if she's in a bad mood when she gets back here, well, you can kiss your phones and your freedom goodbye."

The phones! I'd almost forgotten about them. I still had to convince AJ that he needed to put his phone back.

"When, exactly, do you think she'll be getting back?" I asked.

Joaquin lifted his shoulders. "You think they confide in me? I'm only one level above you guys. Deb tells me where to be and when. That reminds me—she had me pick up some sandwiches in town, so don't get too excited about dinner. I had to trash everything in the fridge."

Sandwich was not the word I'd have chosen to describe the piles of soggy bread and slimy deli meat that greeted us at the Snack Bar.

I pulled AJ aside. "What does he mean, the network might pull the plug. Cancel filming? Would that mean we have to leave the island?"

AJ was looking rough. His shirt was torn, he had smears of blood on his shorts, and his expression was tight. He shook his head. "I don't know. Probably. But what the hell? We've only been here, what, a week? I can't even think about leaving, not now, not when we're so close."

I tried to bring up his phone, but he cut me off.

"There's no way I'll even consider turning it in. Not now. If the show is canceled, these photos are all I have to prove the shrine and the markers exist, so you better believe I'm going to hang on to them."

Well, that was one problem settled. It was obvious I wasn't going to convince AJ to return the phone, so I didn't need to waste my time trying. And as for telling him I had a way to save his photos, well, I wasn't about to show him my satellite now. He was so terrified this might be the end that he'd do anything to save himself. He'd sell me out in a second, no doubt about that. I'd just have to let him keep the phone and hope that Deb didn't follow through on her threat.

I left AJ to his bad mood and his doomsday predictions and grabbed the satellite. I went to my usual spot even though it wasn't necessary to be so elusive—there was hardly anyone around to catch me.

Annoyingly, the battery life had dropped to nearly half, which was definitely a concern. It was also ridiculous, because what kind of espionage satellite designed for use in a remote location barely held a charge? My four-star review shrunk to three.

I logged into the forum. The envelope icon at the top of the screen was blinking. Uh oh. That was strange—I never got messages on this site. I clicked on it. Three messages from DeadSea asking again where I was, but this time he went further and offered help. *You need someone who knows how rare shrines are,* he wrote.

A person I'd never met was offering to drop everything and join a search that for all he knew was across the world. Well, that wasn't weird at all. I stared at his message, processing what it meant, and I couldn't come to any conclusion other than what we were finding was so unusual that it was even freaking out DeadSea. DeadSea! He was a seasoned hunter. He had seen it all.

What if . . . no, I didn't want to think about it.

But I had to. What if Deb had faked the whole thing? What if the shrine wasn't real, and this whole thing had been a giant wild-goose chase designed to bring an element of drama to the show?

I felt sick. If that was true, Deb had played us, and it meant I was going to look like a giant idiot on the show. Once again, I'd be the butt of a public joke.

I was trapped in a nightmare of repetition. Even worse, it was one of my own making. Would I ever stop getting myself into these same terrible situations?

DEB NEVER SHOWED up the rest of the day, or that night, either. Most of the sick players were still missing, too, but a small batch of them arrived by boat the next morning. If I hadn't seen the boat slide onto the beach, though, I wouldn't have realized anyone had returned because every single one of them had beelined for their beds and showed no signs of emerging.

It was just as well, because it didn't seem as if filming was going to resume anytime soon. There weren't any cameras here today, and it was strange how we'd gotten so used to them. At this point, their absence felt odder than their presence. Even odder, though, was that the crew didn't seem inclined to hold our hands while the show was on hold. Periodically they'd dropped by with supplies—matches, new towels, food, a small amount of news—and then head back to their own village. Two days ago we'd been put to work doing a bunch of fake chores, but now it looked like we were actually going to be running the place.

Rohan, the only one of us who knew his way around the kitchen, had designated himself the resident chef. Last night after taking one look at the "sandwiches," he'd somehow managed to summon one of his local friends and put in a request for specific groceries. When the bags were unceremoniously dropped off at sunrise with a pile of breakfast burritos, he'd disappeared to the kitchen to start food prep.

AJ and I were headed back to the fourth marker, so I stopped by the kitchen before we left. "Got any snacks I can take with me today?" I asked.

Rohan put a couple of granola bars on the counter. "These survived the purge, but if you hold off on leaving, the chili is almost done."

I shook my head. "AJ's waiting for me."

"You guys still living the treasure dream?" Rohan asked. He chopped up a bunch of onions lightning fast. I made a mental note not to ever get between him and his knife.

Cody, who was sitting at one of the tables, put in his two cents. "Y'all better be! When Deb gets back, I think we might have to hedge our bets and show her the shrine, so unless you find something soon . . ." He drew a line across his throat. I knew the gesture wasn't meant to scare me, but the threat was still there. We really did have limited time.

AJ and I got going right away, proceeding carefully to the fourth marker. We stopped frequently to listen for sounds we weren't alone, just in case the other treasure hunter was real and not a stunt of Deb's. I hadn't shared my theory with AJ yet, so he was more on edge than I was. Even so, I didn't want to linger if there was still a chance we'd be in danger.

"Let's be quick," I said, when we finally got there. "Find the shovel and—"

But we didn't need the shovel. MrJackSparrow had been back since yesterday, and he'd cleared the marker off. I waited for AJ to go nuts, but he contained himself admirably.

Still, he tossed me the paper and pencil more aggressively than he needed to after he'd taken a few pictures. "This guy is obviously working quickly, so let's step it up. I'll stand guard," he said. "You do the rubbing."

It was another simple marker—even plainer than the last one. There was a large letter *F* carved into it, and then under-

269

neath that, a smaller letter *M*. Underneath the *M* was the word *south*.

This was our third time, so we fell into our routine, and AJ had pulled out his Cipher before I'd even finished the rubbing. It was hard not to get excited when he told me what he learned. "The *F* means this is the final clue. This is it, Riley. We figure out these instructions, and they'll lead us to the treasure, and if we do it soon, we might be able to get there first!"

We shared a minute of happy jumps and I was glad for the lack of the cameras. Two gawky people, hopping awkwardly to celebrate a discovery that may or may not be real—it would have been prime embarrassment footage. Still, I felt a thrill. Fake or not, we were still solving this puzzle, and it had been damn hard. Maybe solving a sham hunt didn't make me the butt of a joke. Maybe . . . maybe it actually made me look smart.

We went to work deciphering the marker's clues. *M* was the Roman numeral for one thousand. Since it was below the *F*, that meant we were supposed head south. And even if the positioning of the letters wasn't clear, the word *south* made it a pretty straightforward reading.

AJ strapped on his pack. I paused. Straightforward. That word was literally the opposite of every clue thus far. Why would the final clue—arguably the most important one—be the most obvious?

"I know that look," AJ said warily. "What's wrong?"

I got everything out of the pack again. I held up the map. "Seems odd that the last clue is so easy. I mean, look at that marker. Picture some random guy out for a hike, not knowing anything about any of the clues that had come before it. With a small amount of work, he could easily figure it out. Don't you think that scenario violates the spirit of the map? The last clue should be just as tricky and hard to read as all the others, if not more so."

AJ sighed. "Well, when you put it like that . . ."

"The map has to come into it somehow. It *has* to. Something about this map needs to give us a different reading of the marker. That's the only thing that makes sense."

AJ was the first to get a lightbulb moment. "The word *south*," he said. "Why use it at all? Everyone knows the way these symbols are laid out we should go south. The word isn't necessary."

I was beginning to see. "Or maybe it *is* necessary." I put my finger on the cross at the top of the map. "Because this cross says to reverse all explicitly stated directions."

"Bingo," AJ said.

"That means we go north."

AJ nodded. "We go north."

And so we did, walking nearly a mile, but when we got to the spot we'd assumed it would be, we were disappointed. There was no sign of any action. We'd gotten so used to MrJackSparrow arriving first to dig up the markers, that it felt oddly anticlimactic when there wasn't any signs of digging. But it was good news, too, because it meant we were finally one step ahead. At least, that's what we thought when we arrived, but after two hours without any luck, we weren't so sure.

"I don't get it," AJ said. "There's nothing here. Nothing at all, not even any rocks or natural landmarks, which makes it a strange choice for such an important hiding spot. Could we have read the marker wrong?"

Time ticked on, and when another hour went by without any progress, we called it a day. Either we'd read the clues wrong, or something else was going on. I spun the fake theory around in my head. Was it a coincidence that MrJackSparrow, our constant nemesis, had suddenly disappeared? He'd been so tantalizingly close, and now nothing, right when the crew suddenly seemed uninterested in doing their jobs. I spent most of the walk back to camp wondering if I should share my theory with AJ or not, but when we were almost there, I made a decision.

"Hold up a sec," I said. We were close enough to smell something delicious floating from camp, and based on the number of toys scattered on the beach—footballs, the volleyball net, cornhole boards—most of the players had come back to life.

"I've been thinking about something," I told AJ. "What if . . . well, what if it was all fake?"

"What was fake?

"The shrine. The markers. All the clues."

AJ looked skeptical. I kept going. "Remember how you found the immunity coin right near where we found the shrine? You said you'd told Deb that was where you planned to start searching, so she'd obviously planted it there for you to find. What if she planted everything else, too? Starting with the shrine itself. Some of us running around on a treasure hunt would definitely add drama to her show. Rohan was right, she's been working behind the scenes this whole time in every other way to get us hyped up. It makes sense she'd try to do it with the treasure stuff, too. And remember, looking for the treasure wasn't part of her original description of the show. She added it. Why? Maybe because she suddenly had this great faux plotline."

"You think the shrine is fake?" AJ looked stricken. Then he smiled, relieved. "It's not a terrible theory, I'll give you that, but we had a camera with us only once, so it's not like there's a ton of footage. If Deb had gone to all that effort to fake us out, she'd want every second on film."

I'd been thinking about that, too, and something had hit me last night when Willa showed me some of the pictures she'd taken during our adventure. When I'd been arguing with Maren at the second marker, I'd thought Willa had just walked away, but she'd managed to take a few pictures of us first. I hardly recognized myself. There was actual, visible emotion on my face and my arm was extended forcefully. I was so used to thinking of myself as background noise, wallpaper, but the girl in those pictures was vibrant and almost compelling. Like someone who'd look perfectly natural showing up on Willa's Instagram. Like someone who—what had Deb said that first day? I looked like someone who mattered.

But I hadn't even realized Willa had been photographing me, which had got me thinking: Why were we positive that the giant cameras Harry and Lou lugged around were the only ways we were being filmed?

"Maybe Deb did film us, but we didn't know it. We know they use drones sometimes. That's not a secret. But who says they don't have tiny little hidden cameras everywhere? They obviously have access to some high-level technology. Harry could have stalked us with a really pro camera. We would have been really easy to follow. We weren't that careful."

"I don't know." AJ still looked doubtful.

"The other thing is, why would they give us these phones? I know Deb said it was to use our pictures and videos to supplement the official footage, but really? Seems like a risky thing to do. Willa can definitely handle herself on both sides of a camera, but how many of the rest of us can even take a decent photograph? I can't imagine that any pictures I took would be good enough to be used in the show."

AJ swallowed, hard. I could see his mind racing. "But you saw it, that shrine had to be legit."

"Was it? We weren't there very long, it was pretty dark in there, and it was so exciting that we weren't exactly inspecting it for authenticity. Remember, we're here for a TV show, with people who are used to creating props and sets. They seem pretty good at it. That arena changes into something new for every single challenge."

"Oh my God," AJ said. "Oh, my freaking God. If this is a

hoax, I am going to kill someone, I swear. The treasure is why I came here. If it turns out not to be real—"

"Maybe the reason there was no treasure at the spot is because Deb is so busy that she didn't get a chance to plant it yet."

"No." AJ shook his head. "I refuse to believe it, and you know why? This show can barely keep its own shit together. They're barely remembering to feed us—you think Deb could come up with clues like this? They're hard, and they follow the proper methodology for sign interpretation. No way she managed that. And why make us think there's someone else searching? Way more dramatic and worthwhile if we have to dig up the markers ourselves instead of someone basically handing them to us."

"But—"

"Nope." AJ help up his hand. "Not buying it."

I wished I was as confident as he was. I hadn't used my old question test in a while, but this was the perfect time.

AJ: self-deluded, or confident?

I watched him walk to the boys' cabin. He was actually whistling. No doubt if asked, he'd choose the second answer, confident, and wasn't what he thought of himself really the only thing that mattered? If the treasure hunt did turn out to be a sham, he'd still probably find a way to make it work for him.

26

NEARLY EVERYONE MADE IT TO THE SNACK BAR FOR Rohan's shredded chicken tacos. It was one of the best dinners we'd had so far, but it wasn't enough to put us in a good mood.

Rohan was partly to blame. "Eat up," he advised. "The word I'm hearing is that this show is hanging on by a thread. One more bad thing happens, and the studio might pull the plug."

The fact that Taylor didn't react with screams and an endless repetition of *Oh my God* was even more depressing, because it meant even she had seen the writing on the wall.

After dinner, Cody made an executive decision and signed both of us up for dish duty, which was really just an excuse for him to convince me to drop the treasure hunt.

"Let's hold on to the shrine as our ace in the hole," he said, pulling plates from the soapy sink water and handing them to me to dry. "If the show gets yanked, we'll tell Deb about it and claim the two hundred and fifty grand. But the treasure prize isn't worth risking the show right now. You got me? No distractions. We all put everything we've got into making sure this TV show keeps going."

I agreed. Now that there was a possibility the clues had been faked, the show was all I had. No gold, and no Porter. If I wanted to leave with something to show for the experience, I needed the show just as much as everyone else.

Anxiety over our future meant the gathering at the fire pit was rowdier than it had ever been.

Justin collected some wood to get the fire started. "At the hospital, I heard Deb and Katya talking," he told us. "Did you guys know the losers are all stuck in a bunkhouse in the crew village on Challenge Island? Deb's keeping them there so they can't go home and tell everyone any show secrets. Can you imagine how much that sucks? I thought the benefit of getting voted off would be that you'd get to go to a hotel with a real bed and Internet access."

"You'd leave for a better bed?" Maren asked. "Lame. You should vote yourself off for that. No one will stop you. I'll even applaud."

"I had no idea I bothered you so much. In that case, I think I'll stay."

Who was Justin going to tell he wanted to leave, anyway? There was no one in charge. I'd gotten used to seeing crew members in their black *Reality Gold* shirts scuttling around camp all day long, but in the past two days we'd barely seen any of them. Even Joaquin had started to shed his costume, and in his T-shirt, shorts, and flip-flops he was starting to blend into our group of players. I was more used to seeing him that way, and occasionally it was hard to remember that he wasn't actually our age and a player on the show. I'd tried to watch him for signs of the perviness Alex had been so worried about, but he seemed fine. One of us. A little lost without a shooting schedule and a clear purpose, but that wasn't enough to set off any alarm bells. What else was the guy going to do?

Porter was the only one missing, but my heart flipped when I saw him walking on the beach. Three full days he'd been sick. That was three days I'd spent getting used to not having him around.

Turned out that wasn't long enough to keep my insides from dissolving into mush when I saw him.

"No need for a standing ovation," he said when he arrived, although Cody stood up anyway and gave him a hearty handshake and a *Welcome back, son.*

Something was different about Porter. He was wearing a T-shirt instead of his usual button-down, but that wasn't it.

"Hey, Frisco," he said, coming over and standing between me and the fire.

Oh. That was it. He was talking to me again. Nice, but also a little annoying. I tried not to look as if I thought him coming over was the best thing that had happened to me in three days, which wasn't easy.

"Hey."

"So . . . I think the game was getting to me the other day. Either that, or I'm turning into some kind of whacked-out conspiracy theorist."

"Is that an apology?" I asked. "It's hard to tell because there are some words missing."

He scratched his neck, looking rueful. "I was thinking I could just come over here and say *hey*, and then you'd say *hey* back, and then we'd forget about all that other stuff and you'd move over so I could sit down and tell you all of the amazing things that came out of my body in the past few days."

"I might agree to some of that, if . . ."

"If . . . ?"

"If . . . you know." I gave the universal hand signal for keep talking.

He sighed exaggeratedly. Always had to be the funny guy, I remembered Maren saying. Well. Was there something so wrong with that?

"Okay, okay. I'm very sorry I accused you of plotting to conspire against me on national television, now scoot over."

I did, and he sat down on the log next to me. There wasn't much space so we were sitting hip to hip. I realized that the crew must have been slowly removing logs as people got eliminated so that we always had to cram next to each other. I hadn't even noticed. Tricky.

"Is that what you did, accuse me of conspiring against you? Because I was a little confused, it happened so fast."

"Eh, maybe we can move on. Can I interest you instead in a conversation about vomit? Because I've become quite an expert on the subject."

"Hmmm. Charming."

"You know, I've actually been called charming before. Quite a bit, although sadly it's usually only the moms at our country club who think so. Girls my age usually just call me hot."

I couldn't help it, I laughed.

Cody interrupted everyone with a loud whistle, the kind that used both fingers.

"Alrighty, y'all," Cody said. He hitched his thumbs into the belt loops at the waist of his jeans. Add a cowboy hat and boots and it was easy to picture him the way he must look on his ranch. "Our friend Rohan here has used his great influence to procure for us a bottle of the finest vodka, which I will hand off to you, good madam."

Cody gave the bottle to Alex, who was closest.

"Please do us the honor of starting us off and then passing this fine bottle around this most excellent campfire."

Cody was slurring, and doing that overexaggeration thing people do when they're drunk. He'd obviously already become very familiar with the contents of that bottle tonight.

"But our contract with the network says no drugs or alcohol," Maddie said.

"Feel free to pass the bottle along to someone else if you want to, Maddie. No harm, no foul. But I believe we're entitled to blow off a little steam after what we've been through so far, wouldn't you agree? I think most of us will be partaking. Joaquin, my friend, what do you say to passing the bottle around?"

"I say cheers!"

No surprise. Joaquin was having a great time. He was probably one of those guys who went back to visit his old school on vacations and hung out in the student center, eventually doing that year after year until he'd been there long enough to befriend kids who hadn't even gone there when he had.

"The drinking age in Brazil is eighteen," Joaquin pointed out. "So for most of you this is perfectly legal, and for those of you who are close? Well, let's just say that the network hasn't exactly had my back here, either, so it's not as if I'd be free with any information. Loosen up, have some fun for a change. All work and no play, et cetera, et cetera."

That little speech right there was exactly what my mom would call *Peer Pressure* and what my friends and I would call *hashtag peer pressure*. Joaquin reached for the bottle, and then for the can of soda that had started circulating as a chaser.

"Good man," Cody said as Joaquin took a drink.

Porter held off. "I think my stomach and I would permanently part ways if I tried anything like that tonight."

I took two swigs. One for me and one for him. It hit me fast, though, and I realized it had been almost a year since I'd gone to a party. I took a third sip to deal with that nice bit of reality and then took a turn with the soda.

Willa decided it was the perfect time to teach us all how to "runway walk," even getting Maren to try. The boys were the best, though. Justin, Porter, and Cody did their Zoolander impressions down the strip of sand Willa had lined with tiki torches, and AJ showed off some moves that immediately disproved the myth that nerds couldn't dance.

Then the cornhole boards came out, but it didn't take long until most of the beanbags were accidentally flung into the darkness. Maddie had definitely taken a few drinks after all, because her usual Little Miss Bubbly personality was quadrupled.

"Let's play Murder in the Dark!" she suggested. And then suggested again, and again, louder and more manic each time until we finally agreed, mostly so she'd stop talking about it. Plus, Cody miraculously produced another bottle of vodka, which upped the interest level dramatically.

Only half of us had ever played the game before. I vaguely remembered playing once at my summer camp in Maine, but not enough to remember the rules. Something about passing out cards, and whoever gets the ace is the murderer. Everyone else walks around quietly in the dark while the murderer sneaks around and finds people when they are alone and whispers *you're dead* one by one until either everyone fake-dies or the detective, the jack, yells *Murder in the dark!* Upon which everyone tries to guess whodunit.

Joaquin passed out the cards, and we played one exuberant, if not skillful, round. I hid with Willa in the Sol hammock, but the murderer/Cody heard us flip out of it and collapse into laughter, and he fake-killed us right away.

After the cards had been passed out the second time, Porter took me by surprise.

"Come on," he said, close, right in my ear. My neck prickled, and a tingly feeling of anticipation rolled all the way down my body. *Omigod.* Everyone was dispersing to their hiding places, so it was easy to slip away on our own. Once we were past the Snack Bar, Porter turned backward so he was facing me, holding both of my hands. We walked like that for a few seconds, smiling at each other like one of us had told a funny story or a secret, and it felt like every single part of me was on high alert waiting for the moment he would pull me in closer.

In the distance, Taylor screamed—leave it to Taylor to scream during a fake murder—and we both laughed for real, instinctively moving nearer, and then suddenly we were *together* together. I wasn't the most experienced girl in the world, so I wondered—in the seconds before a hookup, is it just me who thinks *Is this really happening?* And then, when it does: *Oh my God, yes it is.*

There's something about the first few seconds of any kiss. It's this tiny, fleeting, rare speck of time where two people are choosing each other wholeheartedly and there's no denying that you are essentially both saying to each other *I like you, you like me* and I don't know, it's a little strange, but also a little amazing. All the dancing around and posturing has suddenly disappeared and all that's left is this expression of pure honesty, because you can't really claim you aren't into it, that you didn't want to be there. After those first few seconds—hey, anything can happen and things can and do definitely go wrong. But not then. Not at the beginning.

Someone, I think it was Alex, yelled, "Murder in the dark!"

"Should we go back?" I asked, not meaning it.

"Definitely not," he answered, and there it was again, a flutter of amazement that he was here with me. Not Willa, or Alex, or anyone else. Me.

It seemed like only a few minutes went by and then some urgent sounds started coming from camp. People yelling, and then a crash, like glass breaking.

"Uh-oh," Porter said. "Is that Rohan?"

"Do they have bar brawls in Florida, like in the movies? I could see him starting fights. Pushing people just so they'd get mad and start fighting."

I waved my fists around. The vodka was starting to hit me. I lost my balance, even though I was standing still, leaning against a tree.

"Whoa, how much did you drink? You might need to call it a night."

"No, no, no." Now I could hear myself slurring. "I'm finnnnnne."

"Actually, you know what, I'm not feeling too great."

"Poor wittle baby. Your tummy feeling bad?" I really did

not know where that came from. It had sounded funnier in my head.

"Okay, okay, settle down. I'm predicting that I feel only half as bad now as you're going to feel tomorrow."

Porter held my hand and we started to walk back. Wow, Rohan was really yelling now. *I told you, get the hell away!*

It wasn't easy to walk in the woods in the best of times, but the vodka hadn't helped. I tripped and fell, nearly pulling Porter down with me. There's a point in the arc of any drunken evening where things aren't hilarious anymore, where you know you are acting stupid but you are too far gone to really stop, and I had found that point.

Porter helped me up and there was a fair amount of *sorry* and *don't hate me* and generally a lot of other things I wish I hadn't said. We made it back to camp to see Rohan and Justin circling each other in the Snack Bar, just like a real bar fight. Chairs had been knocked over, tables pushed to the side. There was even blood spattered down Rohan's shirt.

Taylor was screaming at them to stop. "You guys, we are on the same team! We are supposed to be *friends!*"

Willa was crying, but when she saw us, she looked hopeful. "Porter!" she called frantically. "Help!"

I think he asked me if I was okay before he ran off to answer her call of distress. Later I would pull this moment up and try to re-create it, looking for signs he hadn't ditched me and run to her, but honestly, I'm not sure there were any to find.

I had enough sense to realize I needed to avoid what-ever was going down and put myself to bed. Unfortunately, I didn't have enough sense to go the right way, and I wandered off toward the boys' cabin instead.

Whoops. I was about to redirect myself when I saw Cody in the trees. That was weird. Why wasn't he trying to break up the fight?

I tried to back up quietly. That didn't go so well, because I crashed into a bush and lost my balance, which sent me into another bush. When I finally straightened myself out, Cody was staring at me as if I was some kind of stalker. That was ... weird. Usually his *howdy ma'am* demeanor made him the friendliest of the group.

"Heyyyy, Cody," I think I said. Or something equally elo-quent.

I heard a bang, like the sound of something hard drop-ping. He stood up, looking a little mad, or was it guilty? Hard to tell—I wasn't in the best mindset to read facial expres-sions, but what I could definitely appreciate was what a very big guy he was. Talk about bar fights—if anyone got into one, it would be him.

There was a full bottle lying on the ground next to him.

"Aha! So this is where you keep your stash." I finished extricating myself from the bush. "I know your secret now."

Cody looked at the bottle and then at me. "A man who controls the supply, controls the minds of men," he said, very seriously, probably quoting someone famous.

I nodded, as if this was the wisest thing I'd ever heard. And in the moment, it kind of was.

"You know what? You're . . . smart," I said, not so smartly. But it was true. The patents, the brainy quotes, the secret hiding spot. He liked to talk and dress and play up the redneck thing, but that wasn't real. It was just a front.

He wagged his finger at me, and returned to his usual self. "And you know what else? You're drunk. That's okay, darlin', but I think you might need to call it a night. You might not even remember tomorrow, but just in case, how 'bout this: I keep your secret, and you keep mine."

That made me think it was a good idea to start saying "Shhhhhh," crack myself up, and then say "Shhhhhh" again, a cycle that repeated several times during the walk to my cabin, where Cody—quickly—steered me inside and said goodnight.

I made my way to my bed. The bottom bunk had been a good call, although I could have moved to another spot if I wanted because there were so many empty beds now. That made me sad. So many things empty. So many people gone. So many mistakes, and so many failures. I could cry, the world was so full of loss and betrayal, and then suddenly I *was* crying.

I wish that sober me could harness the thought process displayed by sad drunk me. In less than a minute I blurred the timeline between now and last year, so that empty beds and people leaving the island had morphed into old worries about empty seats next to me in the lunchroom, people deleted from my phone and gone from my life. Maybe it was a form of PTSD; the last time I'd had a drink was the last party I'd been to, the one where I realized my old friends were never going to accept me. I knew people who couldn't drink certain kinds of alcohol because it had produced a bad night once. No doubt I was destined to forever associate the taste of vodka with loss.

I'd already had quite a lot of it—both vodka and loss—before I worked up the nerve to go to Maria Kang's Christmas party. She lived in a double-wide Victorian with a full-floor basement on Divisadero Street near Alta Plaza Park. Izzy and I always went over together, but she hadn't texted me. The lack of a message was a message of its own.

"I guess you're still mad," I said, when I found Izzy by the Ping Pong table, sorting Jell-O shots onto trays. Even though Izzy had left school before me, she'd stayed in touch with everyone. It was different for her—no one had any bad feelings toward her. If anything, they felt sorry for her.

"Why would I be mad?" Izzy asked.

"We always go to Maria's parties together, and tonight we didn't, because you didn't text me, so . . ."

"You didn't text me, either," she pointed out. All her attention went to lining Jell-O shots up perfectly on the tray.

She finished with the shots and looked at me. "I thought you might have made your own plans. You seem to be doing that a lot lately."

That was unfair. Practically the entire class had tried to get me kicked out of school. Of course I'd pulled back. Was I just supposed to pretend I didn't notice that everyone hated having me around?

"So you *are* mad," I said.

"Wrong word."

"Then what? Fine, I didn't text you tonight, you're right. But everyone keeps telling me how it's not fair that you got kicked out and I didn't."

"Am I the one focusing on things being fair? Or is it you?"

Wait, stop. This memory was wrong. That wasn't what we had said.

Or was it? In this version, Izzy didn't seem to be mad at me for not being kicked out. Instead, she seemed angry that I'd pulled away from her.

I had finally reached my bed. Stumbling in, I bonked my head on Maddie's bunk. Ow, that hurt. Words hurt, too. Izzy's words. What were they again? I tried to remember but everything was fuzzy.

I pulled my covers up to my neck. *Focus. Remember.*

"You've been keeping me in the dark lately," Izzy was saying, back at that party. "So maybe I've always been in the dark about you. Maybe we were never friends the way I thought we were."

Dark.

I opened my eyes. The room was spinning. The room was dark.

No, wait. That wasn't the darkness I needed to think about. Someone had been talking about dark, being in the dark.

The shrine was dark. The woods, too. Someone was hiding something I wasn't supposed to see. Another person was hiding behind a tree. I knew them, but they kept slipping away before I could catch up.

"Stop," I mumbled.

"Stop what?" It was a real voice. Not one in my head. Not a memory. There was a face above mine, but it was blurry, as if I was looking through a kaleidoscope to see it. Dark hair. Silver earrings. A nose and mouth.

"You missed all the excitement," the mouth was saying.

"Izzy, no," I said. It was hard to get the words out. "You don't understand."

I needed to make her understand. I also wanted to keep my eyes closed. The blurriness, the spinning. Too much.

"I didn't know that you weren't mad at me. I thought you were."

Words were coming out of the mouth again. Laughter, too. "Dude, you are such a lightweight. Go to bed."

"Will everything be better? All better when I wake up?" I asked. It felt important I fix this, whatever it was, before I went to sleep.

The face, the brown eyes and dark hair, hovered for a second.

"Yes," the mouth said. The voice was kinder, nicer than

it had been a second ago. "Go to sleep. Everything is fine. You'll be fine."

For the first time, I felt like things might be.

"Tomorrow we'll catch that person in the woods," I said. "I think I know who it is."

And then I fell asleep.

27

I HADN'T HEARD THE GONG IN DAYS, BUT THAT'S WHAT
woke me up. Not once, and not twice. Many times, over and over, as if someone was beating the heck out of it.

That someone was Deb, and she was mad.

She was waiting for us on the beach with Joaquin, Phil, and Katya, all of them standing in a grim line. Scuttling around the huts doing cleanup were more crew members than I'd seen in days.

"All right, children, playtime is over," Deb said. Did my head hurt, or was she yelling? I squinted. The beach was so bright, it made it hard to think. "And if you object to being called children," Deb was saying—no, she was yelling, definitely yelling—"Then don't behave that way. I'm going to pretend I don't know what went on here last night, and I'm going to pretend that my surrogates had the handle on the situation that I assumed they did, and we're going to move on. We've had a rough few days but we have to make up quite a bit of lost time. It's our tenth day today. We don't have a lot of time left, and there's a lot we need to do. Therefore, we're going to be doing two challenges back to back. One today, and one tomorrow. Furthermore, everyone is confined to camp. By that I mean *everyone*, and by camp, I mean *this beach* and *these cabins*. That's it. No one is to go one step further or I will personally escort them off this island and out of the game, is that understood?"

Deb's hair was loose today, wilder than usual, as if her outrage was powering jolts of electricity through her body.

"First thing we are going to do is have some confessionals to explain to our future audience the sudden appearance of the black eyes and the bloody noses, so everyone who participated in Fight Club last night, which most definitely includes Justin and Rohan, meet me at the boat," Deb ordered. "You're coming over first. The rest of you will join us in exactly one hour. Do not make the second boat wait even a single minute for you, or you're out. Oh, and no one will be checking out a Demon today, which means every single one of them needs to be accounted for at the charging station or it's bye-bye. Got that?"

The phones! I had one last chance to tell AJ to return his. He hadn't been around last night, so I'd forgotten all about it. There was a lot about last night I wished I could forget. I hadn't felt nauseous before, but I certainly did when the memories starting flowing back. The baby talk with Porter.

Tripping over myself—I guess that explained the skinned knee—and oh, wow: telling Cody *you're smart*. Had I really said that? I wanted to die.

Well, that thing with Porter was fun for the five minutes it lasted. He'd ditched me pretty fast when I started acting so dumb. What did he say, his stomach hurt? Well, I couldn't totally blame him. Maybe I would, later, when I started feeling better, but for now all I could think was how great it would be if there was any way to ditch myself. I vaguely remembered dreaming about Izzy. Oh, God. Had I been talking to someone about her?

I was definitely going to hide in the cabin for the next hour, and that seemed to be everyone's plan. I followed Alex up the beach, with Willa, Maren, and Maddie trailing behind.

"Hey, Frisco, don't you want some nice, gooey cheesy eggs and grease-pit bacon?"

My stomach lurched, and not in a good way, even though the call-out meant Porter wasn't pretending I didn't exist.

He waved at me from the Snack Bar. "Come sit."

He hadn't been lying simply to make me queasy—he did have all that food. Oh, right. He was the only one who stayed sober last night. Lucky him.

"Yum. Orange juice?" He held out his glass.

I shook my head violently.

"You look about as good as I thought you would."

"You and Maren are both really good at giving compliments," I told him, sitting down. "Whenever I'm feeling bad, I'll be sure to find one of you to make me feel better."

"If you want a hospital recommendation, I know of a good one." I made a face and Porter shook his head. "You know, now that I think about it, I don't know why I was so surprised you plowed through those drinks. I forgot about Quiz Night—you were the one who almost got expelled. Shoulda known you were trouble. Sure you don't want some eggs? These are really good."

I moved my chair away from the table. No way.

"Yeah, about that," I said. I definitely didn't want to bring up the op-ed, but he did deserve an explanation. "The expulsion thing is kinda sorta related to why I got so drunk so fast. It's a long story, but first I got suspended, and that led to problems with my friends, which led to other bad things like me getting homeschooled since January, so I haven't exactly gone to a ton of parties lately. I guess I'm out of practice."

"You can say that again." Porter finished and waved his plate under my nose before putting it on the neighboring table. He was definitely finding humor in torturing me. "But say no more. I get it."

"How? I didn't tell you anything yet."

"You don't need to. You said it was friend troubles, right? That means girls. And I don't understand anything girls do to each other and I never will, but I don't doubt that something nuts happened."

"Oh. Sexist much?"

"No, seriously. Take our first vote. I thought Alex and

Chloe were friends. Or at least liked each other, but Alex was dead set on Chloe leaving. Made Cody and me promise we'd vote her off. Had to be Chloe, and she didn't care about anyone else. It made no sense. I'm sure the girls in your story are equally messed up, so whatever your side is, don't worry, I'm taking it. I don't even have to hear it."

My surprise quelled my feminist ire for the moment. Alex had insisted on voting Chloe off? Porter was right, that didn't make any sense at all. They had seemed really friendly to each other in the beginning. I was starting to think Alex might be doing a lot of game manipulation. Was there no one trustworthy here?

Hopefully Porter was.

"You know, sometimes it's a letdown when someone takes your side without hearing the story," I told him. "Because you really need to have someone nod along as you give all the details and then jump in to say how horrible the other person is. That's basically the most important part. You don't really get the same satisfaction if the listener just admits up front they're going to agree with everything."

"Oh, good to know. Do I need to get really mad and say things like *I'm going to kill her!* Or will a simple *that sucks* suffice?"

"*That sucks* is perfect. But don't think you can space out and stop listening," I warned. "Because you have to say it at the right time, and say it like you really mean it."

"Got it. Thanks for the lesson. Now let's hear it."

"Hear what?" My brain was fuzzy this morning.

"The story about your jerk friends. Or, wait, I meant the story about your friends who I definitely haven't decided are jerks yet."

I wasn't really ready to go into it, which was a good thing because we were interrupted.

"Riley," one of the trees said. Or rather, someone hiding behind one of the trees. It was AJ. "I need to talk to you."

Porter waved his fork. "The jerk friends can wait. Go strategize. I don't want to see you getting voted off."

Oh. I smiled. But then I felt sick. Nothing like reality to burst your bubble.

AJ pulled me into the woods. "The shrine is real," he said excitedly. "Look, I took my time and examined everything. The statue, the marker. I got a ton of pictures. There's no way they faked it."

His excitement was catching. I grabbed his hand. Real! Not a ruse of Deb's.

"But if it's real, then why couldn't we find anything where the fourth marker sent us? Maybe we really do need to go south. Maybe the idea to flip the directions is wrong. We should go south a thousand paces—"

I grabbed his arm. "Wait, we can think about that later. But right now, we have to deal with your phone," I said. "You have to return it. We can't let Deb take the phones away."

He shook his head violently. "That's a hard no. We're keeping this thing no matter what—it's got our only proof on it. All those pictures. We need them."

It was the way he said *we* that made me decide to trust him. Until now, there had always been an element of selfishness that made me worry if it came down to it, he wouldn't hesitate to toss me to the side.

"I've got something to show you, but we've got to be fast," I told him. "Come with me."

He was desperate enough to follow me without questioning why my big solution involved a trip to the girls' cabin and a makeup compact. Once we were safely in the woods out of view, I opened it up and his face changed. AJ was a tech guy. He knew a satellite when he saw one.

If I'd been worried he was going to be angry at me for holding out on him, his reaction showed otherwise.

"Oh, baby." He shot an admiring look at me while I hooked up his phone. "You, my friend, are full of surprises. Have you had this the whole time?"

I winced. "What if I said yes?"

"Why are you acting so weird? We're all here to do whatever it takes, right?"

It was an echo of what Maren had said back on the helicopter that first day. Was this how everyone felt? For the first time, I wondered if I was too rigid, too black and white. I'd let myself sink under the weight of the article and the *"Can't Even" Girl* because I'd been so upset that those portrayals were false representations. That wasn't *me*, I'd wanted to shout from the top of the Golden Gate Bridge. What I was seeing here on the island, though, was that it might sometimes be okay to not always be yourself. Or, rather, maybe being yourself didn't have to mean always being the same in every situation.

I tried the question game. Me: Slavishly fixated on defining myself and those around me, or just someone who likes to know where people stand?

Two weeks ago, I would have said the latter, but now I wasn't so sure.

We downloaded the pictures and put AJ's phone back, making it to the beach just in time to load into the boat.

I WAS DEFINITELY not the only one who was cursing the fact that we always had to travel to Challenge Island by boat. The waves were higher today than I'd ever seen them, and I felt like heaving every time the hull slapped the water. No one threw up over the side, but I saw Alex lean over once.

Rohan and Justin were waiting for the rest of their team by the usual Sol platform in the arena. They were standing pretty far apart, so I guessed whatever they'd been fighting over hadn't been resolved.

The whole place was buzzing with action. Joaquin's costume was back on, and his accent, too. We were back in business.

"Good morning," he said. "Here we are, at our fourth challenge. How's everyone feeling today?"

There were some muted murmurs.

"No way," Deb said forcefully. "That's not going to cut it,

not by a long shot. I want enthusiasm and action, and I want it now."

I was glad we put the phone back. Deb was showing us her bad side, and I didn't ever want to be on it.

Joaquin repeated his greeting, and this time we all summoned a little more energy. It wasn't just that I didn't feel great. The fakeness was starting to get to me. The game, the whole show concept, the people.

It was going to be a tough challenge. Sol still had seven players to our four, so we had to hope that the upcoming challenge was skewed in our favor. Knowing Deb and how this show worked, that wasn't a crazy possibility.

It turned out to be true. In the next breath, Joaquin announced that Sol would be required to choose three people to sit out the challenge so that the numbers were even. Well, okay. Things were starting to look up.

"And those three people will not include Justin, Rohan, or Willa," Deb called out. She was definitely not playing today.

"Why don't you just handcuff us together?" Rohan exploded.

"Don't tempt me. I might."

Obviously this meant the boys had been fighting over Willa. No surprise there, although I was definitely going to find out exactly why.

The Sol team chose Porter, Cody, and Alex to sit out, sending Taylor to join Deb's new least favorite trio. That seemed like an odd choice to me, since Taylor wasn't exactly the strongest competitor, but then again, what *wasn't* odd anymore? Odd was the new normal.

"Not fair," Porter called out. "I always wanted a shot at winning a Tri-Wizard tournament."

"I'm warning you, Porter," Deb replied. "I'm not in the mood for your nonsense today."

The challenge wasn't bad. Not too hard, but not too dumb, either. Each team had to search for four parts of a map inside a maze, an actual maze made to look like a jungle, with vines and trees and small lagoons. Once we found the four parts, we had to put the map together, solve the clues, and the prize would be revealed.

Drones zoomed overhead and a cameraman followed us inside the maze. I couldn't see what was going on in the Sol maze, but occasionally I could hear them arguing. Good. We really needed them to lose.

It took a while to find the map pieces. The last one was in a log, half submerged in a lagoon. AJ swore it didn't happen, but I thought I saw Harry signal him to take a second look. Once we had that last corner, AJ had no problem reading the map, so the rest was easy. The clues led us to a gold crown buried beneath a vine-wrapped tree, and just to mess with her, we chose Maren to be the High Priestess so she'd have to wear it at Council. It went well with her T-shirt: hot pink with the word *Extra* scrawled diagonally across the front.

"Obviously we're sending the vote to Sol," Maren said. "Let those idiots choose someone for once." I wasn't about to point it out, but the crown seemed to be putting her in a decent mood. She wore it even after the challenge ended.

Everyone knew it would be Sol staying for a vote. It was also pretty clear, even to Taylor, that she was probably going to be one of the two to leave. She was incredibly weepy on the boat ride over.

"I had the best time with you guys, you know?" she wailed. "Promise me we'll be friends forever, no matter what, no matter who leaves tonight."

And then before Council started, she hugged everyone on her team and told them she loved them all *so much.*

"Girl, get your shit together," Maren muttered, adjusting her crown.

There were just four of us left on Huaca—me, AJ, Maren, and Maddie. We sat by the fire pit and made bets on who besides Taylor was likely to leave. The guesses were split between Justin and Rohan. Porter seemed safe, which was a relief, but there was no way both Justin and Rohan could remain—they were each too bitter. My money was on Rohan, the pot stirrer. AJ and Maren both backed Justin, but I doubted that would happen. Justin belonged to Willa, and no one was going to vote against someone she wanted.

But I was wrong. Later, when they returned, Justin wasn't in the boat. As predicted, Taylor was the other player voted off. Oddly, I missed her. When I went back to the cabin for a sweatshirt, Katya was stripping her bed. I stood there for a second after Katya left, thinking about all the things I'd been crying about last night. The empty beds, the disappearing friends.

It was only going to get harder from here on out.

"Bye, Taylor," I said softly to her empty bed, turning off the light as I went out.

28

THE PHONES HAD BEEN COLLECTED AND DOWNLOADED while we were at Council, and on my way to the fire pit for the evening I saw Phil bringing them back to the charging station.

"No cameras will be at camp tonight," he told me. "I'm headed back to the editing room, because it's all hands on deck. Encourage everyone to take pictures and videos with their Demons tonight, so we get something to use from camp."

"Will do." I signed my phone out and signaled to AJ at the fire pit that I had it. He excused himself, saying he was going to get more firewood, and we looped back around the huts to my usual satellite spot.

"Ah, my old friend Internet." AJ cracked his knuckles. "For my first order of business, I really need to see if Sean really did set himself on fire. What's that dumb name he uses?"

"Boom_Sean_alaka," I reminded him.

"Oh," he said quietly a few seconds later.

"What?"

"See? There's a new video," he said. "From the hospital, it looks like."

With a few stops and starts, we were able to watch it. Sean's friendly, goofy personality was nowhere to be seen. He was in a hospital bed, wrapped in bandages and attached to some ominous-looking tubes, and he was very serious.

"Listen, he's talking about his fall," AJ said, turning the volume up. Sean described the beach and his climb to the top of the cliff.

"And then something happened up there," he said. "I was pushed. Intentionally. Someone tried to kill me, and I have no idea why." He held up a bruised hand, his forefinger and thumb almost touching. "I was this close to the end. Just one centimeter to the right, and I'd have broken my neck. The doctors told me I'm lucky to be alive."

The video cut out. AJ whistled.

"Whoa," I said. "Did he just say someone—someone *here*—tried to kill him?"

AJ shrugged. "He's a full-time Youtuber, which means he lives on ratings. Who knows what happened up there. Maybe it's just a stunt."

Maybe, but I was doubtful. That was a pretty serious accusation to make up.

AJ shook his head when he saw how little battery was

left. "A little less than half? You couldn't have let me in on this before you drained the juice?"

We didn't stay online very long, just long enough to search for alternative ways to read a map that might explain where we'd gone wrong. We made a brief stop at Smokey Joe's, and I was relieved not to get any more messages from DeadSea. I showed AJ the MrJackSparrow conversations. We both agreed that the fact he hadn't been online lately meant he could be the treasure hunter who was here right now. He certainly had intimate knowledge of the island, which showed he knew how to get access.

"We'll figure out that marker," AJ told me on our way back to camp. "Hopefully we can get up there tomorrow. We're so close to cracking it, and I'm feeling lucky."

"We can't tell Cody we're searching for it, though," I said. "I heard him apologizing to Deb for the party and telling her that we're all totally dedicated to making sure the show continues. If it does get canceled, he wants to announce the discovery of the shrine, but in the meantime, he doesn't want anyone doing anything that could jeopardize things with the main challenges."

"What, he's the boss now? It's not that hard to sneak off. Even if we have another challenge, we'll manage," AJ said. He decided to go to bed early. We bumped fists and said good night.

"Tomorrow's our lucky day!" he said, pointing at me as he walked backward on the path. "Plan to bring it."

I ARRIVED BACK at the fire pit to discover Joaquin was our designated chaperone for the night, and he must have been irritated at Deb for shaming him because as the night went on, he didn't demonstrate any interest in enforcing lights out. He had even taken off his costume as a symbolic act of rebellion.

"Deb's still fighting off the network," Joaquin explained. "They don't have any confidence this'll be any good, so she's putting together a teaser reel to prove them wrong."

It was worrisome that things were still so dicey. I'd thought since everything went well today it meant we were back on track. Tomorrow couldn't come soon enough, and I really hoped we didn't have another challenge. We needed to crack that marker before MrJackSparrow figured it out.

The mood was definitely not as festive as the night before. It was actually tough to lose two people at this point, good friends or not, so everyone was dealing with it in different ways. I had thought Willa might stay in the cabin, mourning Justin, but instead she stayed by the firelight looking weepy and pretty. Annoyingly, she'd perched herself on Porter's other side.

"I wanted a little more time with Justin," she said at one point, putting her head on Porter's shoulder. Ugh. I didn't like that at all.

"I know what we need," Maddie volunteered cheerily. "More vodka!"

"Well, look at you," Porter said. "Little Miss Sunshine has turned into Little Miss Party Girl. Too bad you guys drank it all last night."

Joaquin leaned in conspiratorially. "I know Cody has a bottle hidden somewhere."

Maddie brightened up. "I'll go ask him."

"I know where he keeps it," Joaquin said. "Let's go get it ourselves before he comes back. Then he can't say no."

That left me, Porter, and Willa at the fire pit. Maren was immersed in her sketches over in the Huaca hut, AJ was probably already asleep, and Alex was writing in her journal at one of the tables in the Snack Bar. I really wished Willa had someone else's shoulder—literally—to cry on. She and Alex were friends, right? Why wasn't Willa in the Snack Bar with Alex taking "we survived the fourth challenge" selfies?

Cody and Rohan were further down the beach with a football. I wondered what Cody would think when he got back and saw Joaquin had retrieved his stash of vodka. Of all of us, Cody was the one who wanted the game to proceed without any issues. Another party would definitely count as an issue. This show was something else—there was something wrong when the teenagers were more concerned with rules than the chaperones.

Wait a minute. There was more than just one thing wrong with this scenario. Joaquin and Maddie had gone off together. Maybe I should run this by Alex, because that was the kind of thing she'd been hinting at.

On Porter's other side, I heard Willa say, ". . . and I had no idea it was coming. He was standing at the edge of the stage, scanning the audience, and it felt like he saw me. I felt a connection, and then suddenly this huge guy tapped me on the shoulder . . ."

Oh, God. She was telling him about how her Instagram fame started after Justin Bieber picked her to be a One Less Lonely Girl at one of his concerts. Those of us in the girls' cabin had heard it as a bedtime story a few times already. It even had a name: Maren had dubbed it "The Rise of Willa Kisses."

And then it hit me—Joaquin had said he knew where Cody's hiding place was. I'd been a little out of it last night, but not out of it enough to forget that the stash was somewhere behind the boys' cabin. Joaquin and Maddie had gone in the opposite direction.

I really didn't want to leave Porter now, and I really, really didn't want to leave him with Willa, but I had to.

"I'll be right back," I told Willa and Porter. "Like, right back. Five minutes, max."

The full version of Willa's story went on for at least that amount of time. She still had to cover how once people had blown up her Instagram she changed the look of her photos, made them sexy *and* artsy—which is apparently very hard to do, much harder than people realize—and how she'd moved to LA full-time, blah blah. That would take at least five minutes.

"Wait," Porter said. He grabbed my wrist and pulled me onto his lap. I felt a surge of heat and I understood why attraction was described as electric. It felt as if there was a crackling bit of energy surrounding us. I didn't need to be worried about Willa. There was definitely something happening between us.

"Where are you going?" he asked. "Stay here."

"I'll only be five minutes," I said, undoing Porter's arm from around my waist. I felt better about leaving, although I wanted to leave even less than I had before.

"Hurry up," Porter said, adding *I'm begging you* under his breath. Willa had only reached the part where the bodyguard had brought her onto the stage. There was a lot left to tell.

I went to the Snack Bar. "Hey, Alex." I was nervous. It was a strange subject to talk about. Maddie and Joaquin . . . together? Surely if they were, then Maddie wanted to be with him, which meant it was fine. Wasn't it?

Alex looked at me funny. "You okay?"

"I don't know. It's probably nothing, but . . . remember that night in the bathroom? When you said if I ever felt weird about Joaquin?"

Alex put her pen down and looked around. "Yeah, of course I do. Why? Where is he?"

"He and Maddie went to—"

She stood up quickly. "Let's find them," she said.

We walked around camp, but there was no sign of them until we stopped at the usually locked Quack Shack. There was a little bit of light creeping out from under the bottom of the door. Alex pushed open the door, and they were inside. Together. Fully clothed, but still. Joaquin had spread a blanket out on the floor and it was obvious where things were headed.

"Hey!" Maddie said to us. "A little privacy?"

"Privacy?" Alex said. "Joaquin, are you kidding me? Maddie's underage, in case you forgot, and you're what, twice her age?"

Maddie looked indignant. "Love knows no bounds," she said. Her arm was around his neck and I could see her hand gripping his shoulder tightly.

"Alex, Riley. Girls, come on," Joaquin said to us. He turned on the full range of his charming personality, smiling that cute dimply smile and spreading out his arms as if to say *nothing to see here*. "There's really no need to make a big scene."

"Did you say love?" Alex ignored him and addressed Maddie. "You met Joaquin ten days ago."

"Sometimes you just know," Maddie said. "Like Willa and Justin, and Riley and Porter. I didn't get in the way of either of their romances, so don't get in the way of ours!"

Romance. It was such an old-fashioned, strange word to use, and it made me realize that something had been happening right in front of us over the past ten days and we hadn't noticed. All the teasing, the piggyback rides, the late-night card games—they'd all been part of a courtship. Although,

311

was that really the right word to use? Maddie would turn eighteen in a few months, so the age thing really didn't bother me. It just felt a little squirrelly. More like teacher/student. Boss/employee.

Alex was comfortable—happy, even—to confront Joaquin, but all I could think about was how awkward it was going to be tomorrow when we had to face him in the light of day. Shouldn't we have kept everything light to preserve the illusion that all of this was fine?

I tried that approach. "I'm really sorry, Maddie. We didn't mean to interrupt, but we came to find you because, um, we wanted you on the beach. Girls game. Cornhole."

"No, thanks," she said firmly. Her arm was still glued to Joaquin's shoulder.

"Oh, it's fine," Joaquin said, extracting himself from Maddie's embrace. He stood up and stretched, as if all of this was perfectly fine, perfectly normal. "I wouldn't want to interfere with Alex and Riley's important plans. Go on, play their little game. We can see each other tomorrow."

"No!" Maddie said. She looked at us in frustration while Joaquin picked up his walkie and called Katya to take his place for lights-out duty. I'd never seen Maddie angry before, but her face was bright red and her arms were rigid at her sides, her fists balled. "Thanks a lot!" she hissed at us.

Joaquin folded up the blanket, tossed it casually over his shoulder, and walked out of the Quack Shack, calmly and slowly. I was really starting to regret all of this. Surely if there was something illicit going on, he'd be acting worried. Wouldn't he? Maddie hopped along beside him on the path to the beach, trying to convince him to stay.

Alex and I followed. At first I was surprised she hadn't wanted to retreat to the girls' cabin after the confrontation. But really, why did it matter where we went? We had nowhere to go that was off limits to Joaquin, because he was the one in charge of making sure no trouble happened at camp. No thought had been given, obviously, to a situation where the chaperone might be the trouble.

Alex and I stood at the edge of the tree line, watching them as they walked down to the water to meet Katya's boat. Maddie gestured toward us and made some exaggerated hand motions. Her body language looked apologetic. At one point, she shook her head and then tipped it into her hand, in a can-you-believe-that pantomime.

She stormed back the way we'd come, walking angrily toward our cabin.

"Wait!" I ran to catch up with her. "Whatever was going on with him seemed sketchy, but isn't it up to Maddie to decide if it was or not? She's obviously not mad at him, so maybe there's nothing to panic about."

"There is, and you know it. She's seventeen with the maturity of a twelve-year-old. This is a girl who wears unicorn pajamas to bed! He took advantage of her intentionally, and right now she's displaying classic symptoms of victimization. Not that anyone would ever really know how to recognize the true signs, because if you read the newspapers or the court reports, a victim can only be someone who cries. Someone who falls apart and is so clearly devastated that she can't function. A victim immediately points her finger at the attacker and never wavers, and if she does change her description of the events, even a tiny bit, then she's a liar and made the whole thing up. Oh, and she can't ever talk to the jerk, and God forbid she does, to try to keep peace and attempt to maintain any civility around him, because that's definitely not allowed. Real victims would *never* do that."

"Oh." It sounded like Alex knew a fair bit about this. I got the feeling she wasn't talking about Maddie anymore. She had to be talking about herself. I didn't even really know what to say or how to say it, but I felt like I needed to try. "How do you know all this?"

"Trust me," she said, suddenly looking very old and very tired. "You don't want to know."

29

KATYA QUICKLY SHUT EVERYTHING DOWN AND SENT US

all to our cabins for lights out. She had Cody's support, so I didn't even get any time with Porter.

Morning came quickly. By now, our eleventh day here, we knew the drill: gong, stumble out for breakfast, suck down coffee, then gather by the boats to listen to Deb outline the day's schedule. Joaquin was there, standing behind her. How had I ever thought he was attractive? His smile this morning seemed smarmy, not sincere.

"The boat leaves in half an hour for the challenge." Deb was all business, although her clipboard had become something of a mess—scrawled notes and miscellaneous papers jammed under the clip every which way. "Oh, and you'll need your bathing suits," she added, without providing any other details. "Dismissed. Get your game faces on and meet back here in thirty."

Nearly everyone left immediately to get themselves camera ready, but not Maddie. I watched her set a course for Joaquin. I was glad Alex had already left to get changed; I didn't think she should interfere.

But then I changed my mind, and immediately wished Alex was there, because when Joaquin saw Maddie coming toward him, he gave her a quick nod and turned to talk to Deb, leaving Maddie hanging. Ouch. It was a sharp contrast to the mornings when he'd ruffle her hair or give her a playful arm punch.

Maddie stood still, a confused look on her face. I had a very bad feeling about this.

"Maddie, come on," I called out to her. "Let's go get our bathing suits."

THE CHALLENGE WAS basically a repeat of the last one, but this time instead of running through a maze we were looking for broken pieces of a gold statue in a submerged shipwreck. It was fascinating how the challenges themselves could be so lame but the actual sets so elaborate. Maybe it was a television thing—the backdrops dazzled the viewers so much they didn't notice all the action was being recycled.

Each team had its own floating dock, and Joaquin had his own smaller one between the teams. Before the challenge started, Katya came to our float to show us how to use the scuba equipment. Having once had to go through an entire scuba certification course, I wondered whether this was a good idea. This show really played fast and loose with safety and supervision, though, so I shouldn't have been surprised that this wasn't any different.

Joaquin went through his usual pre-challenge speech. "As usual, there will be an immunity coin hidden in the depths," he told us in full host mode, accent and all. "I don't have to remind you how many treasure seekers have lost their lives in their pursuit of gold. Be safe, players."

"You going to jump in and rescue me if my tank runs out of air?" Porter called out.

"Sure, Porter. If you need help, I promise to personally save you."

Deb used her megaphone to inform all of us that divers were positioned nearby and our lives did not, in fact, rely on Joaquin's possibly rudimentary swimming skills.

"Doesn't mean I don't love you, though, man," Joaquin said.

"How about me?" Alex called defiantly. "Would you jump in for me?"

I cringed, thinking he'd take the chance to get back at her for last night, but his reply was milder than it could have been. "Sure, Alex, if you really needed it."

Willa was next to ask if he'd jump in for her.

"Definitely," Joaquin promised. "But only if you promise to post a pic for your millions of followers."

"Would you rescue me?" Maddie called.

Oh, God. This was starting to spiral out. Say yes, I silently begged Joaquin. Just say yes. But he didn't.

"Guys, don't worry, you're in good hands. No one will need saving."

Anyone watching wouldn't realize he'd just ignored her, but the contrast to their previous interactions was striking. Yesterday there was no question that he would have singled Maddie out to say he'd jump in first for her.

Maddie knew the difference. I knew it. Alex, too. But we were probably the only ones.

Deb was getting frustrated. She picked up her megaphone again. "As I told you, Joaquin is not going to be saving anyone. Furthermore, none of you is going to need saving because all of you are going to pay very close attention right now as Phil and Katya go through the instructions."

I probably had more experience scuba diving than Katya, but I listened anyway. Then she went into the specific rules of the game.

She held up a weight belt. "Everyone needs to put this on before going in, and you'll need to clip this tether onto it. When you have sixty seconds left on your time, we're going to tug the line once. At thirty seconds, we'll tug it again twice, and when your time is up you'll feel three quick tugs in a row. That's the signal to come up. Anything you do after that will be disqualified, so don't bother trying to stay down any longer. You have plenty of air to stay, so it's not dangerous, but there's no point. Just come up when you get the signal."

I WENT FIRST on Huaca. The shipwreck was hyperrealistic, and by that I mean it was what someone who had never seen a shipwreck would imagine it to look like. In real life, the ships are covered in sand and algae and barnacles, barely more than lumps on the ocean floor. But I got it—rotting pieces of green wood wouldn't impress anyone, so instead we had two precise halves of a new ship that had been split and submerged in perfect condition under the clear blue waves.

The thing I love about being underwater is the thing most people hate. I love hearing my breath. The heavy rasping in and out. Breathing is something you never think about, you just do, but when you're underwater that's almost the only thing you hear. There's something about the weightiness of everything underwater, too, that makes me appreciate being above the surface. Everything feels a bit lighter and more wide-open after a dive.

Our strategy was for me to simply get the layout of the wreck so we could decide as a team which sections to search. The boat really was elaborate—sleeping cabins, a galley, living quarters. I made some mental notes on the more complex parts of the wreck—the galley was full of compartments— and when I felt the tug letting me know my time was up, I kicked my way to the surface.

AJ was next. The clock was paused while we were on deck, so the transition wasn't as rushed as it usually was.

"Start in the galley," I told him, unhooking the tank and weight belt. He took the tank from me to test the airflow. "There are a lot of doors and places where things could be hidden, some tables and chairs all piled up, too. Something could be under those."

"Will do. Wait, where's the belt?" AJ asked. He wasn't quite ready to go. The goggles were on his forehead, and his flippers still off to the side.

I looked around. That was weird. I'd unhooked the belt and let it fall, but it wasn't anywhere on the deck. Then I heard a splash off the side of the boat.

"Why is Maddie going?" Maren asked. "Isn't it AJ's turn?"

There were a few long, drawn-out seconds where I tried to process what was going on. Missing belt, Maddie jumping in out of turn without all the equipment. Oh, God. She was testing Joaquin. She wanted him to save her. I could almost imagine the romantic fantasy she'd cooked up in her head—Joaquin urgently diving down to pull her from the depths.

"Give me the tank!" I said to AJ.

"What the heck? We agreed I would go second." It wasn't really hitting AJ yet, either, what was going on, but despite his complaints, he handed me the tank. Katya was on the radio, frantically calling Deb.

"Did she jump in on purpose? Is she trying to sabotage us?" Maren demanded. And then she smiled. "You know, if that's true, I almost have some respect for that girl now."

320

I didn't have time for any of that. I stepped off the float and plunged feetfirst into the water.

Maddie had sunk almost straight down, which is actually hard to do. You need to know how to let the air out of your lungs and you need to do it slow enough so that you keep sinking rather than pop to the surface. She was staring upward, toward the floats—ominous black squares above us that blocked out the sunlight.

I made it down to the wreck near where she was standing, pulling out my mouthpiece and giving it to Maddie.

"Breathe," I ordered, the word coming out as a blob of sound accompanied by a stream of bubbles. There was a minute where I wasn't sure she would take it, but she did, taking a breath and then passing it back to me. She looked so scared and confused.

Two wetsuited swimmers in full scuba gear appeared. One of them pulled the weight belt off Maddie and hooked arms with her, kicking upward. The remaining diver pointed up and I nodded.

Things on the surface had devolved into chaos. Deb's boat was moored to the Sol float, and the swimmers had taken Maddie over there. I grabbed a towel and sat on our float between AJ and Maren, watching the whole thing. Cody was pacing back and forth, obviously concerned what the disruption of the challenge meant.

Alex was standing between Maddie and Deb, loudly insisting that Maddie needed to see a doctor.

"I told you guys she'd be the last one standing when the zombies get here," AJ said, nodding at Alex. "That chick is a closet badass."

Maren shook her head in defeat. "Yeah, too bad that badass is on the other team, because guess what, we just lost. One of us is leaving tonight."

She was right, but I couldn't shake the idea that we'd lost more than just a challenge.

30

BACK AT THE HUACA HUT, AJ COULDN'T UNDERSTAND
why I didn't want to sneak off and run up to the marker.

"I don't get it," he said. "Are you with me, or what? I can't tell."

If AJ were a painter, he would dip his brush in a single color.

"I'm with you," I said. I didn't want to get into it, since Maddie was crashed out on the couch nearby, but I didn't think we should leave. Things at camp felt . . . unsettled, and if Deb came by to check on things and found us gone, I had a feeling it would be the last straw. "I think there are other things that might be a little more pressing—"

"There aren't," AJ shot back.

"I want to go home," Maddie said. Until that point, she'd been completely silent. I'd actually thought she was asleep. "Where's Deb? I need to tell her I'm quitting."

"Whoa, whoa, whoa, hold on there," AJ said. "Quit? Your little stunt back there was cray, but nothing to quit over."

"Cray is definitely not on your approved list of words," Maren told him. "And if she wants to quit, let her."

"Why do you care, anyway?" Maddie asked. "You were probably going to vote me off tonight, so I'll leave now and save you the trouble."

I cringed. Maddie had been the natural choice to go— AJ, Maren, and I had a partnership—but after today's events it felt mean to vote her off. She was obviously going through something.

Maren pointed out that Maddie had single-handedly lost the challenge for us. "So heck yeah we're going to vote you off. But sure, quit and save us the trouble of a vote."

Maddie sank even further into the couch. Maren had spent most of her time with her sketch pad last night, so I wasn't sure how much she knew of what had gone on.

"Fine. I'm going to pack," Maddie announced. I accompanied her to the cabin.

"This is your fault," she told me. "He's ignoring me because you and Alex embarrassed us. And now he doesn't want anything to do with me. You saw him! He won't even speak to me."

It was obvious that Joaquin was acting so terribly toward Maddie because he knew it had been wrong, and he was shutting it down now that others knew about it.

"I'm sorry, I really am. But I think Alex is right. Joaquin really shouldn't have been—"

"Now I'm going to have to watch myself be humiliated

on TV when this show comes out," she interrupted. "I wish I could smash every camera to pieces and shred every single bit of film so it's as if I were never here—"

She started to cry. This was all very familiar, very painful territory. How many times this year had I wished I could disappear? Not leave. Not kill myself. Simply cease. That's all I wanted: not to be visible anymore. Exiting was too much work and in its own way, too public. I'd just wanted to be erased from the world.

I understood, too, why Maddie was worried about having to watch the show. Seeing it was going to be hard. Sometimes when I'm online, a meme of me pops up, and every time it feels as if I've been physically slapped.

We reached the cabin.

"I can't stand the idea of getting voted off in front of Joaquin. I'll be so embarrassed. I can't deal with that, I really can't. It'll make me feel like such a loser."

Maddie yanked her duffel bag out from under the bunk bed and began to fiercely cram her clothes into it. I left when she took her album of pet pictures out of the safe. I hated the reminder of that first day. When she'd told me about it, she'd been so cute and innocent.

So much had happened since then.

I MADE IT back to the Huaca hut just when Phil came by to give us some bad news.

"If Maddie quits now, your team will still have go to Council for a vote. I'm sorry, but that's the way—"

"Yeah, okay, you delivered your tidings of joy," Maren told him. "Now get out of here and leave us alone."

Strangely, he did.

"That really sucks," AJ said after Phil left. "I can't believe one of us is going home tonight."

"No freaking way," Maren said. "That's not happening. Let me tell you how this is going to go down. Maddie wants to leave, and we want to vote Maddie off, so it's simple: we force her to suck it up and stay for Council."

I shook my head. "We can't do that."

"Why not? Council is in two hours. She can't stick it out here for two more hours? Of course she can."

"It's not that," I said. "Something happened with Maddie and Joaquin last night."

"What?" AJ asked.

Maren frowned in disgust. She knew what I meant. "What a turd," she said.

"What am I missing?" AJ looked back and forth between the two of us, confused. "What happened with Maddie and Joaquin? I don't get it."

"I always thought that guy was sketchy," Maren said. "Why has he been hanging out with us at night when he could be with people his own age at the crew village? And he was always with the girls. It was weird. Getting the picture now, AJ?"

"I guess so," he said hesitantly.

Maren rolled her eyes. "Of course you don't really know what we're talking about. Freaking guys."

I was of the opinion that AJ didn't get it because he was, well, AJ. But I saw her point.

"We can't make Maddie sit through Council and then vote her out. That would be really mean."

Maren nodded sullenly, and then lashed out, kicking the chair Maddie had been sitting in earlier. It toppled over. "Well that sucks, because if we let her walk, then I know you guys are going to vote me off," she said angrily. "You two have this whole treasure thing going on."

"I don't know what we'll do," I said, the same time as AJ said, "Probably."

Maren let out a shout of frustration, loud and sudden enough to stun AJ and me into silence.

A minute or two passed and then Maren spoke. "Can I say one thing?"

Her voice sounded so different when she wasn't on the defensive. Suddenly, I remembered the other night, when I'd been passed out on my bunk. Maren was the one who'd been talking to me, I realized. The face who'd reassured me everything would be fine. I felt an unexpected burst of affection for her.

"I came here to win. I really wanted that prize money. I'm sorry if I came off aggressive sometimes, but it's just me and my mom, and I don't see how going to college is possible, financially."

Oh, God. I tried to say something but only a squeak came out.

"And you know how bad student loan debt is. Well, maybe not you."

She meant me, obviously. I understood the animosity now over my father's treasure hunts, which suddenly seemed incredibly frivolous. And so did my op-ed, for that matter. Even my infamy wasn't the most horrible thing a person could go through, I was starting to realize. It was like here on the island I'd blinked and my vision had cleared, showing me something I hadn't seen before. No one would ever convince me that my exit from Shaw and the subsequent deep freeze of my social life wasn't unfair, but maybe, just maybe, I hadn't needed to let it ruin everything. I listened to Maren's story while I thought about Alex and Maddie and all the things we had all been through, all I could think was *What was wrong with me?* What urgent need had compelled me to insist to everyone that I was in the right? The whole thing would have faded away if I'd just taken my suspension and resumed school without complaint. Sure, it hurt that my classmates were so willing to force me out, but I could have privately acknowledged their concerns that my father's donor status had helped keep me at school and moved on.

"If Riley and I find the treasure, we could split the prize with you," AJ offered. "This game has a lot of rules, but I never heard one say that a winner can't decide to split the prize. We can ask at Council."

Rules. Council. This game had a lot of protocol. Suddenly, I got an idea. There might be a way to use the rules of the game to our advantage. The three of us could stay, while sparing Maddie the embarrassment of an ugly voting ceremony.

"Hold that thought," I said. "We can come back to it later, but right now I think I know a way we can convince Maddie to get voted out at Council without it being embarrassing for her."

FOR THE FIRST time at Council I didn't look around and silently make fun of the decor. Instead, I appreciated the solemnity of the ritual in a way I hadn't before. Still, I could barely stand to look at Joaquin, so I couldn't even imagine how hard it was for Maddie. She'd agreed to come to Council though, once I explained the plan. If it worked, I'd found a way to let Maddie go home without the embarrassment of withdrawing.

It all hinged on the immunity coin.

"Here's what we'll do," I had laid out the strategy ahead of Council. "The three girls will vote for AJ, and AJ will vote for Maddie. That would normally mean that AJ would be voted out because he has more votes, but instead, he'll present the immunity coin."

"How could I have forgotten about that thing?" AJ smacked his forehead. We'd all gotten so caught up in the treasure hunt we'd forgotten about the immunity coin from that first day.

"That means AJ can't be voted off, and so the person who will end up leaving is Maddie, even though she only got one vote. We all get what we want. The three of us stay. Maddie wants to leave, so she does—but she goes out with dignity."

Maren looked surprised. "That could actually work."

Maddie liked the plan, too, enough to not mind seeing Joaquin as much as she'd feared.

"You four don't seem as worried as I'd expect," Joaquin said to us after everyone from Sol had filtered out. The firelight made his face almost ghoulish, or maybe it was just that I'd never look at him the same way again.

"Does that disappoint you?" Maren asked.

"I'm intrigued, more accurately. Emotion has run high at every other Council, but at this one, arguably the most important one, you four are calm and collected."

"Can we get this over with?" Maddie said.

Joaquin had the decency to look stunned, but it only lasted a second. "If that's what you want."

He called the camera crew and they all slid into position. After Joaquin gave his usual Council talk, we got our marbles and quickly cast our votes. Usually there was another question and answer session about how we felt about our vote and all that, but not tonight.

"I have an announcement," AJ said. "I would like to use my immunity coin tonight."

Joaquin looked confused. His eyes did a quick flit toward Maddie and he frowned. Phil must have told him that Maddie wanted to go home, and so he'd expected her name to be the one announced.

"The immunity coin is sacred, AJ. Meant to be used only once, and only when you are in personal jeopardy."

"I think I am, obviously."

"All right, if that's what you want to do, please bring it to the altar."

"Oh, I don't have it on me," AJ told him.

Joaquin's expression was condescending. I wasn't sure how I'd ever thought he was charming. "I'm not sure I understand," he said. "In order to use the immunity coin, you must surrender it."

"I am going to surrender it, but first I need a boat ride back to Black Rock to get it from my safe."

Joaquin dropped the host act. "Deb? Phil? A little help, please. AJ needs you to explain the rules."

The crew flipped on some of the giant lights, and Deb approached the altar.

AJ did not, in fact, need a refresher on the rules. He'd gotten one earlier, when we had summoned Phil back to our team hut and we'd grilled him on the mechanics of using the immunity coin. We'd asked the question ten different ways to make sure, but Phil had never said that the coin had to be present at the Council during voting.

"Are you really going to allow this?" Joaquin said to Deb,

after she gave a nod for AJ to get it. "He's banking on a loophole. You're the rulemaker. Tell him he got it wrong."

Deb wasn't concerned. She was a lot less stressed tonight, probably because she felt like she'd finally gotten things on track after the food poisoning.

"It isn't a loophole, because he's right," Deb said. "No one ever specifically said the coin had to be physically present to be used. It was assumed whoever had the immunity coin would bring it, but he didn't, and it's not of major consequence, so I'm going to allow him to go get it. What's it to you, anyway? This Council isn't nearly as long as usual. Let him get the coin, and we'll still finish up at a decent time. Does everything have to be debated? Can we get through a single day without a screw-up? For once. Please."

I was amazed by Deb's ability to remove herself so completely from what was happening around her that she was unaware of a serious undercurrent of chaos flowing through this Council. Her attention was mostly on the curled and crumpled sheaf of papers pinned to her clipboard. The show was what mattered; always the show. Or rather, *only* the show.

AJ left, and with Deb scribbling away at her notes, that left Joaquin to face Maren, Maddie, and me on his own. I felt some satisfaction that he couldn't make eye contact with any of us. No fun bantering tonight. No folksy, fake conversations, either. It was a stark change from previous Councils, and I wondered why no one from the crew seemed to notice that things between Joaquin and the players were not proceeding as usual. None of them noticed that for the first time he'd joined them outside the Council area during the filming break instead of plopping himself down with the players.

In the distance, I heard the motor from the island shuttle, quickly followed by the thud of pounding feet getting louder and closer. Someone was running, hard.

AJ burst through torch-lined Council entrance. He called my name.

The crew was caught off-guard by his sudden entrance, and they scrambled to get into position. Deb called for the bright stage lights to be turned off in favor of the set lighting. "Torches only, please!"

AJ was out of breath. Something was definitely wrong. He wasn't triumphantly waving the coin around. In fact, he looked about as far from triumphant as a person could get.

"Riley, it wasn't—"

Joaquin, back at his place at the altar, scolded him. "AJ, please take your seat. As always, we'll need to observe the rules of silence for the counting of the votes."

AJ ignored him. He was still working to catching his breath—doubled over, hands on his knees. "Listen to me. Someone stole the immunity coin. They did it while we were here. I saw it in my safe before I left the cabin, but when I went back, it was gone."

"What?" I was sitting between Maren and Maddie, and the three of us looked back and forth at each other in confusion. How was that possible? Our whole plan depended on that immunity coin. AJ had three votes and Maddie had one. Without the immunity coin, AJ would be voted off and Maddie would have to stay.

"It's gone, you guys. Someone is messing with us, and I'm out. Riley, I left all my notes and files for you in a pile on my bed. Take them and go back to the fourth marker. The answer has got to be there somewhere."

"What? No," I said. This couldn't be the end for him. Not now. How had everything fallen apart so quickly? Worst of all, it all fell on me. Messing around with the vote had been my idea.

Maddie was going to hold me to account. "What's going on?" she asked me.

I wasn't sure what to say. Maddie wouldn't have even been here if I hadn't convinced her to come. *Do this and you'll leave with dignity,* I'd told her. "AJ couldn't find the coin—"

"I couldn't find it because it was stolen," AJ interrupted. "I looked everywhere, but it was gone. Someone knew how to break into my safe, and they took it."

From his position at the altar, Joaquin continued to call for silence and we continued to ignore him. Finally, he lost patience and hit the gong. He waited for the reverberations to stop before addressing AJ. "This is your final chance to present the immunity coin."

"I don't have it," AJ told him. "But then, you probably knew that. Or someone did, because this whole game is fixed—"

"You really don't have the coin?" Maddie said. "But . . . but we all voted for you. That's three votes, and only one for me."

She seemed to be finally understanding the consequences of a lost coin. "Wait, no!" she cried, as Joaquin reached for the jars to begin the voting ceremony.

He tipped my jar over first. It was empty. "Riley, you have zero votes."

It was the same for Maren's jar.

I watched in horrified silence when Joaquin picked up Maddie's. I put my arm around her. What else could I do? It was obvious what was about to happen.

Joaquin tipped the jar over and a single marble rolled out. "Maddie, one vote."

I felt her tremble, and the shaking only grew worse after three marbles came from AJ's jar.

"AJ, three votes," Joaquin announced. "Your teammates have voted you out. I'm sorry, but it's time—"

Maddie shook off my arm. "That's not right," she said.

"I'm sorry?" Joaquin asked her. He either couldn't summon the jovial, friendly host personality, or he'd never had one in the first place and we'd only seen what we wanted to.

"*I'm* the one going home," Maddie said. "Not AJ. Me. I'm the one leaving tonight."

She turned to me. "That's what you said. You told me I'd be the one voted off."

"Maddie, I tried—"

I had no explanation, other than we'd been blindsided. There was nothing for any of us to do except watch as AJ approached the altar for his goodbye blessing. Maddie joined him.

"I want to trade places with AJ," Maddie said to Joaquin. "Give me the goodbye blessing, please."

Joaquin didn't display any emotion at all. "I'm afraid that's not possible," he told Maddie coldly.

And that's when she lost it. There was no doubt in my mind that when the show aired, there would be a clip of me assuring Maddie she'd go home with her dignity intact would accompany her meltdown. There was crying, some screaming, and things disintegrated into enough of a mess for Deb to finally step onto the Council floor and get involved.

She tried to calm Maddie down, to no avail. "Maddie, what's going on here? You're all mixed up tonight. Most people get upset when they're voted off, not when they get to stay."

"She's not mixed up," Maren called out. "She's messed up. There's a huge difference, and if your boy Joaquin had kept to himself—"

Deb's entire demeanor changed in the two seconds between *Joaquin* and *himself*. Her hand dropped from Maddie's back, and her entire body straightened and tensed, as if something was expanding on the inside. "Joaquin, I swear to God, you had better pray you haven't ruined my show."

That was it for me. Enough with the precious show. I

started in on Deb, and Maren didn't need any encouragement to let her insults fly, too.

"How dare you let this happen!"

"You only care about one thing!"

"If my parents had any idea what was going on here . . . !"

The altar, set up to be a sacred space for meditative thought and reflection, instead played host to an explosion of angry accusations.

"Enough!" Deb screamed at me and Maren. "Get yourselves back to camp. Get out of here right now, or I won't wait for the network to shut us down. I'll do it myself!"

MAREN AND I left for Black Rock without the usual post-Council niceties.

"What a freaking mess. Who could have taken the coin?" Maren asked. "Deb? To make the show more dramatic?"

I shook my head in frustration. "No idea."

I'd been spinning through all the possibilities the entire boat ride. It had to be someone from the show, someone who could have gotten a master key or known how to override the thumbprint requirement. Deb was high on the list, but it could have been anyone on the crew. I wondered, though, if the goal for stealing it was to create drama for the show or whether there was some sort of treasure manipulation going on. Had someone wanted AJ out of the way to affect our search for the treasure?

"And what was that business at the end, about the network shutting us down?" Maren said. "I was hoping all those rumors were just talk."

Same. I hadn't truly realized we were that close to the show actually getting canceled, and it was taking all I had not to fall into a panic. Not only was the brainy half of our partnership gone, leaving everything up to me, but now I might have a lot less time to accomplish anything.

When we got to Black Rock, Maren and I split up and I hurried toward the boys' cabin. I wanted to get to AJ's safe before someone from the crew came to pack up his things. I nearly crashed into Lou, who was waiting outside the front door.

"Whoa, what are you doing here?" I asked. "Isn't filming done for the day?"

He lifted his camera to his shoulder. "Guess not. Phil told me to get over here, so here I am."

"Whatever. I'm getting something of AJ's. It's really not going to be that exciting, but if you want to film it, fine. Let's do it."

I went inside and flipped on the light.

There was a scream, first from someone else, and then from me.

Willa and Porter were in the cabin. Together. It was nearly a repeat of last night, when I'd seen Joaquin and Maddie, and my brain was having trouble processing it.

They split apart when the lights went on, but not fast

enough. It must have been a coping mechanism, because my mind zeroed in on seemingly inconsequential details like Willa's brown leather sandals on the floor, one of them upside down as if it had been kicked off in a hurry. Porter's navy sweater was in a heap on the floor. There were two Snack Bar glasses on top of a safe. I saw it all, understanding the implications and rejecting them at the same time.

It felt like the ground was tilting, or maybe it was that my legs were getting weak, but something was making it very hard to stay upright. I backed up, not quite in control, bumping into a bed and sending a lacrosse stick clattering to the floor on my way out the door.

I thought I'd been betrayed before. I thought I had experienced the worst of what that emotion brought. But nothing I'd ever been through compared to what I was feeling right now. Their treachery was affecting me in a real, physical way—squeezing my chest and violently churning my stomach.

I *trusted* Porter. I didn't trust anyone, and I'd trusted him.

Had he been using me the whole time? And what about Willa? In some ways, her deception was worse. She'd encouraged me to go for Porter knowing she planned to as well. She'd acted as architect of this twisted triangle. Why—because she could? She had thought it would be fun?

From inside the cabin, Porter was calling my name. It took everything I had, but I left without answering.

31

WAKING UP THE NEXT MORNING WAS BRUTAL. I'D
dragged a blanket from the Huaca hut last night to sleep
on the beach, and when I opened my eyes I marveled at the
bright blue sky and the soothing swish of the waves. Last
night circumstances had been savagely altered—relationships destroyed, hopes burst, and trust mangled, yet somehow in the face of all that, the world was proceeding as usual.

I felt something tap my head. "Rise and shine, butter-
cup," Maren said.

I pushed her foot away. "Get your dirty toes out of my
hair," I mumbled. "And go away. Today has been canceled."

"Make sure you stay out here looking like a pathetic loser
for at least another five minutes. The other team is going to
breakfast soon and I'm sure you want them to see you like
this, right? Especially Porter and Willa."

Ugh. I wrapped myself in the blanket and waddled into

the hut to collapse on the couch. "Who? I don't know anyone with those names."

"That's the spirit."

Last night, Maren had done something that had completely surprised me. When I made it back to the Huaca hut, I hadn't even finished the Willa-Porter story before she had stormed out of the cabin to tell them off. Maren, of all people. It felt odd to even think it: Maren had made that grand gesture for me without a second thought.

"About last night," I started to say. "Thank you. Again. I'm—"

Maren frowned. "Don't ruin it by getting all sappy. We're teammates. The last two teammates left of Huaca, actually, and that's what teammates do. Bring each other coffee, too." She pointed toward the table where a *Reality Gold* branded coffee cup sat steaming. "Your turn tomorrow."

"If we're even here tomorrow." I traded the couch for a seat at the table. I had work to do if I wanted to figure out this final clue. Somehow, AJ and I had read the marker wrong, and I needed to figure out how.

"Thank God we're our own team," I said. How things had changed! I never thought I'd be saying that to Maren. "I really can't face those two."

"Oh, yeah. About that . . ."

I looked up sharply. "What?"

"I got a heads-up from Katya while I was getting coffee that we're merging into one team." She made a face. "Sorry."

"Well, isn't that perfect." A few days ago, I would have been thrilled to hear I'd be with Willa and Porter. But now that was bad news.

Maren flopped down on the couch with her sketch pad. "I still can't believe Willa and Porter did that to you. What a wild night. It was like one of a hundred crazy things that happened. Maddie trying to quit, someone stealing AJ's coin, and all that stuff with Joaquin. Gross."

That reminded me. I was still stewing about Joaquin. Now that we knew what he was really like, I suspected there had been other issues. I wanted to look him up online. Normally, I'd sneak off to my satellite spot. But Maren had shown me last night that I could trust her.

"I've got something else crazy to show you," I told her. I'd hidden the satellite in the couch cushions last night, since the safe wasn't as secure a hiding place as I'd thought. Unlike AJ, she didn't recognize it for what it was, even when I opened it up and got the connector cord ready.

"It's a satellite. I've been using it to get online."

Maren's eyes got huge. "You cheater!"

"I didn't think it was cheating at first," I explained. "I brought it so I could check for advice about treasure hunting—and remember, before we got here none of us knew that searching for the gold would be part of the show. I was going to do it on the side, so I figured using the satellite for that wouldn't matter."

"You keep telling yourself that," Maren said.

I hesitated. "Are you mad?"

Maren rolled her eyes. "You might be the most touchy-feely person I've ever had to deal with. *Do you like me, are you mad, can we be friends?*"

I must have looked hurt.

"Oh, God. Moving on. Where'd you get this thing?" She picked it up and examined it. "It's totally cool. Being rich does have its perks."

"Oh. Um. About that . . ."

"Forget it." She looked embarrassed. "Actually, it felt good to let all that stuff out. Sorry it was all directed at you, but confronting someone turned out to feel really good. Now that I've said all of it, it's like it's not inside me making me mad anymore."

"You're so touchy-feely," I said, which actually made her crack a smile. "Now for something not so funny. I want to look up Joaquin and see if he's ever done anything shady before."

It took a while, but sure enough, we found something on a celebrity gossip site, which led us to another site, and then another, and it quickly became clear that if anyone had bothered to investigate Joaquin, they'd have known something was up. Not only that, but he was in his thirties. I'd thought he was a lot younger.

I was steaming mad. Had he been hired *on purpose*? How could Deb have not known his history. I couldn't sit still. I got up and paced.

"Hey, calm down," Maren said. "Show me this treasure site of yours."

When I logged in I noticed that I had a new message. DeadSea again, most likely, but I was oddly disappointed he'd only sent one message instead of multiple.

But it wasn't from him. It was from MrJackSparrow, and his message was short.

MrJackSparrow: Get off Black Rock Island. Now. Before you get hurt. Don't say I didn't warn you

I clicked the off button as fast as I could, a habit I picked up when I was constantly being confronted with things on my phone I didn't want to see.

Oh my God.

Maren was staring at me. She'd read it, too. "What in the fresh red hell was that about?"

I shook my head. My heart was racing. Someone—MrJackSparrow, probably—knew I was AnonGirl, and he knew I was here. That explained why MrJackSparrow had never been on any of the chats the way he usually was. He was here, watching me. I frantically cast my memory back, trying to remember if he'd ever given any clues about who he was.

He had to be one of the crew members. It was the only explanation. But how? Phil had said they all came straight from Alaska—oh, wait. It hit me. Deb had described her B-team as out of work actors and friends and relatives of the crew. How had I forgotten that? MrJackSparrow could be here as a B-team member.

Once again, I felt vulnerable because it was another example of how a person in charge of protecting us had ulterior motives. I felt sick.

"I've got to get out of here," I told Maren.

I didn't know where I was going, but I couldn't stay in the hut. I felt like a target here.

"But—"

"Look Sean up. Watch his hospital video, okay?"

"Okay, but—"

I practically ran to the water's edge, the urge to escape was that strong. The only thing stopping me from going full tilt was that Porter and Willa were up at the Snack Bar so they'd have a good view of me losing it.

Someone called my name. "Riley!" It was Alex. She hurried down to meet up with me. "Are you okay?" she asked. "I mean, I'm sure you're not, but relatively speaking."

I wasn't, actually. I was tired of being jerked around. Tired of thinking things were one way and finding out they were the opposite.

"Listen," I said to her. "Can I trust you? I sort of think I can, because you got involved and helped Maddie, but on the other hand, you've done some sketchy things, so I'm not sure."

"What things?" Alex asked, offended.

"Like how you insisted on voting Chloe out even though you guys were friends."

"Oh." Guilt flashed across Alex's face.

"Yeah. *Oh*. She probably trusted you as much as I do, so you see my problem, don't you?"

"I did want Chloe out. I felt bad about it. I liked her a lot, but she lives near me. Or more accurately, where I used to live."

"So?"

"The other night you asked how I knew so much about how slimeballs like Joaquin behave. It has to do with that. There was an . . . incident. Everyone was on his side. They said I asked for it, because I snuck out to go to a party with him. Because I was drinking, I deserved it. My parents didn't want to believe it, but they had to, eventually. And when the police refused to charge him, we didn't have a choice. We moved. I didn't want to hide my name, so it was all public."

I really didn't know what to say. *I'm sorry* was ridiculously inadequate.

"I didn't want to deal with all of it on camera if Chloe remembered who I was. It was pretty big news, at least in Ohio."

"I wish I hadn't doubted you. You were so straightforward with us about Joaquin. I should have trusted you for that alone."

But even more than feeling sorry about Alex, I was mad.

346

Deb had pulled us together on purpose, all of us exiled misfits, and for what? Not because she cared. She wanted us to find one another, all of us as unstable as sticks of dynamite.

"I have a story, too. I used to think it was the worst story in the world, but now? Not so much. Come on. Let's go find Deb. I'm tired of her putting us in danger."

WE GOT ROHAN to convince one of his crew friends to bring us to the crew village. It took some doing. Not only were we not allowed there, but we weren't supposed to be transported anywhere without Deb, Phil, or Katya signing off on it. Great, they cared about some rules, but only the ones that made things inconvenient.

The crew village was extremely disappointing. I'd pictured it having all the same beach decorations that we had. Instead, everything was ugly and cobbled together, as if the set designer had spent all the budget on our camp and had to resort to slapping wood slabs together with duct tape over here. I inspected every crew member we passed for signs of a reaction, but we came across very few people and none of them seemed interested in our presence.

It wasn't hard to find Deb—we followed the yelling. She was inside what must have been her office, screaming into a phone. Her clipboard was facedown on the floor, its pages scattered in all directions as if it had come to life and thrown a tantrum.

Her mood didn't improve when she saw us. "What are you doing here?"

"We came to see about Maddie," Alex said. "We're worried about her. Is she okay?"

"Okay-ish," Deb said. "She seems to be mad at the two of you, actually."

Deb was so matter-of-fact. All her manipulating had led to this, and she didn't seem to care.

"We're not the ones who did anything wrong. Your host did, and I'm sure you know what I'm talking about. How do you live with yourself?" I said. "She is literally the sweetest girl, and you're the one who hired Joaquin and put her—us—in his way. Alex with her history. Me with mine. You had to know I'd feel flattered by the attention. And who knows what everyone else is dealing with that he was ready to exploit. You wanted fireworks. You were hoping something like this would happen. The only thing you care about is the show."

"Yeah? You think so?" Deb asked angrily. "You should write an op-ed about it. That would be an awesome idea."

"Maybe I will." We stared at each other for a minute.

"Are you done?" she finally asked. "Because I have a question for you. If I only cared about the show, would I have fired the host?"

"You fired Joaquin?" Alex asked. "Because of Maddie?"

"Yes. He says nothing happened between them, and she claims the same, but it's obvious that his presence was causing her to act irrationally and put herself in danger. I fired him. Whether there was impropriety happening yet, it was likely headed that way."

"So . . . is there still a game?" I asked uncertainly. "We can't do the show without the host."

"You see my dilemma," Deb said flatly.

Wow. I wasn't sure what to say.

Deb picked up her clipboard and started to sort the papers. "There's a lot we can do during editing. I'll pull together some film magic. I poured my heart and soul into this show, and I'm not going to walk away from it now. I never should have let myself be convinced it was a good idea, but I did, so now I've got to fix it. And if I could find outside funding and convince the network to keep us going after a major accident and an outbreak of food poisoning, I can figure this out. I'm going to need a day or two to figure out the best way to restructure the remaining challenges, but after that we'll be good to go."

She tucked the neatened papers under the clip. "If I didn't know better, I'd say that curse is real. This island has been against me from the start. Equipment broken, things stolen, unpredictable weather. Maybe firing Joaquin was the sacrifice I needed to make for Lady Luck to get some wind at my back."

Deb shooed us out the door. "Now go on back. I've got challenges to re-design."

I'd come over here ready to reveal my satellite and the fact I knew someone on the crew was messing with me, but now I couldn't. It didn't feel as if I needed to, either. I'd been wrong—she did care about us, she just wasn't that good at executing the details.

"Well, that went better than I expected," Alex said on our way to the boat.

I nodded, and now that Deb was going to re-do the upcoming challenges, it meant I'd have time to search for the gold at least once more. I'd have to convince Cody it wasn't interfering with the game. If he was with me, I'd feel safe. And the best way to mute MrJackSparrow's threat was to find the gold first.

32

MAREN WAS WAITING FOR ME AT THE HUACA HUT WHEN
I got back. "Where have you been? I thought you'd tried to swim home."

She had watched Sean's video. "I think it's time we take a little bit more control of things. I'm going to call a team meeting."

We went to the fire pit and she banged the gong. "Announcing our first all-team meeting!" she called. "If you want to survive another day, you'll get your butts over here, and I'm not even exaggerating."

There were so few of us left, it didn't take long for everyone to arrive. I tried not to care that Porter was looking at me and trying to signal that he wanted to talk. I wasn't even going to consider it, especially not after Willa came up and hugged him from behind.

He shook her off in annoyance, but it was too late.

"There's some very messed-up stuff going on," Maren said when we had all gathered close enough to talk. "And I know we don't all like each other, but too bad. When you hear what Riley has to say, you're going to freak. Let's get this out in the open," she went on. "Last night, someone stole AJ's immunity coin out of his safe. And it wasn't me or Riley, which means it was one of you." She pointed at each of the Sol team members one by one. "So which one of you did it?"

"How could we get into his safe?" Rohan said. "You're crazytown if you think any of us did that. If someone actually took it, and you're sure that dingbat didn't just lose it somewhere, then it had to be someone on the crew."

"Maybe," Maren said. "Or maybe you convinced one of them to do it for you. That's your MO. Don't even try to deny it."

"No one is going to admit it, but we'll know who did it when they try to use it," Cody pointed out.

"Or maybe someone took it to screw AJ," Maren countered. "And then they chucked it in the ocean. Then what? How will we know who it is?"

"Forget it, Maren. Cody's right. No one's going to admit it," I said.

"I don't care if anyone admits it. I just want everyone on notice. I'm watching."

What good did watching anyone or anything do? I felt like all I'd been doing this entire time was watching everyone and it had gotten me exactly nowhere. I gave a quick report on the other things that were happening, starting with Joaquin's exit. When it came to telling them about Sean's video, I couldn't tell them I had my own Wi-Fi connection, so I let them think I'd seen it at the crew village.

Alex looked confused because she knew that wasn't true, but she let it slide.

"You know, I thought something fishy happened to that guy," Rohan said. "I'd seen some of his videos. He was never as lame as he was on top of that cliff. You don't get a million views if you're uncoordinated enough to slip and mess up a pretty straightforward jump."

"He really thinks someone tried to kill him?" Cody asked. "For real?"

"That's what he said in the video. He seemed pretty sure of it."

Out of all of us, big strong Cody looked the most concerned by this news. "Did he say anything else?"

"Yeah, he gave a weather report right after sharing the details of his attempted murder," Maren said sarcastically. "What other things could possibly be important enough to talk about after that?"

"It is very strange how so many things are going wrong," Rohan said. "I told you how people on the crew are quitting. They're scared. Not because of a so-called curse. They're scared they're going to get blamed for some of it. A drone is missing, and remember that camera that got smashed our first day? It cost something like a hundred grand, and someone here had to have done it."

"It's hard to say what is really going wrong, and what's being manufactured to make us think is going wrong. Deb could have been stirring up problems on purpose. Rohan wasn't wrong when he said they were pitting us against each other and hoping for drama."

"That's a little paranoid, don't you think?" Willa asked dismissively.

I stiffened.

"I mean, why bother? There's plenty of drama during the challenges."

That really wasn't true. The teams had been so mismatched on a few of the challenges that Deb had admitted she was going to have to resort to television magic.

"You're insane," Rohan told Willa, saving me the trouble of responding. "Or you're being intentionally argumentative. Out of all of us here, you're the one most familiar with Hollywood. You have to know this is how it works."

"I'm not an actress," Willa countered. "I'm an *influencer.* A trendsetter. It's a thing."

"Yeah? Well, you can literally go throw your trendsetting butt off Sean's cliff if you actually believe Deb hasn't been playing with us the whole time," Rohan said. "Someone's screwing with us, and it's only a matter of time before something goes really wrong, and one of us joins Sean in the hospital."

"Dammit," Cody said. He put his hat on and off, off and on. "Dammit!"

"Dude, chill," Maren said.

"It was me," he said. "I broke the camera. I also wrote up a couple of reports on stuff that happened after hours, when the cameras weren't around."

Everyone's expressions of outrage were perfectly synchronized.

"I didn't think anyone would get hurt! Man, this is terrible. I've been used."

"Who asked you to do it?" I asked. "Deb?"

"That's the thing," Cody said. "I don't know."

"Good idea," Maren said. "Play dumb. That'll really help."

"I mean it. I didn't actually see anyone. I got instructions of what to do and went through a hiding spot in the woods. Before we got here, someone left an envelope of cash—ten grand—at my house, with a note telling me I could keep the money no matter what, but if I wanted another ten grand after the show was over, all I had to do was a couple of things. I assumed it was a producer asking. If not Deb, someone at the network. It had to be. Who else would go through all that effort? When Rohan talked about creating drama, it all made sense. I just figured it was part of the show."

"I saw you there," I said, thinking back to that night. "Didn't I? That night we got so drunk."

"The night *you* got so drunk, yes. That day there was a note with those bottles, and all it said was 'Enjoy.'"

"Did you push Sean?" Maren asked. I tried to remember if I'd seen Cody on the beach, but I couldn't recall.

"No, ma'am. I certainly did not. That was someone else."

I looked at Maren. I'd just remembered something. "What if Sean saw someone at the cliff? Or what if he didn't actually see anything, but someone thought he did? Remember, the boat was on the other side. Sean might have had to walk past it to get to that cliff. Whoever was there might have thought they'd been seen, and they pushed him so he wouldn't tell."

"So what, though?" Rohan asked. "What's the problem with being seen? Yeah, if they weren't part of the film crew they weren't supposed to be there, but it's not worth killing someone over."

"Maybe it was," I said. "If it was someone who'd be out of place or someone we knew and we could tie them back to doing something they shouldn't be, it might be enough trouble."

"Yeah, I see your point," Rohan said, "but no show is worth injuring Sean like that. No way."

"What if we're looking at it wrong? What if it's not someone trying for ratings?" I asked. "What if it's someone who is here for the treasure? They may have killed before."

Cody nodded. "Maybe. Which is why we're going to continue to leave that treasure alone."

"Or maybe we can—"

Cody shook his head. "The game has to be our priority now. The gold is bringing too much trouble. It's gotten dangerous."

Before I could argue my side, Willa interrupted. "Blah, blah," she said. "I'm so over this treasure. You said yourself it would be impossible to find. I'm going to lie out before the afternoon rain arrives. Anyone want to come? Porter?" She got up and leaned over, flirtatiously reaching for his hand to pull him up.

The disconnect was stunning. We were sitting there talking about life and death and Willa was thinking about her tan.

"You go," Porter said impatiently to Willa. "I want to figure this out. It's important."

"Suit yourself," Willa said, and when she'd gone, Porter shot me a look as if expecting a reward for not running after her. Too little, too late.

I decided to get my notes to show Cody. He just needed some time to understand that at this point, a treasure hunt wouldn't be interfering with the show. Deb had plenty to do to occupy her for the next day or so. Our absence from camp wouldn't matter.

A few minutes later when someone came up the beach, I assumed it was her. But it wasn't. It was Phil. He was panting and out of breath. He'd rowed a canoe over by himself.

"Deb got a call from the network boss," he announced between gasps. "He found out that Deb fired Joaquin. Everyone has to leave the island tomorrow. No more show, no more game."

We were stunned into silence.

"I'm sorry guys, but this is the end."

33

"HOLD UP," ROHAN SAID. "NO GAME? NO SHOW?"

"Deb's on her way to tell you herself, but she needed some time to digest it," Phil confirmed.

"No money, either," I realized. "If there's no game, there can't be a prize."

"Exactly," Phil said. "But hear me out, because even though the show is history, I have a plan. I know you guys found something having to do with the treasure, something big, so let's follow up. Why not, right? This is our only chance."

We looked around at each other, shocked.

"Don't worry, I don't want treasure, but I can't have this show ruined. Something has to come out of it. This is my career, I'm totally stalled. Anyway, I can't split the reward with you; the crew had to sign a contract."

Cody turned to me. "It looks like the only way we can

come out of this mess with something good is if we find the gold. Do you think we can do it?"

I nodded. "I do. I really do."

"Then what are we waiting for?" Cody asked. "Let's go."

The only one who objected was Willa, but it didn't matter, because by the time we packed up our supplies the clouds had started to roll in. Once tanning wasn't an option, she realized if she didn't go she'd be left all alone.

I wasn't happy she was actually coming, especially when I saw her stuffing a fleece jacket into Porter's backpack. I sighed. So they *were* together.

Let it go, Riley.

Before we left, I pulled out the satellite. I didn't have AJ's email, so I sent a message to his Facebook instead. *We're going to the fourth marker. If you can, meet us there.*

Cody, the tracker, easily led the way to the fourth marker. When we got there, I pulled everything out: the map, AJ's notes, the Cipher. All of it. AJ and I had been so sure that flipping the direction from south to north was the right thing to do. But why hadn't we found anything?"

Going south from this point was the safer choice. Maybe the mapmaker was so tricky that he'd slid in a boring, easy clue to throw everyone off.

It was so hard to decide. If I chose wrong, it would be a classic example of Riley's Law—me, leading everyone astray on our final night here and throwing away our last chance.

I rubbed my necklace and thought of Miles. If anyone had been in tune with the island, it was him. A little too much, but still. He wouldn't choose a route that felt so counter to the spirit of the map. He'd never pull a move like Riley's Law.

But then I realized—I hadn't pulled a move like that in a long time, either. In fact, I'd been doing pretty great, and part of it was because I'd started to trust myself again.

And I felt like I should trust the reading of the map that was closest to its spirit, to the ways it had directed us thus far. North. We were going to go north a thousand varas, exactly the way AJ and I had, and maybe with this big group of people we'd see something that the two of us had missed.

How was it fair otherwise? Someone with a passing knowledge of treasure signs could stumble on this marker, interpret it straightforwardly and find the gold. That went against every bit of secrecy and trickery this hunt had stood for thus far.

No, a close reading of the map definitely advised flipping the directions, so that's what we would do.

"This way," I said, pointing north.

"Hold on," Cody said. "Look. The other guy, whoever dug this marker up first, went in the other direction." He showed us some divots in the dirt that revealed the path they'd taken.

"The exact opposite way?" Alex asked. "Yikes. What if we're wrong? If we go in the wrong direction, it's all over. This guy will find the gold and Deb will find us."

"Thanks for the vote of confidence," I said. Alex was right, though. I hesitated. Whoever was searching—MrJackSparrow or whoever it was—had been right on everything so far. What made me think I was smarter than him?

Not smarter, I thought. Just someone who pays attention. Who notices things and processes them. Just like Deb had said. And when I looked at the hunt as a whole, it didn't make sense not to include the map in the interpretation of this final marker. I stood by that.

"But I'm sure. Or nearly sure. It's northwest. That's the direction we're going to go."

And so we did, pushing through the scrub and under-brush. This time, there was no path to follow, not even a slight one, so it took longer. It was getting darker, too, and not only because the day was getting late. This time, a storm was definitely on its way. The forest had gone still, other than the small insistent whispers of wind that hinted bigger gusts were on their way.

"Do you guys hear that? Is that a drone?" Rohan called out. We all stopped and listened and stared up at the sky through the swaying palm fronds. Even through the sound of the wind I could tell it was definitely the buzz of a drone.

"Phil, I thought you said the show was finished? No more filming," Cody said.

"Yeah," he answered distractedly, scanning the sky. "The show's definitely dead. Deader than dead. Along with my career."

But he didn't seem overly upset about it. When the drone

came into view he quickly unzipped his rain jacket and began swinging it over his head.

Cody yanked it out of Phil's hand. "Not cool," he said. "It could be Deb looking for us. We didn't hightail it out of camp so some search-and-rescue team could jump in on the action."

Why had Phil tried to signal the drone? He was the one rushing us out of camp before Deb came by to stop us.

Cody and Phil went back and forth, getting heated, but it didn't sound like Phil was offering a real explanation. Maren didn't hesitate to jump in with her two cents, either. She had never seemed to like Phil.

Porter used the distraction to tentatively approach me. "Frisco," he said.

I clenched up hearing the nickname. "Nope. No way. You don't get to call me that anymore."

"Riley," he corrected. "Can you listen to me for a minute?"

The drone zoomed out of view. It wasn't clear if it had seen us—usually the drones hovered above for a minute or two after spotting its target. This one hadn't stopped moving, so maybe we were clear.

Cody backed away from Phil. He spun his finger in the air. "Let's move."

I fell in behind Cody. Porter didn't take that as a deterrent. He kept up, walking beside me and even moving a little bit ahead to hold back branches that Cody was pushing through.

"It wasn't what it looked like the other night," he said. "I swear. Willa told me she wanted to talk to me, she had something really serious to discuss, and the cabin was one of the only places it was private."

"Private," I repeated, looking at him incredulously. I stepped hard on a branch and it cracked. Cody turned and gave me a look of disapproval.

"Leave no trace," he warned. "Seriously. It's good etiquette."

"Did you really just say etiquette?" Maren called out. "As in what, forest manners? No one's here. No one is coming back. It's only us. Who are we being polite for?"

"The forest gods." Cody held his arms out wide, palms facing the sky. "Or Mother Nature, I don't know. It's a show of respect. You just do it, you don't ask why."

"Yes, privacy," Porter said to me, determined to press on. "And I said sure. Why wouldn't I? We're friends, and I didn't know what she wanted to talk about. It seemed serious."

I pushed through a branch, not holding it for him. He ducked.

"And you needed to talk in the dark?" I asked.

"It wasn't dark! I mean, it was when you arrived, but that's because the lights went out right before you got there. And then suddenly she was all over me, and then the lights went on again, and you were there . . ."

Willa had managed to move up the line, past Alex and Rohan and Phil, and now she was directly behind us. "Come on, Porter," she said, almost lazily. "You know that's not how it happened."

Porter jerked his arm. I hadn't seen it, but Willa must have reached out for him. "Willa, what the hell? You know I liked Riley this whole time. I *told* you. We talked about it. Why are you doing this?"

Porter's expression was a bit wild—angry and confused. "Riley, please, I don't know why she's doing this, but don't listen to her."

"Yes, Riley, definitely don't listen to me." She rolled her eyes exaggeratedly, batted her eyelashes, and twisted a strand of hair around her finger, amping up her usual flirtatiousness to a level that bordered on absurd. "Why would you? I'm sooooo unattractive. There's no way Porter would be interested in me, right?"

"Okay, wow," I said. Even Porter was looking at her in disbelief. "This is all getting a little too nuts."

"That's what I've been trying to tell you," Porter insisted. "It *is* nuts." He lowered his voice. "Specifically, *she* is nuts."

I held up a hand. "I need both of you to stop talking."

I wasn't sure what to do. Porter seemed sincere, and the fact that he was disputing Willa's account right in front of her made me think he was telling the truth. He certainly wasn't trying to play both of us. But even if his story was accurate, it still left me feeling disappointed. Why would Willa have turned on me like that? She'd gone after Porter with such brutal precision, knowing what it would do to me.

And it had hurt. Possibly even more than Porter's role in the whole charade.

I couldn't deal with the two of them, but luckily we had reached the clearing that AJ and I had been so sure held the treasure. "Let me finish this, okay? I promise I'll listen later, but right now, I really have to do this."

I put everyone to work. "We're looking for anything unusual. Something man-made, for example. If this truly is the site of the treasure, then there will be a marker with a triangle on it."

But our search didn't produce anything. Was this how it would end? A wild-goose chase with nothing to show for it? Alex came over to see the map. "How do you know there will be a triangle symbol at the treasure site?"

I showed her the line of text and symbols on the map. "See that bisected triangle? That's what that means."

"So treasure symbols are universally recognized? If someone on another hunt saw this, they'd interpret it to mean the same thing?"

"Yes. But sometimes signs can have multiple meanings. It's all about context. If it's in a certain spot it might mean one thing, but when it's paired with another symbol, the meaning could change."

Alex seemed impressed. "How do you know all this stuff? It's pretty amazing. Show me something else."

"Okay, well see this bottom line of text? It's separate from the others, so that's a clue to look at it carefully. And because the triangle is there, it probably means this line of text is about the final step. The word *dig*, well, that's obvious. The circle with the dot in it means gold."

Alex laughed. "Funny, it's such a boring sign for gold. Look at how fancy the eagle is, but the gold is just a plain old circle."

"It might be plain but it does double duty. It also means three, because—"

I stopped. Signs that mean more than one thing. Context. I flipped through the Cipher for the page that discussed the number three, and there it was: symbols for three, depending how they were used, could also mean triple the distance.

"You guys, I figured it out! We stopped too soon. We're supposed to triple the distance—a thousand varas—which means we need to go another two thousand."

The wind was gaining strength. Leaves and bits of twigs rushed along the ground, swept up in a current of air. It almost appeared as if the forest was picking itself apart and fleeing.

"Did you say we have another two miles to go?" Willa asked. "In the dark, in a storm? No way. That's it—I'm out."

Her tone startled me. A few minutes before, she had been simpering and pouting but in an abrupt shift her voice had become clear and decisive. Even her demeanor was different; all that flirtatiousness had evaporated.

"I'm not getting paid enough to do this crap," she said. "There's no camera here, and even if there was, it's not like anyone is going to see any of the footage anyway. What am I mucking around in the jungle for when I could be over at the crew village, hanging out with Justin? Phil, I'm sorry, but the deal's off."

Everyone seemed as shocked as I was. None of us said anything, aware that something big was being revealed but not quite sure exactly what.

Finally Rohan did the honors. "Hey, man," he said to Phil. "You'd best spill it."

At least Phil had the decency to look embarrassed. "Well, uh, you see—"

"Deb paid me to come here," Willa cut him off. She said it factually. Not ashamed or embarrassed, simply said it, the way she might have said *I live in Los Angeles.* "I'm not really a player. She brought me in to add a little spice where it was needed, make things interesting."

"Making you what, a lightning rod?" I asked.

Willa cocked her head. "More like a lure. They gave me all your names ahead of time so I could look everyone up online. Facebook, Instagram, Twitter, VSCO, Snap. I found out what you guys like—brunch, hunting, hiking, and yes, football. Of course I knew about Murch's stupid blog, by the way. A basic search gave me *that.* I didn't even have to try."

A certain amount of pride seeped in as she described her cyberstalking skills. She must be better at reading people online than she was in person, because I sensed a wave of anger gathering from the rest of us and it didn't stop her from talking. Or maybe she didn't care.

"But more importantly, I could tell what most of you were missing."

She pointed to me. "Friends."

I guess we weren't sugarcoating things at this point, but strangely, I didn't mind. My time on the island had apparently given me some protective armor. I nodded. Why not? It was true.

Porter was next. "To be treated normally. Not to have anyone pity you as *the guy who broke his back.*"

Porter's cheeks reddened, but I was probably the only one who noticed because Willa had moved quickly to Alex.

"Unconditional support," Willa said, and then softened. "I was glad to know about your past, Alex, because you didn't deserve any of that. I tried to be there for you."

Alex was spitting mad. "And now what? I'm supposed to be grateful? Are you kidding? Phony support doesn't count," Alex shot back. "That's the worst kind."

"But it wasn't phony!" Willa exclaimed. She scanned our faces, seemingly noticing for the first time we weren't impressed with her revelation. "Oh, come on. Don't hold this stuff against me. All of you came here to play a role, too. I'm just one of the few who got paid for it."

"Well, I certainly can't be mad at you, darlin'," Cody said. "I haven't exactly been straight with y'all."

"Thanks, Cody." Willa gave him a hug, circling his waist with both arms.

"So you're admitting it!" Porter exclaimed. "The whole

thing with me and you in the cabin was a setup, exactly like I've been saying. Tell her. Come on, tell Riley that's what happened."

Willa nodded. Again, I had to admire how little shame she had. "It was."

I thought back to the night when he first started ignoring me. I wondered if that had something to do with Willa, too. "The night of the truth game," I said. "Why were you so mad?"

"Willa said she heard something about how you were on the show because you knew Deb, and she'd given you information about all of us to create story lines."

"So, basically, she accused me of what she was actually doing and then you believed her without asking me about it?"

"Well, when you put it like that . . ." Porter looked away sheepishly.

Maren did a slow clap. "That's not for you, faker," she said to Willa. "It's for me, for being the only person here not to get taken in by a con artist."

"Actor," Willa corrected. "But I get it. No hard feelings on my end. This might surprise you, but I was rooting for you. After everything you went through—"

"Oh, no you don't," Maren said. "I'm shutting that down right now. You don't get to talk about me. You can root for me silently if that's what you're into, but I'm done." She smeared her palms together and then flicked her fingers toward Willa. "Buh-bye."

It wasn't the first time I was jealous of Maren's ability to be so quick and decisive. I, on the other hand, was all jumbled up. My mind went back to the second night on the island when we'd gone swimming, the first time Willa and I had done anything together. I thought I'd felt the tiny seeds of a new friendship growing. And then that day we'd searched all day for the treasure, when she'd encouraged me to go for Porter. It had felt genuine. How could I have been so stupid? Was I doomed to trust the wrong people no matter where I met them?

I locked eyes with Willa. "Was any of it real?" I asked her.

"Riley, come on," Maren said. She tugged at my arm, trying to break my eye contact with Willa. "Don't waste your time looking at the *why* behind all her tricks and lies. The reason she did those things didn't matter. She did them. That's the important part."

But I disagreed. The w*hy* was important, and I was thinking of my own history. I *had* written that op-ed. It was a fact; I'd done it. And now that I had some time and space to reflect on it, I could see how the message could have been interpreted the way it was. But the *why* in my case should have mattered a little bit. My intention hadn't been interpreted correctly and that should have been part of the story.

Willa came over to me and gently put both her hands on my shoulders. The gesture felt motherly, an odd way to describe it, considering she'd just spent the last twelve days conspiring against me and, in general, behaving like the least maternal inhabitant of our little lawless island.

"Riley, I thought you of all people would be able to figure out what was going on. Boys are dumb—"

"Hey!" Porter objected. We ignored him.

"—so I knew he'd never notice any inconsistencies, but honestly, I kept waiting for you to call me out on it."

Maybe it was because I'd been starved for compliments for so long, but I took it in without even considering a *buh-bye* brush-off.

She reached for Porter's backpack, sliding it off his arm as if she had every right to it. Oh, right. Her fleece jacket. "Sorry to leave you all. Not. But you'll be fine without me."

"You can't go back," Phil said. "It's late. And dark. What if you fell and hurt yourself? What if you got lost? How would we find you?"

Willa pulled a small black disc about the size of a quarter from her fleece pocket. "Lucky thing you gave me a tracker." She pressed a button and a light blinked red. "There. Problem solved. Deb will be monitoring me, so if I stop or anything terrible happens, she'll know. I'll be fine."

"Pirates," Phil blurted.

Willa patted him on the cheek. "You're sweet, but I'll be fine, and honestly, at this point I'd rank a pirate raid as only slightly worse than whatever this is."

Seeing the tracker reminded me how curious it had been when the drone had found us the other day, way over on the other side of the island. Now I knew how we'd been discovered—Willa must have brought her tracker along.

"It's been fun," Willa told us. "And it's been real, but I'm sorry to say it hasn't been real fun."

"Wait," I said. "Can you do something for me?"

She considered it. "Depends."

"You owe me one, Willa. You owe all of us."

"I'm listening."

"Find AJ when you get to the village. Tell him to check Facebook. It's really important. I sent him a message, because I don't think he should miss out on this."

Willa laughed and looked around at the darkening sky and the branches that had nearly hit us. "Oh, yes, that would be a real shame," she said. "But fair enough."

"And tell him this, too: we're tripling the distance of the last sign. Okay? Got it?"

"Got it." She saluted us and turned to leave.

"One other thing," I called. "You said you were one of the few who were paid. We already know about Cody. Was there anyone else?"

"Sean." Willa didn't elaborate, and in a few seconds, she was gone, swallowed up into the jungle.

Maren turned immediately on Phil. "Was there anyone who *wasn't* paid to be here? Because right now my bank account is feeling a little ignored. You don't think I would have spied for you like Cody did? Ten grand? I'd have done whatever you wanted for half that."

I caught Cody's eye and gave him the signal to get moving. We'd wasted enough time.

Before addressing Maren, Phil stared regretfully after Willa. "I still think she should have stayed," he said, although he didn't think so strongly enough to go after her. He fell in line behind Rohan and I moved quickly to join him. I wasn't ready to talk to Porter yet.

"Are you going to explain yourself or what?" Maren demanded of Phil.

"You should be happy we inserted some paid moles into the game," Phil said. "It meant better odds for each of you. As paid employees, Willa and Sean were ineligible to receive any prize, so it worked in your favor, if you look at it that way."

"I'm not looking at it that way, just so you know," Maren replied.

Phil sighed. "You have to understand we'd never done this before. We had no idea if anything would come of collecting twenty kids on an island in front of a bunch of cameras. What if nothing interesting happened? We needed to make sure we could pull together some story lines."

Story lines. That was the word Porter had used with me the night of the Truth challenge when he suspected Deb of feeding me story lines. I remembered how she fell apart after Joaquin's departure, and how she said it had been a mistake when she'd allowed herself to be convinced to do this show.

"Phil, who persuaded Deb to film the show here? Was it you?"

"What?" He looked uncomfortable. "Why would you ask that?"

Someone laughed. It was an eerie sound and it came from behind us; I turned, expecting to see Willa. Had she changed her mind, and come back to taunt us?

But it wasn't Willa.

It was a woman, and I recognized her immediately—the cast member at the truth challenge who'd seemed so familiar. She laughed again, casually, as if it was the most normal thing in the world for all of us to come across each other in the middle of the jungle on a night where a storm was brewing. "Just tell her, Phil."

"Who the *F* are you?" Maren demanded. "Phil, what's going on here?"

I didn't need Phil to answer. I knew where I'd seen her before.

"Serena," I said in surprise. "Right? You're Miles's girlfriend, Serena. Oh, wow. This is . . . unexpected."

I could hardly believe it: Miles Kroger's girlfriend—or more specifically, his treasure hunting partner—was here on the island.

Things were starting to make sense.

34

"HELLO, RILEY," SERENA SAID. SHE HAD THE ADVANTAGE of surprise, and she was holding a drone controller, which must have been how she found us.

"Whoa," Maren said. "You guys know each other?"

Serena nodded. "We spent some time together two years ago." She smiled again at an inside joke. "But we've talked since then."

I was slow today. "Wait, are you . . . ?"

"MrJackSparrow, at your service."

"But . . ." I trailed off.

"The *mister* threw you off? You can be anyone you want online. You of all people should know that. I was surprised to see you on the forum. I warned Phil that someone was popping up on Smokey Joe's thread, asking all kinds of specific questions. We thought it was AJ. The girl I met two summers ago wasn't particularly interested in treasure."

"How do you know Phil?"

"We're cousins. The show was my idea, actually. I needed to get back here, Phil wanted to get out of Alaska, and voilà! It was perfect."

"Did Deb know?"

"Deb? No. No one knows. I was searching for the treasure during my time off."

Oh, that explained the boat.

"It took me a long time to find all those clues that you guys breezed through. The last one—I couldn't figure it out. I was sure we should go south. Why'd you decide to go north?"

I wasn't going to give anything away. Sure, I knew her, and now that I saw who MrJackSparrow was, we weren't in danger, but that didn't mean I was ready to trust her.

"I followed the signs."

"So did I," she said insistently. "But my reading said south. So why do you think we should go north?"

I ignored her question. "Why did you threaten me? With that message on the site."

"Threaten you? That wasn't a real threat. Just some motivation. I wanted some time to catch up. But it's a good thing you didn't listen because I may have been headed in the wrong direction."

Serena was a lot more intense than I remembered. She had been the normal, reasonable one when I'd been here last. Now she seemed as intense as Miles had been; she'd picked up his torch and was carrying it for him. But there was an important difference between the two of them. She didn't seem to be doing it for Miles or for any sort of duty to the gold. She was doing it strictly for herself.

"So we're just letting her join us?" Cody asked. "I mean, sure, why not? Everything else is crazy."

"Let's just find the gold," I said. "That's what's important, and Serena knows things. She might be able to help."

We arrived at a rocky area near the northernmost point of the island. This was more like it. Lots of places a marker, and a treasure, could hide. Our best shot was along the rock wall.

Beside me, Cody stiffened.

"Did you hear that?" he asked.

We all stood still, listening for something other than the sound of the forest. Then, without warning, there was a whoosh from the woods and Cody and Rohan were body-slammed to the ground. It happened immediately and in slow motion at the same time. It was hard to understand what was happening.

Men emerged all around us.

"Stay where you are! We've got you surrounded," one of them called out.

He turned on a flashlight and waved it toward the water. There was an answering light in the distance.

Pirates.

35

THE MEN QUICKLY OVERPOWERED THE REST OF US. THEY
tossed our bags in a pile on the nearby beach, and then tied
our hands together and forced us to splash out to the waiting
boat. It was larger than the motorboats that had shuttled us
back and forth to Challenge Island—this one had a cargo
area beneath the deck that was accessed through a square
hatch. One of the men flipped the hatch open and pushed
Cody toward it first.

"Now the rest of you. Get down there and stay quiet," he
ordered.

What would happen to us? Panic had turned my blood
ice cold. Were we going to die? Was this *it*? I thought about
all the times in the past year I wanted to disappear. Now I
couldn't imagine not fighting to stay alive.

I nearly slipped down the ladder, bumping into Alex. She
barely reacted, and her face was blank, defeated. What had

happened to that fighting spirit? We needed her to snap out of it and become her warrior self again.

From the noise overhead, it was clear some of them were leaving. One of the larger guys sat at the top of the ladder where he could watch us and keep an eye on the island. He wasn't huge, but he could definitely give Cody a run for his money. The others had taken the gun, but he wouldn't need it; he was strong enough to handle a bunch of bound prisoners.

"Against the wall," he told us, almost unnecessarily. There wasn't too much space for us to go anywhere else. I was next to Porter, so close that I could feel his body moving in and out with each breath. I put my head on his shoulder. A few hours ago I'd been doing my best to avoid him, but now everything had changed. I didn't even want to consider that we might not have time together outside this dungeon.

"What do you want?" Phil asked the pirate.

"What do you think we want? The gold."

So much for AJ's conviction that pirates were simply ordinary robbers. These guys had been watching and waiting, and they wanted the treasure. I tried not to worry that none of them had covered their faces. It was a bad sign they weren't afraid we could identify them.

"Which one of you is going to show us where to find it?" the pirate asked. "And don't lie. We know you are following the map."

Phil reluctantly raised his hand and I felt a flush of gratitude, and then fear. I didn't want one of the only adults to be separated from us. Phil pointed to Serena. "I need her, too."

"But—" I started to say something, but Phil shook his head sharply, signaling me to be quiet. I didn't particularly want to leave the safety of my friends, but on the other hand, these bandits weren't going to let us go until they had the treasure. If I helped, it might go faster. But Phil shook his head again and mouthed the word *no*.

The pirate pulled Phil and Serena up and pushed them on the deck. There was a splash and then the sound of all three of them walking through the water.

A few minutes later, we heard the guard come back. He paced on deck, not bothering to come below.

"Y'all, our best chance is to get this guy down here and then rush him," Cody said.

Rohan disagreed. "At least one of them has a gun, you saw that, right?" he pointed out. "Maybe this guy does, too."

"Who needs a gun?" Alex said. Her voice was tinged with hysteria. "We're all tied up. If they want to kill us, they could bring the boat out to deep water and sink it. We'd all drown!"

That shut everyone up. What would we say? Each of us seemed to be coming to the understanding that our situation was dire. My satellite had a tiny bit of juice left. If I could get to our bags somehow, I might be able to use it. I wondered if Willa had made it back to camp, and if she had, if she'd bothered to give AJ the message.

"If Willa told AJ—" I started to say.

The man on deck stomped above our heads, a command to keep silent, and we stayed that way for what felt like an eternity. It could have been an hour, or two, or four. There was no way of knowing. Then suddenly, on deck, the guard called out to someone. There was a thud as someone jumped on board, and then words were exchanged in Portuguese.

"Shhh!" Rohan said.

His mouth dropped open. "Hey. They aren't pirates," he hissed.

"Say what?" Cody asked, voicing my own disbelief.

"I think they were hired," Rohan said, listening again. "Wait, this is crazy. Serena and Phil aren't prisoners. It sounds like these guys are actually working for Serena." He paused again, his expression turning from disbelief to anger. "You've got to be kidding me. All of them are looking for the gold right now, together. Phil, Serena, and the pirates. Jesus."

"What about us?" I asked.

"Hold on." Rohan listened intently, and then explained what he heard. "This whole kidnap thing was a show. They staged it so we wouldn't know they were in on it."

Maren snorted. "A show within a show. The irony here is killing me."

"Don't say *killing*," Alex snapped, momentarily coming to life.

"Actually, this is the best news we could get," I said. "If they went through all this trouble to get us out of the way, then they must be planning to let us go. It would have been much easier for them to get rid of us without the charade. Right? Do you see what I'm saying? I'm right, aren't I?"

Cody nodded. "Logical," he said. "And, yes, hopefully true."

"We can't sit here and let them get away with it," Alex said. I was glad she was getting her spirit back.

The voices outside stopped, then there was another voice in the distance.

"Shhhh," Rohan said, listening. "Hold up. I think they found something. Someone's asking for an axe and a shovel."

Something was dragged across the deck, followed by more splashing. We all held our breath and tried to figure out if they'd left.

"Are they gone?" Alex asked. "Both of them?"

"Sounds like it," Rohan said. "No footsteps."

Then there was a scuttling noise overhead, moving quickly across the deck. It grew louder as it came closer. I recoiled, prepared for the worst. Suddenly, the door slammed open.

It was AJ. Willa had pulled through! She'd told him where we were.

AJ scurried into the cabin. Nearly all of us cried out in relief when he began to cut our ties loose with a pocketknife.

"Got your message," he said when he reached me. And then in typical AJ fashion, he focused right away on the treasure. "I told you the smart money was north. Deb's here, too, with Harry and the infrared camera. Deb's in a rage about

Phil. At first we couldn't figure out what was going on, so we watched them for a while, and man, I would not want to be that guy when Deb finally gets her hands on him. It took me a long time to figure out where they'd stashed all of you. But guess what? It looks like they found the final marker, the one with the triangle."

I told AJ about Serena, and how she was Phil's cousin, the mastermind of the whole plan, as well as MrJackSparrow.

"She's toast," AJ said. "Come on, let's go."

I was torn. Phil and Serena had found the triangle—the final sign! Everything we'd been working for. But who knows how close to death we had just been. Shouldn't we escape while we had the chance?

"Me and Cody can take these guys," Rohan said, cracking his knuckles. "They got us before because they caught us by surprise, but now it's our turn."

"Alex and I will go to the crew village and call the police," Maren offered. "We'll tell them exactly where to go."

Alex nodded. "We'll take the dingy tied to the stern." She appraised Maren. "As long as you can handle some speed rowing?"

"I can handle it," Maren said.

"Wait! the satellite," I remembered. Maren knew what I meant—no one else did, not yet anyway—and she got my backpack off the beach.

"There isn't too much battery left," I warned. "Save it until you're far enough away and you know you can get a signal."

"Aye, aye, Cap'n," Maren said. She and Willa boarded the dingy and disappeared into the night, just a couple of badass girls on a routine rescue mission. I turned to Porter.

"What are you looking at me for?" he said. "I'm going wherever you go."

"Very sweet," AJ said. "That means you're coming with me, because if I know Riley, she needs to go find the treasure."

"Oh, don't you worry," Porter said, pulling me close so my face was pressed against his chest. His heart was thumping almost as fast as mine. "I know Riley just as well as you, and of course she's going to find that gold."

I was standing between two people who had just said they knew me. They *knew* me! And so did Willa and Maren and . . . it was overwhelming. I'd come here lost and alone, but now I was part of a group who actually cared about me.

"Ready?" AJ asked me, holding out his hand. "Fist bump."

I took a breath before holding out my own.

"Ready," I said. I took a breath. "Let's finish this."

36

DEB AND HARRY WERE HIDING IN A GROVE OF TREES BY
the sheer rock wall. The same place, most likely, where the
pirates had concealed themselves before they'd jumped us.
Harry lowered his camera—that's how happy he was to see
us—and Deb squeezed each of us tight. It was ironic, but
throughout most of the game I'd trusted Joaquin way more
than Deb. He turned out to be a slime, and she was the one
who'd had our backs the whole time.

"You guys . . ." she said in a whisper. The wind had all but
disappeared. "I had no idea that Phil . . . you've been in such
danger." She threw her hands up. "I don't even know what to
say."

"Say it later," AJ advised. "Right now we've got gold to
find."

We watched Phil and Serena for a few minutes, evaluating our next move. It was clear Serena was in charge. Phil

had the gun now, but she was the one giving the orders and directing everyone else. She was getting more and more agitated. The gold fever had definitely passed from Miles to her.

"It should be here." She was visibly angry.

"We've looked for hours. It's not here, but you still owe us our money," one of the men told her. "You need to pay us."

"No one is leaving until we find it, so keep looking. Harder."

The pirate left her to talk to his men. None of them looked happy. The air was oddly quiet. After thrashing around for hours, a strange stillness had arrived, as if we were in the eye of a hurricane. It felt eerie, as if the storm was holding its breath and getting ready to let loose even harder.

"Serena, calm down," Phil said.

"Never in the history of being told to calm down has anyone ever actually calmed down, Phil, so shut it."

"I'm just trying to say—"

"I knew it was a mistake to involve you," Serena ranted. "Don't even start, Phil. We are not giving up. None of us. Not them, not you, and definitely not me."

"It's the middle of the night, it's dark out, we'll never find it," Phil said. He sounded reasonable, as if none of this was bonkers. "Let's get back to the boat, untie the kids, tell them we escaped."

"Quit, you mean?" Serena snapped.

"The film equipment needs to be packed, the arena dismantled. You can come back while all that's happening. The kids will have gone home, so it'll only be you here."

Deb cursed under her breath. "That bastard," she said. "Using our show—*my* show—like this. I'm going to kill him."

Porter looked around. "Uh oh. Look—the pirates are drifting off. What if they go back to the boat? If they find out we're gone, we'll lose our edge of surprise."

"We should sneak attack Phil and Serena now," Rohan said. "I'll count to three, and then we rush them."

"They've got a gun, Rohan," Deb said. "I can't authorize a move like that."

"I'm with Rohan," Cody said. "We jump 'em now, before they're expecting it."

Serena was still berating Phil. "You don't get it, do you?" she said. "I am not leaving this spot without the gold. I've been waiting for it for six long years. It was almost mine. It would have been, if he hadn't—"

Serena broke off. I realized it then. She had killed Miles. Of course she had. Miles always intended to give the treasure to the government and collect the bounty. Serena, as I well knew, had plans to splash the gold around on the black market. She and Miles must have argued about it and things had gotten heated to the point of no return, or even worse, she'd plotted his death. How she did it hardly mattered; she'd been the one responsible, and then she'd plotted her chance to get back here.

Cody had started to count. "One, two . . ."

Rage blew up inside me and I felt a force pushing me to move, and before the third count, I was pushing my way out of the bushes.

"You!" I said, to Serena. "You killed Miles!"

Phil looked from me to his cousin in shock, and taking advantage of his surprise, Serena lunged for the gun. They struggled.

Suddenly, there was a loud crack, and I watched in horror as Phil slumped over. Blood started to seep onto his Hawaiian shirt, turning the white flowers black. He clutched his side.

Porter grabbed me from behind and threw me to the ground.

The only pirate who'd stayed behind made an attempt to grab the gun from her, but there was another shot, and then he, too, collapsed.

Rohan and Cody ran for Serena. Her hands were shaking, but she still had the gun.

"Don't do it, ma'am," Cody said, holding his hands out. "Just put the gun down. Nice and slow. No one else needs to get hurt."

"No," Serena said. And then she repeated the word over and over as she backed into the woods. "No, no, no."

Phil was starting to cough up blood. We looked at each other. Go after Serena, or help Phil? There was no choice. Even Deb came over to help. Each of us dropped to our knees beside Phil, and Cody quickly tied a tourniquet around Phil's bicep. He'd been hit in the arm just above his elbow, a deep wound, and the bullet had gotten his side, too.

"Keep pressure on this," Cody told Rohan. He had me rip up the injured pirate's shirt, and instructed Porter on how to tie additional tourniquets.

"Help me with this guy," Cody said. The pirate was unconscious, but he was still breathing. "Jesus. He's in bad shape."

There were lights in the distance—a boat. Rescue was imminent. And then, even better, the sounds of a helicopter. A few hours ago this man had kidnapped us, but now that he was so near death, I hoped he got help.

"There might be a doctor on the helicopter," I said. "They'll know what to do."

Cody shook his head. "I don't think he's going to make it."

I didn't know what to feel. To be so close to someone about to die was overwhelming. Cody sat back on his heels. "I'll take it from here," he said. "I've seen plenty of life and death on the ranch. It's not pretty."

I leaned back on my heels, unsure of what to do. "Go," Cody said. "Just go."

I stumbled up to my feet. Porter and Rohan were busy with Phil, who was conscious—that was a good sign. I wasn't quite ready to think of Phil as someone who'd betrayed us. To me, he was still the easygoing Phil I'd known from the past two weeks, and I didn't want that person to die. If he lived, there would be time enough to be angry at him.

AJ hadn't given a thought to either Phil or the pirate, as far as I could tell. He was busy examining the rock face.

"The gold should be here somewhere," he said, pointing to a triangle carved deeply into the stone. "I don't understand it. That sign tells us it's nearby."

Out of the corner of my eye, I saw Rohan stand up. He shook his head. "The pirate didn't make it."

A light from the helicopter flashed across the rock face, and for a second it glinted off my pendant. I touched it. *Come on, Lady Luck.* A gust of wind from the helicopter's blades knocked a branch into the rocks, and it sliced off a chunk.

Wait, what was that, in the rock wall? Was there something there? A crack, maybe. I walked over, as if in a trance. There was a light illuminating it, but it almost seemed to be coming from inside the rock, not from the helicopter's searchlight.

Seven must die. Six had died already. I looked at the motionless body of the pirate. Now there had been seven.

Was the island finally ready to reveal its hiding place?

I pressed my face to the crack and looked inside. A cavern, much like the one housing the shrine, and inside that: gold. Piles and piles of coins and statues and chalices, and yes, jewelry, too. All glowing gold.

We'd done it! We'd found the treasure.

One Year Later

THE LIMO CAME TO PICK ME UP AT THE AIRPORT, A GIANT

hulking thing that was more of a bus than a car. I was the last to arrive in LA, and before I'd even reached the sidewalk, Maren and Alex and Maddie were leaning half way out of the windows screaming my name.

Everyone was inside the car, and why not—there was plenty of room. I squeezed past AJ, Cody, and Rohan. I hugged all of them, saving a smile for Porter who was sitting in the back row. I didn't need to hug him yet; we'd just seen each other last weekend. We spent virtually every weekend together now. Willa was a frequent guest in my New York City apartment, too—we'd become friends after the island, real friends this time. She still lived in LA but she was applying to art school in New York, so if I stayed there for another year we planned to get an apartment together. People asked me afterward how I had forgiven her, but I didn't consider her behavior on the island a personal betrayal. Finding out she'd been placed among us to push our buttons explained away so many inconsistencies. I chose to focus on the good moments we'd shared together.

She'd meet up with all of us later tonight, which was going to be interesting. Not everyone—Maren, specifically—had forgiven Willa. Of course, of all my new friends Willa had been the one who'd loved the meme backstory the most. She'd known about it ahead of time through her sleuthing, but she hadn't realized how much the online notoriety had bothered me.

"You've been looking at it all wrong," she told me the first time I'd visited her in LA after the island. We were at the Santa Monica pier, doing some of those things I'd imagined us doing. "You and those losers at your old school are the only ones who care about why this meme was created in the first place. The rest of the world doesn't care about that. That picture just means *I can't even* now. That's it. Nothing more. You should embrace it. I mean, why not? It's classic."

In fact, it was Willa who had helped me pick out the red dress I was wearing today. "That's your color now," she'd told me. "Make it your own."

I adjusted the strap nervously. I'd gotten used to the color, but it was a little more form-fitting than I would have chosen if Willa hadn't been there pushing me. We were going to an early screening of Deb's new documentary, the one I'd spent the past year working on. It was a story of the gold, but it was our story, too.

My parents were flying down from San Francisco. Everything that had happened between me and my father felt very small in comparison to what I'd just gone through, so we'd been able to move on after I'd returned, triumphant. Although that's the funny part about families: when we were reunited after the island, it was hard to remember that there was anything to move on from. I was sure issues would bubble up again, but for now, my father and I had managed to find respect for each other and our different ways of doing things. It helped that I'd found the gold, too, of course.

Phil would be at the theater tonight as well. It had taken a long time, but he'd recovered from the gunshot if not his cousin's betrayal.

I had gone to see him in the hospital after that crazy night.

"I had no idea Serena was capable of any of this," Phil had said. His throat was raw. Deb told me he'd spent much of his first few days out of recovery crying.

"My father believes that gold fever catches certain people and doesn't let go. It happened to Miles first, and Serena became a victim, too. I felt it a little bit, myself."

"I had no idea she was so far gone. I think she arranged the food poisoning, too," Phil said. "Some of the crew was hit, but not her. She was happy—and prepared—for the extra time to search."

"You're a good guy, Phil, but things got out of hand. Do you think she was . . . intentionally . . . aiming for you?" I asked tentatively.

"I don't even know. Maybe. Maybe not."

"I guess it's up to you to choose what you want to believe," I told him.

Belief and the power of choosing what to believe was a major part of my own story, it turned out. I'd worked it into the documentary, too, and it made sense: all treasure hunters, in their own way, choose the signs to follow.

Serena was still on the run, but I had no doubt that wherever she was, she would have followed the reports of the treasure's discovery. The cave had been full of amazing things. Statues, masks, chalices, and jewelry. I thought back to that first conversation with Sean back on the helicopter after we'd found out we'd have the option to search. As it turned out, there would have been a few things for him to pocket, but he was doing just fine without any of the gold. He'd recovered, and his role on the show seemed to have brought him a wave of new followers, which were probably more valuable than treasure to him anyway.

I could relate to that sentiment. Willa had come to the cave the next day—everyone had, all the players and crew—and after we'd all had a chance to marvel and exclaim over our discovery, she'd directed a mini-photo shoot like the one she'd fantasized about. Her sharp visual eye was the reason that an Internet search of my name now would immediately pull up a picture of me smiling in amazement amidst the gold: holding it, wearing it, and draped in it. And yes, there was a crown. *I can't even* had a whole new meaning now.

After the discovery, the rest of the night had been a blur, but the next day we met with representatives from the Brazilian government to show them what we'd found. Deb had never gotten the proper permits—intentionally—but after the discovery she had negotiated with the government for their usual bounty payment. She'd worked it out so that it was split between me, AJ, Maren, Alex, Cody, Porter, and Rohan, with her production company getting a share as well. We were each going to clear a little over two hundred and fifty thousand, a substantial surprise, considering we'd expected to all split that amount. I'd planned to give my allocation to Maren, but she'd refused it. She had enough to pay for college and beyond, so I'd asked to have my slice of the reward go to a charity in San Francisco that focused on mental health. I'd given it in Miles's name.

I looked around at all of us sitting in the limo. It was a nice bookend to our arrival on the helicopter. We'd all come so far since then—me, especially. I'd been right, finding the treasure did help shift my reputation, but that wasn't even the best thing to have come out of the experience. The best thing was that I'd found myself again.

"Now that the movie is done, what are you going to do next?" Maren asked me. She was wearing a special T-shirt, picked out just for the event because it had a couple of "fancy" references. This shirt was a wordy one: *Ain't no party like a Gatsby party, because a Gatsby party don't stop until two people are dead and everyone is disillusioned.*

I touched Maren's hair. It was brown now, not black. I'd gotten my answer after all.

She pulled back and slapped my hand away. "Hands off the goods, creeper," she told me. She'd kept the colored tips—pink, today—admitting that the black dye had been "a little extra."

"To answer your question, I'm going to Black Rock one last time," I said. "Deb and I are going to do some wrap-up interviews."

"Ugh, better you than me." Maren shuddered. "I'm happy I'll never have to see that place again."

I felt differently. My time on the island had been a turning point. It was why I hadn't hesitated when Deb had asked me to work on the film with her.

"I have all this footage," Deb had said. "I have to do something with it, and I think it's better suited for a documentary anyway. I can tell the story. Yours, mine, Phil's. Our stories are all intertwined with the treasure now. It's only fair that we be the ones to tell it. You've got a storyteller's eye, and I want you to help me."

Agreeing had been one of the best decisions I'd ever made. That, and choosing to give Porter a second chance. I'd learned I could trust other people again—including myself.

Porter had heard Maren's question. "So what *are* you going to do next?"

"Probably join AJ at Harvard," Alex guessed. "After the gap year you had, and the résumé you have now, any school would be crazy not to admit you."

"Yeah, I don't know about that. Harvard's pretty far out of reach," I said. "But that's okay. You know what? I love New York. NYU has a pretty amazing film school, and one of the film editors I worked with said she'd write a rec for me there, so I might have a shot . . ."

I shrugged. I didn't really know what I was going to do, but for the first time, I wasn't worried about it. I'd figure it out as I went.

Life is funny like that. You might think you've got everything all mapped out, but a single minute, a single decision, can change everything. But that's the magic. It's your reality. *Yours.* Interpreting what it means is up to you.

I thought about my question game. Where did I see myself now? Riley Ozaki: mixed-up teen or misguided optimist?

Both, I think. A little of both. And that's the way it should be.

About the Author

TIFFANY BROOKS lives in San Francisco with her family and a bunch of rescued pets, who luckily don't object to being featured on her Instagram because her kids refuse. The best thing about living on the West Coast is she can find out what happens on *Game of Thrones* three hours ahead of airtime. That, plus not having winter weather, means she'll never move back east, although that doesn't stop her New England family from asking when she'll be moving "back home" to NYC or Connecticut. *Reality Gold*, her debut novel, kicks off the Shifting Reality Collection, a YA trilogy.

Visit Tiffany's website at
WWW.TIFFANYBROOKSAUTHOR.COM
to learn more about Riley, all the *Reality Gold* contestants, and a behind-the-scenes look at what it takes to film a reality show.

Reviews are "gold" to authors!
If you enjoyed this book, please consider
reviewing or rating it on Goodreads.

Please visit
WWW.DUNEMEREBOOKS.COM
to order your next great read.

DUNEMERE
Books